D1022702

The action-packed story line is a thrill a page
without scrimping on a warm romance.
Very Highly Recommended."—*Harriet Klausner*

YOU ONLY LOVE TWICE

"This book is an absolute joy to read. I loved every
minute of it! We are given humor, a murderer,
sensuality, scintillating dialogue, and characters
to cheer for. What more could you want?"—*Rendezvous*

"If you love mystery, murder, and mayhem along with
your romance, then *You Only Love Twice* will be your
cup of tea."—*Romantic Times*

THE BRIDE'S BODYGUARD

"Cleverly plotted intrigue."—*Publishers Weekly*

"This witty Regency romance/mystery will keep you up
all night."—*The Atlanta Journal/Constitution*

"A rich, satisfying blend of suspense
and passion."—*Brazosport Facts*

MORE PRAISE FOR ELIZABETH THORNTON

"Elizabeth gives you delicious stories filled with
mystery, sensual romance, and dynamite characters.
I have been reading this woman's wonderful
stories for years and years. I hope she never
stops writing."—*The Belles and Beaux of Romance*

"Fast-paced and full of suprises, Thornton's
latest novel is an exciting story of romance,
mystery, and adventure . . . a complex lot that
exuberantly carries the reader. Thornton's firm
control of her plot, her graceful prose, and her
witty dialogue make *Dangerous to Kiss* a pleasure
to read."—*Publishers Weekly* on *Dangerous to Kiss*

LADY FUGITIVE

"Rosamund, I'm not going to let you get behind me."

Her eyes jerked up to meet his. He wasn't smiling, but she was almost positive there was a glint of amusement in his eyes, only this time she could have sworn he wasn't laughing at her.

It was mortifying. She was twenty-six years old and felt as skittish as an adolescent girl.

With brows down, she wrapped her arms around him, and fumbled with the bandages. When her breasts brushed against his chest, he flinched.

"I'm sorry," she said, "but the binding must be tight."

He had that strange look on his face again, as though someone had just stabbed him in the back. "I didn't mean to hurt you," she murmured.

He didn't say anything, but just stood there, staring at her. The silence lengthened.

"You . . . ," he said.

She couldn't drag her eyes from his. "I . . . ?" she said.

They edged closer. His hands wrapped around her arms. She touched a hand to his bare chest. His skin was warm. She could feel the thundering of his heart. Or was it her own heart? It seemed the most natural thing in the world to lift her face to his.

Also by *Elizabeth Thornton*

THE
PERFECT
PRINCESS

ELIZABETH
THORNTON

BANTAM BOOKS

THE PERFECT PRINCESS
A Bantam Book/November 2001

ISBN 0-553-58123-6

Published simultaneously in the United States and Canada

Bantam Books are published by Bantam Books, a division of Random
House, Inc. Its trademark, consisting of the words "Bantam Books" and
the portrayal of a rooster, is Registered in U.S. Patent and Trademark
Office and in other countries, Marca Registrada. Bantam Books, 1540
Broadway, New York, New York 10036.

PRINTED IN THE UNITED STATES OF AMERICA

OPM   10 9 8 7 6 5 4 3 2 1

THE
PERFECT
PRINCESS

Prologue

Richard Maitland decided that he wasn't ready to die yet. Not that he had much say in the matter. A black mist was closing in on him. *So this is what it's like to die,* he thought. His brain was telling him to give up and go to sleep. Why was he fighting it?

He was fighting it because his death would be ignoble, and his murderer or murderers would get away with it. They were clever and he'd played right into their hands. He was a lone wolf—a fatal character flaw according to Harper. In this instance, Harper was right. No one knew where he was. He hadn't thought to tell anyone because it wasn't important and had nothing to do with his work at Special Branch. Though his friends wouldn't accept the neat little scenario that had been laid out for him, they wouldn't know where to begin to look for answers to why he had to die.

He wasn't sure he knew himself.

Who would want him dead?

His laugh turned into a dry, rasping cough, and he

clamped his arm across his chest to stifle the stab of pain. He'd made enemies in his time, scores of them. Soldier, agent, chief of staff of Special Branch—a man in his position attracted enemies like flies to a rotting corpse.

Hard on that thought came another. *Lucy.*

The black mist faded as his mind grappled with a burgeoning fear. Lucy. Where was she? What had they done with her? He remembered the boy . . .

He could smell the blood. The air was ripe with it. Lucy's blood. His blood. He had to open his eyes, had to get his bearings.

It seemed to take forever before his lashes lifted. Lights flickered. Shapes advanced and retreated. He frowned as he willed everything to come into focus. He was staring at a bed, and the half-clothed body of the young woman who lay on top of it. Lucy.

He thought his lungs would burst as he tried to scream his protest. This should never have happened. She was innocent. Her only crime was that she had known him. She was a prop in this grotesque drama. That's all she was to her killers, a prop to make his own murder seem more plausible.

It was all coming back to him: the boy who had been waiting for him at the top of the stairs; the bastard who had stuck a knife in him; how they'd dumped him in this chair in a corner of the room and had left him to bleed to death. His hand was splayed against his chest, and something warm and sticky oozed between his fingers. He looked down. A large crimson stain was spreading across his shirt. If he didn't do something soon it would be too late.

He couldn't pull himself to his feet, so he sank to the floor, on his knees, and used one arm pressed tight against his chest to staunch the flow of blood. Now that he was more awake, sensation was coming back, and his chest felt as though a red-hot poker was lodged in it. Ignoring the pounding inside his head, he propelled himself forward on his knees, inch by painful inch, till he came to the edge of the bed.

He groped with his free hand and found the pistol that had fallen between the mattress and the footboard. He had very little strength left, and though he knew it might be the death of him, he took his arm away from his chest and used both hands to cock the gun. Bracing his back against the bed, he aimed for the window and squeezed the trigger.

The report of the shot sent waves of sound echoing from wall to wall. There were shouts from below, then the thundering of footsteps on the stairs. He had no way of knowing whether he'd summoned help or his would-be murderers. Not that it made much difference.

The mist was becoming thicker and he had no more will or strength to fight it. It sucked him under like a great black wave.

Chapter 1

Why do you want to marry me, Michael?"

She immediately regretted asking the question. She knew she was going to refuse him. Now she would have to appear interested in his answer.

"Prince Michael," he corrected automatically. "Because, Lady Rosamund, I think you'll make a perfect princess."

A perfect princess. The words grated on Rosamund. That's what they were calling her in the newspapers, ever since Prince Michael of the diminutive principality of Kolnbourg had made her the object of his attentions. And the depressing truth was, she probably *would* make a perfect princess.

She was the daughter of a duke. She'd led a sheltered existence. From the day of her birth, she'd been trained in all the feminine arts, the ones that were essential for the wife of some gentleman from her own sphere. She'd never been to school like other girls, or had beaux, or been kissed or had adventures.

If only she'd been born a boy, things would have been so different! She had two brothers, Caspar, the elder, and Justin, who was three years younger than she. They'd done exciting things such as having a Grand Tour, and fighting for king and country. They'd also done other exciting things she wasn't supposed to know about . . . *La Contessa* was what everyone was calling Caspar's latest mistress, who was haughty, expensive, and had the temper of a tigress.

Rosamund's smile was fleeting. La Contessa's temperament would never do for a duke's daughter, of course. She'd been raised to be polite to everyone from His Majesty down to the lowest menial. She knew the rules of protocol back to front and inside out. She always knew where to sit at the dinner table, or to whom she should curtsy and whom she should not. Small talk was her forte, except when her mind wandered, as it did from time to time, and she forgot where she was. If she had to describe herself in one word, it would be . . . *bland.*

Bland. It was a word that had stuck in her mind ever since Lady Townsend's ball, where she'd overheard some of the younger women discussing her character. No one could possibly dislike her, someone said, because she was as bland as a blancmange. And everyone laughed.

Her mother had been anything but bland. By all accounts, Elizabeth Devere had been impatient with the constraints her exalted position had placed on her, and saw no reason to follow them slavishly. In the end it was her downfall. She'd gone out riding alone and had taken a tumble while jumping a fence. It wasn't the accident that killed her, but the fact that she hadn't been found till the following morning. She'd come down with a fever and had quietly slipped away.

Maybe if her mother had lived, her grief-stricken father wouldn't have been so strict with his only daughter. And maybe, if her mother had lived, his only daughter wouldn't be feeling so restless right now.

All that happened twenty years ago, but she still missed her. She wondered what her mother would think of the way her daughter had turned out if she could see her now.

"Lady Rosamund?"

Uh-oh. She'd done it again, forgotten where she was.

She looked at Prince Michael and sighed. There must be something wrong with her, she thought. Prince Michael of Kolnbourg was tall, dark, and handsome. He was also titled and legions of women had tried to lead him to the altar. Then why didn't he appeal to her?

Perhaps because she, too, was tall, dark, and handsome as well as titled. She was also wealthy in her own right and no fool. It didn't take much intelligence to deduce that this was why Prince Michael had chosen to court her. Meanwhile, next month, she would turn twenty-seven, and she knew her father was becoming desperate for her to accept one of her suitors.

What she wanted, however, was a beau, not a suitor, someone who would like her for herself. Suitors, in her experience, were bookkeepers—every asset was noted in their mental ledgers before they made an offer.

Michael, *Prince* Michael, was definitely a suitor. He was only fourth in line to the throne and hadn't a sou to his name, a tragic circumstance when one considered his expensive tastes. Marriage to her would solve all his problems.

They were in the conservatory of Twickenham House, the ducal mansion in Twickenham, just outside of London, and Rosamund took a moment or two to set the mood by staring at the vista through one of the windows. Autumn was ripe and mellow, and the trees were ablaze with color.

"I'm an English girl," she said. "I could never be happy transplanted to a foreign shore."

She looked over her shoulder and caught him in the act of studying his watch. Evidently, she bored him as much as he bored her! It didn't surprise her: Lady Rosamund Devere was a boring sort of person. As a duke's daughter she'd been *raised* to be as bland as a blancmange. Which was exactly the kind of wife Prince Michael wanted.

The perfect princess, the bland blancmange, who could be counted on never to put a foot wrong, say a wrong word, or have an original thought.

Without awkwardness or embarrassment, Prince Michael slipped his watch inside his vest pocket and gave her one of his engaging smiles. "I have no objection to your remaining in England after we are wed," he said. "In fact, I may decide to make England my home. The climate agrees with me."

So did the actresses, but she wasn't supposed to know about them. She gave him one of her own engaging smiles. "I'm almost tempted, but . . ."

"But?"

"Well, you can't play chess, Your Highness. You see, I could never marry a man who cannot play chess."

❧

Mrs. Calliope Tracey put the teapot down with a thump. *"Chess?"* she said. "What has chess to do with anything?"

Rosamund gazed at her friend over the rim of her teacup.

Last night, she'd put up at the Clarendon, where she normally stayed whenever she came up to town to do a little shopping or escape her father's temper. The duke, her father, had not been amused when she'd told him that she and Prince Michael would not suit. There had been a scene, if one person ranting and raving could be called a scene. And her brothers had not got off scot-free either. It seemed that His Grace had raised three thankless children, if persons of their advanced years could possibly be called children. Not one of them was married. At this rate, their line would die out. Then where would they be?

As usual, she and her brothers had listened to Papa in sympathetic silence, then made their escape to do precisely what they wanted to do. With Justin, it would be chasing petticoats, racing his curricle to Brighton, dueling, gaming, or whiling the hours away with friends. With Caspar, it would no doubt be La Contessa. There wasn't much a duke's daughter could escape to, but she could always count on her one and only friend to lend a sympathetic ear. So here she was, in the breakfast room of Callie's house in Manchester Square.

That was another consequence of being a duke's daughter. She had legions of acquaintances, both male and female, but they were not friends. They were so intimidated by her rank that they treated her with a deference that made her squirm. They never contradicted anything she said. Whatever she suggested was always accepted without argument. It was such a bore.

Callie was the exception. Her late father, a widower, had been the duke's steward, and he and Callie arrived at Castle Devere, the principal residence of the Duke of Romsey, not long after the tragic death of Rosamund's mother. She and Callie had known each other from the time they were children. They'd even been educated together, not at school, but by Rosamund's governess. This arrangement had suited both the duke and his steward, since Callie would have the advantage of a superior education her father could not afford and Rosamund would have the benefit of Callie's company. Though the idea was that they'd both be treated equally, it hadn't worked out that way. Callie had always been allowed more freedoms than Rosamund.

And after Callie married and moved away, there had been a succession of chaperons, most of them edging toward their dotage. Over two months ago, her father had relented and had hired a young woman of Rosamund's age to be her companion, Prudence Dryden, but things hadn't worked out the way Rosamund had hoped. Miss Dryden was hard to get to know. And since she was hard to get to know as well, they were like polite strangers.

"Roz?" Callie slapped her open palm on the table to get Rosamund's attention. "Hallo? Hallo?"

Rosamund blinked. "What?"

"Where do you go when that look comes over your face? What are you thinking?"

"I was thinking that ordinary girls have an easy time of it. They have so many choices. They can do what they want or go where they want. Look at you."

Callie laughed. "Nonsense," she said. "The sad truth is, no female has an easy time of it. We are tied to some man's leading strings from birth, first a father's, then a husband's or a brother's. It's only when a woman becomes a widow that she is truly free. You should follow my example."

Rosamund obligingly smiled. This was one of Callie's oft-repeated jests, that life for a female began only when she became a widow, and in Callie's case, it was true. When her unlamented tyrant of a husband choked to death on his own vomit during a drunken stupor, Callie had come to live with his brother in Manchester Square, and she'd found her true vocation as Charles Tracey's hostess. She was amusing; she was outrageous. An invitation to one of her parties was highly prized, and she was invited everywhere. Callie had no shortage of beaux, either.

She was the kind of woman, Rosamund thought, that would appeal to men. She had expressive brown eyes, and dark brown hair that curled naturally to frame her face in tiny ringlets. And she was as dainty and as finely sculpted as a porcelain figurine. God forbid that she should alight from a carriage without some male rushing to her assistance or that she should carry a hatbox or drop a handkerchief. It wasn't that Callie expected these courtesies. It was simply that men thought she was fragile. And nothing could be further from the truth.

It was true that men showed her, Rosamund, the same courtesy, but that was because they wanted to curry favor with her father. The only time she felt tiny was when she was flanked by her father and brothers. That was one thing she particularly liked about her companion. Prudence was as tall as she.

"Why are you smiling?" asked Callie.

"I was thinking of Prince Michael. At least he's taller than I am."

"You still haven't explained what chess has to do with anything. What did the prince say after you told him that you could never marry a man who did not play chess?"

"Not 'did not play chess' but 'could not play chess.' There is a difference. What could he say? I'd beaten him at chess, you see. If he hadn't looked at his watch, I would have let him down gently. But after he slighted me like that, I didn't care how brutal I was." To Callie's blank stare, Rosamund elaborated, "He's a chess player. He fancies himself an expert. But I let him know he was no match for me."

"Then what happened?"

"He clicked his heels and took off like one of Congreve's rockets."

Callie stared, then hooted with laughter. At length, she said, "You chess players are a breed apart. I never had the patience for it."

"No. I remember."

There was an interval of silence as Callie replenished their teacups. Without looking up, Callie said, "All this talk of ordinary girls makes me think that you're finally thinking of establishing your own home."

"I've thought about it, but I don't know what good it would do. I'd no sooner move in than so would my father and brothers. Or, if they didn't move in, they'd visit me so often, I wouldn't know the difference."

Callie sighed. "I'm sure you're right. Your father and brothers are too protective of you. If they were my relations, I think I'd shoot them or shoot myself. Thank God my male relations know enough to keep their distance, except for Charles, of course, and he's a dear. I never regretted my decision to come and live with him."

Rosamund did not doubt it. Though there was an unmarried aunt, Frances, who lived with them as well, Callie had the run of the house. She also seemed to have the run of Charles, who, according to the duke, should put his foot down more often.

Callie said suddenly, "Where is your chaperon, Miss What's-Her-Name?"

"Miss Dryden," said Rosamund, slightly irritated because, in two months, Callie had never taken the trouble to learn the girl's name. "She came down with a bad cold, and is confined to her bed."

"I'm surprised at your father. I've never known him allow you to travel alone." Callie finished her tea, and put down her cup and saucer. "Not that Miss Dryden is much of a chaperon. She's so insipid."

"Reserved," said Rosamund, bristling. "Miss Dryden is reserved, not insipid. And I didn't travel alone. I came in the ducal carriage, with a full complement of coachmen and postilions, all of them armed to the teeth. And now that I'm here, *you* can be my chaperon."

Callie rested her chin on her linked fingers. "You know, Roz," she said, "if I were you, I would get married. No, no, hear me out. It could be the ideal solution. Maybe you were too hasty in refusing Prince Michael.

From what I hear of him, he'd make an ideal husband."
Her eyes danced. "He'd marry you and forget about you.
You'd be free to come and go as you please. No more
leading strings. What more could a woman want?"

"What about the right man?" responded Rosamund
dryly.

"The right man?" Callie laughed. "Roz, he doesn't exist. If he did, you would have met him by now."

"Now, just a minute! I'm not exactly in my dotage."

Callie sat back in her chair and studied Rosamund's
lowered brows. Finally, she said, "I'm all ears. Describe
this romantic figure who can do what no other man has
done and lead you to the altar."

Rosamund gazed down at the dregs in her teacup as
though she were a fortune-teller reading the tea leaves.
A solitary tea-leaf bobbed on the surface. With an index
finger, she pushed it under. A moment later, it bobbed
right up again.

"Drat," she said, "I can't get rid of him."

"Who?" asked Callie, baffled.

"The one who is tall, dark, and handsome."

"Well, I hope he is tall. Nothing looks more ridiculous
than a woman dancing with a man she stands head and
shoulders above. What else?"

Rosamund carefully set down her teacup and gave
one of her bland smiles. "Why," she said, "he'll be just
like you, Callie—you know, blunt to the point of rudeness. I won't have to wonder what he's really thinking because he'll tell me straight-out, to my face. He won't
think of me as a duke's daughter. He won't care about
my fortune. He'll contradict me at every turn. He won't
try to curry favor with my father or my brothers, and if
they cross him, he'll tell them to go to the devil. And . . ."

"And?"

"And when we play cards or chess or whatever, he
won't sulk just because a female has beaten him."

Callie laughed. "I think you mean every word."

"Oh, I do. But since this man has yet to show his face, I'll just have to make do with you. Now, tell me what we're going to do this morning."

Callie adjusted the clasp of her gold bracelet as she spoke. "I'm afraid you'll have to entertain yourself for an hour or two, because I have an appointment I must keep." She looked up and smiled. "I'd invite you along, but your father would have a fit if he ever found out."

Rosamund was beginning to be annoyed. "I thought you knew my father better than that. His bark is worse than his bite. He's all bluster. And if I had paid attention to his fits, as you call them, I would have accepted Prince Michael, wouldn't I? So let me worry about my father and tell me where we are going this morning."

Callie shook her head. "No. All teasing aside, it's not the sort of place you would feel comfortable in."

"Let me be the judge of that."

"Fine. I'm going to Newgate."

"Newgate? *The* Newgate?"

"Yes. The prison."

Rosamund had a ghoulish vision of a public execution. She gave her friend a sharp look as a thought occurred to her. This was typical of Callie. She'd established herself as an original, someone who would dare the devil just for the thrill of it. That was one of the reasons she was so much in demand. She had a fund of stories that kept her audience both shocked and enraptured. Callie was never dull. She attended masqued balls that ladies weren't supposed to know about; she'd been on a balloon ride. But a public execution? That was going too far.

Callie's delicate brows winged upward. "I don't know what's going through your head, but I'm sure you've got it all wrong. This is a mission of mercy."

She got up and went to the sideboard. A moment later, she returned with a folded newspaper and passed it to Rosamund. "Front page, Richard Maitland," she said. "The trial has been going on all week. You must have read about it. He's been found guilty and sentenced to hang."

Rosamund glanced at the paper, then looked up at Callie. "Isn't he the man who murdered one of the maids at the George and Dragon? Wasn't she his mistress?"

Callie shook her head. "He denies that she was his mistress. He says that they were only friends. Her father served with him in Spain, and after he died, she asked Maitland for help. He said that she was already dead when he entered her room and one of her killers attacked him."

"Killers?"

"A boy and a man. Haven't you read the papers?"

"Yes, but I can't remember the details."

Callie made a small sound of impatience. "The boy was part of the plot. He lured Maitland into Miss Rider's room so that the real killer, who was hiding behind the door, could finish him off."

"I thought this was a crime of passion. Isn't that what the prosecutor said? She was going to leave him for someone else. There were witnesses who said as much."

Callie expelled a quick breath. "Oh, yes, witnesses, if one can call barmaids and chambermaids credible witnesses."

There were times when Callie could be downright irritating, as now. When she made up her mind about something, she would say anything to win her point. Rosamund had followed the trial in the newspapers, but not very closely because her own name was being bandied about as the future Princess Michael of Kolnbourg and her mind had been preoccupied. But she remembered thinking that Richard Maitland was as guilty as sin.

"Barmaids and chambermaids," she said, "are respectable people, and the jury believed them."

"Hah! There was nothing respectable about that lot. I

could tell just by looking at them. Oh, yes, I was there at the trial. I never missed a day."

It didn't surprise Rosamund to learn that Callie had attended the trial. It was quite common for ladies of fashion, at least the bolder ones, to attend such events, and Callie was bolder than most. After a moment, she said, "Why would these witnesses lie?"

"Maybe someone bribed them. Or maybe they're frightened to tell the truth. Maitland said that he had powerful enemies."

Rosamund shook her head.

"What?" demanded Callie.

"Why are you so determined to believe that this man is innocent?"

"Because of who he is. He's an officer and a gentleman. He is . . . was chief of staff of Special Branch. I'd rather believe him than barmaids and chambermaids. And I'm going to tell him so, to his face. Oh, don't look so shocked. He'll be shackled. We won't come to any harm."

Rosamund didn't know enough about the case to argue the point, and she knew, too, that when Callie's mind was made up, nothing could change it.

"Who is 'we'?" she asked.

"Oh, Aunt Fran. And we're to meet Charles there. So you see, I'll be well chaperoned."

This was one occasion when Rosamund thought Charles should definitely put his foot down. Not that Callie would listen to him.

Callie was studying Rosamund's face, and she let out a soft sigh. "Listen, Roz," she said, "I feel sorry for the man, that's all. His friends have all deserted him. I just want him to know that someone believes in him. So I'm going to give him a royal send-off—champagne, roast duck, truffles, that sort of thing. Don't look so worried. He may not agree to see me. Then I shall just leave my basket of treats with the keeper."

There was an interval of silence, then Callie went on, "I don't suppose you ever ran into Maitland when you were in Lisbon?"

"Was Maitland in Lisbon?"

"He served all through the Spanish Campaign. His war record is spotless. It was all in the papers."

"No, I never met him. But that's not surprising. My father and I were guests of the ambassador. The only soldiers I met were pretty high up in the chain of command."

Callie got up. "If you want to tidy yourself before we go, the lavender room is free. Shall we meet back here in say, oh, half an hour? If you don't want to go, I won't take offense. I know how difficult your father can be when you forget you're a duke's daughter. Make yourself at home. We should be back in an hour or so."

Rosamund slumped back in her chair, something she would never have done if someone had been there to see her. Callie, she reflected, had the uncanny knack of making her feel less than adequate. Her eye fell on the newspaper Callie had offered her. After a moment, she reached for it and shook it out with enough force to tear the page. It was dated August 28, 1816. She began to read.

Maitland Guilty! Sentenced to Hang!

Colonel Richard Maitland, Chief of Staff of Special Branch, was found guilty today at the Old Bailey of the murder of Miss Lucille Rider. There was speculation that the jury might recommend clemency in view of the defendant's distinguished war record, but no such recommendation reached the court. Before passing sentence, Chief Justice Robarts said that this was a particularly brutal crime, and that crimes of passion must never be tolerated in a civilized country. After donning the black cap, he pronounced the sentence of death.

Maitland's expression remained stoic throughout. No sound was heard in the packed courtroom as the sentence was read. Colonel Maitland, who has always protested his innocence, was led away in chains.

There were many on the steps of the Old Bailey who expressed satisfaction with the verdict. The general view seemed to be that no one was above the law, and a man in Colonel Maitland's position, a man who was sworn to uphold the law, should be dealt with severely. Many expressed their sympathy for the victim, a maid at the hotel where the murder took place. It was the testimony of Miss Rider's friends that was largely responsible for the conviction. Though Maitland always insisted that his relationship with Miss Rider was innocent, their sworn statements to the contrary undermined his defense.

A highly placed source at Special Branch, who wishes to remain anonymous, commented that the colonel was an intensely private person who ran the department with a rod of iron. When asked about rumors of Maitland's sometimes brutal and unorthodox methods, the official refused to confirm or deny them.

The execution has been set for August 30 at 8:00 A.M. outside Newgate Prison.

Rosamund read the article again, then laid the paper aside. It did not seem to her that there was anything here to stir her sympathy for Richard Maitland. Many soldiers had distinguished war records, but that was no excuse for murder. Even his own colleagues at Special Branch had nothing good to say about him.

His defense, as she remembered, was that his enemies had engineered the whole thing. He was the real target, not Miss Rider. They killed her to make it look like a crime of passion, and so deflect suspicion from themselves, then her murderers had stabbed him and left him for dead. It was too bad for Maitland that the prosecutor produced a physician who claimed that the stab wound to Maitland was superficial and not life-threatening. A self-inflicted wound, the prosecutor averred, to convince the authorities of his innocence. Then Maitland had thrown the knife out of the window so that it would not incriminate him. But the knife was found and Maitland's plot failed.

The execution was to take place tomorrow morning. A shiver ran over her. Now her sympathies *were* stirred. A mission of mercy—

If her father knew of this proposed visit to Newgate, he would absolutely forbid it. On the other hand, she was twenty-six years old and life was passing her by.

She dwelled on that thought for a long time. Her decision suddenly made, she headed upstairs to the lavender room.

Chapter 2

*E*nglish justice was nothing if it was not swift, re-flected Richard Maitland. He'd been charged with murder one week, tried and convicted the next, and sentenced to hang two days later. Tomorrow, in fact. It hardly gave a man time to plan his escape.

He adjusted his long length in the hard barrack bed, and allowed his gaze to stray to the grated window high in the wall, too high for anyone to see out. Three floors down was the Felons' Quadrangle, but no sound reached him through the closed window. No sights, no sounds, no fresh air, and damn little light. There was nothing for a man to do in the condemned cell but reflect on his life or go mad.

This wasn't the first time he'd faced execution. In Spain, he'd been caught working behind enemy lines. He was a spy. He'd known the rules of war. But his death would have been honorable because he was fighting for king and country. There was no honor in hanging for a crime he did not commit.

Last time, he'd been saved at the eleventh hour by the cavalry. Where, in hell's name, was the cavalry now?

When he tried to sit up, he winced. The wound in his chest was healing, but it hadn't completely healed yet. Newgate wasn't exactly the place to be if a man wanted to recover his health. Sanitary conditions were appalling. He was lucky he hadn't come down with blood poisoning. And the authorities weren't interested in exerting themselves for a man who had been condemned to death. The young orderly who had examined him that morning had cracked a joke to the effect that the only cure was plenty of rest. He would have all eternity to laugh at the orderly's little joke if he didn't get out of here fast. And once he was free, one way or another he would clear his name and discover who had murdered Lucy Rider.

He could never think of the girl without his rage turning inward. He'd had plenty of time to think in the last little while, and though he'd belatedly come to realize that Lucy must have been part of the plot against him, he couldn't bring himself to believe that she'd really understood what she was getting into. To his enemies, she was just a pawn, and they'd given her up for a greater prize. If he'd had his wits about him, he could have prevented Lucy's death.

He could not believe how stupid he'd been. He'd trusted her, he, Richard Maitland, who could count on one hand the number of people he trusted; he counted them off on the fingers of his right hand—Harper; Hugh Templar and his wife, Abbie; Jason Radley . . . He stopped. That was four. After a moment's consideration, he added himself.

He was surprised to find that he was smiling, because there was damn little to smile about in these dismal surroundings. There wasn't enough room to swing the proverbial cat. The only relief from boredom was the occasional visitor who came to say their final farewells.

But those were not his friends. In fact, he'd warned his friends to stay away, not only from Newgate, but from the trial as well. He'd done the same with his parents. He didn't want them making the long journey from Aberdeen to London just to see him like this. He'd seen how things were going. He'd known he would be found guilty, and he had no intention of passively accepting his fate. If he escaped, anyone who was close to him would come under suspicion.

Massie, who was now acting chief of staff, had visited him that morning to say a somber farewell. He'd also visited before the trial.

"I know you're innocent," Massie said, "and I know you're the victim of a plot. I want to help. Tell me where to begin to look for these conspirators."

Richard liked Massie. He was a good agent. They had much in common. The intelligence service was their profession. Unlike many of their colleagues, they had no connections in high places to help them up the ladder. Everything they had, they'd got through their own intelligence and hard work.

There was, however, one major difference between himself and Massie. Massie followed the rules.

But he hadn't taken Massie into his confidence. Good agents weren't always what they seemed to be, and if Massie was working for his enemies, his offer to help might be nothing more than a ploy to find out just how much he, Richard, knew, so that they could cover their tracks.

Cover their tracks? He almost laughed. The man and the boy had disappeared without a trace. They'd covered their tracks so well that he didn't know where to begin to look for them. All the witnesses were telling the truth as they saw it. Lucy had done her part well. It was a conspiracy. But who was behind it?

He'd come at that question from all angles since the night Lucy died, and he was no nearer to answering it now than he'd been then. It wasn't because there was a lack of suspects. There were too damn many.

His head jerked up when he heard the key turn in the lock. A moment later, the massive studded door slowly swung open. Framed in the doorway was a uniformed turnkey, a vicious-looking character with monkey features and bushy eyebrows set in a scowl.

"Harper," said Richard, a slow grin spreading across his face. "What kept you?"

"I was waiting until the coast was clear. Well, move your arse. We haven't got all day."

Sergeant Harper was one of the few people Richard trusted, which was just as well, because Harper was Richard's bodyguard. This explained why Harper was more surly than usual. The man he was sworn to protect had gone off, so he said, half-arsed without a word to his bodyguard, and look where it had got him.

Richard and Harper had known each other for a long time. In Spain, they'd both served in His Majesty's Secret Service. They hadn't always seen eye to eye, but the cases they'd worked on since had given each a profound respect for the other. They were comrades. In private, they spoke freely, though Harper perhaps a little more freely than his chief would have liked. It did no good to remonstrate with Harper. He did not answer to Richard. His appointment had come from the prime minister, as a reward for services rendered, and he never let Richard forget it.

Harper looked down the length of the passageway, saw that it was empty, and stepped into the cell. "Let's get these fetters unlocked," he said, "but mind, don't take 'em off till you're in the closet."

Now that the moment of escape had arrived, Richard felt a surge of energy at every pulse point in his body. The nagging pain in his chest vanished; his mind was crystal clear. His breathing quickened.

As Harper unlocked the fetters on his hands and

legs, Richard reviewed each step of the escape plan. Harper, the brass-faced villain, really was a turnkey, having secured the position with a little help from his unsavory friends even before Richard was convicted of murder. A born pessimist was Harper, and sometimes, as now, it paid off. The first step of the plan was to disguise Richard as a turnkey as well. Harper would escort him to the water closet at the end of the passageway, where a uniform was waiting for him, and inside the tricorne hat would be a pistol, fully loaded. Once he had changed, they would descend the three flights of stairs to the Felons' Quadrangle and act as though they were guarding the prisoners and their visitors. Soon after, a new shift of turnkeys would arrive to replace them, and they would march to the turnkeys' lodges beside the keeper's rooms and the last locked door to freedom.

And here was the tricky part. They hoped that in the confusion, with so many turnkeys coming and going, no one would notice them entering the keeper's rooms. Once inside, they would take the keeper hostage and force the turnkeys at that last door to open it for them.

And so to freedom.

Naturally, Harper had thought of everything that could go wrong. Their plan depended on no one recognizing Richard. On Harper's advice, he'd refused the services of the barber that morning, and a fine stubble now darkened his chin and cheeks. It was to their advantage, also, that Newgate was as dark and gloomy as . . . well, Newgate. It had been built to be impervious to light. Freedom could not come too soon for Richard.

"Ready?" said Harper.

Richard smiled. "Lead on, MacDuff."

❧

When Rosamund entered the breakfast room half an hour later and found Charles Tracey in heated debate with Callie and Aunt Fran, she knew something was very wrong. Charles was supposed to meet them in Newgate.

He was thirtyish, tall, and willowy, with blond hair receding at the temples. Rosamund had never entirely warmed to him, perhaps because he seemed always aggrieved about something. The only thing he didn't judge and find wanting was Callie, whom he clearly adored. Rosamund felt sorry for him, but all the same, an hour in Charles's company never failed to depress her.

At the moment, Charles was venting his anxieties about the outing to Newgate.

"Too many things can go wrong!" he said.

"Nonsense," replied Callie. "It's all arranged. I'm not going to let a little thing like that stop me."

"A little thing like what?" asked Rosamund, adjusting her shawl as she came up to them.

Silence. She could tell from their faces they were all surprised to see her.

Charles recovered himself first. "Lady Rosamund," he said. "So that was your carriage and coachman I saw in the square."

Callie said, "I thought you had made up your mind not to go."

Rosamund answered Charles first. "How are you, Charles? It's good to see you again." She responded to his formal bow with a slight inclination of her head. To Callie she said, "I don't remember saying I wouldn't go with you, but if the trip is off, I won't be disappointed."

"The trip is not off," said Callie. "I'm not going to allow an unruly mob to tell me what to do."

"Mob?" Rosamund looked at Charles.

He nodded. "They've called the militia out to disperse them. We're talking about riots, Lady Rosamund. There are thousands of people out there on the streets of London. At the prince regent's house, when they learned he was not there to receive their petition, their mood turned ugly. They threw stones at windows then tried to set his house on fire with fireballs."

"What are they petitioning for?"

"Fair wages. Lower prices. Work for the workless." Charles shrugged. "Most of them are orderly, but there are always one or two agitators who try to stir things up."

Callie said, "The prince regent's house is miles from here, and even farther away from Newgate."

Aunt Fran, who had been fussing with the basket she carried over one arm, looked up. "Newgate," she said. There was a quaver in her voice. "I remember the riots in the summer of 1780. The mob went on the rampage and burned private dwellings, then they marched on Newgate and freed all the prisoners."

"That was almost forty years ago," said Callie. "The authorities know better now than to let the mob get out of hand."

"Aunt Fran has a point, though," said Charles. "I doubt there will be a driver in London who will take us to Newgate."

"Oh." Callie thought for a moment, then her face brightened. "Then we'll go in Rosamund's carriage. With her armed coachmen and postilions to protect us, the mob will think twice about meddling with the duke's property. And I'm sure that's how he'd want Rosamund to travel anyway."

Charles was losing patience. "Rioters don't meddle. They throw stones and fireballs."

Rosamund, who'd had every intention of offering the duke's carriage, now balked. She had a ghastly vision of her father's face should his spanking-new carriage, built by his own hands to his own specifications, be returned to him as a burned-out shell. Carriage-building was not a hobby with the duke. It was his vocation.

"Why can't we take your carriage?" Rosamund asked. "We could still use my postilions."

"Didn't I tell you? It's being repaired."

Aunt Fran was beginning to look worried. "Does that mean we're still going?"

"Yes," said Callie. "Charles, would you mind ordering the carriage round, Lady Rosamund's carriage? Now, stop worrying. It's built like a fortress. We'll be quite safe."

As Charles went out, Aunt Fran cleared her throat. "Couldn't we postpone . . . no, no, how silly of me. If we don't go today, it will be too late."

Aunt Fran looked no more eager to visit Richard Maitland than she was, thought Rosamund. But her own case was different. She was testing herself. She didn't see why Aunt Fran had to be miserable.

"Miss Tracey," she said, "are you feeling all right? You look deathly pale."

Aunt Fran seized upon that opening like a hunted rabbit darts into a hole. "Well, I do feel a little under the weather," she said. "I didn't sleep a wink all night."

Callie sighed. "Why don't you go back to bed, Aunt Fran? Rosamund and I can chaperon each other."

Aunt Fran didn't need to be told twice. She deposited the basket on the table and practically tripped over her skirts in her haste to get away.

Callie shook her head. "I had no idea she felt like that. Well, it's you and I, Roz, just like the old days. Are you game, Miss Fainthearted?"

And just like the old days, Rosamund found herself rising to the bait.

Old habits were hard to break.

❧

At Rosamund's insistence, they left the ducal carriage with its complement of coachmen and postilions in the stable yard of the Magpie and Stump. If there was a mob on the loose, she told her companions, and it turned violent, her coachmen might come under attack. Better for them and Papa's carriage and prize horses if they were out of sight. Besides, they had only to cross the road and walk a little way to reach the prison.

Callie was not pleased by the delay. They were late enough as it was, she said. The keeper would think they were not coming. The streets were deserted. She did not see why the carriage could not wait for them outside Newgate's doors.

Charles took Rosamund's part and voiced the thought that was going through her mind. "The streets are deserted," he said, "because word of the riots has probably spread. Sensible folk are in their homes, with their doors and windows bolted. And that's where we should be."

"Not a word about riots to the keeper," said Callie severely, "or he may cancel our visit."

They entered Newgate by the private door to the keeper's rooms. Callie need not have worried. Mr. Proudie was waiting for them. He was affable and effusive, and positively fawning after the introductions were made.

"Lady Rosamund," he said, "the Duke of Romsey's daughter! Well, well! This is an honor. Newgate, if I do say so myself, is becoming quite the rage among the aristocracy. You'd be surprised how many fashionable people pass through our doors."

"Yes," said Rosamund, "crime is rampant among all classes, so I've heard."

The keeper looked baffled, and Callie quickly interposed, "And Colonel Maitland? Has he had many visitors?" She pinned Rosamund with a "this is no time to be funny" look.

The keeper chuckled. "Ah, no. He's not glamorous, you see. He's only a common murderer. Now, if he were Jack Sheppard, or a highwayman like Dick Turpin, his well-wishers would be lining up in droves to shake his hand. Well, well, come this way."

In single file, they followed the keeper along a windowless stone corridor with a watery light shining at the far end. Rosamund pulled her shawl more closely around her shoulders. It wasn't only the cold of that gloomy, cheerless place that was affecting her. The atmosphere was foul, as though the prison were a closed box and the prisoners and their goalers had been breathing the same air since time began. The smell was nauseating, too, a horrible combination of boiled cabbage and stale urine. And every time a gate clanged shut at her back, a shudder passed over her. She had just arrived and she could hardly wait to get out. *If I had my way, I'd lock him up and throw away the key.* How many times had she used that hackneyed expression? *Never again,* she promised herself.

The last gate they passed through took them to the Felons' Quadrangle. It was open to the elements, but the walls were so high that no sunlight penetrated to the few prisoners and visitors who were strolling about. At intervals around the walls, stone benches had been set out, and it was to one of these benches that the keeper now led them.

"We're not going to visit Colonel Maitland in his cell?" asked Rosamund.

"Ah, no, Lady Rosamund," replied the keeper. "Not suitable for a lady. Highly unpleasant." He laughed. "Grown men have been known to weep when they enter the cells for the condemned." He nodded to the uniformed turnkeys who were stationed at every few feet around the perimeter of the yard. "Safer here, too. Most of my men are former soldiers. They shoot to kill and ask questions later. But there are no violent prisoners here to cause you alarm. Coiners, embezzlers, libelers, that's what we have here."

"What about debtors?" asked Charles.

"Oh, they're housed in another part of the building entirely."

With that, he beckoned over the nearest turnkey and

told him to accompany him to the prisoner Maitland's cell.

As the keeper and turnkey made for one of the staircases, Callie seated herself on a stone bench; Charles mumbled something under his breath and set down the basket they'd brought for Maitland; and Rosamund took stock of the people in the prison yard.

The three females present had to be wives and daughters, she thought, because female prisoners had their own quadrangle. One wife was telling her husband off in no uncertain terms; the other two were weeping. They all looked harmless enough, harmless and pitiable. There was no laughter or joy in this place. What it must be like for the men and women who were under sentence of death was beyond imagining. If she had her way, prisons like Newgate would be razed to the ground.

Her gaze moved to the turnkeys. They didn't look like former soldiers to her. They looked more like brigands. Their uniforms were shabby and ill-fitting; their tricorne hats were askew. They were talking among themselves. She'd known soldiers, and this lot simply did not look disciplined.

There were two in particular that her eyes kept straying to. The older man had a face that reminded her of the faces of the gargoyles on the pediment of Twickenham House, and the younger man . . . he had what her father would call "presence." He wasn't particularly handsome, or particularly tall, but he had that look of intense virility and power that could be quite intimidating. He didn't fidget; he didn't glance from side to side or look up or down. He had the nonchalant stillness of a predator who waits at a watering hole for its prey to show up.

He moved his head slightly and their eyes collided. She felt the power of that look as though he'd touched her with ice. He didn't like her. No. It was stronger than that. He despised her.

She tore her eyes away and said something to Charles, she didn't know what, but her mind was still on the hard-eyed man who'd made no attempt to hide his disdain. And no wonder, she thought. She and Callie were dressed to the nines, Callie with her white rabbit-skin collar and matching muff, and she with her high-heeled kid shoes studded with glass beads. He probably thought that Callie was wearing ermine, and that the glass beads in her shoes were precious gems. If she'd only known she was coming to Newgate, she would have dressed more modestly.

The hard-eyed man must think they were curiosity-seekers, bored aristocrats who had come to Newgate to titillate their jaded palettes. He wouldn't believe it was a mission of mercy, and neither did she.

What on earth was she doing here?

Much the same thought was going through the mind of the hard-eyed man. What in Hades was *she* doing here? An arrogant, overdressed aristocrat, with nothing better to do than visit the condemned, was going to skew his plans. But for her, the keeper would be in his rooms. Now Proudie would discover that he, Richard Maitland, had escaped. At any moment, he was going to come clattering down those stone stairs and raise the alarm. And he would be prepared for trouble. The element of surprise would be lost, and it was highly unlikely that they could take him hostage. Then the prison would be locked up as tight as a drum. There would be no changing of the guard, and he'd be caught. And all because of Lady Rosamund Devere.

He'd recognized her, of course, *la belle dame sans merci*. That's what they'd called her in Lisbon. Not that she was merciless, merely indifferent. God forbid that she should speak to anyone below the rank of a colonel, or mix with the officers' wives. He'd once admired her beauty, but that was before he'd come to see that those finely sculpted features and cool gray eyes concealed an over-weening conceit.

He'd heard enough to know that he was the object of her visit, but that didn't make sense. They'd never met. In Lisbon, ordinary soldiers like him—and he was only a lieutenant then—were not considered fit to kiss the hem of her gown. And if he had tried, he was damn sure that her elegantly shod foot would have lashed out and connected with his teeth.

He had a bad feeling about Lady Rosamund's motives in coming here. A very bad feeling.

Harper was becoming restless. From the side of his mouth, he whispered, "You're the commanding officer. What do we do now?"

"We wait," said Richard.

"For what?"

"For all hell to break loose."

"Then what?"

"Then, in the confusion, we take ourselves a hostage, Harper, and barter our way out of here."

Harper turned his head. "Not the duke's daughter? Not Lady Rosamund Devere?"

"Who else do you suggest?"

"But she's almost as tall as you are. Why not take the other lady? She'll be a damn sight easier to control. She's as dainty as a doll."

"Yes, but she's not a duke's daughter, is she? Her currency isn't high enough. And . . ." A faint smile touched Richard's lips.

"And?"

"I've always wanted to get my hands on Lady Rosamund Devere. This may be my only chance. Listen! Here comes trouble. Easy, Harper, easy. Do nothing until I give the signal."

The turnkey who came hurtling down the steps and into the yard could hardly get his breath. "Lock up the prison," he croaked out, then louder, "lock up the prison. All prisoners back to their cells! Visitors remain in the yard! Prisoner has escaped. Watch out for Richard Maitland!"

The turkeys in the yard drew their pistols and waved them threateningly at the inmates and their visitors. There were cries and shouts as women clung to their husbands and guards pried them apart. Rosamund was numb with shock. Richard Maitland had escaped.

Then she knew, she *knew* why the hard-eyed turnkey had seemed so intimidating.

Callie was on her feet. "But he can't have escaped. No one escapes from Newgate! Rosamund, what's the matter? What are you staring at?"

Rosamund took a quick step back, then another. Richard Maitland, and she was sure it was he, was coming straight at her with pistol drawn. She wanted to scream, but all she did was gulp. The nonchalant predator had sighted his prey. At any moment, he would pounce.

Several things happened at once. She took another step back, tumbled over the basket Charles had set down, and struck her head on a paving stone. A shot rang out. Screams. Shouts. Richard Maitland fell on top of her, and she knocked her head again.

His voice was as hard as his eyes and touched with a hint of Scotland. "Fight me and I'll kill you, do you understand?"

She couldn't fight him even if she wanted to. His weight was crushing her; she could hardly breathe. The fall had dazed her and tears of pain stung her eyes. She looked at her white gloves and saw that they were spotted with blood. "I think I've been shot," she said.

"Up there! Up there!" shouted Harper, pointing to one of the staircases. "He's getting away! And there's another one!"

At these words, the panic intensified. Some turnkeys

ran for the cover of the stairs; others began to herd the prisoners and their visitors into one corner of the yard, out of the line of fire.

Richard got to his feet. "The duke's daughter has been hit," he shouted above the din.

Callie was shouting, too, but her voice did not carry. Rosamund sat up and looked around for Charles. Somehow, he'd become separated from them. He was in a corner, with the other prisoners, with his hands in the air. Then, before her horrified eyes, the gargoyle-faced man stuck a pistol in Callie's ribs. Whatever he said made a profound impression. Callie stopped screaming, nodded, and sank down on one of the stone benches. She looked petrified.

Rosamund cried out when Maitland yanked her to her feet, then swung her into his arms. He lowered his head and for her ears only hissed, "If you so much as say a word, one of my comrades will kill your friend, then I'll kill you. Understand?"

One of my comrades? How many of them were there?

"Did you hear me? I'll kill you."

Rosamund nodded. She believed him. He had the face of a killer—there was a vicious twist to his mouth, and his eyes were as hard as flint. And he had nothing to lose by killing Callie or her. He was going to hang anyway.

She winced when his companion opened his mouth and bellowed, "Make way for the duke's daughter! She's been hit! She's been hit!"

She was still groggy from striking her head on the paving stone, but she'd realized that she hadn't been hit. The only pain was in her head. It wouldn't matter to Maitland whether she was hit or not. She saw what he was up to. He was going to use her as a hostage to make his escape.

Don't panic! Don't panic! she told herself. Her ordeal

would soon be over. Once he was out of the prison, he would have no use for her and would let her go. All she had to do was keep her head.

And maybe he wouldn't get away. Maybe the turnkeys would refuse to let him pass. Maybe one of them would recognize him. Maybe he would be captured and returned to his cell.

And, quite forgetting her aversion to Newgate and its horrors, she decided it would give her a great deal of pleasure to be present when they hanged him in the morning.

She was appalled at how easily he got past the turnkeys. No one recognized him because he held her high against his chest and kept his head well down, and the gargoyle did all the talking. The turnkeys were reluctant to let them pass. They didn't know that Maitland had escaped, but they knew about the lockup and assumed some of the prisoners had gone amok. However, they recognized her as the lady whom the keeper had fawned over, and all doors opened like magic for the duke's daughter.

Before they came to the keeper's rooms, her abductors had a conference. They'd never get away, Maitland said, by pretending she was wounded. The turnkey would want to send for the prison doctor to examine the wound. They'd have to change their story. They'd say that the Duke of Romsey's daughter had fainted, and the keeper had ordered them to take her to her carriage.

"Where is your carriage?" Maitland asked in that hard-faced, hard-eyed way of his.

There was no point in lying, so she told him.

And once again, these bold as brass, bare-faced villains got away with it. The turnkey took one look at her dazed expression and he unlocked the last door.

When they were out on the street, Maitland seemed to stagger under her weight. She wasn't surprised. Though she didn't have an ounce of fat to spare, she was, after all, five foot seven in her stockinged feet. If he'd wanted a pocket Venus, he should have picked Callie.

As if reading her mind, he said, "I should have taken the other one." He dropped her on her feet none-too-gently. "I think I've broken my back. A regular Amazon, isn't she?"

She took instant umbrage, but it was muted by fear. There was no sense provoking the villain at this point. He could still hurt her.

"What's that?" he asked.

They lifted their heads and listened. It sounded like distant thunder, or a stampede of horses.

"Rioters," she said with relish. "They're marching on the prison. I suggest you make yourself scarce. Well, good-bye, Colonel Maitland. Perhaps I shall see you again some day." At the end of a rope, she hoped.

Those nasty eyes narrowed on her again, making her pulse jump.

"You're not going anywhere," he snarled, "until I know why you tried to have me killed back there."

She was speechless, but only for a moment. "You're out of your mind! One of the turnkey's guns must have gone off in the panic."

He fettered her by the wrist in a grasp that made her flinch. "You'll tell me, if I have to break every bone in your body." Then, to the other man, "Where are the horses?"

"Behind the church."

They started off at a run toward the Church of the Sepulchre. She could hardly keep up with him. A time or two, she stumbled, but the brute just yanked hard on her arm, dragging her along behind him.

She was suddenly angry, cat-spitting angry, with the kind of anger that drives out fear. She'd played the game his way, and this was her reward? Without her compliance, he would never have made it out of Newgate. If she went on like this, she'd end up just like his first victim.

At that moment, a wave of people surged into the street ahead of them, and she knew what she had to do. With an energy born of desperation, she lunged for Maitland and slammed into his back. As he fell to his knees, he relaxed his grip on her wrist. She tore herself free, and leapt past him, then she raced to meet the rioters as if they were the cavalry come to her rescue.

"Bloody hell," said Harper. "They've cut off our line of retreat. We'll never get to the horses now."

Maitland got up. He looked behind him. "We can't go back, either."

A stream of armed turnkeys were pouring out of Newgate.

"Here," said Harper, "where's she off to?"

As they watched, Rosamund veered off to the side, avoiding the surging mob, and she darted into a lane behind the Old Bailey.

"Where did she say her carriage was?" asked Richard.

"The Magpie and Stump."

A looked passed between them.

Ducking a hail of rioters' stones and turnkeys' bullets, they took off after Rosamund.

Chapter 3

osamund ran for her life. She didn't have to
think about where she was going. The Old
Bailey was right there at the crossroads. There
would be judges and lawyers and officers of the law to
protect her from Richard Maitland and his henchman.
And she would warn them about how wily and dangerous
he was so that, unlike the turnkeys in Newgate, they
would be prepared.

The man was not only a killer, he was deranged as
well. Everybody was his enemy; everybody was trying to
kill him. He saw treachery and conspiracy in every
chance encounter. But how he could suspect her, a
duke's daughter, of conspiring to have him shot, in
Newgate of all places, was beyond belief.

The man was insane. There was no other explanation.
And there was no reasoning with madmen.

She ran down the back of the Old Bailey and stopped
at the first door she came to. It was locked. She used
both fists to hammer on it. There was no response. Her

breathing was so erratic that her cries for help were like the pitiful mewlings of a drowning cat.

She looked over her shoulder. The mob was streaming toward Newgate and there was no sign of her pursuers. But the danger wasn't over yet. She hadn't spoken more than a few words to Richard Maitland, but she'd taken his measure. He wouldn't give up easily.

Ignoring the stitch in her side, she picked up her skirts and ran on. Then, ahead of her, like a river in spate, the mob, coming from another direction, surged into the alley. The trampling of their feet, their murderous yells, their savagely angry faces made her blood run cold. There was the sound of rifle fire, and the mob went wild.

She darted into the shelter of the nearest door and hammered on it as well. This time, there was a response. Someone yelled at her from a window above the door. Then a pistol was pushed through the bars and was aimed straight at her.

"You must help me," she cried out. "I am the Lady Rosamund Devere and—"

When she saw a thumb pull back the pistol's hammer, she gasped and flattened herself against the wall. Windows shattered as rioters threw stones. And from the Old Bailey itself, the defenders retaliated with pistol fire, warning shots over the heads of the mob, but this only enraged them more.

She stood there trembling, her mind in a whirl. She didn't know which way to turn. And even as she debated with herself, two figures turned the corner of Newgate Street and raced toward her: Richard Maitland and the gargoyle.

Panic swept over her. This could not be happening to her! Nothing ever happened to her! She could hardly turn around but she was falling over chaperons. If she went shopping in Bond Street, there were always one or two footmen in attendance to ensure that no one looked at her the wrong way. If she went out riding, a groom was always on hand to watch over her. If she went for a drive in the carriage, the coachmen and postilions had orders to shoot to kill if highwaymen waylaid her.

Yet here she was, totally unprotected, with a deranged murderer and his accomplice on one side, and an enraged mob on the other. This was England. These things could not be happening.

And she shouldn't be dithering like this. Maitland or the mob, she had to choose one or the other.

She chose the mob.

As soon as she'd made her decision, her panic ebbed a little and her brain began to function. On the other side of that mob was Fleet Lane and the Magpie and Stump, where she'd left her carriage. *Her carriage. And her armed postilions. And her armed coachmen.* They would blow Maitland's head off if he so much as touched her. All she had to do was fight her way clear of the mob and she'd be safe from a deranged killer.

With her pursuers hot on her heels, she went tearing over the cobblestones and dived into the crush. She was too frightened to care about the niceties. Pure animal instinct had taken over, and she shoved and elbowed people out of her way as though they were no more than scarecrows in a field of corn. When they snarled at her, she snarled back. And once in a while, she chanced a quick look over her shoulder to keep her enemies in sight.

They were gaining on her.

She plowed on blindly, and shoved once too often. Great beefy arms clamped around her. She'd been stopped by a man who had the brawny physique of her father's blacksmith.

"Whoa," he said, "you're going the wrong way, little lady."

Little lady, he'd called her, and compared to him she was the pocket Venus she'd always wanted to be. But not now, not when Maitland was almost upon her. She wanted to be the Amazon he'd taunted her with being, one of those legendary female warriors who could hold her own against any man.

But not this man. Those arms were like iron shackles. "You's been hurt," he said. His voice was rough but not unkindly, and she stopped squirming. "Who did this to you, little lady?" He was looking at a cut on her arm that she hadn't noticed until then.

She screwed her neck round and sucked in a breath when she saw how close Maitland had come. He was so close that she could see the laugh lines at the corner of his eyes, his cold blue eyes. She couldn't imagine this man laughing. His jaw was tensed; his lips were flattened; his features looked as though they were carved from granite.

And he was still wearing his turnkey's tunic.

Her brain worked like lightning. This was not the time to go into long explanations of who she was and why Maitland was after her. Her nice blacksmith obviously wanted to rescue her. She didn't think he'd be so eager if he knew she was a duke's daughter.

"That man is after me," she sobbed. "He's a militia-man and he was taking me to Newgate."

Her words had the desired affect. "Militia!" roared the blacksmith. "What militiaman?"

She pointed with a trembling finger.

The blacksmith thrust her behind him and immediately began to shoulder his way toward Maitland. When he reached his quarry and fell on him with flying fists, Rosamund allowed herself a small sigh of relief. *One down and one to go.* She searched the sea of faces, but there was no sign of Maitland's henchman. Praying that he'd met with a similar fate to Maitland's, she pushed into the angry rioters and forged ahead.

When she burst into the inn's stable yard, her lungs were burning; her legs were cramping. In the mêlée, she'd lost her reticule, her bonnet, her shawl, and one of her shoes. She didn't care. Her one thought was to reach her carriage and escape before another catastrophe overtook her.

The inn and stable yard were choked with people, rioters who—she gathered from the catcalls and comments flying back and forth—had decided to take a respite from their labors and fortify themselves with the inn's beer and ale before returning to the fray. There were no angry faces here. Everyone seemed to be having a grand time. It was just like a party.

She frowned when she saw the ducal carriage. There were no postilions and no coachmen guarding it, only a stableboy holding the lead horses' reins. She'd told her coachmen that she'd be back in an hour, but she hadn't been gone that long. She didn't have to search her mind too hard to come up with the answer to where her coachmen had taken themselves. Obviously, they'd joined the party and were probably in the inn's taproom having a grand old time.

Newgate! The Old Bailey! And now her own coachmen! She must have done something terribly wrong somewhere to be punished like this.

Dodging ostlers and tipsy customers, she hobbled over to the boy at the horses' heads. She was so out of breath that it took her a moment to find her voice. "My coachmen," she finally managed, "fetch them for me at once."

"*Your* coachmen?" The stableboy made an insulting appraisal, from her ramshackle hair to her unshod toes, and he snickered. "Arsk me when yer sober," he said.

Rosamund was about to annihilate him with a few polite, well-chosen words, when he snickered again, and her hand, with a will of its own, suddenly grabbed him by the collar and hoisted him to his toes. She was a lot taller than he. Lowering her face to within inches of his, she said in a voice that mimicked the duke's voice exactly when he went on the rampage, "Fetch my coachmen or I'll see to it that you spend the rest of your misbegotten life rotting in Newgate Gaol."

Satisfied with what she read in his face, she gently lowered him and let him go. Eyes as round as bread plates, he touched his forelock and practically fell over himself as he went racing toward the inn. Rosamund absently took over his job of calming the horses, but she was thinking that never in her whole life had she addressed anyone in that tone of voice, especially someone who was not in a position to answer back. She had an inexhaustible supply of patience, or so she'd always thought. She'd left this very coach barely an hour ago, and she'd returned to it a changed woman. From this moment on, she promised herself, she would never more complain of all the checks her father imposed to keep her safe.

Just thinking of the last hour gave her the shudders. But she felt safe here in this crowded stable yard with her coachmen nearby, and now that her panic had lost its edge, she could think of Maitland without wanting to murder him. She didn't wish him well, but she didn't want him to hang either. If only he could be transported to the colonies, she would feel that justice had been served.

She'd set the blacksmith on him, but she didn't think the blacksmith would do more than thrash him. Or perhaps break his leg. The thought was vastly comforting. At any rate, she'd bought herself some time.

Her thoughts were interrupted when someone shouted for silence. "Listen!" the voice cried out.

An uneasy tension held everyone in its grasp. A moment later, the unmistakable sound of rifle fire rippled through the silence. The word *militia* came from every side. There wasn't a panic, but the party was over, and the yard quickly emptied as people took cover.

Then she saw him, Maitland, under the spreading branches of a horse chestnut tree. He was drinking from a tankard of ale. He was still wearing his turnkey's uniform, but he'd ripped off the frogging so that he looked like one of the rioters. There wasn't a mark on him, no bloody nose or broken jaw, and no broken limbs. Evidently, her blacksmith had possessed more brawn than skill. The hope that Maitland would take her for one of the rioters—she knew she looked a fright—was dashed when he raised his tankard in mock salute.

Well, she wasn't as defenseless as he thought she was. Her father had taught her what to do if ever she was waylaid by highwaymen, and she lost no time in putting his drill into practice. She lunged for the coach door, yanked it open, and hoisted herself inside. When the coach jerked as the lead horses stamped restlessly, she momentarily lost her balance, steadied herself, then she reached for the pistol that was always kept in the holster in the lining of the banquette. She knew how to shoot a pistol.

She crouched down in front of the coach window and peered out. Maitland was no longer under the horse chestnut tree, but this came as no surprise. He would be creeping up on her, maybe from the other side, hoping to take her off guard. Keeping her head well down, she inched toward the other door. That's when he came in the far door and lunged for her. She brought her pistol up and, contrary to Papa's strict instructions, aimed for his shoulder and not his heart. She simply did not possess the killer instinct. But he was too quick for her. His foot lashed out and connected with her pistol just as she pulled the trigger, and the bullet went wild. Someone on the roof of the coach let out a furious oath. Then Maitland fell on top of her, and for the third time in less than an hour, she cracked her head on something hard. The horses, maddened by the shot, reared in their traces and tried to make a bolt for it.

"Harper!" roared Maitland.

Harper! She knew that name! Harper was Maitland's

bodyguard. She'd read about him in the papers. Some bodyguard! Whenever Maitland didn't want his bodyguard around, he simply assigned him to other duties at Special Branch, and that's where Sergeant Harper was when Lucy Rider was murdered.

A voice from above roared back. "I've got 'em. I've got 'em."

Rosamund wanted to scream, but Maitland's weight crushed the breath out of her. Her head ached, her wrist ached, and though she was dazed, she knew what was going on. Harper was in the box and he had taken over the reins. She gritted her teeth as the horses jolted forward, then she went rigid with fear as Maitland pressed the barrel of a gun to her temple.

"Stay down or I'll blow your brains out," he gritted. When she didn't answer, he lost patience. "Did you hear me?"

She nodded vigorously.

Finally, he shifted, and she could breathe again, but not very easily because, as he raised himself to the banquette, he planted his booted foot right on her chest.

What was he waiting for? What was he watching for?

"Spring 'em," he suddenly yelled, making her wince.

She heard the crack of the whip, and as the horses sprang forward, the coach lurched into motion.

They wouldn't get far, she told herself. Papa's horses were notoriously hard to handle. The postilion who rode the lead horse wasn't there only to protect her, but to keep those high-strung horses from bolting the first chance they got. One man on the box would not control them for long. The horses would bolt, and the carriage would overturn, and it would be all over for Maitland and his lackey.

And if the horses didn't bolt, they'd be hemmed in by the mob or the militia. Either way, it would be over. All she had to do was grit her teeth and wait.

She couldn't see, but she could hear plenty as the

coach careened out of the stable yard—yells, curses, and the man on the box alternately cracking the whip and laughing like a maniac.

The coach tilted as it turned a corner, then it came down with a hard thud on the cobblestones, making her teeth rattle. At least the gun was no longer pressed against her temple. Maitland was looking out the window, his pistol cradled in the crook of one arm. Her own gun was somewhere on the floor, useless now, unless she could reload it, and that wasn't going to happen as long as his foot was on her chest.

When his eyes suddenly narrowed on her, she sucked in a breath. "What," he asked in a dangerously mild tone, "are you plotting to do to me now?"

Thoughts of boiling oil and thumbscrews danced in her head, but, under the circumstances, she decided to be diplomatic. "You've got the wrong idea about me," she said. "There is no plot. It's all in your imagination."

Those thinned lips flattened even more. When he bent over her, she edged away. "It's all in my imagination," he said.

"Yes."

"And I suppose I imagined that you tried to kill me when I entered your carriage?"

"You were pursuing me! And anyway, I aimed for your shoulder."

In the same deadly tone, he went on, "How does a duke's daughter come to be so handy with a gun?"

"Because," she said, "my mother's coach was attacked by highwaymen once, and she barely escaped with her life. After that, my father insisted that I learn how to defend myself."

"That's how to get yourself killed!"

"And that's exactly what I'm going to tell my father once you let me go."

He didn't take the hint. His dark brows rose, then he looked away so that she could not read his eyes. She had the oddest sensation that he was laughing at her, and the lump of fear in her throat dissolved. Laughing at *her*! A *Devere*! Whose ancestors were as heroic as the heroes of the Trojan war: Caspar Devere, who'd fought with the Black Prince at Poitiers and who'd blown kisses to the ladies, years later, just before the executioner chopped off his head when those upstart Lancastrians came to power; Lady Margaret Devere, who'd defended her husband's castle against Cromwell's Roundheads, then chased them off at the head of her own army; her own father, another Caspar Devere, who'd rescued dozens of French aristocrats during the Revolution; and her own mother, Elizabeth Devere, who'd thrown herself at a highwayman who'd pointed his gun at her son. Her family tree was weighed down with heroes.

Then what was she doing, cowering on the coach floor like this, allowing a no-good, detestable thug, who probably didn't have any ancestors, lord it over her with his boot planted firmly against her breasts?

The coach hit a pothole; her teeth and bones chattered like castanets, and that was the last straw.

"Get off me, you . . . you scoundrel!" she snapped.

She swiped at the offending boot with her balled fist, and much to her surprise, he did as she asked.

He pointed his pistol straight at her. "Stay on the floor," he commanded.

There wasn't a hint of a smile in his eyes or voice. She'd been mistaken to think that he was laughing at her. This man didn't have a sense of humor, and the laugh lines at the corners of his eyes weren't laugh lines at all. They were squint lines from narrowing his eyes in that unpleasant way of his to strike terror into the hearts of his victims.

And it was working.

She used her hands to push herself to a sitting position, but mindful of the gun, she didn't disobey his order to stay on the floor.

He chewed on his bottom lip. Finally, he said, "Begin at the beginning and tell me exactly what brought you to Newgate."

She delayed answering, as though she were putting her thoughts in order, but she was straining to hear sounds of pursuit. The streets of London were supposed to be swarming with militia. Then why hadn't they stopped the duke's carriage with the distinctive Devere coat of arms emblazoned on its side? And why hadn't Papa's high-strung horses bolted when there was only one man controlling the reins? And why—

"I'm waiting, Lady Rosamund."

Her eyes jerked up to meet his. "There's nothing sinister about my going to Newgate," she began. "My friend, Mrs. Tracey, invited me to accompany her. She felt sorry for you. You see, she believes you are innocent. All she wanted was to tell you so and give you a basket of small luxuries to brighten your last hours of life."

"But you didn't feel sorry for me, Lady Rosamund, did you?"

"Oh, I did, but that was before I met you."

Now he did smile, but there was nothing pleasant about it. It was as intimidating as the wicked-looking pistol in his hand. He said, "I might have believed you if I hadn't seen you give the signal to have me shot."

"What signal?"

"You dropped your reticule, then someone fired at me."

"Dropped my reticule? *Dropped my reticule?* I lost my shoe, and my shawl, and my bonnet as well. Were those signals to have you shot?"

He was doing it again, chewing on his bottom lip, and she experienced the same odd sensation. If he was laughing at her, gun or no gun, she would go for his throat.

He grunted, then said, "But you recognized me. I saw it in your eyes. That's when you gave the signal."

The man wasn't only deranged, he was stupid as well.

"You were going to be hanged," she said slowly, patiently. "Why would anyone in her right mind have you killed when all she had to do was wait a day, and His Majesty's executioner would do the job for her? If they'd only hanged you yesterday, none of this would have happened to me. I'd still be in Twickenham. And I didn't recognize you, not at first. How could I when I've never set eyes on you? You seemed different from the other turnkeys, that's all. And when the guard shouted that you'd escaped, I put two and two together."

He frowned. "Different from the other turnkeys? Then why didn't they notice? Why you and not them?"

She wasn't going to tell him that it was a female thing—how she'd been struck by his virility, his presence, his broad shoulders. Then he *would* laugh at her. "Because," she said, "you had shifty eyes. I could tell just by looking at you that you were a killer."

The words were out before she could stop them. She tensed, expecting him to retaliate in some way, but all he did was grunt.

Finally, he said, "Let's start again. Tell me about your friend, Mrs. Tracey. Leave nothing out. I want to know why you came to town, and why a duke's daughter would lower herself to visit a convicted murderer. You'd better make this convincing, or it will be very much the worse for you."

That closed expression, those ice-cold eyes promised swift retribution if he caught her out in a lie. Well, she had no motive to lie, but this man was so delusional that he wouldn't recognize the truth if it came from the Deity himself. He was compulsively suspicious. She'd bet her last farthing that he looked in every closet and under every bed before he lay down to sleep at night.

Her eyes strayed to the window. There wasn't much to see from her vantage point, but she knew they were in town because the coach was still rattling over cobblestones. Where were they going? What would he do with her when they got there? He wouldn't want to keep her with him, because she would only slow him down.

She thought of what he *could* do to her and waited for the panic to come. There was no panic. She didn't know why, but she didn't fear him half as much as she had when he was pursuing her. He still looked as mean and as fierce as ever, but she sensed something, she didn't know what. But her intuition was telling her that either he had softened toward her or that his bark was worse than his bite.

He would let her go once he reached his destination, she silently assured herself, and on that resolute thought, she embarked on her story. "It began," she said, "with Prince Michael of Kolnbourg."

ᴥ

Thirty minutes later, Rosamund was gnashing her teeth together, and calling herself all kinds of a fool for thinking he had softened toward her. While he and the gargoyle were comfortably ensconced inside Papa's carriage, deciding what to do next, she was flat on her back, handcuffed to the inside of an upturned rowing boat, somewhere outside London, on the banks of the river Thames.

At least the upturned boat protected her from the pelting rain.

She was no longer debating whether he would kill her or not. She was debating when and how she would kill *him*. Boiling oil and thumbscrews no longer satisfied her thirst for revenge. He would pay, she vowed, not for the first time, for all the indignities he had made her suffer. She was cold, she was hungry, and most mortifying of all, she knew that if he didn't return soon and release her so that she could answer nature's call, her bladder would burst. Hateful, despicable, spiteful man! What, oh, what was keeping him?

What was keeping him was the thorny problem of

what to do with Lady Rosamund Devere. "I'm not having her along at any price," said Richard. "She's nothing but trouble. If she doesn't return soon to dear Papa, he'll have the prime minister call out the army to look for us. I'm not joking, Harper. That's the kind of power the duke wields."

"And whose fault is that? It was your idea to bring her along. We should have left her back there, in Newgate."

"I thought she might know something."

"Know something about what? You was due to be hanged, wasn't you? Why would anyone want to kill you when they had only to wait till tomorrow?"

Richard grinned, and his eyes crinkled at the corners. "That's what she said."

"And she's right. I think Newgate must have turned your brains to mush."

There was a pause in the conversation as Harper passed an opened bottle of brandy to Richard, a bottle they'd found in the storage compartment under one of the banquettes. They'd also found a set of silver cups, a silver chamber pot, and warm woolen blankets.

After taking a swig of brandy, Richard passed the bottle back. Maybe Newgate *had* addled his brains. Now that he'd questioned the woman, his suspicions seemed absurd. She was bewildered by how her ordered existence had suddenly blown up in her face, bewildered and angry. And she blamed him for it.

A faint smile curled his lips as he remembered her indignant words. *If they'd only hanged you yesterday, none of this would have happened to me.*

Harper was right. There was no plot and no conspiracy. When that shot had gone off, he'd jumped to the conclusion that his enemies had somehow got wind that he was planning to escape and had come to prevent it. He wasn't going to mention his suspicions to Harper, because only three people besides himself knew about the escape—Harper, and his good friends Hugh and Abbie

Templar. They would be insulted because it would mean that he suspected that one of them had talked indiscriminately.

God, he was tired, and the pain from the knife wound in his chest seemed to be on fire. Just a short walk away, a snug cottage was waiting for him, a cottage that Hugh had outfitted with supplies—a change of clothes, money, food, and other necessities. The plan was that they'd conceal themselves there and slip away when darkness fell. They were to meet up with Hugh at Lavenham, just to change horses and let him know that all had gone well. But that was before he'd rashly brought Lady Rosamund along.

He stirred and adjusted his shoulders to ease the pain in his chest. "I say," he said, "that we leave her on some deserted road and let her find her own way home."

Harper scratched his chin. "Oh, yes, I can just see it. We leave her on some deserted road, she's set upon by footpads and murdered, and her doting father will be chomping at the bit to shake your hand."

"Have you got a better plan?"

"As a matter of fact, I has. We knows that the duke will be hot on our trail looking for his carriage, so I'll lead him on a false trail. Then I'll get rid of the carriage and horses, get fresh mounts, and come back for you and Lady Rosamund."

"What am I supposed to do with her until then?"

"Hide out in the cottage. Make yourself comfortable."

Richard turned his head and stared hard at Harper. "Why don't you hide out with her and let me take the carriage?"

Harper laughed. "Sounds to me as though you're afraid of her. She's only a girl. What can she do?"

"Look at the powder burns on my coat and say that."

"Is that all? She just about blew my arse off. If those horses hadn't moved when they did, she would have unmanned me!"

Richard's shoulders began to shake, and he adjusted his position again. "I still say I should take the carriage."

"No. If you was caught, you'd hang. Besides, you'd never manage the duke's horses. I was Mr. Templar's coachman, remember? If you can handle his cattle, you can handle anything."

Richard had forgotten about Harper's stint as Hugh's coachman. Soldier, agent, coachman, bodyguard— Harper had had a varied career. They'd all three served in the Secret Service at one time. Now Hugh was retired; he, himself, was due to hang; and Harper was a fugitive. A fine ending to three brilliant careers! And the prime minister had sworn that he owed them a debt of gratitude that could never be repaid.

Well, where was the prime minister when they needed him?

"So, are we agreed?" asked Harper. "I take the coach and you take the girl."

Richard was beginning to feel like a fractious child, but he really didn't want to be left alone with Lady Rosamund. She was resourceful and she wasn't easily cowed. Feeling as he did, he didn't know if he was up to it.

"She's dangerous," he began, "and—"

Harper threw up his hands. "You was the best His Majesty's Secret Service had to offer, wasn't you? If you can't handle one inexperienced girl, then all I can say is, God help England!"

"All right!" Richard let out a resigned sigh. "You come back with the horses. Then what do we do with her?"

"Then, when dark falls, we takes her to Mother Danby's place, with instructions not to let her go till morning, then we'll be on our way."

"Who is Mother Danby?"

"You don't want to know. Oh, she keeps a decent house. And she's an Amazon, just like Lady Rosamund.

So all our troubles will be over." He turned his head. "What was that?"

It sounded as though a fox had got into the hen house.

"Lady Rosamund," said Richard. "I'd recognize her voice anywhere."

Harper grinned. "I best be off, then."

Both men alighted from the carriage. When Harper was in the box, Richard said, "Good luck and take care."

Harper looked over at the upturned boat from which issued a stream of orders. "Remember she's a lady," he said, and with a crack of the whip and a wink, he took off.

Richard had a bottle of brandy under one arm, his pistol, fully loaded, in the other hand, and a blanket draped over his head and shoulders to protect him from the rain. Heaving a sigh, he walked over to the upturned boat.

Chapter 4

*H*er bladder didn't burst. He returned in the nick of time, unfettered her, and pointing to a wilderness of bushes, told her to be quick about it. She needed no second telling. Mustering her dignity, she hobbled into the bushes and took care of her most pressing problem. Only then did she give her mind to other things.

She'd heard the coach and horses move off, so that meant she had only Maitland to deal with. If she could just get away from him, she could hide herself in the underbrush until it was dark. By her reckoning, they weren't far out of London. They'd taken back roads to avoid the tollgates, but she knew they'd passed through a village not long ago. She could—

"What are you, a cart horse? You've had more than enough time. Get back here or I'll come and get you, ready or not."

And he would, too! There wasn't an ounce of delicacy in him. A cart horse indeed! First an Amazon, now a cart horse. No one had ever addressed her so rudely. If her father were here, he'd have Maitland in chains and thrown into the dungeons at Castle Devere. She longed to give him a piece of her mind, but she didn't intend to stay around that long. It was now or never.

He loomed up in front of her with the silence of a panther, and all she could do was stand there, stupidly gawking at him. Well, she wasn't completely stupid. She had the presence of mind to step out of her one remaining shoe and inch it behind her. If their pursuers followed them this far, her shoe would confirm that she had been here and they were on the right track.

"Come!" he commanded, "and take your shoe with you."

She clenched her fists and set her chin, but one look at that forbidding countenance made her decide to choose her fights with care, and this fight wasn't worth the effort.

But, oh, how her pride stung. He was so insufferably self-confident, and gave orders as though she were his lackey. But pride was only a part of it. Her sense of fair play was outraged, too. While he was protected from the rain by a blanket he had purloined from her father's coach, she was soaking up water like a thirsty sponge.

There were worse things that could happen to her. She must never forget that her captor had already murdered one woman. He had nothing to lose by doing away with her, too.

When they came out of the bushes, he pointed in the direction he wanted her to take. She balked. The path was no more than a narrow bog that led into a dense thicket of bramble bushes. It was an excellent place to conceal a body. *Her body*.

His hand touched her shoulder, and she shied away, slipped on the mud, and sat down heavily among the bramble bushes.

"For the love of God!" He sounded thoroughly annoyed. "What did you think I was going to do to you?" He stared hard at her, then shook his head. "If I'd wanted to kill you, I would have done it when you went into the bushes to relieve yourself. Have you no sense, woman? Hold still till I get these thorns out of your clothes."

He thrust his pistol into the waistband of his trousers, set down the bottle of brandy, and began to detach the prickly thorns from her gown. She sat there in miserable silence, with her knees drawn up to her chin, as the rain cascaded over her like a river in spate. Was it only yesterday, she wondered, that she'd longed for a little adventure? If this was the Deity's idea of a joke, she was not amused. In fact, she was seething at the injustice of it all. Not that she blamed the Deity. No. Richard Maitland, and he alone, was responsible for all her troubles.

Having released her from the brambles, he straightened and gave her another searching look. "Are you all right?" he asked.

"Am I all right?" she said pleasantly. "I wonder you should ask. What could be more agreeable than to be held at gunpoint, abducted, and tossed into a thicket of brambles in a downpour of rain in the middle of nowhere?"

"You fell into the brambles," he said. He stooped to pick up the bottle of brandy.

Was that a smile on his face? Her temper ignited and before she could think of the wisdom of what she was doing, she lunged for his booted foot, gave it a hard yank, and sent *him*, his blanket, and his brandy bottle flying into the bushes. Before the first oath was out of his mouth, she was on her feet and stumbling down the muddy track toward the boat. A push from behind sent her sprawling, and her momentum carried her forward. But she wasn't done yet. She was still clutching her stupid shoe, so she lay there in a heap, awaiting her moment. It came when he went down on one knee, and grasping her shoulders, raised her to her feet.

"Will you be sensible—"

She aimed for his face. As he threw up his arm to ward off the blow, his elbow inadvertently connected with her jaw.

"Bloody hell!" he muttered, and caught her as she began to sink to her knees.

❧

The path led to a one-room derelict cottage behind a dry stone wall. By the time Richard had carried her up the steep incline and deposited her on the bed, he was gasping for breath. Two weeks in Newgate hadn't improved his health, nor had carrying the Amazon from one end of the prison to the other and now up the hill to the cottage. The wound in his chest was beginning to throb.

As he stepped back from the bed, he took a good look at her. The perfect princess, the newspapers called her. Well, the perfect princess looked as though she'd been caught in a mangle.

How had it come to this? It was an accident, of course, though he didn't expect her to believe it. He had never struck a woman in his life. He didn't want to hurt her or terrorize her. He just wanted her to behave herself until they could go their separate ways.

He reached for the threadbare blanket at the end of the bed and draped it over her to absorb some of the damp, then he went to a cupboard in the fireplace wall. When he discovered that everything was just as he'd hoped, he said a silent thank you to Hugh Templar for providing everything a man on the run could possibly want—a fresh set of clothes, a fat purse of money, a medicine box, dressings for his wound, a razor, food, and a bottle of brandy to replace the bottle he'd lost.

There were two tin mugs on a table in front of the fireplace. He half filled one, took a healthy gulp from it, then crossed to the bed. He held her head as he dribbled brandy between her lips. Thankfully, she swallowed it without a protest. When her eyelashes fluttered and she stirred, he breathed a sigh of relief. She was going to be all right.

Which was more than he could say for himself. His head was swimming; his muscles ached. If he didn't get a grip on himself, he would give in to his fatigue, and with this girl, that could be a fatal mistake.

He thought about changing the dressing on his wound, but he decided that this wasn't the time, not when the girl was coming round. He'd wait till Harper got back. Surely two grown men could handle her, two grown men who, in Harper's words, were the best His Majesty's Secret Service had to offer?

He shook his head. Lady Rosamund was no ordinary woman. Most females would have been reduced to a quivering jelly by now. This one had pluck. Even when she was frightened, she kept her wits about her. She'd braved rioters and gunfire outside Newgate in her determination to get away from him, and only a few moments ago she'd attacked him with nothing more than a shoe. If she were a man, and he were still chief of staff at Special Branch, he'd offer her a job on the spot.

The thought made him smile, but the smile faded as his eyes roamed over her. The thin blanket clung to her wet form, emphasizing her lush curves. Though she was tall, she was perfectly proportioned. He was, after all, a male, and had noticed that much about her when she first entered the Felons' Quadrangle. Now that he had the leisure to examine her closely, he found other things to admire: her abundant dark hair; the finely arched brows and delicate features; the softly molded mouth.

When he realized he was staring at her mouth, he forced himself to draw in a slow, deep breath. This woman was dangerous! He shouldn't be softening toward her or lusting after her! He had too much to lose.

He had to make her fear him. It was the only way to get her to behave herself.

All the same, it didn't sit well with him. It went against everything he'd ever learned at his mother's knee. Females were the weaker sex. A man who took advantage of that fact was nothing but a brute. Besides, this female was innocent. Her one mistake was to be in the wrong place at the wrong time.

And that kind of thinking could get him sent back to Newgate and the gallows.

He had to make her fear him.

On that sobering thought, he stripped out of his wet clothes, dried himself off with a towel, then quickly donned the fresh set of clothes Hugh had left for him.

❧

When she came to herself, her jaw throbbed and her mouth burned with the taste of brandy. She was lying in a bed, but she knew it wasn't her own bed. The mattress was lumpy. Straw, she thought, then *Maitland*, and it all came back to her. She hauled herself up.

He was going through a cupboard on one side of a blackened stone hearth. Her gaze moved to take in other things, a small table and two wooden chairs; blackened pots and pans on a shelf; small windows on either side of the door. It was a one-room cottage with an abandoned air about it.

When she pushed back the blanket and swung her legs over the side of the bed, the bed creaked. Maitland straightened and walked toward her. He was spotless. She couldn't believe it. The last time she'd seen him, he was covered in mud. He'd washed himself and changed his clothes. But that wasn't all. He looked quite handsome. His light-brown hair had obviously been combed. And the sinister cast of his features was no longer there. And then it came to her. He had shaved.

His immaculate appearance made her all the more aware of her own bedraggled state. Mud squished between her toes and her rain-soaked garments hugged her in a soggy embrace.

She got to her feet, and eyed him warily as he came up to her. Seeing her expression, he nodded. "Don't make me use force to restrain you," he said.

His narrow-eyed gaze was almost more than she could bear. She wanted to look away, but her pride wouldn't allow it. There was nothing better this man would like than to see her cringe.

"I know your capacity for violence," she said, and touched a hand to her sore jaw.

He muttered something under his breath, combed his fingers through his hair, and took a step back. Finally, he said, "Listen to me, Lady Rosamund. If you behave yourself, no harm will come to you. Harper will be back soon with horses, then we're going to take you to a coaching inn and Harper and I will be on our way. You'll be back with your family before you know it."

Things were beginning to take shape in her mind. Someone had gone to a great deal of trouble to find this out-of-the-way cottage and supply it with whatever Maitland needed to make good his escape. But the cottage was so run-down, it was obvious this was not his ultimate destination, just a stop on the way to rest up and make sure the coast was clear before going on.

He said that Harper would soon be back with horses, then they'd take her to a coaching inn. If only she could believe him!

"I've looked out a change of clothes for you," he said. He went back to the cupboard and returned with a bundle of dry garments. "They're Harper's clothes, but they'll do until your own clothes dry out. And boots. Harper's boots. His feet are quite small."

Chills were breaking out all over her, and she would have gladly exchanged her wet garments for a suit of horsehair, but she didn't like the idea of stealing Harper's clothes. She feared him almost as much as she feared Maitland.

There was more to it than that, though.

When she didn't respond, his voice changed, became harder. "Five minutes," he said. "I'll give you five minutes, and if you're not dressed by the time I come back, I'll put you into these clothes myself. Oh, and don't think of escape. I'll be standing right outside that door. Did you hear me, Lady Rosamund? You'd better be in these dry clothes by the time I come through that door."

"I won't be," she said.

Frustration roared through him. "You're soaked to the skin! Your teeth are chattering! I'm not having you come down with a lung fever. Do you understand?"

"Perfectly. It's you who doesn't understand."

"Then enlighten me, ma'am, if you would be so kind."

She lifted her shoulders in a tiny shrug. "I can't undress myself without my abigail."

"Without your—"

"Lady's maid."

There was a silence. Two spots of color bloomed in her cheeks. Her eyes dared him to laugh at her. His brow puckered, then comprehension slowly dawned. She couldn't undress herself because, as he remembered, the buttons on her gown marched in a straight line from the back of her neck to the base of her spine.

"I'll be your lady's maid," he said.

She went rigid. "That won't be necessary. If you'd just give me a knife, or a pair of scissors, I'll cut my way out of my gown."

"A knife or a pair of scissors?"

She nodded.

"Do I look crazy? Turn around. I'll act as your lady's maid."

Her eyes went wide, and that got his temper going. He knew exactly what was going through her mind. "Lord have mercy! You don't think I'm going to have my wicked way with you? If you could only see yourself in a mirror, you would know how ludicrous that idea is." Then again, "Now turn around."

Her delicate nostrils flared, but she obeyed him, all the same.

The buttons were tiny and his fingers seemed to be all thumbs. At this rate, they'd be standing here till dooms-day. He grasped the edges of her gown and yanked. But-tons spilled over the stone floor and rattled into corners and under the bed. The back of her gown gaped, reveal-ing creamy white shoulders and her lacy stays. Her waist was surprisingly tiny, no more than a man's hand-span. His hand-span.

Where did that insane thought come from? "Five min-utes," he ground out, then left her.

She waited till the door closed, then she yanked off her frock, then her stockings, and used the blanket to dry herself off.

"If you could only see yourself in a mirror," she said, mimicking his tone of voice exactly. Well, if she was not mistaken, he was no Romeo. He couldn't even unbutton a woman's gown. It didn't surprise her. What woman in her right mind would have Richard Maitland? Not this one. Not even his mistress wanted him. Poor Lucy Rider.

If she could only see herself in a mirror! What did he expect after all she'd been through? When she was all prettied up she was, so her father said, a raving beauty. Of course, her father was prejudiced, but even allowing for exaggeration, she wasn't the hag Richard Maitland made her out to be.

She didn't know why his barb stung. So he didn't fancy her. So much the better. It was one thing less to worry about.

Her underclothes were damp as well, but she couldn't remove her chemise without first removing her stays, and they tied at the back. Her arms were aching by the time she undid the strings and slipped the stupid garment over her head, then her chemise. She didn't know how ordinary women managed to dress and undress themselves.

She pulled on a white lawn shirt that fell well below her knees. She was past caring about appearances. It was dry. That's what mattered, not Richard Maitland's opinion of her. The black pantaloons fitted her no better. The waist was too wide; the legs were too long; it was too snug around her bottom. She was glad there was no mirror in that crude cottage, or she would be tempted to smash it, and she couldn't afford any more bad buck.

As she stepped into Harper's boots, her mind flitted to this and that. Was it likely, she asked herself, that Maitland would clothe her if he was only going to do away with her? She had only to wait . . .

Could she trust him? *Should* she trust him?

Of course not, she thought, as she leaned over to turn up the legs of her pantaloons and her jaw began to ache.

She was reaching for the last article of clothing, a blue superfine jacket, when Richard came through the door. They both froze, he because Harper's black knit pantaloons were molded to Rosamund's form, revealing her lush bottom and the long length of her shapely legs. Before he could prevent it, a crude picture formed in his mind.

She froze because he looked as though someone had just stabbed him in the back. She half expected him to keel over and fall on his face.

He frowned and said with irritation, "Can't you do something with your hair? Or do you require the services of your lady's maid to dress it for you?"

Well, of course she needed Nan's services to dress her hair. That's what lady's maids were for. And if she ever decided to do without her maid's services, then where would Nan be? She would be out of a job, and her widowed mother and younger brothers and sisters would have to make do without her wages. This man was so dense, he didn't understand how the world worked.

As he went to the cupboard and unlocked it, she combed her fingers through her hair. It was supposed to be her best feature—thick, silky, and dark. Now it was a mess of tangles, and she had no idea what to do with it, except brush it back over her shoulders.

And why was he so angry?

When he turned from the cupboard, he was holding a picnic hamper. After depositing it on the table, he untied the string holding the lid down and crossed to her. She jumped when he suddenly reached for her hair.

"I have never met such a helpless female," he said. "Hold still."

He twisted her hair into a rope and tied it with the string. That done, he pointed to the fireplace. "You light the fire and I'll get our meal ready."

She looked at the kindling in the grate. She had never lit a fire in her life, but she'd watched others do it, and it didn't appear to be too difficult. Her eyes strayed to the mantelpiece. There it was, the ever necessary tinderbox. All she had to do was strike flint on flint to get a spark that would light the tinder. Then she would put the tinder under the kindling and the fire would blaze to life.

"Go on. Get the fire lit and we'll get your clothes dried off."

Orders, orders, orders! she mouthed to herself as she moved to the fireplace. She didn't talk to her servants like that. Their feelings would be hurt.

After several unsuccessful attempts to get the tinder lit, her respect for chambermaids took a gigantic leap. This wasn't a difficult job. It was impossible.

Richard Maitland's fingers closed around hers and he took the tinderbox away from her. "Are you completely useless?" he said in exasperation. "If you had to fend for yourself, you would starve to death, that's if you didn't freeze first. You highborn ladies . . ." He expelled a long breath. "Watch me."

And she watched, as flint struck flint, time after time, to no effect.

He scowled. "The tinder must be damp."

She would have smiled into his glowering face if her jaw hadn't hurt. Instead, she raised her brows, the only rebuke that she allowed herself when her servants displeased her. "I know the feeling," she said. "I miss my servants, too. If only Harper were here."

⋆

She enjoyed every morsel of that meal, in spite of the fact that there was no blazing fire to warm them, or burning candles to take the edge off the gloom. She and Maitland were both hopeless. They'd tried repeatedly to light the tinder in the box and had finally given up. She didn't mind. His glowering face gave her all the warmth she needed.

Even the fact that her left hand was handcuffed to her chair didn't dim her spirits. The ache in her jaw had subsided. Though it was cold, the food was as good as anything her own cook could produce, and her fear of her captor was ebbing as the minutes passed.

Maitland, on the other hand, was restless. He would suddenly get up and go outside to check on things, as he said. He was worried—not that he talked things over with her. But she had eyes in her head. She could see, feel the tension mount in him. And the more tense he became, the more she relaxed. Maybe rescue was just around the corner.

"We're moving out," he said.

"What?" She put her fork down. "I didn't hear Harper come back."

"He hasn't. That's why we're moving out. It shouldn't have taken him this long to get horses."

She didn't know if this was good news or bad, and she said slowly, "Does this mean you're letting me go?"

He was moving between the cupboard and the bed, stuffing a saddlebag with odds and ends. He didn't look up when he spoke to her. "Hardly. You would only lead the militia straight here."

"But you said that you would take me to an inn and leave me there."

"Only if we had horses. And Harper was going to procure them. Without him, that plan won't work. We'll have to think of something else."

A moment ago, she'd felt relatively safe with this man, now she didn't know where she was. It was like being on a seesaw. One minute she was up, the next minute she was down.

"What if," she said, "I promise not to tell the authorities anything?"

Now he did look at her. "Why should I believe you?"

Her chin came up. "Because I'm a Devere."

He was on the point of answering her curtly, but changed his mind when he saw her expression. There was pride there, but it was touched by fear.

Of course she was afraid! He was her ruthless abductor and she believed him to be a murderer. She didn't know what to expect. Naturally, she would promise anything to get away from him.

What surprised him was how much he wanted to believe her.

Gentling his voice, he said, "I can't let you go until I'm sure I have a headstart on my pursuers, but if you give me your word that you won't try to escape or try any tricks, I'll put the pistol away and dispense with the handcuffs."

For a moment, it looked as though she might agree, then she shook her head. "To a Devere, his word is sacred," she said. "Is there anything sacred to you, Richard Maitland?"

Her answer rankled. His whole life had been devoted to serving his country, and his country had turned against him. Why he should have expected more from this chit of a girl was beyond comprehension.

She didn't trust him. It didn't matter because he didn't trust her either. She'd practically told him not to. Fine. Then he was back to being her ruthless abductor.

He gave a small, twisted smile. "My life is sacred to me," he said, "and you would do well to remember it."

She watched him turn away to go on with the packing. She had the strangest feeling that somehow she'd failed him, and that was nonsense. She was the innocent party here. Her word was worth something. This man was a murderer. His word wasn't worth anything.

Then why did she feel as though she'd let him down?

She said quietly, "What are you going to do with me?"

"I'll think of something."

At these chilling words, so carelessly uttered, her head cleared. His warning was well taken. The only thing that mattered to him was his own life and she would do well to remember it.

She swallowed hard, wondering what might happen to her, and swallowed again when she thought of her father. He would know by now that she'd been abducted and he would be ravaged with worry. So would her brothers.

She looked at the window. It would be dark soon. She would have a better chance of escaping in the dark.

Chapter 5

*T*he news of Maitland's escape from Newgate and his abduction of Lady Rosamund traveled through London with the force of a comet. Though many balls and parties were canceled as a consequence of the riots, the gentlemen's clubs in St. James's were busier than ever. In White's, Mr. George Withers listened intently as Charles Tracey gave a first-hand account of how Maitland had escaped. He'd been there, Tracey said, with his sister-in-law, and Lady Rosamund had insisted on going with them.

Tracey, Withers thought cynically, was enjoying all the attention, though he'd hardly acted the part of the hero. He would have liked to ask Mr. Tracey a few pointed questions, but the man was so hemmed in by his audience that he could not get near him.

It was just as well, because Withers doubted that he could remain cool and collected. Already, his heart was pounding and his breathing was becoming audible. One of his rages was coming upon him, and the last thing he

wanted was to betray himself to the wealthy and aristocratic patrons of White's, who had accepted him as one
of their own.

They knew him as George Withers, a son of England
who had made his fortune in South Carolina, where he
owned a sizeable plantation. His credentials and letters
of recommendation were genuine. He really was one of
Charles Town's leading citizens. What no one knew was
that the real George Withers had died a long time ago,
before the man impersonating him had moved to South
Carolina.

He managed a smile as he scraped back his chair and
said that he was for home. There were a few nods, but no
one at his table tried to persuade him to stay. They were
too interested in what Tracey had to say.

It was only a short walk to his rooms in Bond Street,
but try as he might, he could not keep his rage at bay. If
he'd met a stray dog or a beggar, he would have vented
his rage on them, but the only person he passed was the
night watch, and to this burly fellow, he merely tipped
his hat.

Richard Maitland has escaped from Newgate. The words
pounded inside his head. *Richard Maitland has escaped
from Newgate.*

No one could accuse him of understimating Richard
Maitland, but escaping from Newgate was something he
had never imagined. This was Lady Rosamund's doing.
Maitland had used her as a hostage, Tracey said, to make
his escape, aided and abetted by his former bodyguard.

He should have killed Maitland when he had the
chance, when he walked into Lucy Rider's bedchamber.
But that wouldn't have suited his purposes. He'd wanted
Maitland to survive and be publicly humiliated before
they hanged him. He'd wanted to even the score. He'd
plotted, schemed, dreamed about having Maitland in
the palm of his hand—and now this.

It wasn't over yet. It wasn't nearly over.

His rage began to ebb when he pictured Maitland on the run, hunted from pillar to post, and he would be hunted, now that he had taken Lady Rosamund hostage. He had no friends, no one to help him—he had seen to that. His recapture was only a matter of time.

He had no fears that Maitland would come after him, but it pleased him to imagine how the man who was reported to have the keenest intelligence in His Majesty's Secret Service must be adding things up, as he tried to fathom who was behind his downfall. He would never figure it out, not in a million years.

The more he thought about Maitland cooped up in some filthy rat hole, trying to figure out who had put him there, the lighter his mood became. When he entered his rooms, he felt in command of the situation again and dismissed his manservant with a smile.

He made straight for his book room, poured himself a generous measure of brandy, and went to warm himself at the fire. Above the mantel was a mirror, and his eye was caught by his reflection. No one looking at him, he decided, would ever guess that he was a killer. He wasn't handsome, but his face was pleasant, friendly, the kind of face that people trusted, especially women. And it helped, too, that he looked older than his years. His brown hair was liberally laced with silver and the lines on his face were etched permanently by the brutal winters he'd endured in the fur trade in the wilds of Canada.

He would never have had to spend those soul-grinding, dismal years in Canada if it hadn't been for Maitland.

It struck him as odd that only two people had ever mistrusted him, his father and Richard Maitland.

"I didn't kill the kitten, Papa! I didn't! It was a fox, and I frightened it away." And real tears rolled down his cheeks.

His father wasn't entirely satisfied, but his mother had

intervened, and her protestations of her blue-eyed boy's innocence carried the day.

Women had always been putty in his hands—his mother, his wife, Lucy—he smiled when he thought of the boy. This was something different. He'd never had an apprentice before; he'd never had someone who looked up to him and applauded his cunning and his successes. He found it liberating to be able to take off the mask and reveal himself as he truly was. And the boy was an apt pupil. They could have a bright future together.

Maitland had had the opposite effect on him. From the moment they'd met, he'd felt uncomfortable in Maitland's presence. *A dour Scot,* he'd thought, but there was more to it than that. He'd find Maitland's eyes on him, unsmiling eyes that missed nothing, and he'd find himself trailing away in the middle of a sentence. He'd tried to make friends with Maitland, tried to win him over, but Maitland had ignored every overture.

Maitland held no fears for him now. He would never work things out. And Maitland had a failing that he, himself, did not possess. Maitland followed a code of honor, something singular to himself and slightly tarnished around the edges, but a code of honor nonetheless. Maitland would stop at murder, whereas he would not.

His mind sifted through this and that and finally focused on Maitland's friends. A cautious man, Maitland, and that was something he understood and respected. The chief of staff of Special Branch couldn't afford to let people get close to him. The only friends who amounted to anything were Hugh Templar and Jason Radley. He knew that Radley had gone off to Paris before Maitland's world collapsed around him, and as far as he knew, he was still there. As for Templar, he had deserted his "friend" the moment he went to trial.

Or had he?

On reflection, he decided that it was too risky to stand

aside and let the authorities track Maitland on their own. He had no faith in the authorities. *Bumbling* and *incompetent* were the words he would use to describe them, else they would never have convicted an innocent man—Maitland—while allowing someone who was guilty five times over—himself—to walk away unscathed.

His first kill had shocked him, though he'd planned it down to the last detail. It was odd how easier it became with each successive kill, easier and more pleasurable. The rush of power was like nothing he had ever experienced. When he killed, he felt like a god.

He felt the rush of power now just thinking about it. But good as those kills had been, they were as nothing to the pleasure he anticipated when he finally watched Richard Maitland dangle at the end of a rope.

Careful, he warned himself. Maitland wouldn't be as easy a kill as those others. The man was born with a suspicious nature. Until Maitland, he'd got by on his cunning and natural charm. After Maitland, he'd learned to use his brains as well. He had to think things through, had to pull things apart and piece them together on the remote chance, the very remote chance, that Maitland would work things out.

When he heard voices in the corridor, he got up. He was expecting his visitor and wanted answers to the questions that had been running through his mind. Where were Richard Maitland's friends? Where could he be hiding? What would he do next? Who was this bodyguard who had helped him escape?

And who would be in charge of tracking Maitland down?

&

Harper leaned his elbow on the bar counter, took a long swig from his tankard of ale, and wiped the foam from his mouth with the back of his sleeve. He was beginning to realize that abducting a duke's daughter wasn't the wisest thing his chief had ever done. The road to Chelsea was choked with troopers. He'd only come a mile or two along the road when he was spotted, and a troop of cavalry had given chase. If he hadn't been driving the finest and fastest rig he'd ever had the pleasure of handling, he'd be on his way to Newgate by now. As it was, he'd just managed to ditch the duke's equipage and take refuge in the Cocked Hat, when the militia surrounded it.

And here he'd been as dusk fell and the lanterns were lit. The taproom was packed, and a soldier guarded each exit. They'd found the duke's coach and now they were looking for the girl and her abductors. Everyone in the vicinity had been rounded up and ordered to wait in the inn until they could be questioned. If the king had been abducted, there couldn't have been a bigger rumpus.

It could be worse, much worse. Those soldiers could have come from the Horse Guards, where Special Branch was quartered. Then someone might recognize him, and the game would be up. But these soldiers came from Richmond, and they didn't know him from Adam.

They hadn't started to question the patrons yet. Harper didn't think he was going to hang around for that. Though he knew he had a glib tongue and could talk his way out of just about anything, it could take hours before they got around to him. He had to get horses and get back to his chief. Just a little while longer and he would make his move. He'd cause a distraction and be out of here like a shot.

If his luck held.

When the door opened and two men entered the bar, he realized that getting back to his chief was the least of his worries. He casually turned his back on them so that they wouldn't see his face. He didn't know whether they would know him or not, but he sure as hell knew them. Everyone at Special Branch knew them, Digby and Whorsley, the two thugs from upstairs. They all worked under the same roof and came under the umbrella of His Majesty's Secret Service, but some sections were more secret than others. Digby and Whorsley worked for Section C, commonly known as the Spanish Inquisition. These were the spies who spied on spies.

They were forever sticking their noses in where they were least wanted. Colonel Maitland had bent those noses out of joint a time or two. Digby hated the chief because he thought he'd stolen his promotion. He would make him pay for it now, if he ever caught him.

He turned his head slightly, and from the corner of his eye saw that they were leaving with one of the officers. They couldn't know about the cottage, could they? He shook his head, answering his own question. Only he, the chief, and Mr. Templar knew where the cottage was, and they wouldn't tell anyone. But now that they'd found the duke's carriage, the men from upstairs would know that the chief must be hiding close by.

He had a very bad feeling in the pit of his stomach.

"Look!" a woman shrilled. "They're bringing in the duke's carriage! And ain't that the duke and his sons?"

There was a surge toward the windows as everyone tried to get a better look. From his vantage point at the bar counter, Harper had a clear view. They were standing directly under one of the lanterns.

They made a striking group, the duke and his sons, as darkly handsome as gypsies, and as graceful. But there was something about their bearing, not arrogance exactly, but something close to it, that commanded respect. And Digby and Whorsley were certainly giving them respect, bowing and scraping like trained dogs in a circus.

"*Toadeaters,*" muttered Harper under his breath.

The door opened and a soldier entered. "His Grace, the Duke of Romsey," he cried out, "is offering a reward of five thousand pounds for information leading to the safe return of his daughter."

A hush descended, then everyone started talking and

shouting across each other. One of the soldiers left his post at the door to quell an argument that had broken out between two patrons. The distraction Harper had been waiting for had arrived.

He idled his way to the door and pushed it open, then froze when he heard someone calling his name.

"That's Sergeant Harper! He's one of them!"

Digby's voice! So the man from upstairs had recognized him after all. He didn't look back. He charged down the corridor, through the back door, and into the inn's courtyard. And after him streamed a horde of shrieking patrons, all determined to get to him first so they could claim the reward.

As they surged into the courtyard, soldiers cocked their pistols.

"There he is!" yelled Harper, pointing. "He's getting away!"

It was the same trick he'd used at Newgate, and he hoped to hell it would work here as well.

He untied the first horse he came to and jumped onto its back. A volley of shots rang out, but none of them was aimed at him. The soldiers were firing at the imaginary target he had pointed out. It would take them precious seconds to reload their pistols.

He dug in his heels and in a bounding leap went thundering onto the road to town. A bullet whined right past his ear. There was always some clever blighter who held his fire until he was sure of his target. That's what he'd taught the men under his command to do, so he shouldn't be complaining.

"Hold your fire!" yelled Digby.

"After him, fools!" Whorsley's voice this time.

There was no thought in Harper's mind now of rejoining his chief. He knew what he had to do, and that was lead the enemy as far from Colonel Maitland as possible.

Chapter 6

His Grace called for Digby and Whorsley and, without waiting to see if they were following, led the way into the inn. As soon as the innkeeper showed them into a private parlor and bowed himself out, he pointed to chairs. "Sit," he said.

Digby and Whorsley exchanged a veiled look, but when the duke's sons each took a chair at the table, so did they, only they sat ill at ease on the edge of their seats.

His Grace stood in the middle of the room, his feet apart, clenching and unclenching his hands. He was a tall man, well over six feet, with dark hair graying at the temples. Harper had likened him in his own mind to a gypsy, but the duke was not dark-skinned. He was tanned by the sun, the result of an active life spent outdoors. He was in his early sixties and was generally taken for a much younger man. At this moment, he looked older than his years. Every line in his grief-stricken face was deeply etched.

His sons, Lords Caspar and Justin, so closely resembled their father that no one could have mistaken the relationship. Rosamund had been spared the square jaw and aquiline nose, but they all shared their father's wide-set gray eyes, intelligent eyes that looked at the world in a clear-eyed, reflective stare.

After several moments of silence, Caspar said gently, "Father, sit down."

"What?" The duke looked at his elder son, made a considerable effort to come to himself, and took the chair Caspar indicated.

He was never at a loss, always in command of every situation. His hair-raising escapades in France during the Revolution had made him a legend in his own time. But this was different. This so closely resembled the grief that had consumed him when his wife died that the fear was almost paralyzing. He'd forgotten how fragile he was until two strangers, Major Digby and Captain Whorsley, had arrived at the house and broken the news of Rosamund's abduction. Her coach had been found abandoned in the environs of Chelsea, they'd said, and without more ado, he'd mounted up and ridden out with them. Now he wanted a fuller accounting of what had happened to his daughter.

Caspar and Justin, he knew, felt as lost as he did. They'd been in London when militiamen had tracked them down and given them the news. They'd arrived at the Cocked Hat within moments of each other.

Just looking at his sons brought a measure of calm, though he did not always see eye to eye with them. Caspar, the heir, against his father's wishes had fought in the Spanish Campaign, and had returned to England a changed man, with a steel in him the duke secretly admired, but could not always tolerate.

Justin, not to be outdone by his older brother, had joined him in the last weeks of the war. But Justin's experience was different from Caspar's. He'd been feted by the Belgians, he and his fellow, dashing hussars. To Justin, the war was glory and glamour. Caspar's long years in Spain were much darker. All the same, the duke was counting on both sons now to see them through this terrible calamity.

They believed that Maitland was no fool, and that he would use Rosamund to barter his way to freedom. He prayed they were right, but what he'd read of Maitland in the newspapers made him fear the worst. If he thought he'd get away with it, he would kill Rosamund without compunction. They had to find him before it was too late.

The duke's eyes moved to Digby and Whorsley. Though they were military men, they looked as if they spent much of their time chained to their desks, studying reports. They were both lean, fortyish, with lines of concentration furrowing their brows, and they reminded the duke of his own bookkeepers. If a penny went missing, they worried at it until it was found. He hoped it was a good sign.

They'd said they were from Section C of His Majesty's Secret Service, and seemed proud of it. The duke, however, was not reassured. The Secret Service was so fragmented that the right hand rarely knew what the left hand was up to. If it had known, someone like Richard Maitland would never have been appointed as chief of staff.

Everyone was staring at him, waiting for him to speak. "Major Digby," he said, "who is this Harper fellow?"

"Maitland's bodyguard, and now evidently his accomplice. He helped Maitland escape from the prison. That's all we know at this point, Your Grace."

The duke nodded. "And what fool took a shot at him? I mean that final shot that barely missed its mark?"

Digby spread his hands. "I don't know, but when I find out, the man will be disciplined."

This seemed to satisfy the duke. "Now tell me about Richard Maitland," he said. "How did he come to be tried in a civil court and not by the military?"

"Because," said Digby, "the civil authorities got to him first and refused to give him up. We could have insisted, but public opinion wanted him tried in an open court. They thought we would be lenient with one of our own, I suppose. At any rate, our superiors decided not to make a fuss."

The duke grunted. After a moment, he said, "So, who is this Maitland? What can you tell me about him?"

"With all due respect, Your Grace," said Digby carefully, "time is wasting. Maitland can't be far away. We should be organizing a search, house by house, and street by street."

The duke lifted his head. His voice was suddenly harsh. "An excellent idea if there were anyone left to organize. But your men are pursuing a fugitive. And let's hope no one else takes a shot at him, or our best chance of finding Maitland will be gone."

Digby bit down on his lip.

"So," continued the duke, "while we wait, tell me about Richard Maitland. How did such a man come to be the chief of staff at Special Branch? Who are his friends? His family? Who can he turn to for help?"

"I believe," said Digby, "his family lives in Scotland. His father is a lawyer of some sort, but not well-known or distinguished in any way. A modest family, you might say. Their son was ambitious. He did well at school, and went into the army on graduating from university. Eventually, he transferred to British Intelligence in Spain."

When Digby paused to gather his thoughts, Lord Caspar said, "He sounds like an admirable fellow. So what went wrong?"

"What went wrong," said Digby with feeling, "is he got too big for his boots. He didn't become chief of staff through his own merits, but because he was lucky. He was in the right place at the right time."

He seemed to realize that he was becoming too passionate, and after a short pause, spoke in a more moderate tone. "You may have heard that there was a plot to assassinate the prime minister?"

"Yes, I heard," said the duke. "Are you saying this Maitland fellow prevented it?"

"No. Only that he took the credit for it, he and his faithful hound, Harper."

"I see," said the duke. "Go on."

"As a reward, Lord Liverpool appointed him chief of staff. If Section C had been consulted, we would have argued against the appointment. Maitland is not one of us. He doesn't fit in. He doesn't play by the rules, but thinks he is accountable to no one. As for his friends, he doesn't have any, not what you and I would call real friends. He has colleagues and acquaintances, that's all."

"Well," interjected Lord Justin laconically, "this bodyguard—what's his name, Harper?—seems to be a true friend. Loyalty like that cannot be bought."

Digby allowed himself a small smile. "Sergeant Harper!" he said. "An enlisted man, then a coachman, bodyguard, and now Maitland's partner in crime. A true and fitting friend indeed, for the likes of Maitland."

The duke's brows came down. He counted among his friends his own coachman, Sellers, now retired, but living in comfort at Castle Devere. He didn't like the tone of Digby's remarks; he didn't like his sneer; and he was coming to the conclusion that he didn't like the man, either.

He looked at the other agent. "Well, Captain Whorsley, what have you to say?"

"Oh." Whorsley looked at Digby. "I agree with everything Major Digby says, Your Grace."

Digby said, "He won't get away with this, Your Grace.

He has nowhere to go and no one to turn to. We'll catch him, and when we do, he'll pay for his crimes."

When the duke stood, everyone respectfully got up as well. "Now listen to me," he said. "Catching Maitland and making him pay for his crimes is not our object. Our object is the safe return of my daughter, and if, God willing, she's still alive, we'll give Maitland whatever he wants to get her back. If he demands a ransom, I'll pay it. If he wants a safe passage out of England, I'll arrange it. If he wants amnesty, he can have it. Whatever Maitland wants, he can have. Is that understood?"

Both agents nodded, Whorsley at once, Digby with obvious reluctance.

The duke's gaze wandered to the small-paned window. "But," he said, his voice low and thick, "if anything happens to my Rosamund, Maitland will answer to me for it, and to no one else."

The silence that followed these chilling words was broken by the sound of horses' hooves clattering over cobblestones. The duke strode to the window and looked out. "Your men are beginning to return, I believe, Major Digby," he said. "And empty-handed, I think." He turned from the window. "I'm making this inn my headquarters for the present. You will inform me of all developments. That is all."

When the agents looked at him blankly, he said, "You were going to organize a search, I believe? Well, go to it."

Digby and Whorsley bowed themselves out of the room.

❧

They were silent as they descended the stairs, but on entering the stable yard, they both let fly with an obscene expletive.

"Did you hear him?" asked Whorsley incredulously. "We're to give Maitland whatever he wants."

Digby was seething. "Safe passage out of England! A ransom! They're going to reward that murdering swine? Not if I have anything to do with it."

Whorsley shook his head. "There's nothing we *can* do about it. You know our orders. We're to do nothing without consulting the duke. And those orders come directly from the prime minister."

"There are ways around orders."

They'd been walking toward a group of horsemen who had just dismounted, but at these words, Whorsley stopped in his tracks. "You have a plan?"

Digby let out an impatient sigh. "Of course I don't have a plan." He turned to face his companion. "All I'm saying is that we can't consult the duke if he's not there. And no one can predict what will happen when we corner Maitland. Soldiers panic. Guns go off. Who is to say who fired the first shot? And if the duke's daughter is returned unharmed, who will care?"

"And if she's not unharmed?"

"We'll blame Maitland for it. No one is going to listen to what he says anyway."

He felt humiliated by the duke and his sons and took his wrath out on the soldiers who were returning after a fruitless chase. *Maitland!* he thought. *Always Maitland!* The duke and his sons should have reviled the upstart. They should have been out for his blood. But it was Maitland whom they seemed to admire, albeit reluctantly, and himself who was made to feel small.

Well, he was done with living in Richard Maitland's shadow. He'd proved he was the better man. Maitland had brought nothing but shame to the honor of the Service. If he had been made chief of staff, as was his due, Maitland would have been relegated to some insignificant post where he could do the least harm.

And now they would all be watching him—the prime minister, the home secretary, his colleagues—to see how he handled the Maitland affair. Let them! He was more than a match for Richard Maitland, and this was his chance to prove it.

&

Upstairs, in the duke's private parlor, the atmosphere was considerably more relaxed. Caspar and Justin were lounging in armchairs, and the duke was standing in front of the fireplace, smoking a cheroot. Justin fished in his pocket, withdrew a cheroot, and lit it from the candle in the center of the table. The duke watched him light it, but kept his lips firmly sealed.

His sons, he reminded himself, were grown men and answerable to no one but themselves. He could hardly object to them smoking when he, himself, enjoyed the odd cigar. And there were worse things than smoking. His glance flicked to Caspar.

He was too handsome for his own good. Too good-looking, too much money, and too many fast women—that was Caspar's trouble. When was he going to settle down?

And why was he worrying about such trifles when his daughter's life could be hanging in the balance?

Justin exhaled a plume of smoke, caught his father's eye, and said, "Did you say something, Father?"

"No," barked the duke. "Just open the window."

Caspar stretched his legs. "The more I listened to Digby," he said, "the less hostile I became to Maitland. I wonder if Digby knows that every time he opens his mouth, his envy shows? The man is consumed with professional jealousy."

"And," added Justin, "conceit. *He's not one of us.* You know what that means? Maitland didn't go to the right schools, or get into the right clubs."

Caspar said, "Well, he went to the right university. I heard that he went to Cambridge for a year, but left under a cloud. So maybe that's when the corruption started."

The duke said, "Just as long as you remember that he *is* corrupt. And dangerous. I don't like Digby or Whorsley any more than you do, but they weren't convicted of murder, and they didn't abduct your sister." He paused, then went on, "All the same, I don't think we'll leave everything up to those two. They didn't strike me as particularly clever, and we're dealing with someone who is razor sharp. His escape from Newgate was brilliantly executed. He doesn't panic when things go wrong; he uses circumstances to his advantage. He couldn't have known Rosamund would be there, but when he was cornered, he used her to get away."

He looked at his sons steadily, trying to impress his words upon them. "Don't underestimate him. Remember, he has killed once. He has nothing to lose if he kills again."

Caspar said quietly, "What do you want us to do, Father?"

"We need more information. It's nonsense to say that Maitland has no friends. Harper is loyal to him, isn't he? There must be someone else, someone who can provide him with shelter, and money to live on. A friend from the past, a fellow soldier perhaps."

"Shall I start with his colleagues at Special Branch?"

"No. Those Whitehall types are notoriously tight-lipped. Start with Callie. I still don't understand what she and Rosamund were doing in Newgate. Maybe she can give us a lead on Maitland.

"Justin, I want you to take a message to Twickenham. If Maitland wants to barter for a ransom or whatever, he may leave a message there. Tell my secretary where I am, and he's to let me know at once."

"Done."

"And we'll need our own men."

"How many?"

"A dozen should do it."

Justin grinned. "That's no problem. Half our footmen and groundsmen are former soldiers."

"I hope they make better soldiers than they do footmen and groundsmen," muttered the duke. "Yes, yes, I know. Times are hard and the least we could do was give them employment when they came home from the war."

The duke walked his sons to the door. "I'll keep an eye on things here, but get back as soon as you can."

Casper clasped his father's hand. "Rosamund is safe, Father. She is Maitland's trump card. He won't let anything happen to her."

"I know," said the duke. "I know."

But when he was alone, he wasn't sure he knew anything at all.

ை

The duke was right about Callie giving them a lead on Maitland, though it took Caspar some time to get the information out of her. She was so enraged at what she perceived as Maitland's betrayal that she broke off at every other sentence to demolish his character. And, of course, she was full of self-recrimination. She was the one who should have been abducted, not Rosamund. It was all her fault.

If she was looking for sympathy from him, Caspar thought, she would be disappointed. Even as a child, Callie always had to be the center of attention, so much so that visitors to Castle Devere had often mistaken *her* for the duke's daughter. Caspar had been impatient with her then, and he was impatient with her now. He didn't want to know how she felt when Maitland took Rosamund hostage. He wanted to know about Rosamund. He wanted facts. He wanted to know how Maitland managed the escape and who else besides his bodyguard could have helped him. Finally, he got what he wanted. A name. Hugh Templar.

It was a name Caspar recognized. He'd met Major Templar, as he then was, at various receptions in Lisbon and Madrid. *The scholar-soldier* they'd called him because of his interest in Roman antiquities. Since then, their paths had crossed in London, and they'd exchanged the odd friendly word, but that was the extent of their acquaintance.

"I don't know if they were friends," said Callie, "so much as colleagues. They served with Wellington, you know, in Spain."

"Many men served with Wellington," Caspar said. "That doesn't make them friends or mean that they keep up with each other after the war."

"I'm aware of that. But they've been seen together. Maitland has been a guest of the Templars, here and at their place in Oxfordshire. There's something else. Maitland's bodyguard. Well, he was Templar's coachman before he became Maitland's bodyguard, and he was in Spain as well."

"Who told you all this?"

"I can't recall. Does it matter? It's not a secret. I must have heard it at some ball or other. Anyway, they're not friends now. Templar did not even come to Maitland's trial. Oh, how I wish I had taken a leaf out of Templar's book!"

"Yes," Caspar said sharply, "so do we all wish it! Now tell me where I can find Mr. Templar."

Templar's house was in Berkeley Square, only a few minutes away from Callie's house. The streets were quiet now, but there were still troopers patrolling on horseback. Caspar's thoughts were preoccupied. He was thinking of Templar and Maitland. He knew next to nothing of Maitland, but from what he knew of Templar, he could not see him deserting a friend or fellow officer in his darkest hour.

So what was Templar up to? What was so important

that it had kept him away from Maitland's trial? And how did Harper fit into it? The go-between? What?

His hopes of questioning Templar were dashed when he arrived at the house only to learn that Templar was not there. His master, the butler said, had taken his wife and young son to Staines to view the ruins of a Roman villa.

Caspar did not need a map to fix Staines's position in relation to Chelsea. It was a small village on the Thames, on the way to Windsor.

"When was this?" Casper asked.

"Two days ago, your lordship."

Two days ago, Richard Maitland had been found guilty of murder and sentenced to hang, and Templar had conveniently left town.

He smiled at the butler. "Mr.—?"

"Soames," the butler supplied, startled.

"Why don't we go inside, Mr. Soames, and you can tell me all about it?"

Chapter 7

He said they were moving out, but they didn't go very far. After loading the boat with two bulging saddlebags, he ordered her into the boat, then he rowed to the other side of the river, where he rested his oars under the dripping leaves of a weeping willow. And here they'd remained as the darkness closed in around them.

She'd considered her chances of escape if she jumped into the river, but she hadn't liked the odds. For one thing, her hands were handcuffed, making it impossible for her to swim. For another, he'd given her Harper's coat to wear and she was warm and dry. She hadn't given up the idea of escape, only she preferred to make the attempt when she was on dry land.

His mood had turned ugly again, and they had hardly exchanged two words in she didn't know how long. The silence was beginning to grate on her.

She cleared her throat. "What are we waiting for?"

"Harper, of course."

She looked across the river but could see nothing. "How will he know we're here?"

"He'll know."

She swallowed her next question. Of course Harper wouldn't be able to see them in the dark. This must have been arranged beforehand. The boat had to have been there for a purpose. If something went wrong, they could slip away by boat.

This man overlooked nothing. Back at the cottage, he'd removed everything that might have betrayed their presence there. Her ruined shoe and popped buttons were now in one of his coat pockets. The picnic basket with the remains of their meal and her tattered clothes was now weighed down with stones and thrown into the river. She was beginning to see just how formidable a foe he would make.

If he was so formidable, how had he managed to bungle a murder? He was practically caught in the act. Caught, convicted, and sentenced to hang. So maybe he wasn't so formidable after all.

On the other hand, he'd escaped from Newgate, hadn't he? To her knowledge only one other convict had escaped from Newgate, and that was before she was born.

"Colonel Maitland—"

"Quiet!"

She pressed her lips together. If he didn't want to talk, it didn't matter to her. She was used to amusing herself with her own thoughts. Sometimes, she spoke to herself, even when she was hemmed in by a crowd of people. Not that anybody noticed. People didn't talk *with* her, they talked *at* her. They weren't interested in her replies, only in the fact that she was a duke's daughter. If she'd been a mechanical doll, they wouldn't have noticed the difference.

So, to entertain herself, she sometimes played a game. In her mind's eye, she turned the people around her into chess pieces, some of them her allies, and some her enemies who tried to check her as she made for the nearest exit.

It wasn't chess, of course, but it appealed to her sense of whimsy. If chess pieces could talk, who knew what they would say? They might rant about always having to shuffle back and forth on the same old board, going through the same old motions, day in, day out. What if one of them were to rebel and make a dash for freedom?

With Maitland, it wasn't a game. He'd really done it. She settled back and thought about it. Newgate. The Felons' Quadrangle.

The turnkeys and prisoners and their visitors had to be pawns, and were cluttering up the center of the board. That wouldn't last for long. The pawns were always the first to be sacrificed.

The real players were moving into position.

Maitland. She toyed with the idea of making him the black king, but it just did not fit. In chess, the king was far too passive, always hiding behind a pawn or his bishop or his queen. Maitland would go on the attack. He had to be the most powerful piece on the board, and that was the queen. Harper could only be his right-hand man, his rook.

She was the prize Maitland wanted, the white king. Once he had her, the game would be over. He would have won. Her queen was supposed to protect her, but in this game her queen—and who was more aggressive than Callie?—hadn't decided yet whose side she was on, and her rook, Mr. Proudie, had been taken out of play in the opening gambit. The only thing that stood between her and Maitland were her pawns.

The turnkey panicked them. *Prisoner has escaped! Lock up the prison!* Pawns were getting in each other's way. Harper scattered them. *Up there,* he'd shouted. *He's getting away.* And her pawns cleared the board.

Where was her bishop? Her knight? Where was Charles? He was in a corner with his hands in the air. And when her queen finally rallied, it was too late. Harper disabled her.

Nothing now stood between Maitland and her. Checkmate.

Then the shot rang out, and she toppled to the board.

The sequence was wrong. It hadn't played out quite that way. There was something out of place. What? Where? How? It was coming to her.

"Damn!"

The boat rocked and she rocked with it.

"Damn!" he said again.

She looked at Maitland's shadowy outline, then looked out across the river. There were no people to be seen but she could see their lanterns flickering as they climbed the path through the bushes to the cottage. Not Harper, then, for there would be only one lantern. These must be her rescuers, and among them could well be her own father and brothers. She drew in a breath to scream, but froze when she felt the cold barrel of his pistol pressed to her temple.

"Scream, and it will be the last breath you exhale." His free hand closed around her throat and tightened. "And it will achieve nothing, *nothing*, do you understand? They can't reach you. They have no boats. All I have to do is throw you in the river, and you'd drown within minutes. Is that what you want?"

Tears welled in her eyes. "No." The hand around her throat slackened and she choked out, "But you don't understand what my father must be going through."

This was not the time to defy him. Fear and frustration were riding him hard, and he was more brutal than he meant to be. "I don't care! Can't you get it into your head that all I'm trying to do is survive? If I have to choose between you and me, I'll choose myself every time. Remember that!"

He forced her down on her knees. "Facedown," he told her.

She lay curled in a heap, her face pressed against one of the saddlebags. Her tears had dried. All she could think was how much she hated this man.

≈

Richard didn't have as high an opinion of his prowess as Rosamund did. As she huddled in the bottom of the boat, he silently cursed himself for his sheer incompetence. His first mistake was in abducting a duke's daughter. His second mistake was in allowing Harper to talk him into keeping her for a little while longer. And his third mistake, he could blame on his parents. They were the ones who had raised him to treat all females with deference and respect no matter what the provocation. So now, he felt guilty for the way he had manhandled her.

But bloody hell! This woman was no shrinking violet. She could take care of herself. What they should have done was unhitch two of the duke's high-spirited horses, ridden hell for leather to meet Hugh, and left Lady Rosamund Devere to her own devices. As for the hypothetical footpads Harper had mentioned, he wouldn't like to be in their shoes if they tangled with Rosamund.

When he realized he was grinning, he let out a soft oath. This woman had addled his brains! He shouldn't be admiring her, he should be concentrating on putting as much distance between himself and his pursuers as he possibly could. Things couldn't be much worse. God only knew where Harper was; Hugh must be thinking the worst; and he wasn't fit to row a boat.

Every time he drew on the oars, he could feel the pain in the left side of his chest. He could well be bleeding to death. And because he was on the point of collapse and couldn't row worth a damn, he was letting the current take them downstream, in the opposite direction to where he wanted to go.

He had to get rid of the girl, but he had to do it so that he gave himself plenty of time to get away. He needed to dress his wound; he needed a horse; but more than anything, he needed to rest.

❧

He beached the boat under an abandoned ferry dock, and they walked the short distance to the village of Kennington. Across the river, the lights of the city winked on and off. Kennington was in a rural area and boasted one main street, and one coaching inn, The Black Prince.

He examined her critically before they entered the inn, and he adjusted her hat for no good reason that she could see. Her hair was still tied back, and was now covered by Harper's greatcoat.

They were to pass themselves off as brothers, Maitland told her, attorneys who had come into the area to act for one of their clients. That's if anyone asked. But on no account was she to open her mouth. He would do all the talking, and just to get his point across, he put a gun to her ribs.

No one asked. No one was curious. No one gave her a second glance, or noticed the appeal in her eyes, or the silent messages she tried to pass. No one noticed that she wasn't a young man but a woman in men's clothing. And no one noticed that beneath the saddlebags he held loosely over one arm, Maitland concealed a pistol. The landlord, a dull, shabby fellow, brightened only when Maitland placed a sovereign on the counter and ordered sandwiches, coffee, and hot water to be brought to their room. The landlord didn't even ask how they had got there, but seemed to assume that they'd arrived on horseback and had left their horses in the livery stable.

Though she had traveled extensively, Rosamund had never once stayed at an inn. Her father wouldn't hear of it. The Clarendon, His Grace's London address, didn't count because the duke's suite of rooms was on the

ground floor and had its own entrance. God forbid that
she should mix with any of the hotel guests! And on her
various journeys, there were always friends or acquaintances of the duke to welcome her into their homes and
see to her comfort. She had chafed at these restraints because she was always surrounded by old people, and
Callie had fired her imagination with tales of the Pelican
and the Castle, superior inns on the road to Bath, where
manners were free and easy, and one could sit down to
dinner with perfect strangers and be fast friends by the
time the last course was served.

One comprehensive glance informed her that the
Black Prince wasn't the kind of inn Callie had in mind.
The ceilings were low, the floor was crooked, and there
was hardly enough room for two people to pass on the
stairs. As for the patrons, the few that she saw coming
and going, they looked like horse thieves and spoke in a
dialect she could hardly understand.

The landlord rang a hand bell. When no one
answered it, he bellowed, "Becky!" and rang the bell
again.

A moment later, a young woman in a mobcap came
from the back of the inn, drying her hands on her
apron, muttering to herself all the while. When she saw
Maitland and Rosamund, she stopped dead and her eyes
widened.

Rosamund's heart lurched. *This is it*, she thought. *Rescue at last!* Maybe Becky recognized her, or maybe she
recognized Maitland. Yes, it must be Maitland, because
Becky could hardly tear her eyes from him.

The landlord said something, but Rosamund didn't
hear. She was waiting for the maid to scream; she was
thinking ahead, trying to figure out what she should do.
Should she run? Should she swoon? Should she throw
herself at Maitland? She chanced a quick look at him.

Why was he smiling?

Becky didn't scream. She fluttered her eyelashes; she simpered; she picked up a candle and told them to follow her.

They were flirting! Maitland and the chambermaid were flirting! Maitland, who couldn't open his mouth without uttering a threat, was exchanging pleasantries and blandishments with the chambermaid as though he were a beau at one of Almack's fashionable assemblies, and Becky a highborn lady.

Naturally, there were no blandishments for her. Only the barrel of his pistol, now digging into her back as she trudged up the stairs.

Becky entered the room first and lit the candle on the mantelpiece from her own candle, then she put the flame to the kindling in the grate.

"This is our best bedchamber," she gushed. She patted the only bed. "Our beds are clean. You won't find no bugs in this here mattress."

Bugs? Bugs in the mattress? thought Rosamund, horrified. She'd never heard of such a thing! It didn't matter. There was only one bed. Maitland could have it. She would make do with the floor.

"And," said Becky, opening a closet door with a flourish, "the commode, you know, with the—ah—convenience in it." She giggled.

"Charming," enthused Maitland, flashing the maid a warm smile. He turned to Rosamund with the vestiges of his smile still creasing his cheeks.

She hardly recognized him. He really was quite handsome when he smiled. Now she began to understand why the maid was so giddy. Thank God she had more sense than to be taken in by the scoundrel's smile or his baby-blue eyes that were crinkled at the corners. She was equally immune to his broad shoulders and hard, muscular body. Her own brothers could give him a run for his money, and they were taller, too.

If Casper were to walk into this room, Becky wouldn't even notice Maitland.

Still, the villain did have something. Presence. That's what she'd thought when she'd first laid eyes on him. Presence. Virility. Power. He was a man to be reckoned with. And now, it seemed, he was a flirt as well.

Revolting!

She jumped when his arm suddenly encircled her shoulders and he squeezed hard. "My brother has an inflammation of the throat," he said, "and has lost his voice, so I'll answer for him. We're attorneys on a rather delicate mission, and I'm afraid I can't tell you more than that."

He pressed a coin to the girl's hand. "For your trouble," he said.

"Oh," breathed Becky, and "Oh" again when Maitland sketched an exaggerated bow and opened the door for her.

She gazed raptly up at him. "The taproom will be open for another hour. If you wants me for anything, anything at all, that's where you'll find me."

Maitland sighed. "Unfortunately, my brother and I have a mountain of work to get through before we meet with our client tomorrow, but if you could bring the sandwiches I ordered, the coffee and hot water, I'd be more than grateful."

Becky beamed. "I'll do that right away."

Maitland shut and locked the door. He looked at Rosamund and his smile vanished. "Why are you pouting?" he asked.

"Pouting!" She gasped, and her chin came up. "I am *not* pouting. In fact, I've never been more amused in my life."

He tilted his head to one side and regarded her quizzically. "Is your aristocratic nose out of joint because the maid didn't fawn all over you? How could she know, after all, that you're a duke's daughter?"

He'd got that backwards. It wasn't Becky's behavior that annoyed her, but his. She didn't want to tell him that, so she said, "I assure you, I never give a thought to the fact that I'm a duke's daughter."

He gave a hoot of laughter. "Thousands might believe you, but I certainly wouldn't. I remember you, you see, from Lisbon. I was there, at a ball you attended. You were lovely to look at, but God forbid that you should lower yourself to mix with the other ladies. You might as well have been a marble statue."

She longed to defend herself, to tell him that she wasn't haughty and cold, but shy and tired of being fawned over. Knowing that he wouldn't believe her, she simply turned her back on him, tossed her hat on the bed, and threw off Harper's greatcoat. Then she went to stand in front of the fire.

She turned to face him. "Colonel Maitland," she began, and stopped. His teeth were clenched and his eyes were closed. He'd removed his hat, but he hadn't moved from the door. He was slumped against it, and his face was ashen. She was alarmed at the change in him.

"What is it?" she cried out.

His eyes opened. "Sit down," he said, and pointed to the bed.

She did as he said, but she kept her eyes on him. He looked as though he was going to faint.

He slung the saddlebags on top of the table and set his pistol down within arm's reach. When he shrugged out of his coat, then his jacket, she stared. His shirtfront was matted with dried blood. And when he slowly, painfully, pulled his shirt over his head and tossed it on the floor, she gasped. There was a white linen dressing tied around his back and chest and it was blotched with fresh blood just above his left breast.

"Who did this to you?"

He didn't look up, but opened one of the saddlebags and produced a number of items that he began to set out in careful order: a bundle of clean linen rags; scissors; a jar of something; and a silver flask. "Who do you think did it?" he said. "Whoever murdered Lucy Rider."

It took her a moment to make the connection. He was referring to the night his mistress was murdered, the night he claimed her murderer had stabbed him, too. "But I thought that wound was superficial," she said.

He looked over at her. "It's not life-threatening, if that's what you mean. I'm not at death's door. It's just that the damn thing won't heal."

The prosecutor, as she remembered, had made the case that, after killing his mistress, Maitland had stabbed himself to support his story that some unknown person had tried to kill them both. He couldn't just slip away from the girl's room, the prosecutor said, because too many people saw him go up the stairs. That's why he had to make it look as though someone had attacked him, too. As for his alleged attackers, the boy and the man— why had no one seen them?

He'd killed his mistress in a fit of jealous passion, the prosecutor said.

Maitland jealous? Maitland kill a woman in a fit of passion? She just couldn't see it. It was her impression that women didn't rate very high with the chief of staff of Special Branch.

Something else came back to her. Maitland could have avoided a sentence of death if he'd claimed that Lucy had struck the first blow. But this he would not do. Not once had he wavered from his story: there was a boy waiting for him outside Lucy's room, a boy who entered first and walked to the bed. Lucy was already dead. Then someone stabbed him.

"Did you murder Lucy Rider?" she asked quietly.

"No," he replied, "but I don't expect you to believe me."

Their eyes locked and held, then she said in the same quiet voice, "Did you murder Lucy Rider?"

It looked as though he might yell at her, but he combed his fingers through his hair—a gesture she was coming to recognize—and he said simply and quietly, "No. I did not."

She didn't know why she believed him. She hardly knew him. But she knew how she felt, and it seemed as though a dark cloud had been lifted from her mind.

She winced when he pulled the dressing away from his chest and doused the wound with whatever was in the silver flask. His face clenched in pain, and he put the flask to his lips and swallowed. It was brandy, of course. She could smell the scent of fermenting grape. After a moment or two, he breathed deeply, put down the flask, then made a pad with one strip of linen, poured brandy on it, and shoved it under the binding to cover the wound.

"Aren't you going to change the binding?" she asked. "it's loose and soaked with blood. You'll never staunch the bleeding like that."

"What would be the point? I'd never manage to do it up again."

She got off the bed. "I'll do it." When he reached for his pistol, she sat down again. "Fine," she said angrily. "Bleed to death. Frankly, I'm surprised you've lasted this long. No wonder your wound opened. You shouldn't have carried me out of Newgate, and you certainly shouldn't have rowed us here in that leaky rowing boat. Have you no sense? With a wound like that, you must exert yourself as little as possible."

He stroked his nose with his index finger. "I couldn't ask you to row," he said, "because you might have brained me with an oar."

"I'm serious!" She was getting angrier by the minute. He seemed to think she was a simpleton. "What you should have done from the very beginning was find a place close to Newgate where you could have rested up for a few days, to give your wound time to heal. All this dashing about from one end of the country to the other has achieved nothing. We're practically back where we started."

"That's what happens sometimes when you're on the run. And we didn't exactly dash from one end of the country to the other. Chelsea is on the outskirts of London. Tell you what, Rosamund. Next time I break out of prison, I'll let you make all the arrangements."

She didn't share his amusement. "I suppose you're going to hire horses and we'll ride out of here tomorrow morning? Wonderful. I can hardly wait. How long do you think you will last when the bleeding starts again?"

He stared at her with narrowed eyes. After a moment, he said, "Come here."

As she crossed to the table, Maitland moved the pistol well out of her reach. He used the scissors to cut away the binding, then put those out of her reach, too.

He handed her a clean bandage. "Do it," he said.

She looked down at the table. "What's in that jar?"

"Ah . . . basilicum powder."

"Good. At least you've come prepared."

He watched as she unscrewed the lid and liberally sprinkled the powder on a fresh dressing. "How do you know so much about dressing wounds?" he asked.

The only real doctoring she'd done was in her father's stables. Just as building carriages was her father's vocation, taking care of sick horses was hers.

"Well?" he prompted.

She said ironically, "You know how it is, Colonel Maitland. We ladies of the manor are expected to take care of our serfs."

He bit down on his lip, another habit she was coming to recognize.

She dimpled, and moved his hand so that she could apply the fresh pad. When she saw the wound, she frowned. "Nasty" was all she said. But it was worse than nasty. The edges of the wound had separated slightly and

fresh blood oozed from it. But the brandy had done its
work. It had loosened the dried blood. She set down the
dressing with the basilicum and took the brandy-soaked
pad from his hand to finish the job, then she dipped her
head and sniffed. "You're lucky," she said. "It's quite
clean. If you lie down, I'll sprinkle it with basilicum."

He was looking at her oddly. "Lie down," she said.

His eyes crinkled at the corners. "And have you hit me
over the head with that jar? I don't think so. Just bind the
wound, Rosamund."

She sucked air through her teeth, but that was the only
sign she gave of her annoyance. She positioned the dressing over the wound, told him to hold it, then she picked
up a long strip of linen to bind the dressing in place. Only
then did she take stock of the situation. It suddenly occurred to her that he was half-naked, and she would have
to put her arms around him.

Why had her breathing suddenly accelerated?

She said crossly, "We're trying to stanch the flow of
blood, Colonel Maitland. Use the heel of your hand and
press the pad into the wound. Yes, I know, it hurts. But
that can't be helped."

"Yes, ma'am," he answered meekly.

She frowned as she considered the logistics of the operation. Not only would she have to put her arms around
him, but she'd have to press herself against him as well.

"I think," she said, "it would be easier if you turned
around while I wind the bandage around you."

"Rosamund, I'm not going to let you get behind me."

Her eyes jerked up to meet his. He wasn't smiling, but
she was almost positive there was a glint of amusement in
his eyes.

It was mortifying. She was twenty-six years old and she
felt as skittish as an adolescent girl.

With brows down, she wrapped her arms around him,
and fumbled with the binding. When her breasts
brushed against his chest, he flinched.

"I'm sorry," she said, "but the binding must be tight."

She went through the operation again. He didn't flinch this time, but his breathing became audible. "Hold still," she said, and pulling hard on the two ends of the binding, she tied them in a neat knot.

When he remained silent, she looked up at him. He had that strange look on his face again, as though someone had just stabbed him in the back. "I didn't mean to hurt you," she murmured.

He didn't say anything, but just stood there, staring at her. The silence lengthened.

"You . . ." he said.

She couldn't drag her eyes from his. "I . . . ?" she said.

They edged closer. His hands wrapped around her arms. She touched a hand to his bare chest. His skin was warm. She could feel the thundering of his heart. Or was it her own heart? It seemed the most natural thing in the world to lift her face to his.

When his hands suddenly tightened and he thrust her away from him, she cried out.

"Bloody hell!" he exclaimed. "Don't you know you're playing with fire? Hasn't anyone ever told you not to flirt with a man unless you're prepared for the consequences?" His eyes narrowed unpleasantly. "Or did you think you could seduce me into letting you go?"

The haze in her mind instantly cleared. He was back to being the villain again, with his dark eyebrows slashed together, scowling at her.

She put her hands on her hips. "Is this all the thanks I get for trying to help you? And you are mistaken, Colonel Maitland. It would no more enter my head to seduce you than to run off with one of my footmen. Have you forgotten who I am?"

That was the problem. He *had* forgotten who she was. Something was happening between them, something that couldn't be allowed to happen.

He pointed to the bed. "Get over there and *stay away from me!*"

She could scowl as well as he. "With pleasure," she snapped. "And please refrain from calling me Rosamund. I'm Lady Rosamund to the likes of you, and don't forget it," and she flounced to the bed.

❧

Shortly after, the sandwiches and coffee arrived and hot water for their ablutions. Richard did no more than wash the dirt from his hands and face. Rosamund was more fastidious, and took her time in the closet—with the door ajar to give her some light—and she scrubbed herself with the washing cloth from head to toe.

When it came time to have those few hours of sleep he'd promised himself, Richard was dismayed to discover there was nothing in that room he could handcuff her to. Well, that wasn't precisely true, but it meant she would have had to sleep standing up or crouched on the floor. He was tempted, sorely tempted, to lock her in the closet, but it was cold in there with no fire or candle. And it seemed so unjust after the way she'd dressed his wound. She needed her sleep as much as he did. There was nothing for it but to handcuff her to himself.

When he pulled her to the bed, she didn't make a scene. She didn't say a word. In fact, she hadn't spoken since he'd ordered her to stay away from him, and that suited him just fine. Not that she was cowed into submission, not the Lady Rosamund Devere who had put him in his place by pointing out—as though he needed to be told—that she put him lower than one of her footmen. And like the true lady she was, she now behaved as though he were invisible.

She was having a peculiar effect on him, this maddening aristocrat who irritated him one moment and filled him with admiration the next. He was irritated because she wouldn't obey him; because she forced him to act like a monster; and most of all, because she was too innocent for her own good. She seemed completely unaware of her power over men. When she was dressed in the height of fashion, she was stunning; in men's clothes, she was irresistible! Those long shapely legs! That nicely rounded bottom! Not to mention the tantalizing sway of her hips! Couldn't she see what she was doing to him? Evidently not.

Strangely enough, the things that irritated him were the very things he admired about her. She feared him, yet she couldn't be cowed into submission, not for long. She possessed a reserve of strength that nothing could crush. And her innocence went far beyond her ignorance of men's lusts. She'd cleaned and bound his wound when it would have been in her best interest to let him bleed to death. How could he not be touched?

She'd overturned all his preconceived notions about women of her class. Well, most of them, anyway. Maybe she had been bred to be nothing but an ornament, but when she was put to the test, she could turn her hand to just about anything. In that respect, she was not unlike Abbie Templar and Gwyneth Radley.

Except that he had never lusted after Abbie or Gwyneth.

Lust. Is that what it was?

He could handle lust, but what completely unnerved him was the odd yearning that came over him whenever Rosamund softened toward him. Those intelligent gray eyes of hers would gaze steadfastly into his as though she were seeing into his soul.

Did you kill Lucy Rider?

No. I did not.

Did she believe him? He thought, hoped that she did, because . . . because . . .

Hell and damnation! He was doing it again. He should be catching up on his sleep, not brooding over a woman he had only known for a day! For all he knew, she could be a clever schemer who knew how to play on a man's weaknesses. He didn't think so, but he'd been wrong before now. It was trusting a woman that had brought about his downfall. He wasn't going to fall into that trap again. He had things to do, plans to make, and at the top of his list of things to do was to get rid of this troublesome chit.

He turned his head on the pillow and looked over at her. They were so far apart that a coach could have driven down the middle of the bed. His arm ached from this unnatural position. His side ached. He was stiff all over. He'd never get to sleep like this.

He dug in his pocket, fished out the key to the handcuffs, and unlocked them. Rosamund sighed and turned into him. She was sleeping. To test her, so he told himself, he brushed a finger over her lips. No response from her, but he felt the power of that touch all the way to his loins.

Cursing under his breath, he pushed back the quilted cover and got to his feet. After adding a few lumps of coal to the fire, he went to the window and looked out. Across the river, the lights of London were winking out.

Hugh would have given up on him by now. At least he could trust Hugh to do the right thing. Hugh wouldn't try to find him, knowing that he might lead others to him. He would carry on as though nothing had happened.

Only one person knew where he was going, and that was Harper.

It must be the fatigue that was making him maudlin, he decided, but he couldn't help thinking that he must have taken a wrong turn somewhere. He had so few friends that he couldn't afford to lose one of them.

On that depressing thought, he grabbed his greatcoat from the chair, draped it around his shoulders, and bedded down in front of the door. If she tried to leave the room, she would have to get past him first, and that would never happen.

He'd forgotten his pistol. Uttering another oath, he dragged himself to his feet and padded back to the bed. His pistol was on the floor, tucked out of sight under the mattress. After he retrieved it, he stood there, lost in thought, staring down at the sleeping girl.

When he realized he was smiling, he frowned. *Damn few friends and one troublesome chit,* he thought fiercely, and he stalked back to his makeshift bed. Now he remembered where he had taken that wrong turn. It was when he had abducted the Lady Rosamund Devere.

He settled down, closed his eyes, and began to count sheep. A moment later, he sat up and felt his coat for the object that was digging into his side. It turned out to be Lady Rosamund's shoe. Was there no escaping this woman?

The thought stayed with him for a long, long time.

Chapter 8

On entering his rented house at the edge of the village, Hugh Templar removed his wet overcoat, lifted the candle from the hall table, and climbed the stairs in search of his wife. It was very late and there were no servants about, but he knew that Abbie would still be up. He found her in the nursery. She didn't hear him come in, and he took a moment to savor the sight of her. She was rocking his infant son in her arms as she crooned a tuneless lullaby. Abbie couldn't hold a tune. Little Thomas didn't seem to mind. He gazed raptly into his mother's face and cooed along with her.

"Hugh," said Abbie as he came up to her. "I expected you home hours ago." She put a finger to her lips, then gestured to an adjoining door that was slightly ajar. Hugh nodded to indicate that he understood the message. Thomas's nurse might be awake and listening to every word.

"Blame Woodruff," he said. "I waited for hours, but he

didn't turn up. Then my horse went lame and I had to walk most of the way home."

Abbie nodded her approval. There was no Mr. Woodruff. He was the pretext for Hugh being out of the house at all hours, a fictitious dealer in ancient coins.

"Look," she said, "I think Thomas's hair is getting darker."

Hugh obediently studied his son's head. There was no hair, only a silky fuzz, and what little there was of it was as blond as his mother's.

"Mmm," said Hugh tactfully.

"He looks just like you."

This obviously gave Abbie so much pleasure that Hugh didn't argue the point. To him, all babies looked alike. The difference was that when he took *this* baby into his arms, as he did now, something peculiar happened to his insides.

A few minutes later, when Thomas was asleep and tucked up in bed, they tiptoed to their own bedchamber directly across the hall.

As soon as Hugh closed the door, Abbie said, "Shall I get you something to drink? Whiskey? Coffee?"

"No. I've had my share tonight at the Falcon, waiting for our friends to turn up."

"What is it, Hugh? What's wrong?"

"It's all right, Abbie. They escaped from Newgate and they haven't been caught. I learned that much." He removed his jacket and flung himself into one of the armchairs flanking the grate. "But the escape did not go as we'd planned."

Abbie seated herself on the footstool in front of Hugh's chair and gazed up at him. His face was lined with exhaustion, but that came as no surprise. He'd left late that afternoon for the Falcon, in the neighboring village of Latham, with fresh horses for Richard and Harper, and another fat purse of money to speed them on their way. She'd expected him back hours ago.

"Tell me what happened," she said quietly.

He let out a long breath. "I waited for them at the Falcon, as we arranged, but when the hours passed and there was no sign of them, I decided to ride into town to find out what had happened. When I got to the outskirts of Chelsea, I joined a long line of travelers who were being stopped and questioned by the militia. They were looking for our friends and," he smiled a little, "someone they had abducted."

Abbie sat back. "Abducted!! Richard and Harper abducted someone? Who?"

"Lady Rosamund Devere."

Her jaw sagged, then she said incredulously, "Romsey's daughter?"

"That's the one. I got all this from one of the militiamen, you understand. It seems that there were riots in London today, and the mob marched on Newgate, making movement through the streets impossible. I suppose Richard and Harper couldn't get to the horses so they did the next best thing. They commandeered Lady Rosamund's carriage. Trouble is, and I mean *real* trouble, Lady Rosamund was still in it."

When he saw Abbie's stricken expression, he choked off the laughter that threatened to bubble up. And really, he thought, the situation was anything but funny. He put his laughter down to the strain of the last few hours, worrying about his friends. And there was more to tell.

He looked at Abbie. Most men, he knew, would shield their wives from so much knowledge, assuming that they couldn't handle it. They didn't know Abbie. He'd worked with her on a case once, and he was alive today only because she had kept her head.

"There's more, Abbie. They found the coach abandoned on the other side of Chelsea. Harper was driving it, but he got away. There was no sign of Richard or Lady Rosamund, but the soldiers are making a search of the area."

"You think they'll find the cottage?"

"It's possible."

She searched his face anxiously. "Oh, Hugh, what can we do?"

"We behave as if nothing has happened. We'll visit the Roman ruins and the local points of interest, and in a few days, we'll return to town." When she shook her head, he rose abruptly and paced to the window. With his back to her, he went on, "I don't like it any more than you do, but that was the plan, and we're keeping to it. It's what Richard wanted, not only for our sakes but for his as well." He turned to face her. "Richard insisted that if things went wrong, it was every man for himself. That means—"

"I know what it means! And it sounds heartless!"

A muscle clenched in Hugh's cheek. "It's not heartless. It was the code we lived by as agents. We're not out of the woods yet. I'm the first person the authorities will suspect of helping Richard. I thought you understood that. They could be here at any moment. They may be watching us as I speak. I'm not going to risk leading them to Richard."

"I know. I know. I'm sorry." She shrugged helplessly. "I just wish there was something we could do."

He crossed to her and with hands on her shoulders raised her to her feet. "Listen to me, Abbie. Richard was a crack agent. In Spain, he worked with the partisans. There was a price on his head. He always managed to stay one step ahead of his enemies. He'll do it this time, too."

She attempted a smile. "That's what he once told me about you."

"They won't catch Richard, I promise you."

"Then where will he go? What will he do? And what about Harper?"

"I don't know. But you can bet that Richard had it all planned out before he broke out of Newgate. There's a house somewhere, in Berkshire. It was left to him by someone, I don't know who. He may go there."

"It's the first I've heard of it! I thought all he had were his rooms in Jermyn Street. So, where is this house?"

"I don't know, exactly. Richard never mentioned it. But I overheard him in conversation with his solicitor once. When he realized I was there, he closed the door to his office. I think that's where he'll go, and Harper will join him as soon as he can."

"What," said Abbie with some asperity, "is so mysterious about a house in Berkshire that he couldn't tell his friends about it? And it isn't as though he has friends to spare. There's just Harper and us."

"There's Jason Radley and his wife."

"Richard hasn't known them very long, and anyway, aren't they touring France on a belated honeymoon?"

"So I heard. But I know Jason would have been here like a shot if Richard had only let him know of the trouble he was in."

"Then why *didn't* he?" demanded Abbie angrily.

"Because," said Hugh, "Richard is a lone wolf. He doesn't make friends easily. He's like me, Abbie." He pressed a quick kiss to her lips. "Before I met you."

She didn't return his smile as he'd expected, but shivered. "That's what is so awful," she said. "It could have happened to you, to anyone. Wouldn't you think that the authorities would have known that a man of Richard's stature could never have murdered that poor girl?"

"They might, if the scene hadn't been so cleverly set to incriminate him, and Richard is his own worst enemy. He's aloof, uncommunicative. He rubbed the investigating magistrates the wrong way. He wouldn't even communicate with his friends, except to tell us not to get involved."

"Well, thank God," she said with feeling, "his friends did not listen to him. I just wish we could do more."

"I know."

"He's so alone."

"I know."

"It's his parents I feel sorry for. To live so far away and not know what's going on."

Hugh patted her shoulder. "I know."

"If only he were married."

"I don't think Richard will ever marry. He's too solitary, too reserved."

"That could change, if he met the right woman."

"Now, hold on! It's a bit premature to be thinking of that. He's already got one woman to worry about."

Her brows arched. "Oh, yes, he had it all planned out, did he? And where did Lady Rosamund fit into his plans? Mmm?"

Hugh grinned. "That was a complication Richard couldn't have foreseen. But she won't be a complication for long. I'm betting that the first chance he gets, he'll drop her at some isolated inn, then vanish into thin air."

"If I took you up on every idle bet you make," she said crossly, "I'd be a rich woman. What are you grinning at?"

"Richard and Lady Rosamund. They're like oil and water. He's the complete republican who would like nothing better than to see the aristocracy abolished, and she's one step away from becoming a princess. She's everything Richard cannot abide—privileged, haughty—"

Hugh stopped speaking, because Abbie was shaking her head. "You don't think she's haughty?" he asked.

"No. And I don't think she's privileged either."

"Abbie, she's a duke's daughter. They live on a different plane from the rest of us."

"That's just what I mean." She plumped herself down on the bed, then patted the mattress, inviting Hugh to join her. When he did, she went on, "She hasn't spoken to me or anything like that, but I've watched her at the odd functions we've attended, and she strikes me as . . . well, a lonely person. She's never allowed to mix with ordinary people, only with dignitaries and people of her own class. She's always smiling, always polite, but sometimes a look comes over her face—oh, I don't know how to explain it!—but it's as if she were a prisoner, and all the people around her are her jailors, not her friends."

Hugh began to laugh, but stopped when he saw Abbie's expression. "Well, anything is possible, I suppose," he said.

"You're the one who is always telling me that I'm a good judge of character."

"No. What I'm always telling you is that you are quick to think the best of people. And if you hadn't been so inclined, we wouldn't be married. I'd still be that lone wolf."

She pounced on that. "But who knew you were a lone wolf? Not me! Not when all those lovely ladies were throwing out lures to you, lures you were quick to pick up, I might add."

"Abbie, that's old history!"

"I'm only bringing it up to make a point. You say that Richard and Lady Rosamund are like oil and water. And I say they are two of a kind. I wonder how many close friends she has. No more than Richard, is my guess." A thought struck her. "Hugh?"

"What?"

"I hope Richard isn't terrifying that poor girl. I mean, we both know he's a man of honor, but he can be ruthless when he wants to be."

"Don't worry, Abbie. Richard is no fool. He has enough troubles without making mortal enemies of Lady Rosamund's august father and hot-tempered brothers. They're more to be feared than any branch of the Secret Service. Richard knows this, which is why I am confident that Lady Rosamund will soon be back with her family with little to complain about except, perhaps, a few ruffled feathers."

"Poor Romsey," she said softly. "What he must be

going through! He doesn't know Richard as we do. He'll be fearing the worst." Her head suddenly lifted. "Hugh, do you think they'll come after us?"

"You can count on it. But not Special Branch. They won't be allowed to investigate one of their own. It will be another branch of the Service."

"I wasn't thinking of the Secret Service. I meant Romsey and his sons."

"Good Lord!" After a moment's sobering reflection, Hugh said, "It won't come to that. They won't come after us if they get Lady Rosamund back. And I'm sure Richard will release the girl the first chance he gets."

Abbie nodded. "Of course he will."

They both stilled when the front door knocker sounded.

"Could that be Richard?" Abbie whispered. "Or perhaps Harper?"

"At the front door? That doesn't seem likely. Wait here."

Hugh quickly donned his jacket and left the room. The visitor was becoming impatient, and the knocker beat a relentless tattoo. It wasn't Richard or Harper, however, who faced Hugh when he flung open the front door.

"Lord Caspar," he said, then recovering himself quickly. "Well, well, well! Speak of the devil! Come in, come in."

Chapter 9

Rosamund came slowly awake. When she breathed in the aroma of fresh-brewed coffee, her brow wrinkled. That was odd. Nan had made a mistake. It wasn't coffee she drank first thing in the morning, but chocolate, sweetened with a little honey. And why were the candles lit? Nan should have pulled back the curtains to let the sunlight in. She turned her head and stared at the window. Dawn was creeping over the horizon. *Dawn?* She was never awakened before ten o'clock.

Her next thought made her groan. *Maitland.*

He was seated at the table, calmly drinking a cup of coffee, looking as hale and hearty as she'd ever seen him. This was her doing, she thought. She'd bound his wound and stanched the bleeding, and now he was ready for anything.

Was she insane?

He said, "Your coffee is getting cold."

She pulled herself up and said none-too-pleasantly, "What?"

"Your coffee." He indicated the coffeepot on the table. "Get up, Rosamund. There's something I want to say to you. You see, I've figured out how to get rid of . . . how I can return you to your family without any risk to myself."

She stared at him hard. Was this a trick? Could she believe him? Anyway, what choice did she have?

She didn't waste time in arranging her hair or straightening her clothes. All she did was slip into Harper's jacket. When she was seated at the table and drinking her own cup of coffee, Maitland told her his plan.

"It's simple," he said. "I'm going to hire a chaise and tell the postboys to take you to your house in Twickenham. I, of course, shall make other arrangements for myself."

He was certainly in a good humor this morning. And she hadn't missed his nasty, half-finished sentence—*I've figured out how to get rid of . . .* He meant how to get rid of *her*, of course. She was afraid to believe him, afraid of being let down again. There had to be a catch in it somewhere.

He sat back in his chair. "I thought you'd be over-joyed."

"Mmm," she said musingly. "It's the part about sending me home without any risk to yourself that bothers me." She curled both hands around her cup, and went on carefully, "What's to stop me, as soon as the chaise is out of your sight, from redirecting the postboys to the nearest magistrates? They would be after you before you could say your own name. Not that I would do such a thing," she hastened to add. "I'm only trying to see things from your point of view."

"You'll be gagged and tied up." He frowned when she sucked in a breath. "Listen to me, Rosamund, I need time to get away, and I doubt if the postboys will notice you until you reach your destination. That will give me a two-hour head start. That's all I want."

It was true, then. He really was going to let her go. She didn't mind, not really, about the gag or being tied up. From his point of view, it made perfect sense. There were worse things that could happen to her.

She wanted to thank him. She wanted to tell him that she wouldn't cause any trouble, or tell the authorities where he was, not even when she was back with her family. She wanted to tell him that she believed in his innocence, and when she was free, she would do everything in her power to clear his name. But she didn't tell him any of these things because she knew he wouldn't believe her.

He got up. "I'll give you five minutes to get ready, but don't try any tricks."

She sat there, unmoving, as she heard him lock the door on the outside. The thought of disobeying him flashed through her mind, but only because he'd put the thought there. She didn't want to betray him, because then he would surely hang, and in spite of everything, she really did believe in his innocence.

But that didn't mean she had to like him.

Five minutes, he'd said. She made for the closet first.

&

In the livery stable, when he tried to order a chaise, Richard received a setback.

"You'd be quicker walking, guv'nor," said the proprietor, who was also the ostler. "'Aven't you 'eard? Some duke's daughter got 'erself snatched, and the militia have set up barricades on all the bridges. No one and nothing is getting in or out of London unless the militia says so."

This put paid to Richard's plans of sending Rosamund home to Twickenham. Her chaise would be stopped on Westminster Bridge, and that was too close for comfort. The militia would be on his tail like a swarm of hornets. He couldn't change his plans, not if he wanted to meet up with Harper. He'd have to send her somewhere else.

Brighton, he thought. They'd probably stop in a matter of hours to water the horses, and the postboys would find her. By then it would be too late to catch up to him. Yes, Brighton would do very well.

"I want a chaise at once," he said. "See to it." And to soften his command, he tossed a shilling into the air, which the ostler caught with the ease of long practice.

"And," said Richard, "if the chaise is ready to roll by the time I fetch my brother, there'll be another shilling for you."

The ostler grinned. "It'll be ready, guv."

In turning away, Richard almost knocked over a young lad who had come tearing into the stable.

As he steadied him, the boy cried out, "Mr. Bleecher! The militia are coming! I saw them myself. In boats, they was. They found something under the dock, a boat, I think, and now they're knocking on doors and searching people's houses."

Richard kept his expression impassive, but every sense was alive to his danger. He said curiously, "The militia? Here? In Kennington?"

The boy nodded. "Aye."

The ostler spat on the floor. "Militia," he said, "always throwing their weight about." Then to the boy, "Get to work, Danny. And don't you worry your head about no militia. Old Bleecher 'ere knows 'ow to 'andle them."

Richard thought for a moment, then said casually, "Perhaps my brother and I should wait before continuing our journey."

"Why would you do that?"

"The militia . . ." Richard let his words hang on the air.

He hadn't misjudged his man. The ostler said, "You looks like a respectable gent to me. As for that rabble," he spat on the earth floor again, "they've never seen service. All they wants is a scarlet uniform and the glory that goes with it. 'Alf of 'em don't know their elbows from their arses."

Good Lord, thought Richard, *could Bleecher be another Harper?*

He looked at the ostler then, really looked at him, and he no longer saw a grubby little man with a stained leather apron and dirt beneath his fingernails. He saw lines on a face that had been baked dry by the hot Spanish sun; he saw a war veteran, a man who deserved his utmost respect.

He extended his right hand. "What regiment?" he asked.

Bleecher looked at Richard's outstretched hand and wiped his own on his breeches before accepting it. His spine straightened, his shoulders went back. "Ninety-fifth Rifles," he declared.

"One of the best," said Richard, and meant it. He added, "Good luck to you, *Sergeant* Bleecher?"

The other man nodded. "Aye, Sergeant Bleecher, once upon a time. And good luck to you, sir."

When he came out of the livery stable, Richard looked toward the river. The sky was getting lighter by the minute, but he could see no redcoats in the distance. All the same, speed was of the essence, but speed to where? Not only was the road to Twickenham cut off, but with the militia now in Kennington, so was the road to Brighton. There was only one way out of here and that was west, on this side of the river, the route he'd planned to take himself.

He thought of Rosamund and cursed fluently. What could he say to her? That the militia were closing in on them and he'd been forced to change his plans? Oh, yes, he could just picture how that would act on her. She would cause trouble, and he'd be forced to leave her behind, then the militia would surely be on his trail.

He couldn't leave her behind. He'd tell her about the change of plans once they were well clear of Kennington. Or maybe before that, when they were in the chaise. She wouldn't like it, but she was an intelligent woman. He'd make her understand.

On that dismal thought, he trudged back to the inn.

૨ે

She was ready and waiting for him when he entered their chamber. His face was set in a scowl, but there was nothing new in that. In fact, she was becoming so used to his scowls that they had no effect on her. Besides, now that she believed in his innocence, his scowls didn't frighten her, nor his threats, nor the gun he poked in her ribs, nor the prospect of being gagged and tied up.

The simple truth was, she trusted him, but he didn't trust her.

The thought of seeing her father's face when she walked into his arms, with Caspar and Justin standing by, brought the sting of tears to her eyes. She'd been missing for almost twenty-four hours, and she knew it would be the longest twenty-four hours of her father's life.

The chaise was waiting for them in the stable yard, with the postboy already mounted on the lead horse. She was eager to get under way, but Maitland had a private word with the ostler and tossed him a coin before joining her.

She entered first. When she saw the saddlebags on the floor of the chaise, it struck an odd note, but she wasn't alarmed. Without a word, Maitland entered the chaise, duly gagged her and handcuffed her hands behind her back. He didn't even bother to say a few words to mark their parting. She huffed a little at that, but the prospect of going home to her family took the edge off her pique. But when he sat beside her on the banquette, slammed the door shut, and told the postboy to get going, she stared at him in disbelief.

When the chaise took off at a spanking pace, Maitland held up his hands in a placating gesture. "Listen to me, Rosamund," he said. "There's been a change of plan. I can't let you go yet. You see . . ."

That's when she stopped listening to him. They were leaving Kennington and they were going the wrong way. She didn't have to reason things through. She knew at once that this was another of his betrayals, and if she didn't act now it would be too late. She tried to rise to her feet, but Maitland pushed her back and told her to be reasonable. If she behaved herself, he said, everything could still work out for the best.

She stared at him in shock—then, with the panic of a cornered wild thing, she flung herself at him. She lashed out with her feet; she struggled to free her hands; she bucked; she arched; she tossed her head. He did no more than subdue her with the press of his weight, until her struggles gradually ceased.

When she stilled and went limp in his arms, he said in the same placating tone, "All I want from you is a promise that you'll behave yourself, then I'll remove the gag and handcuffs."

Her eyes flashed with an emotion powerful enough to make him draw back. He nodded slowly. "Hate me, then, but until I have your promise, the gag and the handcuffs remain. Promise me, Rosamund. All you need do is nod your head."

Her answer was to struggle to a sitting position, lift her chin, and deliberately stare out the window.

"Have it your own way" was all he said.

They had not gone far when she saw the village of Chelsea across the river. If they kept to this road, they would come out at Richmond, and across the bridge was Twickenham and home.

But even as her hopes revived, the chaise came to a

crossroads and made a turn. They were going southwest, to a place called Morton.

She sat back against the banquette and closed her eyes to hide her tears. To come so close, *so close*, and now this. She wanted to curl up and die.

She heard him sigh, then her gag was removed, and after that the handcuffs. "Don't try anything," he said, "or I won't hesitate to use force to subdue you."

He flexed his hands as though to make his point. It wasn't necessary. She knew just how brutal those hands could be.

She couldn't bear to answer him or acknowledge his presence. She was seething, and ashamed now of how gullible she'd been. She'd helped dress his wound! She'd believed in him! She was going to try to clear his name! And all he'd done was make promises he never had any intention of keeping.

"Look," he said, "circumstances changed. The militia could have surrounded the inn at any moment. If I'd left you there, they would soon have discovered, if not from you, from the landlord and serving girl, that I couldn't be far away. Rosamund, you have to understand how desperate my situation is. I have no intention of being recaptured and sent back to Newgate. But I promise you, when the time is right, I'll let you go."

She gave him a look she hoped would scorch him. He was trying to placate her, trying to bring her round. Well, he was wasting his time. From now on, she was going to suppress her softer feelings and be as hard as he.

She settled back in the corner of the chaise and cleared her mind of everything but her favorite game. At least in her mind she could escape from him.

Richard, meantime, was still debating what to do about Rosamund. Like Harper, he recoiled from the thought of abandoning her on some lonely country road where anything could happen to her. He toyed with the idea of hiding out till nightfall and leaving her at

Morton. It would be hard to track him in the dark. But by that time, Morton could be teeming with militia. He couldn't chance the delay. They had to keep moving.

Surely, there was some hamlet between Morton and his destination on the Berkshire downs where he could leave her without any risk to himself? And if not, what was he going to do with her?

❧

At Morton, he sent the chaise back to Kennington and hired horses for the next stretch of their journey. Morton was the last village they were to pass through. The man seemed to be obsessed with the thought of militia, so they left the roads and traveled through woods and pastures. It was slow and wearisome, and miserable past bearing when it started to rain.

They stopped a time or two to rest and water the horses. All they had to eat themselves was bread and cheese, and water to quench their thirst. She marveled at Maitland's stamina. She was ready to drop, but he pressed on regardless.

Only when the darkness became impenetrable did he call a halt, and they took shelter for the night in a deserted cowshed. But the next morning, they were up with the dawn and moving on.

Once, when they took shelter under a bridge to get out of the driving rain, it came to her that her captor was worse off than she. His face was gray. She could hear a slight hiatus in his breathing; a constant shifting as though to ease his discomfort, and she wondered if his wound had started to bleed again.

She was on the point of warning him that if he didn't rest, he could bleed to death, but he was up and telling her that it was time to move out, and she was just too tired to argue with him.

At first she tried to keep track of the direction they were taking, but as darkness fell again, she lost her bearings, then she lost interest in everything except the thought of a warm bed, and a soft pillow to lay her head.

She suddenly felt herself falling, and came awake with a panicked cry. His arms were there to catch her.

"We've arrived," he said, sounding as groggy as she felt.

As he steadied her—or was she steadying him?—she blinked the fatigue from her eyes. She didn't know where they were or how far they'd traveled.

"Arrived?" Her eyes strained to identify the dark shapes shrouded in lighter shadows. There were no lights anywhere. "Arrived where?"

There was no answer.

She was vaguely aware of him leading the horses away, but she was too tired to care. She didn't care if it was a cottage or a palace.

A bed, that's all she wanted.

He was gone for some time, but she didn't move an inch. She didn't think she had the strength to take another step. She no longer cared for a bed and a soft pillow. She just wanted to lie down on the ground and go to sleep. Then he came out of the shadows, grasped her elbow, and propelled her forward. Like a blind person, she allowed him to steer her along a flagstone path and up a short flight of stairs. Then they were inside the house. Though it was as dark as pitch, Maitland seemed to know where he was going.

Impressions came and went: her boots clicking on what might have been a marble floor; the faint scent of beeswax; Maitland striking flint on flint and, wonder of wonders, getting a fire going. This wasn't a house, it was a Palladian mansion. Then she saw the elegant tester bed, and after throwing off her greatcoat, collapsed upon it.

Chapter 10

When she awakened this time, her mind was crystal clear. She knew exactly where she was and that the man stretched out beside her on top of the bed was Richard Maitland. She wasn't handcuffed; there was nothing restraining her. There was no Harper and no servants. There was only Maitland and her.

Holding her breath, she turned slightly to look at him. Sunlight streamed in one of the long windows, touching his hair with threads of pure gold. He looked younger in sleep, almost boyish. Like her, he'd done no more than toss off his greatcoat before throwing himself on the bed.

She noticed other things. There was fresh blood on his shirtfront; his skin looked clammy; his breathing was labored.

She had to repress the urge to jump out of bed and set to work dressing his wound. This was Maitland! She was his prisoner! She couldn't give up her best chance of escape.

When she slipped from the bed, he moaned, but he did not waken. She had to clasp her hands together to prevent herself from feeling his brow. But her mind was telling her that there was more to Maitland's condition than exhaustion. He was feverish. She should check the dressing. She should get him to drink. She should—

Don't start that! she told herself irritably. If she wakened him, he would only find a way of restraining her, and she would never get away.

She wasn't heartless, though. She'd ride to the nearest village, she decided, and send a doctor to him. Of course, she'd have to come up with a good story so that no one would know who Maitland was. She didn't want him to be taken into custody. She just wanted to get away. And she would never tell another soul about this house, not even her own father. More than that, she could not, would not, do.

Her mind firmly made up, she turned to leave, and caught sight of herself in the cheval mirror. It was the first time she'd seen herself in a full-length looking glass dressed as she was in men's clothing. It gave her quite a jolt. She hardly recognized herself, in more ways than one.

Was it only three days ago, she asked herself, that she was dressed in the height of fashion and smelled faintly of gardenia? Now she looked a fright and stank of horses.

Her reflection should have repelled her, but it didn't. In fact, it did the opposite. Rosamund swallowed hard as she tried to make sense of what she was feeling. She was the same girl she'd been three days ago, yet she was different. It wasn't just her appearance; it was something more profound. On the outside, she looked a fright; on the inside, she felt . . . she felt . . .

She wondered what her mother would think of her if she could see her now.

When Maitland moved, she jammed on her hat. It was time to go.

She was curious about the house, of course. It was much smaller than Twickenham House, but built along the same lines. At any other time, she would have been interested in exploring it, but not now, not when freedom was within her grasp. All the same, as she crept on her toes across the marble-floored hallway to the front door, she took everything in—the intricately stuccoed ceiling; the niches in the walls, with marble statues; the grand staircase with hanging oil lamps. This house could only belong to a rich man.

Then what was Maitland's connection to it?

Outside, on the entrance courtyard, she paused to take her bearings. The stable block was to her left. She lost no time in crossing to it. The horses were in their stalls, as Maitland had left them the night before, with fresh water and feed.

The care he'd obviously lavished on these poor dumb beasts gave her quite a pang. Her own father always maintained that one could tell a great deal about a man's character just by observing how he treated his cattle. And last night, while she had forgotten that the horses existed, Maitland had unsaddled them, fed them, watered them, and in all likelihood rubbed them down.

The man wasn't all bad.

She was becoming alarmed at the direction her thoughts were taking. She mustn't soften toward him! The truth of the matter was, he'd taken better care of the horses than he had of her.

She tried not to think of Maitland as she saddled her horse, but everything always seemed to lead straight back to him. He thought she was useless, and maybe she was in some things. But there wasn't much she didn't know about horses. She could never be a lady's maid, but in a pinch, she could take the place of her father's head groom, and His Grace would never notice the difference.

Except that last night, it was Maitland who had taken care of the horses, and he must have been on the point of collapse even then.

"Go away!" she said angrily, as though he were standing right in front of her.

She led her horse out of the stable, mounted up, and flicked her heels to her mount's flanks. In one bounding leap, they were off.

She'd left him a horse. What more could he ask of her?

I'm free, free, free, she sang inside her head. And how glorious it was to be wearing men's clothes and riding astride. Maitland didn't know how lucky he was! If he had to dress in woman's clothes, he wouldn't manage to dress and undress himself any better than she.

Maitland again! What was the matter with her?

At the top of a rise, she reined in and wheeled her mount around. The house was nestled in a forest of trees, brilliant now in their autumn colors. Behind the house, the ground rose steeply. There were no trees here, only a vast stretch of sward with clusters of sheep grazing on it.

Now she knew where she was. This must be the Berkshire downs. There would be few farms here, with few people, and the nearest village could be miles away.

She turned her head as she scanned the horizon. There were no farms and no fields of ripened corn, only the wilderness of the downs, and way off in the distance, the steeple of a church to mark the nearest village.

Once she reached the village, there would be no going back. She had to come up with a plausible story that would get help for Maitland without betraying his identity. But every picture that formed in her mind ended in disaster for Maitland.

It was impossible.

She looked back at the house. Even now, he could be bleeding to death. He had a fever.

Someone had to look after him.

She had to go back.

&

She marched into the house and made straight for the bedchamber with a step that would have warned her father to watch his own step. When she saw Maitland, she halted. He'd removed his jacket and was now curled up in a ball of pain.

She crossed to him quickly and, with a great deal of heaving on her part and groaning on his, managed to get him on his back. She couldn't pull the shirt over his head so she tore it from throat to hem and pushed the edges aside. The dressing had slipped and his wound had started to bleed again, though not profusely. But it was inflamed around the edges, and that worried her. As she'd done before, she put her nose close to the wound and sniffed. Thankfully there was no smell of putrefaction.

She let out a shaken breath and looked around for the saddlebags. They were on the floor, beside the bed, where Maitland must have dropped them last night before sinking into an exhausted sleep. She found what she was looking for in the first bag she opened. On returning to her patient, she set to work at once, moving the binding out of the way and loosening the crusts of dried blood with a rag doused in brandy. She tried to be gentle, but Maitland suddenly moved, jostling her arm, and the brandy flask tipped, splashing the wound. He let out a yell, made an effort to sit up, then fell back against the pillows.

"Maitland," she said urgently.

No response.

She put down the flask and felt for his pulse. It was accelerated but quite strong. She put a hand to his brow. Feverish. This was more than a faint. But it wasn't a concussion. She would have known if he'd fallen and knocked his head, wouldn't she? The answer was no, she wouldn't. She'd been too wrapped up in her own misery last night to be aware of his.

It gave her the oddest feeling to comb her fingers through his hair as she searched for some sign that he'd injured his head. When she felt the stickiness on her fingers, she sat back. Blood.

This posed a dilemma, because she had no experience in treating a concussion. But the cut didn't appear to be serious. She couldn't afford to worry about it, she told herself. Maitland had the stamina of an ox. A bump on the head wasn't going to slow him down for long. It was the knife wound that was critical.

There was no washstand in the room, but a door on one side of the bed was open. Just as she thought, the door led to a bathing room, complete with copper bath, a thronelike commode, and a handsome mahogany washstand. There was a room just like it off her own bedchamber in Twickenham. The elegance of this room, however, was spoiled by a man's crumpled jacket on the floor, together with a bloodstained towel. While she was gone, Maitland, evidently, had tried to doctor himself. So she was right. The concussion couldn't be serious, or he wouldn't have managed to get out of bed.

She snatched up two of the towels and rushed back to his side. She'd never lost a horse yet, and she had no intention of losing this exasperating man.

She positioned a folded towel over the wound and eased the binding over it to keep it in place. This was only a temporary measure until she'd assembled what she needed to make a poultice for the inflammation.

Her next order of business was to clean the gash on his head. Finally, she began to remove his clothes, which were still damp from the rain. Her hands stilled. Why were his garments still damp while her own were bone-dry? The answer came swiftly. While he had found shelter for her from the rain, he'd taken care of the horses and she didn't know what else. He was always the last to come in out of the rain, the last to eat, the last to rest, and the first to be up and doing. On every stop on that exhausting journey, it was the same story.

She was wrong to think he'd taken better care of the horses than he had of her. It was himself he had neglected.

Shaking her head, she set to work again, heaving and puffing as she adjusted his weight to get the job done. She must have hurt him, because he started to fight her. At this rate, he'd open the wound again and bleed to death. She subdued him by falling on top of him.

He stopped struggling. "Harper?" he said. Then more urgently when she didn't reply, "Harper?"

"Aye."

That one softly spoken word seemed to soothe him. There was no more struggling as she removed his boots, then his trousers. She hesitated a moment or two over the drawers, but reasoned that if she was to bring his fever down, she'd have to bathe him with cold water. The drawers would only get in the way, so off they came.

When she realized that her cheeks were burning hot, she became impatient with herself. She was no novice to male nudity. She'd caught glimpses of her brothers often enough cavorting nude in the shallows of the man-made lake at Twickenham House, and she'd never turned a hair. She wasn't going to turn missish now.

Anyway, it wasn't his nudity that made her stare, but the silvery scars that embellished his chest, and one longer scar that ran across his belly and dipped toward his groin.

He was a warrior, only now he was a fallen warrior, helpless to help himself. All that stood between him and his enemies was herself, and she was no warrior at all.

Maybe she wasn't a warrior, but she made up her mind there and then that she would not desert him until he was on his feet again.

When she got him settled between the sheets, she took a step back. She didn't try to analyze what she was feeling. There was too much to do and her mind was racing ahead. She had to make a warm bran poultice for the inflammation; she had to bring down his fever and make sure he drank plenty of liquids; she had to dress the gash on his head; she had to make sure he didn't move and start the bleeding again.

The poultice first, she decided.

The kitchen was easy to find. One of the doors in the bedchamber gave onto the servants' staircase, and at the bottom of the stairs were the domestic quarters. The kitchen was right next to the still room. It came as no surprise to find that the larder was well stocked with provisions. Though there were no servants or resident caretakers, the house was well looked after. So, where were the servants now?

She'd get to that later. She concentrated on the innocent-looking tinderbox that was sitting on the mantel of the huge, blackened stone fireplace.

She approached it with the same resolute step as when she'd entered the house. This was one battle she couldn't afford to lose.

Chapter 11

He had a way with women. It wasn't something he cultivated, but something he'd been born with. As a child, all he'd had to do was look crestfallen and he could wrap his mother around his little finger. So, it came as no surprise when Richard Maitland's landlady agreed to show him her tenant's rooms on the understanding that he might be willing to take them over.

"Mr. Withers, is it?"

"George Withers," he replied.

He saw no point in giving a false name. If he was found out in a lie, people might take a closer look at him and start asking awkward questions. He'd learned to stick to the truth unless he had a compelling reason not to. In this instance, he had a plausible reason for being here. His rooms in Bond Street were too cramped. He was looking for something bigger.

Mrs. Everett straightened her mobcap, smiled coyly, and led the way upstairs. "I don't know that I ought to

show you the rooms," she said. "Mr. Maitland is paid up
to the end of September. He paid quarterly, you know.
Such a quiet gentleman. But it's always the quiet ones
who bear watching, isn't it? Do you know, there was
something about him I never liked? Cold and distant, he
was. Not what you would call friendly. But murder! I
never thought it would come to that."

She was about fifty, plump, and anything but comely.
All the same, he treated her with the gallantry he would
have shown a society beauty. The stupid cow didn't realize that all he wanted was information. When it became
evident that she knew nothing useful, he induced her to
leave him alone in Maitland's rooms by promising to
stop by on his way out and share a pot of tea and her
homemade scones.

His smile vanished the moment he showed her out.
The magistrates, he knew, had already taken away anything of interest, but he was betting that Richard
Maitland wasn't the sort to leave anything interesting lying around. But that was speculation, and he had
learned the value of caution. He couldn't go far wrong if
he took Maitland as his example, and he knew that if
their positions were reversed, Maitland would be here.

In four days, the search for Maitland had practically
ground to a halt. Or it would be truer to say that the trail
had grown cold. There were horse patrols in plenty, going off in fits and starts whenever someone reported
sighting Maitland or his former bodyguard. But there
was no pattern to these sightings, no single direction to
give them a clue to where they were headed. What *was*
known was that Maitland had hidden out in a cottage in
Chelsea then had slipped away in a boat. It wasn't until
the next morning that the boat was discovered under the
Vauxhall dock, and that's where the trail ended.

There was a rumor going around, a rumor he knew to
be true, that Lord Caspar had enlisted Hugh Templar's
help to track Maitland, and that had raised his hopes.

But nothing had come of it, or they would have found Lady Rosamund by now and the whole world would know it.

Maybe he had misjudged Templar. Maybe he hadn't deserted his friend. Maybe he was playing a delaying game to give Maitland time to cover his tracks so that he could come back and fight another day.

That's what gave him his sense of urgency. Only he had the will and the drive to find Maitland, because he had the most to lose. Not that he seriously believed that Maitland would work things out and come after him. But after their last encounter, he wasn't leaving anything to chance.

He spent the next few minutes walking through the rooms, taking a general impression. He was surprised at what he found. He had anticipated something more Spartan, in keeping with Maitland's character, but these rooms were comfortably furnished in blue upholstery and some fine walnut and mahogany pieces. Only the book room was as he expected—shelves of books, two shabby leather chairs flanking the grate, a desk, and little else.

After this, he went through each room systematically, cupboard by cupboard and drawer by drawer. It was just as he thought: the few letters, papers, and receipts that he found were of no help to him. The only thing that struck an odd note was a small painting in an alcove in the book room. It was in oils, pleasant enough though not very skillfully executed, and depicted a gem of a house, of neoclassical design, in a pastoral setting. The artist was Richard Maitland.

There were other pictures scattered throughout the various rooms, but they were all landscapes—stark mountains and lakes, and heather-clad moors— obviously scenes of Scotland, Maitland's home.

He toured the rooms again, but this time he looked only at the paintings. They were far superior to the painting in the book room, and none of them bore Maitland's signature.

It seemed to him that the painting of the house must have sentimental value to Maitland, or why would he keep it? Something else struck him. The pastoral setting was typical of England, not Scotland.

A memory came to him. In the holidays, everyone went home, but not Maitland. He went to an uncle who had a house on the Berkshire downs.

What was his name? What was the name of the house?

It hardly mattered. When Maitland left Chelsea, he'd rowed downstream, in the opposite direction to the route he would have taken if he were making for Berkshire.

He thought about it for a moment or two, closed his eyes, and pinched the bridge of his nose with thumb and forefinger. A false trail, he thought, to throw them off the scent? What else had Maitland done to throw them off the scent?

He opened his eyes and stared at the painting. If only he could remember the name of that house. After a moment's silent scrutiny, he removed the picture from the wall and took it to the window to get a better look.

It was right there, etched into the masonry above the front portico.

Dunsmoor.

છ

At Dunsmoor House, Rosamund was slumped in one of the armchairs that flanked the grate. She'd managed to snatch a few hours of sleep during the night, but she'd been up since dawn nursing her patient and stoking the fires. *Fatigue* was too weak a word to describe what she was feeling. Every muscle in her body ached. She didn't know if she had the strength to push herself out of the chair now that she'd given in to the temptation to take a few moments for herself.

She glanced at the clock, then at the bed. Maitland was sleeping soundly. In a few minutes, though, it would be time to begin the ritual that she performed every other hour in an effort to bring down his fever and keep his wound clean: change the poultice; bathe the patient with cold water; feed him weak tea, spoonful by spoonful; check the gash on his head; feel his pulse.

The last time she'd added something to the ritual, or rather to the tea. He'd been so restless during the night that he'd torn the poultice, and bran had leaked onto his bare skin. If she'd been there, it wouldn't have happened, but she'd been in the kitchen making his tea. By the time she got to him, the bran had hardened like plaster. It had taken her forever to clean the mess. So she'd added a drop or two of laudanum to his tea to prevent him from thrashing about, and it worked. Only she wasn't sure if she'd done the right thing.

If only there was someone she could share her worries with. Even Harper would do. She thought, hoped, the fever had abated a little, but she wasn't sure. It was the same with the inflammation. And she didn't know the first thing about concussions. A second opinion would be more than welcome.

At least she could say with conviction that her patient's condition hadn't worsened.

She had just struggled to her feet when she heard what might have been a floorboard or a stair creaking. When it came again, her pulse began to race. Someone was creeping up the servants' staircase, someone who did not want his presence to be known. Not Harper, then, or the authorities. They wouldn't come by stealth. A thief, perhaps, who thought the house was empty. Or maybe it was Maitland's mortal enemy, the one who had engineered his downfall.

The fatigue that had weighed her down was swept away as sheer animal instinct took over. There was no chance of hiding Maitland or getting him away. But she

was ready for trouble. Maitland's pistol, primed and
ready, was on top of the dresser. She never went anywhere without it now.

Every nerve was tingling as she curled her fingers
around the smooth butt, then, moving as stealthily as the
intruder, she positioned herself to one side of the door.
When he opened it, she would be hidden from view.

When the door handle turned, she held her breath.
Inch by slow inch, the door opened. There was an excla-
mation of surprise, then a man entered and walked to
the bed.

Rosamund leveled her pistol. "Touch him and I'll
blow your brains out! I mean it! Now drop your pistol on
the floor—gently, mind—put your hands in the air, and
turn around."

ও৯

Harper had managed only a quick glance at his chief
to make sure that he was all right when the strident voice
accosted him. He did exactly as he was told, but as he
turned, he tensed to spring. When he saw his opponent,
however, surprise held him in check. A beardless youth
confronted him, a youth who looked as though he'd just
walked off the battlefield. His shirt and face were spat-
tered with flecks of blood and what looked like mud. His
eyes were red-rimmed; his expression haunted. But the
hand that held the pistol that was aimed straight at
Harper's heart was as steady as the hand on a marble
statue.

"You're making a mistake," began Harper, then
stopped when the youth lowered his pistol and sniffed.

"You took your time getting here," said the young
man, only he didn't sound like a young man now. He
sounded like a female, and one, moreover, who had
come to the end of her tether.

Her words were quick and edged with reproach. "I

could have used another pair of hands. My life has become one long round of applying poultices, bed-baths, keeping the fires stoked, making tea, and emptying chamber pots." She waved the gun in the air. "Not to mention watering and feeding the horses. They have to be watered and fed three times a day, did you know that?"

Harper was seriously coming to believe that he was dealing with a maniac, and would have sprung at her if she hadn't pointed the gun at him again.

"He wouldn't lie still," she said, "and ruptured the poultice, so I gave him laudanum. I think I may have done more harm than good. But you must understand, I've never treated a horse with a concussion before."

Harper felt as though he were lost in a fog. The youth was turning out to be Lady Rosamund Devere. His mind quickly sifted through her unintelligible words. He glanced at his chief, then took a slow inventory of the shambles in the room. Bloodied rags and poultices were stacked on top of the dresser, basins of water were set out on the floor like stepping stones; jars and bottles of he knew not what were set out on a small table; a pile of filthy clothes was heaped in a chair; on another chair, he saw a kettle, teapot and cups, and a half-eaten apple. And—he looked and looked again—a china chamber pot was on the floor beside the bed, decorously covered with a folded towel.

"What horse, your ladyship?" he asked carefully, his eyes never wavering from the chamber pot.

She shook her head, gave a watery chuckle, and said brokenly, "Oh, Harper, I'm so glad you're here."

❧

It was late in the evening when Richard dragged himself from sleep to find Harper hovering over him. Though he felt shivery and had a blazing headache, he insisted on getting up. He frowned when he saw he was naked, but other than that, he made no comment. "Rosamund?" was the first word out of his mouth.

"She's in the room across the hall," said Harper, "sleeping the sleep of the just. I don't think she'll wake for a long time yet."

As Harper helped Richard into a nightshirt and a warm woolen dressing gown, he gave him an account of his own movements since taking off with the duke's carriage. He told him about the reward the duke was offering for Lady Rosamund's safe return, about Digby and Whorsley, and finally explained why he had taken so long to get there. The countryside, he said, was crawling with militiamen, and that had slowed him down. He'd spent the first two nights sleeping in haystacks, the next night in a barn, and last night in one of the shepherd's stone bothies on the downs. He'd only arrived an hour or two ago, to find the colonel blissfully out of things and Lady Rosamund at her wits' end.

He broke off at that point. He didn't think his chief was listening. He was looking around the room, taking everything in. The candles were lit, the curtains were drawn, and every evidence of the mayhem Harper had encountered earlier had been tidied away.

"Sit," said Harper, pointing to a chair beside the fire.

When Richard was seated, a bowl was thrust into his hands. "I'm not hungry," he said.

"Good, because I'm not offering you anything to eat. That's gravy, beef gravy. That should settle your stomach. And you've got to have something. Lady Rosamund says you've hardly eaten for two days."

Richard stared at his bowl, then looked at the door that led to the hall and Rosamund's room. Harper was talking as though Rosamund were an ally, and that didn't make sense to him.

Harper took the chair opposite and took up his own bowl: beef stew, thick and tender, the way he liked it.

When Richard made to set his bowl aside, Harper said testily, "I don't think you knows how lucky you is." He jabbed with his spoon, indicating the door to the hall. "That girl has worn herself to the bone to save your life. She's done as much—more—than I could do if I'd been here, and as we both know, I've had plenty of practice on the battlefields of Spain. She brought your fever down; your wound smells clean; she made you drink kettles of weak tea and did other unmentionable things that we won't go into because it would only embarrass her. And this is how you repay her? You're not out of the woods yet. So act the man, and get that gravy down you. And if it stays down, then we'll see about supper."

Richard's eyes were fixed on Harper.

His chief's expression, Harper thought humorously, was oddly touching, shades of disbelief and horror. Eyes twinkling, Harper said, "Aye, there was no one else here to take care of you, so Lady Rosamund did whatever was necessary, as if you was her own brother, she said."

"And where the devil were *you*?" asked Richard, scowling. Impressions were flitting in and out of his mind. He'd known someone was nursing him, but he'd thought that someone was Harper. *Rosamund?* he thought, and a curious lump lodged in his throat.

"I told you. The militia slowed me down."

Richard stared at the beef gravy, and after a moment put a spoonful to his mouth. Harper's words and his own impressions were still revolving in his mind. After taking several spoonfuls of gravy, he looked over at Harper. "If you weren't here, why didn't she leave when she had the chance? Why did she stay and nurse me?"

"She did leave you, but she came back." Harper offered Richard a thick slice of bread, which he absently accepted. "She thinks you're innocent, you see, and she doesn't want to see you hang."

Richard gave Harper another fixed stare. "She thinks I'm innocent?"

"That's what she said." Harper chuckled. "I'm as amazed as you. But there's no saying how females gets these odd ideas in their heads."

"I *am* innocent."

"Yes, but what I'm asking myself is what you did or said to convince Lady Rosamund of it."

"Nothing. Nothing at all."

"Well, we knows it wasn't your charm, because you don't have any. So it's just as I said. Women get these strange notions, and there's no explaining it."

Richard chewed on the bread and sipped the beef gravy without being aware of what he was doing. He knew he must be terribly ill, because he was beginning to feel maudlin again.

"Would you like more?" asked Harper, removing the empty bowl from Richard's hands.

Richard shook his head. "Did Rosamund make the stew as well?"

Harper stared. "Hardly. She's a duke's daughter, remember? She knows how to boil water, and that's about it."

"Then how does she know so much about doctoring?"

"Horses," said Harper succinctly.

Richard's brows rose. "Horses?"

"In the duke's stables. That's what she told me. Seems like a Devere would be ashamed not to tend his own cattle when they falls sickly. You was lucky you didn't break a leg, or she might have been tempted to put you out of your misery. Permanently."

As his shoulders began to shake, Richard pressed his right arm hard against his chest to ease the ache. "No, not Rosamund," he said. "she is incapable of hurting anyone."

His chief's expression, his tone of voice, and his way of referring to Lady Rosamund by only her Christian name had Harper's mind buzzing. If he hadn't known better, he told himself, he'd be half convinced that a little romance was brewing here. But he knew that couldn't be the case, because he knew his chief too well. Though the colonel never lacked for a pretty woman in his bed, he never became attached to any woman. In fact, he was indifferent to them. Harper had long since decided that his chief had been badly burned once and had no wish to repeat the experience. No one understood better than he. He'd been burned so many times that he'd sworn off women for life.

He'd wanted something better for his chief, though, than to turn into the cantankerous old bachelor he'd become. He'd wanted him to meet the right woman. But not by the wildest leap of his imagination had he thought the right woman would turn out to be someone like Lady Rosamund Devere.

She wasn't the right woman. She was the wrong woman, in every way, and he hoped the colonel had the sense to see it.

Richard said, "Why did I sleep so long?"

Harper shrugged. "Fatigue. Loss of blood. Concussion. And Lady Rosamund gave you a few drops of laudanum to stop you thrashing about." A thought occurred to him, and he went on, "How did you get that nasty gash on the side of your head? Lady Rosamund couldn't explain it."

Richard gave a sheepish grin. "I fell asleep in the saddle, and when I tumbled to the ground, I cracked my head. Just as I got up, Rosamund slipped from the saddle, too, but I caught her as she fell."

Rosamund again, thought Harper, not liking the sound of this. Maybe the fall had scrambled his chief's wits, or maybe the laudanum had weakened his defenses, and in an hour or two he'd be more like himself—cold, reserved, and cynical, just the way Harper liked him. "What made you bring her here?" asked Harper at length.

Richard shrugged. "I kept running into militia, and by the time I was clear of them, I was too ill to think of anything but getting here. I wasn't sure if I could do it."

Harper thought about this and nodded. "So," he said, "what are we going to do about her?"

"Do about her?" echoed Richard. He was staring at the fire with a small, unreadable smile barely touching his lips. "We're going to send her home and forget about her." He bestirred himself and looked at Harper. "She's not going to tell anyone where we are. She could have done it by now if she'd wanted to. Besides, when we send her home, no one will be after me for that reward, and the hue and cry will die down. It's the best solution all round."

All things considered, Harper thought this was an excellent idea.

After a while, Richard straightened and said, "Is there anything to drink around here?"

Harper found the decanter and poured the drinks. When he was seated, Richard took a healthy swallow, then said, "Bring me up-to-date, Harper. Tell me again why you took your time getting here, and leave nothing out."

This was more like the chief. Harper happily obliged.

Chapter 12

*S*he hardly knew what to say when Harper ushered her into Maitland's bedchamber then disappeared. Maitland looked so different, *elegant* was the word, in a blue superfine jacket and black trousers. She thought he'd still be in bed.

Her own gown, which Harper had dug out of somewhere, might have belonged to a governess. It was a gray kersemere and, to her great relief, buttoned up the front. The hem came to her ankles, but only because she'd let it down. Harper couldn't find shoes to fit her, so she was still wearing his boots. She had washed her hair, and since she didn't know how to dress it, it fell around her shoulders in an unruly mop. She brushed it back nervously. He seemed more at ease than she.

"Lady Rosamund," he said, "please take a chair. You must excuse the setting." He smiled wryly and gestured with one hand toward the bed, which was now made up. "But after what we've been through together . . . well, this is the warmest room in the house. If we light a fire in the drawing room, it will take forever to warm up, and someone has to stoke it."

She knew what he meant. Harper had explained the situation to her. Local people had been hired to get the house ready for their arrival, but it was too risky to keep them on. The story that Harper had given out was that his master suffered from consumption of the lungs and had decided to come into the country for his health. He would be bringing his own servants with him. But there were no servants. All the work had to be done by them.

As she perched on the edge of the chair he indicated, and he took the chair opposite, she studied him carefully. He was too pale. She thought he winced when he adjusted his position.

"Lady Rosamund," he began, "I must thank you for—"

She cut him off rudely. "You shouldn't be out of bed. All my hard work will be for nothing if you have a relapse. I know you too well now, Richard Maitland, to be taken in by you. You're not feeling half as well as you pretend."

He breathed deeply and almost glared at her, but one of those sudden, warm smiles lit up his face. "Will you let me finish what I started to say? I've decided to send you home, Lady Rosamund. You leave tomorrow at first light. Harper will take you as far as Windsor, then he'll hire a chaise to take you to Twickenham."

He was back to calling her Lady Rosamund, and she found it oddly hurtful. This was his way, she supposed, of telling her that she was becoming too familiar. She dredged up a smile. "Well, we've heard that one before, haven't we?"

He had the grace to look guilty. "I know it must seem as though I broke my word to you," he said, "but I had no choice. We were surrounded by militia. What else could I do?"

She didn't know why she was being so contrary. She'd already deduced that Maitland and Harper now regarded her as a friend. No one kept watch over her. She could come and go as she pleased. In fact, she'd anticipated that this was how it would end.

She found herself suddenly wishing that she could put back the clock, that she hadn't visited Callie, or made that fateful trip to Newgate, that she had never met Richard Maitland.

He was studying her face. Frowning, he said, "I mean what I say. I'm sending you home."

"I believe you."

"I thought you'd be happy."

"I am."

"Then what is it? What are you thinking?"

She was thinking that she would never see him again. She said, "Where will you go? What will you do?"

He gave her an odd, twisted smile. "It's better if you don't know."

Her back stiffened. "You think I'll betray you? I won't, you know."

He stared at her across the hearth, his eyes wide. "It never once entered my mind. There is no one I trust more than you. Not now." His expression changed, and he went on, "I'm going to clear my name. That's what I'm going to do."

Her response was quick and harsh. "You should be thinking rather of how you can start a new life where nobody knows you."

He answered her just as harshly. "Lucy Rider was murdered. I can't let her killer get away with it. This is something I *have* to do."

"I know, I know," she said softly.

Their eyes locked, and in a single heartbeat, it was as if they were seeing each other for the first time. Everything of no consequence was stripped away—her rank; his prejudice. The clock continued to tick; the windowpanes continued to rattle; the fire to splutter and flare. They were oblivious of everything but each other.

Richard recovered himself first. Looking away, he said in an oddly gruff voice, "I'm sure Harper left us a decanter of sherry. Ah, there it is." He touched a hand to his chest and winced. "Would you mind pouring, Lady Rosamund?"

"Not at all." Her voice was natural, her smile was natural, but when she poured out the two glasses of sherry, her hand shook. She couldn't believe what was happening to her. *Dear Lord, not him!* she prayed. *Anybody but Richard Maitland! Anybody!*

It was this extraordinary situation that was responsible, she told herself. First, he'd terrorized her, then he'd stirred her pity, and now he was treating her as an ally. No wonder she was confused. When she was back home with her family, she'd regain her balance.

Before the silence could become too self-conscious, she said quickly, "So who are your enemies, Richard?" His Christian name had slipped out so naturally that she was taken aback. A quick glance in his direction assured her that he hadn't noticed. He was preoccupied with his own thoughts. "Have you narrowed it down?"

He accepted the glass she offered him and said, "As a matter of fact, I have. A dozen or so."

"Who would have believed you could be so popular?"

He shot her a look from under his brows, saw her impish smile, and chuckled. "That's the number of cases I've worked on since I took over at Special Branch." He took a sip of sherry. "But if we go further back, to the Spanish Campaign, well, agents aren't exactly in the business of making friends."

"So the motive is revenge?"

"Or I may know something I don't know I know, and someone is afraid that one day it will click into place and all will be discovered. But I don't think that's the reason I was targeted."

"Why not?"

"Because Lucy's murderer could have killed me at any time. Why wait? Why engineer this elaborate plot so that I would be disgraced? I think he planned the whole thing, down to my execution."

She shook her head.

"What?"

"The knife wound. You might have died from it."

"Yes." His mouth flattened. "That's what puzzled me. But if he'd wanted to kill me, why not stab me in the back or smash something over my head?"

"Because," she answered slowly as she thought it through, "the authorities would have known that someone else must have been in the room besides you and Lucy."

"And the same goes if the knife wound had been mortal." He flashed her a smile. "Maybe he wanted me to bleed to death. Maybe I'm crediting him with too much imagination, too much foresight. But I don't think so. All the same, I don't think he intended to hurt me as much as he did, but I moved, you see, and the knife slipped. Now drink your sherry before I outpace you."

Her glass of sherry, untouched, was still in her hand. She took a sip, then another, but she did it to please him. She was reflecting on how her view of things had been turned upside down in the space of a few days, and how, now that she believed in his innocence, everything he said made perfect sense.

"Why the little half smile?" he asked, breaking into her train of thought.

She looked up at him. "I remember thinking, when I read about your trial in the papers, that you were as guilty as sin."

The corners of his mouth lifted a little. "What changed your mind?"

She said lightly, "You took good care of the horses."

"Praise indeed."

"And"—she dimpled—"you didn't hurt me. You're not unlike my father. He roars as well. It's quite intimidating to people who don't know him."

His tone was dry. "I shall remember that."

After a moment, she said, "What happened, Richard? I mean, I read about your trial in the papers, but I want to hear your side of the story. What happened with Lucy?"

"You know what happened. The papers carried my version of events as well. The trouble was, nobody believed me."

"Well, I believe you, and I'm listening, so tell me again." When he stared at her, she gave a tiny shrug. "You never know. I'm coming to it fresh. I may see something you've overlooked."

He came close to smiling, but something in her expression must have made him change his mind, for he merely said, "Fair enough, but top up my sherry glass first, then I'll tell you." When this was done he settled back in his chair, and began to speak.

Lieutenant Alex Rider, he said, was Lucy's father, and had served with him in the Spanish Campaign. Their paths had diverged for a time, then crossed again at Waterloo.

"And that's where Rider died. As his commanding officer, I wrote to Lucy informing her of her father's death. After the war was over, I returned to England and met her, quite by chance, in the George and Dragon, where she worked. This was almost a year ago. I dined there frequently because it's only a five-minute walk from my rooms. I always left her a substantial gratuity—for her father's sake and because she'd fallen on hard times—and that's all our relationship amounted to."

He shot her a look, but when she didn't respond to the challenge, he took a moment to gather his thoughts before continuing. As he described the events leading up to the night of Lucy's murder, things she'd forgotten came back to her.

In that last month, Lucy changed, he said. She needed advice; she wanted to borrow money. She made excuses to see him more often.

"The night Lucy died, I had an appointment to see her. She wanted me to help her draft a letter to some lady or other who had advertised for a parlor maid. I was glad to do it. This would be a great improvement on her present situation. So, all unsuspecting, I went to the George and Dragon."

"And the boy?" she prompted when he fell silent.

He took a long swallow from his glass before he answered. "That boy, more than anything in this sordid business, makes me shudder with revulsion. He knew what he was doing. He was in it up to his neck. I shall never forget how he smiled at me when I realized Lucy was dead." He took another long swallow, then went on, "He was waiting for me at the top of the stairs. I thought he was a bootboy or a page. I really didn't think about it at all. 'Lucy is expecting you,' he said, and I followed him into the room. I see now that he was meant to distract me."

He shifted and she could see the tension etch deep lines on his brow and cheeks. "There was a candle on the dresser. She was on the bed—asleep, I thought. The boy stood at the edge of the bed, staring down at her." He shook his head. "I don't know what made me reach for my gun, but I did. Then everything happened at once." He closed his eyes. "I saw the blood. I looked at the boy. Someone put an arm around my throat from behind. I struggled and he stabbed me in the chest. I dropped my gun. Then I was pushed into a chair and my assailant and the boy left." He opened his eyes wide. "I don't know how long I sat there, but it came to me that if I didn't get help soon, I would bleed to death."

"Your pistol," she said, remembering that a shot had been fired.

"Yes. It had fallen between the mattress and the footboard. I finally got off a shot, and that brought people running. I was arrested the next day, after they found the knife that killed Lucy on the ground right under the window of her room. You know the rest."

The rest was that the boy and Richard's attacker had vanished into thin air, and no one believed that they existed. Then the nightmare began: the trial, the witnesses, the conviction, and finally the sentence of death.

Just thinking about it made her skin chill by several degrees. The task of clearing his name seemed hopeless.

"So," he said, his eyes glinting, "give me the benefit of a fresh perspective. Who is out to destroy me, Rosamund?"

She answered him seriously. "Someone who wants an eye for an eye, and a tooth for a tooth; someone who wants you to suffer as he has suffered, and only when you have lost everything that matters to you, your good name, your position at Special Branch, and your friends, will he be satisfied to see you go to the gallows.

"Or maybe not. I think this person is so obsessed with you that he'd be happy to see you a fugitive for the rest of your life. But what if you outlive him? No, that won't do. You have to die, but only when he is finished with you." She looked directly into his eyes. "And I don't think he's finished with you yet."

"I'm willing to accept that the motive for my downfall is revenge, but let's not embroider the facts."

"Do you play chess?"

"I—What?"

"Do you play chess?"

"A little."

"A little? What does that mean? You either play or you don't."

"All right! I play chess! What has that to do with any-thing?"

"This man plays chess, or if he doesn't, he ought to. He doesn't think of one move at a time. He sets up the board, makes his opening gambit, and sees in his mind's eye every possible move his adversary can make and the countermoves he will make, till he has won the game."

"I think," he said, "the sherry has gone to your head."

She was too caught up in her own thoughts to re-spond to this aside. In her mind's eye, she could see how it had played out. "Everything between you and Lucy Rider was innocent until Mr. Sinister appeared on the scene. The game really began that last month. The first thing he did was make Lucy his pawn. No. His queen. From that moment on, she had you hopping from square to square, and you never realized your danger. But Lucy was dispensable, and when the time came, he didn't hesitate to sacrifice her. In fact, he'd planned this move before play started.

"Now let's think of the trial. He has you just where he wants you. Look around the board. You're standing alone with no knight, rook, or bishop to help you, not even a pawn."

His eyes were brimming with amusement. "You're for-getting Harper and Hugh Templar."

"Hugh Templar? I thought he deserted you when you went to trial."

"No. He was helping Harper set things up for my es-cape."

Her eyes shone. "Then that was a brilliant move on your part."

"And then there's you," he added softly.

She took him seriously. "Yes, but that was luck. You can't depend on luck in this game."

"I'm a great believer in luck."

She looked up, saw the laughter in his eyes, and

smiled with him. "You may mock me, but chess is logical, and if you look far enough ahead, you can see where your opponent is going."

"Who's mocking? To tell the truth, I'm fascinated. Tell me more. I'm all alone on the board. What about Mr. Sinister?"

"Oh, he's marshaled every piece he possesses to gather for the kill—the witnesses against you, the prosecutor, the reporters, and, sad to say, public opinion. But the game will end only when they hang you."

A thought occurred to her and her gray eyes sparkled. "Oh, I wish I could hear his thoughts right now! He'll be gnashing his teeth because you outmaneuvered him when you escaped from Newgate! That's one move he couldn't have anticipated. No one ever escapes from Newgate."

"Did I hear right?" He put his hand to his ear. "Are you giving me credit for something?"

She put her head back and laughed. "I think Mr. Sinister may be wakening up to the fact that he has met his match. But don't underestimate him. The law is on his side, and he's bound to have accomplices. Lucy is gone, of course. But the boy was never found. There may be others."

He drank the last of his sherry. "What I don't understand," he said, "is how he persuaded Lucy to become involved."

"You liked her, didn't you?"

"Very much. She was only a girl, really, an orphan, but she never complained about her lot. I still find it hard to believe that she was part of the plot against me, but there's no other explanation for the lies she told."

"I think she must have been in love with him." When he made a face, she smiled. "I know, it sounds farfetched, but some women will do anything for love. And we can't know what tale he spun, only that Lucy took the bait."

She gazed at him earnestly. "If we could only work out who, in your past, believes he was unjustly punished because of you, we would know who he is. He must have lost everything that mattered to him, just as you had to lose everything, too."

"There isn't anyone. I've never sent a man to trial without irrefutable evidence of his guilt." He paused. "Damn!"

"Yes," she said. "Isn't that what happened to you?"

"It doesn't help. I don't know who this person can be."

"There must be someone," she said hopelessly.

"There isn't."

"Don't be so quick to make up your mind! Think about it! Really think about it!"

He was silent for a long time. Finally, he gave his head a little shake, as if he couldn't accept the answer that came to him.

"What?" she asked.

"The only person who fits that description is myself. It happened years ago, and it was my character that was damn near destroyed. So that episode can have nothing to do with this."

"What happened?"

"It's not relevant."

His refusal to confide in her now, after she'd demonstrated her complete faith in him, was like a slap in the face. She felt the color rise in her cheeks, and she half rose from her chair.

"Sit down, Rosamund," he said.

She sat, but she stared at the fire.

After a moment he sighed, then began to speak quietly and slowly. "It happened during my third term at Cambridge. I was only seventeen and was determined to make the most of my good fortune. Cambridge was like a dream come true, one of the best universities in all of Britain. My father could never have afforded to send me there. But I had benefactors, Andrew Dunsmoor and his wife. They spent part of every year in Scotland visiting her family. We were distant relations. They were very kind, very generous, and took a great interest in me. They had no children of their own, you see.

"When I turned sixteen, they invited me to come and live with them here, which I did, with my parents' blessing. They, my parents, could see all the advantages in this arrangement and none of the drawbacks. At any rate, the following year, when Dunsmoor enrolled me in Cambridge, my father was ecstatic. And so was I."

He gave a dry laugh. "It wasn't anything like I expected. I'd been raised all my life to strive for excellence. My father had always taught me that an education was the key to advancement for people in our position. I felt I owed it to my parents and the Dunsmoors to do well. However, the young men I met at Cambridge lived by a different creed. They were there to enjoy themselves, and enjoy themselves they did— wine, women, gaming, and all sorts of high jinks. They didn't care if they were sent down, and many of them were. They had money to fall back on, family connections, that sort of thing. I was an outsider. To be perfectly honest, I was my own worst enemy. I behaved like a monumental prig."

He'd left gaps in his story that were easy to fill in. A young man from a modest background had been thrown in with a set of young men who took their wealth and privilege for granted. He would have felt like an outsider right from the beginning, and when he refused to join in the high jinks he mentioned, he would have been relegated to the outer edges of the fraternity, where his own pride would have isolated him. The young men he referred to would be like her own brothers. They would not have been deliberately cruel, merely indifferent, and that was the worst cruelty of all.

He was staring at his glass, as though it were a crystal ball, not seeing into the future but taking him back to the past. He said, "But as wild as these boys were—and that's all we were, boys—they had a highly developed sense of honor. Anyone who broke that code was considered beneath contempt, and treated accordingly."

"And you broke that code?" she asked softly.

"No, but they thought I had. Things began to go missing—small sums of money, a jeweled pin, I can't remember what. One of the boys, Middler, took it upon himself to set a trap, without telling anyone, and I and another boy were caught in it. We'd both gone into Middler's room, right after each other, both knowing that Middler had cashed a large bank draft from his father. Needless to say, the money was missing. And of course, the thief had to be me or the other boy."

"What were you doing in Middler's room?"

"I'd loaned him a book at the beginning of term and I wanted it back. As for the other boy, Frank Stapleton, he and Middler were always in and out of each other's rooms. They were friends."

She made a small inarticulate sound, knowing what he would say next.

"I don't have to tell you," he said, "whose story they believed. As I said, I was an outsider. So I was the one who had to be punished."

"They beat you?"

"Oh, no, nothing so uncivilized. They told me to leave Cambridge at once and never set foot in it again. To which I replied that I'd leave it in my own good time and not before. So they punished me with silence."

"Oh, God."

"It didn't last long. I knew Frank Stapleton must be the thief, so I set about finding the evidence to prove it. You might say it was my first case." When she didn't return his smile, he shrugged. "At any rate, he'd pawned the jeweled pin and other small articles he'd stolen. To cut a long story short, the pawnbroker identified him and exonerated me."

"And the money?"

"Once it was known that Stapleton was a thief, his friends got him to confess. He'd spent every penny of it on paying off creditors. The irony was, he'd borrowed the money to spend on his friends."

"They would have been much more severe with Stapleton than they were with you."

"How do you know?" He sounded surprised.

"Because his offense was more serious. He let an innocent boy take his punishment. That was cowardly. What did they do to him?"

His eyes darkened. "They tarred and feathered him and left him out all night tied to a tree in the middle of the quadrangle, so that in the morning the whole university would witness his shame. I suppose at the time I felt he deserved it, but it did not take me long to regret what was done. Stapleton left Cambridge at once. I left shortly after, never to return. The next term, I enrolled in Aberdeen University, with my own kind."

"You sound bitter."

"That's because I've dredged up that ghastly memory. If I was bitter, I didn't stay that way for long." He stopped suddenly. "This is all beside the point. You wanted to know if I had ever shamed anyone, and that's my answer. But Stapleton wasn't innocent; he was guilty. So you see, our cases are not the same."

Her shoulders slumped.

"Disappointed?"

"I suppose I am. I thought we were getting somewhere. Whatever happened to Stapleton?"

"I haven't a clue."

"And those other young men who tarred and feathered him?"

"I see the odd one occasionally, but only in passing. We're civil to each other, but we keep our distance. There's an awkwardness there . . . you know what I mean. Anyway, all that happened seventeen years ago.

Do you really believe it has any bearing on what's happening now?"

She heaved a sigh. "No, more's the pity."

After that, they went back and forth, going over old ground, probing every detail in an effort to find some clue that would point them in a new direction—all to no avail. They were interrupted when Harper entered with their dinner. A small table was cleared, and Harper set the tray down.

"Beef stew," he said, "with dumplings and pastries."

He left almost at once. "To see to the horses," he said, and winked at Rosamund.

Much later, when they'd eaten their fill, Rosamund said, "Tell me about this house, and what happened to the Dunsmoors."

"They're both dead," he said, "and I inherited the house."

"Do you think it's safe to stay here? I mean, what if the militia come here looking for you?"

"Besides myself," he said, "only you and Harper know about this house."

"But if this was your home—"

"It wasn't. When I left Cambridge, I never returned to Dunsmoor. Let me worry about it, all right?"

The snub caught her off guard again, and she withdrew into her shell like a little tortoise that had been whacked on the nose. A moment later, she looked at the clock, exclaimed at the time, and pleading fatigue rose from the table. He walked her to the door.

She heard him sigh, then his hands were on her shoulders and he turned her to face him. "Go home, Lady Rosamund Devere," he said, "and forget all about me." His hands tightened on her arms, briefly, then his hands dropped away and he took a step back. "Forget about me, Rosamund," he said.

She searched his face. There was no offense intended. He was perfectly serious and spoke from the heart.

Her own heart cramped. She couldn't give him the answer he wanted, because she knew she would never forget him, or the deadly peril that threatened him. It would be like deserting him, and that she could never do.

She masked her pain with a smile. "Take care, Richard Maitland," she said. "You've made an awesome enemy, and he hasn't finished with you yet."

And before the incipient tears could turn into a flood, she whisked herself out of the room.

Chapter 13

*I*t was still dark when Harper came for her and told her it was time to get going. He'd brought a tray with tea and toast and had laid out a fresh set of clothes.

"Men's clothes," he told her, grinning, "because we have a hard ride ahead of us, and two men on the road won't attract no notice. Women is nothing but trouble, begging your pardon, your ladyship."

"And Colonel Maitland?" she asked quickly, before Harper could whisk himself out of the room. He seemed in an unholy hurry to get away from her. "How is he?"

"Couldn't be better! Top o' the morning! As fit as a fiddle!" and before she could put any more questions to him, Harper made his escape.

She was out of the bed like a shot. It didn't take her long to get ready, and less than ten minutes later, she stalked into Richard's bedchamber and came to a sudden halt. The bed was made up, a fire was blazing in the grate; the remains of his breakfast were on the small table by the window. But there was no Richard.

"We best get going, your ladyship," said Harper from the open doorway.

She whirled on him. "Where is he, Harper?"

Harper looked down at his boots. "I ... er ... think he went for a walk."

"In the dark?"

He frowned, sighed, then went on sheepishly, "I don't know where he is, m'lady, and that's the truth. But he did say that I was to get you away from here before the sun was up."

She stalked by Harper and went marching along the corridor till she came to the next room, another bed-chamber. All the furniture was under Holland covers. It was the same in the next room and the one after that. Harper dogged her heels, telling her to be sensible; that time was wasting; and finally, that it was better this way.

"Think about it, m'lady. What can you say that hasn't been said?"

Plenty. She'd had a sleepless night thinking about what she wanted to say to Richard Maitland. She wanted to tell him that she knew she could convince her father and brothers to believe in his innocence and that they would all work tirelessly to prove it. She wanted to tell him that there was nothing and no one who could ever shake her faith in him.

That was the most important thing: that he should know that there was nothing and no one who could ever shake her faith in him.

That's what had kept her awake last night, not sifting through the details of the crime for which he'd been convicted, but all the gaps he'd left in his story. He'd felt like an outsider when he went to Cambridge. He wasn't one of them—that's why they'd made him their scape-goat. It was the law of the jungle.

They punished me with silence.

She knew what that meant. If he walked into the common room, everyone would leave it. If he sat down at a table, everyone would rise and move to another table. Every day and every night, he would be alone with only his own thoughts for company.

Horrible, horrible boys!

It would have taken more than that, though, to get rid of Richard. Yet he'd left Cambridge shortly after, never to return. He'd done the same with this house. That could only mean that Mr. Dunsmoor had turned against him, too. He must have changed his mind eventually, because he'd left Richard his house. But Richard didn't give people second chances. That was patently clear. And that was his greatest failing.

She cut Harper off in mid-sentence. "Do you swear to me he's feeling all right?"

"Aye. You did a good job there."

She walked on. There was another staircase at the other end of the house, but she was beginning to see how hopeless it was. If Richard didn't want to be found, he wouldn't be found.

"Lass," said Harper gently, "it's time to go."

The pity in his eyes made her own eyes tear. "You don't approve of me, do you, Harper?"

He knew what she meant. "Not for the colonel, m'lady, not a duke's daughter."

She waited till she had command of her voice. "Will you give him a message from me? Tell him I don't give up easily." Then, before she could completely disgrace herself, "All right, Harper, you win. Let's go."

❧

When Richard heard them leave, he tossed aside the notes he'd been making. He was on the top floor of the house, in the little study that had once belonged to him, when he was practically a member of the family. But that was a lifetime ago, before Cambridge, before the estrangement between himself and the man he once called "Uncle Andrew."

He pushed back his chair and got up, then paused as a wave of dizziness enveloped him. He knew he was on the mend, so he put it down to fatigue and the residue of his fever. The dizziness soon subsided, and he walked to the window and looked out.

He'd hoped to catch a glimpse of her, but the darkness was impenetrable. Dawn was only a feeble glimmer on the horizon, and it didn't look like a promising dawn either, but a dreary repetition of the last several days. Whether it rained or not, there would be a pervading dampness that would penetrate to every corner and cupboard in the house. Nothing could keep it out.

Not unlike Rosamund.

His smile was fleeting. He hoped she'd got the message. They were becoming far too friendly, too cozy for his liking. He didn't want anyone or anything distracting him from what he had to do. Besides, he was a dangerous man to know. He'd kept his friends out of this sorry business, so he certainly wasn't going to drag a naive and impossibly trusting amateur into it.

Did you murder Lucy Rider?

No.

And just like that she believed him.

A woman like that was dangerous, not because she made snap decisions, but because of the effect she had on her victims. If his heart hadn't been protected by a layer of calluses, he might have been tempted to pour out all his woes.

He heard another voice asking a similar question, Uncle Andrew's voice. *"Did you steal that money?"*

"No, sir."

"Don't lie to me! I know those boys! I know their fathers! They wouldn't accuse you if you were innocent. So, I'll ask you again. Did you steal that money?"

"No, sir."

"I don't believe you!"

There had been a reconciliation of sorts, but after that, he could never be the same with the Dunsmoors. So he'd returned to Scotland, and right after university, he'd gone into the army. They'd kept up a sporadic correspondence, but he had never been much of a letter writer. When he was in Spain, first Mrs. Dunsmoor died, then her husband, and the house had passed to him. It was the last thing he'd expected. He'd written to the lawyer, telling him to let the house and its acreage, but even when he was back in England, he'd made no attempt to return to Dunsmoor.

It was necessity that had brought him back, and now that he was here, he wondered why he'd stayed away. He'd seen things, done things as an agent that made his quarrel with the Dunsmoors seem trivial. It was more than time to lay these ghosts to rest. If their positions were reversed, if he'd been Uncle Andrew, he might have said the same.

Not everyone was as generous as Rosamund.

Rosamund again! Frowning, he looked at the notes on his desk. He should be sifting through them, trying to find someone who fitted Rosamund's profile, someone who wanted him to suffer as he had been made to suffer. An eye for an eye. A tooth for a tooth.

He sat down at his desk and began to make more notes. Half an hour later, when he was no further ahead, he got up, left the study, and went downstairs to his bedchamber. The bed looked very inviting, but he ignored it. He didn't expect Harper back for hours, so it was up to him to keep the fires going and generally take care of things.

Though he was sure in his own mind that no one could connect him to the house, and he didn't expect trouble, he'd learned caution the hard way and never took unnecessary risks. After banking the fire in his bed-chamber and the one in the kitchen, he donned his caped greatcoat and went outside to have a look around.

Dawn was making a valiant effort to put in an appearance, but it was hindered by the heavy cloud cover, and not only that. A fine mist was rising from the sodden earth, blanketing buildings and trees in a frothy shroud.

He ignored the elements as he ignored the shivers that were beginning to wrack his frame. Head down, shoulders hunched against the breeze, he made for the stable. There was only one horse to see to, but after filling the troughs with water and bran, he felt as though he'd taken care of a troop of horses.

Caution or not, he knew that if he didn't get back to his bed, he would collapse where he was.

He was climbing the portico stairs when he heard the faint rumble of horses' hooves. He stepped behind a pillar and reached for his pistol. Though he could see nothing, he listened intently. One horse and one rider, he decided, and they were in one hell of a hurry to reach the house. A foe would show more caution.

On that thought, he stepped out from behind the pillar. Almost at the same moment the rider emerged from the trees.

"Richard!" she yelled at the top of her voice.

Rosamund! She was low in the saddle and her hair streamed behind her like a wake. He looked past her. There was no sign of Harper. As she reined in, he hastened down the steps.

"You have to get away at once!" Her breath came in rasping sobs. "They spotted us. No, there's no time to saddle your horse. Get up behind me."

"Harper?" he said.

"He tried to lead them away. There's no time to explain! Get up behind me."

He lifted his head when he heard something. She

wasn't exaggerating. It sounded as though a troop of cavalry was galloping along the drive to the house.

Cursing softly, he got up behind her. "Make for the downs," he said in her ear, then he held on tight as their mount leapt forward.

≥

When they cleared the trees and came to a grassy knoll overlooking the house, he made her draw rein. There was little to see. The house was shrouded in mist. All they would see were shadows, but those shadows were moving.

"What happened?" asked Richard.

She was breathing hard. "We didn't get farther than the village. It's a pea-soup fog down there. I don't really know what happened except that someone coming out of the inn bellowed Harper's name. 'Digby!' Harper said, and told me to come here to warn you to get away. Then he took another route to try and lead them away from you."

She wheeled the horse and anxiously searched for a chink in the white fluffy blanket that veiled the downs. There was none. She might as well be poised at the edge of a cliff.

"We can't go on in this," she said despairingly.

Richard spoke quietly in her ear. "There's a shepherd's bothy not far from here. We can take shelter there. Change places with me, and I'll guide the horse."

Dismounting was awkward and she fell on her rump as she slipped out of the saddle. The horse shied and cantered forward. Richard turned it, but kept his distance.

"Now listen to me, Rosamund," he said. "I want you to go back to the house. You'll be safe there. If you come with me, anything might happen when the shooting starts. It's me they want, not you. Go back to the house. Do you hear me?"

Before she could get her breath, he turned the horse and disappeared into the mist.

She scrambled to her feet and went after him. "You bloody fool!" she yelled at the top of her voice. She was really, really angry. Angry and panicked. "I'm your best hope of escaping the gallows! You would have seen it before now if you hadn't been so dense!" She was running now and screeching like a banshee. "You put a gun to my head, and tell them you'll kill me if they try to take you, just like you did in Newgate!"

Tears were streaming down her face. In the last little while, she'd suffered agonies, fearing that he might be captured. He was in desperate straits. He couldn't go far in this pea soup, and when his pursuers caught up to him, he wouldn't stand a chance. He needed her if only to barter his way to freedom.

She went charging into the mist, shouting at the top of her lungs. "You can't get rid of me! Where you go, I go. And you'll be sorry when they mistake me for you in this beastly fog and shoot me dead. They won't know I'm Romsey's daughter. I'm dressed like a man, remember? Do you hear me, Richard? You'll be sorry! You'll go to the gallows with my death on—"

Her words were cut off when she stumbled over a rock and fell flat on her face. Though she was gasping for breath, she quickly pulled herself up to her knees. A hand dangled in front of her nose. She looked up. Richard was astride the horse.

"Thank you" was all she said as she grasped his hand.

Without saying a word, he hoisted her to her feet, then onto the horse's back. His heels touched his mount's flanks and they broke into a canter.

&

She was right about them not getting far, though it wasn't the mist that caused the problem. Their mount stumbled and they both tumbled to the ground. She got to her feet first and tried to catch the horse's reins, but it trotted off into the mist. When she turned back, Richard was on his knees.

She was badly frightened by how weak he appeared to be. He hadn't had a chance to recover from his injuries, and now this. She masked her fear and said, "Where is this bothy?"

"Not far."

She looked back over her shoulder, searching the mist, straining to hear sounds of pursuit. She could see nothing, hear nothing. It was the mist that had saved them, but how long would it last?

Swallowing her fear, she said, "We'll walk the rest of the way. Put your arm around my shoulders."

He did as she said, and leaned against her for support. "I'll be all right when we get to the bothy," he said. "Then I want you to leave."

She didn't argue with him. She couldn't leave him even if she wanted to. The mist was so dense, she wouldn't know which way to go. It was uphill all the way, and they saved their breath for their exertions. Rosamund didn't know how they could possibly find the bothy, but Richard seemed to know where he was going. A time or two, when the mist thinned a little, he stopped and looked this way and that. All she could see were shadows, but to him they appeared to be landmarks, and they went on.

She thought she was lending him her strength, but as time passed, it was she who began to give in to fatigue, and he who encouraged her.

"Not much farther," he said. "Don't give up. We'll rest, then we'll decide what to do."

She didn't know what they could do. Richard wasn't fit to go on. But he was resourceful. He'd escaped from Newgate. He would escape from this, too.

They stumbled upon the bothy just as Rosamund made up her mind that she couldn't take another step.

Its walls were made of stone, its roof was thatched, and the floor was cobbled, just like the streets of London. But it was so small that two people with fingers touching and their arms outstretched could reach the opposite walls.

"Who does the bothy belong to?" she asked.

"Everyone. No one. The shepherds use these bothies in emergencies, when they are caught on the downs in a sudden mist or snowstorm."

There was a narrow bunk with a straw pallet, and a stool beside a blackened grate. On the other side of the grate was a basket of kindling and a pile of logs.

She barred the door and helped Richard to the bunk.

"We can't light a fire," he said. "The smell of the smoke will give us away." He stopped, shook his head, and gave a dry laugh. "They'll find us soon enough anyway. The mist is lifting. Light a fire if you want."

A moment before, she'd been ready to drop, but the thought of the mist lifting sent her flying to the window. "It looks the same to me," she said anxiously.

She turned to look at him just as he sank onto the pallet. "Come here," he said, and he held his hands out to her.

She knelt in front of him and put her hands in his. Her eyes searched his. "Do you have a fever?"

"No."

"Is your wound troubling you?"

"No. Listen to me, Rosamund. There's nothing wrong with me but fatigue. I spent an uneasy night, wondering what to do about you."

"And," she said reproachfully, "you decided to send me away without seeing me again."

He looked down at her hands, then raised them to his lips and pressed a kiss to one, then to the other. "I thought it was for the best."

Her heart clenched in fear. He must have given up all hope if he was letting his guard down like this. She couldn't get words past the lump in her throat. When he smiled into her eyes, her fear turned to dread.

"For my sake, you must be brave," he said. "As soon as we hear them approaching, you're to go outside and let them know who you are. They'll come in here to get me, but no matter what you hear, you have to stay outside. Don't look back. Go home to your family and forget all about me."

She said tremulously, "And what if I don't? What if I stay by your side? Richard, they won't dare touch you with me here."

He spoke slowly and patiently, as though he were explaining things to a child. "Then they'll take me back to Newgate and hang me. Is that what you want? Rosamund, I want to die a soldier's death. Let me die with some dignity."

The moan started in her chest. Her mouth opened, but all that came out was a feeble whimper. Tears drowned her eyes. "I can't . . . I won't . . ."

"Rosamund, Rosamund."

He drew her to him, and wrapped her in his arms. He kissed her gently, then not so gently as she responded. Her arms crept around his neck. When he drew away slightly, it was only to draw back the edges of her coat, then his. Then he wrapped her in his arms again.

She spoke against the hollow of his throat. "That's the first time I've ever been kissed."

He raised his head to look at her. "I find that hard to believe."

She managed, barely, to return his smile. "That's what comes of being a duke's daughter. Men are afraid to approach me. Or perhaps it's me. Perhaps they find me unappealing. It's what you said, don't you remember, in the cottage in Chelsea?"

He threaded his fingers through her hair and brought her face close to his. His voice was husky. "I lied. You are, without doubt, the loveliest and most desirable woman I have ever met."

Even as the words warmed her, the cold finger of fear touched her heart. He wouldn't be saying these things if he thought he could get out of here alive. This, then, was all that they would ever have.

Then she would not spoil it with tears and regrets.

Banishing her fears and anguish, she said with a smile, "If only I had been an ordinary girl, instead of a duke's daughter . . ."

"Yes," he said gravely. "If only you had been an ordinary girl."

She blinked at him through a blur of tears. "If only . . ." she began, but her voice cracked and she couldn't go on.

"Hush." He kissed her again. "Don't torment yourself like this."

She wished there was more light in that small room, because she was sketching his portrait in her mind and heart so that she would remember him till her dying day. But there was more to a man than his looks. She would never forget Richard Maitland.

"You are," she said softly, "the noblest gentleman that I have ever met."

He smiled at this. "Tell me about yourself, Rosamund. I know so little."

He really was interested in hearing about her life, but at the same time, he wanted to relieve some of the tension that gripped her; in short, distract her from counting the seconds until they were discovered.

"Where shall I begin?" she asked.

"At the beginning, of course. What were you like as a child? Happy? Sad? I really want to know."

"I was happy," she said at once, "but not so happy after my mother died."

She began to talk, haltingly at first, then more fluently as memories crowded her mind. Though her mother had died when Rosamund was only five, there was no doubt in Richard's mind that Her Grace had been a powerful influence in her daughter's life, and still was. A picture formed in his mind of a woman who enjoyed her children and enjoyed life, an unconventional woman who had no patience with the restrictions that society tried to place upon her. And the duke, who doted on his duchess, was an indulgent husband.

"When she was gone," said Rosamund wistfully at one point, "all the color in the world seemed to go with her." She added quickly, "You mustn't think that my father neglected me or anything like that. In fact, he did just the opposite. It was the manner of my mother's death, you understand, that made him so protective. He blamed himself for allowing her too many liberties."

When she paused, he said, "And he made certain that his only daughter stayed close to home?"

"Yes," she said, and sighed.

As she continued to speak, Richard began to adjust impressions he'd taken of Rosamund and stored in his mind. He saw now that she'd never been haughty or cold, but only unsure of herself. And who could blame her? The people who loved her best, and whom she undoubtably loved, had gently but ruthlessly quashed every attempt she'd made to establish herself as her own person. Governesses, horses, and chess—that had been the sum of Rosamund's life as she grew to womanhood. But at least her father had had the sense to supply her with a friend. Callie.

She gave him an arch look. "It was Callie's idea to visit you in Newgate. I think she hero worships you, and that's saying something for Callie. She has an acid tongue. But you captured her imagination. No one could say anything wrong about Richard Maitland in Callie's hearing."

"I'm obliged to the lady."

Her smile flashed.

"And what about you, Rosamund? Why did you go to

Newgate? You've already told me you thought I was as guilty as sin."

The arch look vanished, and she said seriously. "It was sheer bravado on my part. Callie challenged me, and I accepted. But I want you to know that that is one decision I shall *never* regret."

Of course, her words moved him. His arms tightened around her, pulling her closer and he kissed the top of her head. "If your mother could see you now," he said, "she would be proud of you."

She looked up at him, her expression arrested. "Do you think so?"

"I know so! You're your mother's daughter, and who should know better than I?"

Her smile was tremulous at best, and swiftly faded when she felt his body tense. "What is it, Richard?"

"Listen!"

Then she heard it, horses' hooves, thudding on the soft turf. A troop of riders was approaching the bothy.

"The mist must be clearing," he said. "It's time."

Her face crumpled. "No! Richard, no! There's so much more I want to say to you."

"Don't panic!" His hands grasped hers. "For my sake, Rosamund, you'll do as I told you." Then more gently, "I would do anything to spare you this, but I can't. If you lose your courage now, think what it will do to me. My dearest girl, everything passes. Even this will pass. I want you to be happy. I want you to forget me. Now go!"

White-faced and trembling, she stumbled to the door. At the threshold, she turned. "It's all right, Richard. I know what you're trying to do, and it won't work. I shall never forget you. And I haven't given up hope, so don't do anything foolish."

"Rosamund—"

But she was through the door.

You fool! he thought savagely. What possessed him to play the romantic hero? If he'd wanted her to forget him, he shouldn't have kissed her, shouldn't have betrayed how much he cared for her, shouldn't have invited her to confide in him.

But how could he help it? A man on the threshold of death could be forgiven for wanting to take something for himself, especially from the only woman who had ever mattered to him. If he lived to be one hundred, she would be the one woman he would never forget.

He smiled grimly at the unconscious irony of his last jest.

When he heard the jingle of spurs as men dismounted, he got up and checked his pistol, then he positioned himself so that the light would fall on him when they came through the door. He hoped to hell that they knew how to shoot straight.

It would have been better if he had left Rosamund in the bothy while he went out to meet them. Better for him, but not for her. He didn't want her to see his end.

Rosamund's voice came to him, strident, commanding, as befitted a duke's daughter. Or maybe as befitted her mother's daughter. She was still trying to save him. He swallowed hard, then braced himself for what was to come.

Many minutes passed, then the door began to open.

"Don't shoot, sir!" said a voice he recognized.

Richard slowly lowered his pistol. "Harper?" he asked incredulously.

Harper chuckled. "You has the luck o' the devil, Colonel Maitland, sir! Mr. Templar is here. And Lord Caspar. They've come to rescue you. Don't that beat all!"

Chapter 14

*I*t didn't feel like a rescue to Richard. When he came out of the bothy, he was surrounded by a horde of mean-faced menacing minions, who looked as though they wanted to kill him.

"They won't hurt you, Richard," Rosamund called out. "They're loyal to the duke."

Loyal to the duke? What did she think this was—the Middle Ages? A closer look revealed that they were all dressed in blue coats and gold frogging, the duke's livery. They were servants, but their livery was misleading. He knew war veterans when he saw them, and this lot looked as though they'd seen many a battle.

Hugh Templar spoke up. "Just do as they say, Richard, and you'll be all right."

Harper said, "Now, don't stiffen up like that, Colonel, sir. They're on our side. Their feathers are ruffled 'cos you abducted Lady Rosamund, but they won't do you no harm." He chuckled. "Or she'll have their guts for garters, and they knows it."

With three of the few people he trusted all saying the same thing, Richard relaxed his guard a little.

"Get his gun and any other weapons he may be concealing on his person."

The speaker was standing beside Rosamund, and Richard had no difficulty in identifying him as her brother, Lord Caspar—tall, handsome, unsmiling, and with the haughtiness of an aristocrat. Richard disliked him on sight.

There was some jostling as two of the Devere men began to search him for weapons. They took away his pistol and the blade he kept in his boot. Someone else stood on his toes. But Harper barked out an order and, like the trained soldiers they were, they fell back and left a space around him.

Rosamund started forward, but her brother's hand shot out and grasped her arm, keeping her by his side.

Hugh came up to him and clapped him on the shoulder. He bore it stoically. He didn't want to talk about his health. He just wanted to know what in Hades's name was going on.

"Richard," said Hugh, smiling. "Thank God, you're all right." His smile faded. "I know, you want an explanation of why I've come after you, but this isn't the time. There's a troop of militia close by. I don't think they know about us, but we can't be sure. We must ride out of here at once."

Rosamund cried out, "But he's not fit to ride. Can't you see he's on the point of collapse?"

No one paid any attention to this outburst. A horse was brought to him, the same horse that had run off when they fell off it. He didn't know if he had the strength to mount it.

Rosamund said something passionate, though inaudible, to her brother, who merely shrugged his broad shoulders; Hugh frowned; Harper cupped his hands and bent down to hoist Richard into the saddle.

"Come on, Colonel, sir," he whispered. "You can do it."

Lord Caspar's bored voice cut across Harper's. "Mount up or hang. It's all the same to me, Maitland."

The men in blue livery laughed.

Richard gritted his teeth, put his booted foot into Harper's cupped hands, and mounted up.

&

Some time later, Major Digby and his troop of militia came galloping up to Dunsmoor's front doors. His face was mottled with fury. His hands on the reins were not gentle, and his mount stamped and whinnied as it felt the pressure of the bit when he reined in.

He was furious because he now saw that Maitland's bodyguard had led them on a wild-goose chase while, in all likelihood, Maitland had made good his escape. But he wasn't sure and he didn't know what to do for the best, search the house or go after Maitland, supposing they could find his trail in this fog. But having encountered Harper, at least he knew that they were on the right track. The information that George Withers had passed on had proved reliable.

He was out of the saddle in an instant, with Whorsley and several soldiers close behind him, guns drawn, taking the stairs two at a time. He hammered on the front door, and when no one answered, ordered his men to break it down.

Once inside, Digby yelled, "Search the house. He may still be here. And watch out for his bodyguard. He may have doubled back and be hiding here, too. And if you find Lady Rosamund, treat her with kid gloves."

It didn't take them long to discover that the house was empty, but had been recently occupied. The fires were still burning. And when Whorsley found the notes in the little study, they had absolute proof that Maitland had recently been there.

Whorsley said, "This is odd." He was reading Richard's

notes. "He's going over old cases. It seems as though he's trying to make a connection between them and Lucy Rider's murder." He looked at Digby. "Is it possible, do you think, that he didn't kill her?"

Digby snatched the notes out of Whorsley's hand and stuffed them in his pocket. Through his teeth, he said, "That's not important. Our job is to find him and bring him in."

"But if he's innocent, shouldn't we pass these notes on to—"

"No! Why muddy the waters? He was found guilty by a jury. That's the end of the matter as far as the law is concerned. Do you really want to see him back as chief of staff? Believe me, we're doing the Service a favor by just doing our job."

"What do we do now?"

Digby walked to the window and looked out. They might as well be marooned on a desert island. They couldn't go chasing all over the downs in this mist.

His sense of frustration brought bile to his throat. If only they'd come straight to the house and not gone charging after Harper! That Maitland had bested him yet again was not to be borne. But Maitland couldn't travel fast if he had Lady Rosamund with him.

He'd find him and bring him back in chains. Then the prime minister would reward him for a job well done. Chief of staff. He'd like that. The reverie was tantalizing.

He said, "We wait till the fog lifts, then we'll begin a proper search."

No more was said about the notes they had found. Digby didn't think they would make any difference to Maitland's conviction, but to be on the safe side, when no one was looking, he threw them in the fire.

❧

Their progress was slow, but not, thought Richard grimly, because he couldn't keep up. It was the fog that

kept them to a snail's pace—and, bless her, Rosamund.
Just when he thought he couldn't stay upright in the
saddle one more minute, she would call a halt and say
that she had to stretch her legs. She was doing it for him,
so that he could catch his breath. He wanted to acknowledge the kindness, but as soon as she dismounted,
she was hemmed in by the Devere retainers. Her brother
was making very sure that there would be no more words
between them.

Reality had caught up to them, as he had known it
would. He had no quarrel with reality. He was used to it.
He just wished there was a way of sparing Rosamund.

He gleaned odd scraps of information at their various
stops. Hugh, he learned, had made some sort of bargain
with the duke, an advantageous bargain, but that would
all be gone into when they reached their destination.
Digby and Whorsley from Section C and a troop of militia were hot on their heels. They had to press on, Hugh
said.

Harper was more revealing. He'd run smack into
Digby and Whorsley, he said, who were holed up in the
local tavern, so he'd sent Rosamund back to the house to
warn Richard, then tried to lead them away, and had run
smack into Lord Caspar and Hugh.

"I didn't know it was them," he said. "I thought it was
all up with me. Soldiers in front of me, soldiers behind
me. Then I heard Mr. Templar's voice calling to me out
of the fog, and I knew I was among friends."

"Then what happened?"

He grinned. "Then I showed them a shortcut to the
house, while Digby and company went chasing off in the
opposite direction."

"But how did Lord Caspar and Hugh know about
Dunsmoor?"

Harper shrugged. "I dunno. You'll have to ask Mr.
Templar."

But that Richard could not do, because Hugh was on rearguard duty in the event of the enemy overtaking them. There were scouts riding ahead as well. This didn't feel like England. This felt like Spain, when he worked with the partisans behind the French lines.

His eyes strayed to Lord Caspar. He had to give credit where credit was due. The man seemed to know what he was doing. And maybe he deserved Lord Caspar's hostility. He had, after all, abducted Rosamund. What he could not tolerate was the man's breeding. Some men truly believed they were born to rule, and his lordship gave every indication that he was one of them.

Hour after weary hour, they plodded on, occasionally passing the odd shepherd or farmer who were tending their flocks. It gradually came to Richard that they were traveling in a north-easterly direction. He had assumed they would go south, toward London, but they were leaving the villages and hamlets behind and entering a more barren terrain.

As they climbed, the fog thinned, but dusk was beginning to chase the light away, so the visibility hardly improved. Suddenly, out of the wispy vapor, there emerged a stark fortress, complete with towers and crenellated battlements.

They were expected. As they neared the gatehouse, porters came running and swung open the massive iron gates—porters, Richard noted, who were wearing the same livery as the men who were escorting him.

The Middle Ages, it seemed, had arrived in the shape of the Castle Devere.

≈

All he wanted was sleep. What he got was a lecture from Hugh, warning him that from now on he was to answer only to the name of Richard Harris, and that he was elevated to the rank of one of Lady Rosamund's rescuers. After Hugh came the doctor, who had fingers like steel claws, and finally the valet, who ordered him into a tub of hot water. Then he slept.

It was a restless sleep. He kept dreaming of chessboards, and pawns in blue and gold livery who were out for his blood. He knew that if he could only capture their queen, he could grasp the king and his nightmare would be over, but she was too clever, too elusive. Just when he thought he had her, she changed her shape and became one of the pawns.

It was the sound of the door latch that awakened him. One moment he was asleep and the next he was reaching for his pistol by the side of his bed.

It was only the valet, who had returned with his clothes all nicely brushed and pressed. He gaped at the pistol that was pointed straight at him.

Richard tucked the pistol under his pillow, and without a word of explanation got out of bed. "Where is everyone?" he asked.

The valet blinked, but spoke as though nothing unusual had happened. "I was to tell you when you wakened, Mr. Harris, that your presence is requested in the yellow salon."

Richard began to dress. "What of His Grace? Will he be there?"

"No. His Grace remains at Twickenham House."

It was the only good news he'd heard in a long time.

Ten minutes later, now fortified with a glass of excellent Madeira, courtesy of the beaming valet, Richard was escorted downstairs by another beaming footman. Every servant who passed treated him to a smile. These were not the men who had escorted him from Dunsmoor to Castle Devere. When he asked the footman who was escorting him where they were, he learned that they were sleeping off the effects of a celebratory dinner Lord Caspar had laid on for them.

In the Great Hall, they passed stuffed warhorses with

plumed knights on their backs. A lion skin, complete
with head and fangs, guarded the cavernous stone
hearth. Tapestries depicting ancient battles adorned the
walls. The silver, the crystal, the intricately carved furniture—all spoke volumes, and what they told Richard was
that he had entered the domain of a proud and privileged dynasty.

As though he needed reminding.

The yellow salon was at the end of a long, drafty corridor. When he was announced, he squared his shoulders, and entered.

Chapter 15

As the others had already dined, Lord Caspar had one of the footmen bring a pot of coffee and a tray of sandwiches for Richard, a courtesy that was much appreciated since it was hours since he had eaten. There were only four of them in that snug study, Lord Caspar, Hugh, Harper, and himself, and as Richard ate, the others explained how and why they came to be there.

Lord Caspar, he learned, had been quick off the mark, and had turned up on Hugh's doorstep less than twenty-four hours after he, Richard, had escaped from Newgate. He also learned that he had Abbie to thank for persuading Hugh to tell Lord Caspar about Dunsmoor.

"You know Abbie," said Hugh. "Though she was well aware that no harm would come to Lady Rosamund with you, Richard, she couldn't bear to think of the torments her family must be suffering. So I made a bargain with Lord Caspar. If you did not release Lady Rosamund within twenty-four hours, I would help him track you down. To be quite honest, I was sure you would return her to her family the first chance you got, and that would have been the end of it. But when you didn't do as I expected, I thought things must have gone terribly wrong. So it was as much for your sake as Lady Rosamund's that I decided to become involved. At any rate, Harper has explained the delay in releasing Lady Rosamund, but all things considered, you're much better off under the duke's protection than you were fending for yourself."

"I don't think there's any doubt of that," answered Lord Caspar dryly. He had a decanter of port in his hand, and after pouring out a glass for Richard, topped up the others' glasses. "Short of granting you a pardon, which is beyond my father's power, you can name your own terms, Maitland."

"Does that apply to Harper, too?" asked Richard.

Harper was elated at the way things had turned out and it showed. "There's no need to worry about me, Colonel, sir. I'm going to be a hero. Seems like you tricked me into thinking you was on a secret mission, and that's why I helped you escape from Newgate. Then, when you wouldn't let Lady Rosamund go, I began to have my doubts, so when your back was turned, I took off and made straight for Mr. Templar to ask his advice."

Hugh took up the story. "And I shall say that I went straight to Lord Caspar, and here we are."

"And," said Lord Caspar, "all we shall tell the authorities about you is that you disappeared into the mist without a trace."

Richard chewed on the last bite of his last sandwich and washed it down with a swallow of port. He was doing more than listening to his companions' explanations and account of events. He was taking impressions, registering little changes in expression and tone of voice, adding up everything that was unsaid. One thing was abundantly clear. Hugh and Harper, whose judgment he trusted, had complete confidence in Lord Caspar. It went some way to allaying his own suspicion that Lord Caspar would renege on the bargain he'd made with Hugh. It would be a stupid thing to do, but Lord Caspar might not know that no one crossed Hugh Templar, former master spy in His Majesty's Secret Service, and got away with it.

He looked at Hugh and an unspoken message passed between them. Lord Caspar, Hugh's look told him, was not a stupid man.

Richard said abruptly, "You have yet to explain, Hugh, how you found me. Who told you about Dunsmoor?"

"Ah." Hugh smiled ruefully. "I eavesdropped on a conversation between you and your solicitor, so I knew about the house on the Berkshire downs. Lord Caspar and I tracked down Mr. Harley, who very obligingly told us about Dunsmoor. It seemed reasonable to suppose that that's where you would make for. I simply plotted your course and there it was—Newgate, Chelsea, Lavenham to see me, then into Berkshire."

Richard said tersely, "If I'd known, I wouldn't have—" He checked himself, sighed, then after a moment said in exasperation, "I can't believe you eavesdropped on a private conversation between my solicitor and me. Is nothing sacred?"

Hugh laughed. "Not to two old hands like us, Richard, leastways not eavesdropping. Besides, you should be thanking me. If we hadn't appeared when we did, Digby would have arrested you, and I don't think you would succeed in escaping from Newgate a second time." Hugh watched Richard's expression change, and he shook his head. "No, we didn't lead Digby to you. In fact, it turns out that we were following *him*. He was ahead of us, Richard, and we only caught up to him because he decided to wait out the fog in the local tavern."

Lord Caspar said, "You must have left a trail and he followed it."

"Or," said Hugh, "he knew about Dunsmoor."

Richard didn't think he'd left a trail, but he'd made the journey when he was at his lowest ebb. It was possible that he'd grown careless. The other alternative, that Digby had known about Dunsmoor, was more disturbing.

He looked up to find Lord Caspar's eyes upon him, assessing eyes that looked faintly puzzled, then the look was gone.

"So," said Richard, "where do we go from here?"

Lord Caspar smiled, the first smile he had cracked in Richard's memory. "Twickenham," he said. "His Grace, as I'm sure you'll understand, is anxious to make your acquaintance."

"We'll be his lordship's footmen," said Harper. His eyes gleamed with satisfaction. "And don't you worry none, Colonel, sir. No one will recognize you, 'cos no one ever gives servants a second stare."

"His lordships's *what*?" demanded Richard between his teeth.

"It need not be for long," Hugh added diplomatically. "This will give you a respite, Richard, time to get on your feet before you decide where you want to go and what you want to do."

Richard held Hugh's stare for a moment, then looked away. He didn't resent the fact that he would be disguised as a footman, but that he would be at his lordship's beck and call, a prospect Lord Caspar seemed to be relishing if his smile was anything to go by. When it occurred to him that he was behaving like a sulky schoolboy, he almost smiled. He had to admit that if their positions were reversed, if Lord Caspar had abducted Rosamund, his lordship most likely wouldn't be breathing right now.

Maybe the duke would make up for his son's omission?

Lord Caspar's next remark went some way to allaying that suspicion. "Naturally, you may depend on my father's support. A Devere's word is his bond, and His Grace will not renege on the bargain he made with Mr. Templar. If you want safe passage out of England, that can be arranged. If you want to change your identity and start fresh somewhere else, that can be arranged, too. But all that can be gone into when you meet with my father."

There was more in this vein, but Richard's mind was appraising the merits of hiding out at Twickenham House, at least until he was on his feet again. The more he thought about it, the better he liked the idea. No one would think of looking for him there, and it would be a great relief not to be watching his back all the time. And, as Hugh said, it need not be for long. A week should do it. Two at the most. Then he would do what he'd always intended to do—flush out the persons responsible for falsely incriminating him.

There was one little problem. Rosamund.

As the conversation went on around him, he let the problem of Rosamund revolve in his mind. He had to talk to her and make sure she understood that what happened at the bothy hadn't meant anything. They'd both been in the grip of powerful emotions. Fear had drawn them together. He'd comforted her. She'd comforted him. That's all it was.

Leastways, that's what he was going to impress upon her. The truth was, there was no future for them. This was her future, Castle Devere and her brother, Lord Caspar. He could no more fit into her world than she could fit into his.

Special Branch—that was his world, and though it was lost to him right now, he wanted it back. And if it wasn't Special Branch, it would be something similar. It was true that Dunsmoor had a sizeable acreage and provided a comfortable living, but that was a far cry from the luxury Rosamund was used to.

Not that Rosamund cared about luxury. What she wanted was a life of her own.

If only I were an ordinary girl.

Her words tormented him because he felt so helpless. He wanted to set her free, but he didn't know how it could be done, short of marrying her, and that was out of the question. It wasn't only her wealth that separated them. The Deveres were a powerful family, and highly connected. If they wanted to, they could utterly crush him. Even now, his fate was in their hands. Besides, he'd only known the girl for a week, and he mistrusted these softer feelings she stirred in him.

What he would like to do was take the duke aside and talk to him man-to-man. There was more to Rosamund, he would say, than the duke realized. Then he would drive home his point by illustrating how resourceful she'd been during her few days of captivity.

He bit back a chuckle when he remembered how she had almost unmanned Harper when her gun went off in the coach; how she had set the brawny rioter on him to make good her escape; how she'd lectured him on what he should have done when he escaped from Newgate; how she'd attacked him outside the cottage in Chelsea, sending him flying into the bramble bushes.

He'd told her that she was the loveliest and most desirable woman of his acquaintance. He should also have told her that she was the only woman who could make him laugh.

Rosamund, he thought. *Ah, Rosamund. If only . . .*

Lord Caspar's voice brought him out of his reverie. "Have I said something to amuse you, Maitland?"

Richard wiped the grin from his face and said sheepishly, "The port. It's made me drowsy." He got up, bid them all a polite goodnight and left.

Lord Caspar followed him out and shut the door. His lordship wasted no time with niceties. "How much money," he said, "will it take to persuade you not to marry my sister?"

Richard felt as though a steel comb had been raked through his teeth. When he could unlock his jaw, he said, "I think you must be confusing me with someone else."

Lord Caspar took a step closer and his eyes narrowed. "Let's not play games, Maitland. How much?"

Richard inhaled a long, calming breath. "If you knew me better," he said, "you'd know that those tactics won't work with me. If I decide to marry Lady Rosamund, I won't be bought off or frightened away. A simple 'no' from Rosamund will suffice."

"And what if she won't say 'no'?"

He decided to put Lord Caspar out of his misery. "There's nothing between Rosamund and me. The question of marriage has never come up, nor will it."

And with that, he stalked off.

❧

There was no escaping the Deveres. When he entered his own chamber, he found a footman waiting for him with a message from Rosamund. Her ladyship wished to speak with him, the footman said.

Fine, because he had a few choice words he wished to say to her ladyship as well.

"Where is she?"

Her suite of rooms was at the end of the corridor. He pushed into a little sitting room and came to an abrupt halt.

"Richard," she breathed out, making a sigh of his name.

"Rosamund?"

He hardly recognized the vision who came toward him, she looked so different now that she'd exchanged her boy's clothes for female garb. Her rose-tinted gown clung to her womanly form and revealed far more than he wanted to see. He could tell that she'd washed her hair. It fanned around her shoulders in a frothy veil. There wasn't a trace of the jaunty boy who defied him at every turn. This was a siren made to break men's hearts.

Rosamund grasped Richard's hands and smiled into his eyes. "Did Caspar give you a hard time?" she asked.

The mention of her brother brought him out of his stupor faster than a douse of ice-cold water. He dropped her hands and put some distance between them. "What," he asked, striving for patience, "did you tell your brother about us?"

She took in the hard jut of his jaw, his brows slashed in a frown, and she said haltingly, "I told him that we loved each other and were going to be married. Now, don't look like that. I had to say something. After Caspar saw that I was all right, when I came out of the bothy, his mood turned ugly. I was afraid of what he would do to you, so I told him—"

The flow of words dried up when he turned his back on her and walked to the fireplace. With one hand resting on the mantel, he turned to face her. "Marriage," he said, "is not in my stars, not to you or any woman. As for love, I may have played the gallant when I thought my last moments had come, but I don't remember using the word 'love,' and it's something I would remember."

"You don't understand," she said. "You see—"

He held up his hand and went on more gently, "Listen to me, Rosamund. What happened to us was natural. We were caught up in a life and death situation. In the little time we had together, we ran the gamut of every emotion known to man. We came to depend on each other. That's all it was. These circumstances no longer apply. In another week, you'll forget all about me. You'll take up your old life, and I'll have plenty to keep me occupied. Let's not end this on a sour note."

At first, she was amused, but by the time he had finished his little speech, she veered between mortification and outrage. He'd completely misunderstood the situation. Marriage to him was the farthest thing from her mind. But that he should dismiss her as though she were a love-struck adolescent was the worst cut of all.

Pain spread through her in waves, and with the pain, the awful realization that she wouldn't be hurting like this if she did not truly love him.

Pain was too weak a word to describe what she was feeling. She was devastated. Everything he had told her in the bothy was a lie. He had only been playing the gallant because he thought his last moments had come.

She wouldn't cry, she promised herself, wouldn't show him how much he had hurt her. She searched for her pride, found it, and tossed her head.

"Marriage! To you!" She laughed lightly. "It never once entered my head. Now you listen to me, Richard Maitland. When I came out of the bothy, Caspar was all for teaching you a lesson for abducting me. He wanted to kill you, but because of my father's bargain with Mr. Templar, he said he would be satisfied by giving you the beating of your life, and nothing Mr. Templar or Harper said could make him change his mind. So I took a hand in things. I knew you were on the point of collapse and couldn't defend yourself, so I told my brother that I loved you and that we were going to be married. I also told him that if he laid a hand on you, I would never speak to him again. And that's why you've been treated with kid gloves."

She forced a chuckle. "Poor Richard. It never occurred to me that *you* would be taken in by my little ploy."

When he looked at her doubtfully, she gave another light laugh, and crossed to him. "I have no intention of ending our friendship on a sour note," she said with a smile, and he would never know how much that smile cost her. "In fact, I shall always regard my adventure with you as something to treasure, and one day I shall amaze my children when I tell them all about it."

She held out her hand. "This is goodbye, then, Richard. We won't be seeing much of each other at Twickenham House."

There was something about this easy dismissal that rubbed him the wrong way, something about her mention of children that did not sit right with him. Whose children? Not Prince Michael's. She'd told him that the prince was not only a dandy, but also a libertine. Was there some other gentleman waiting in the wings to claim her? But what rankled most of all was that he was to be reduced to an anecdote to amuse her children.

The hell he was!

He looked down at her outstretched hand. "Why so formal?" he said. "After all we've been through together, don't I deserve a good-bye kiss?"

With some vague notion of making a lasting impression on her that couldn't be laughed off, he yanked her against him and covered her mouth with his.

For a moment, she went as rigid as a marble statue. That was on the outside. Inside a fire ignited and licked along her veins. This was nothing like those sweet kisses in the bothy. There was desperation here, and heat, and something that was gloriously primitive.

She went on tiptoe and wound her arms around his neck.

In a purely reflexive movement, his hands fisted in her hair, and he dragged back her head so that he could kiss her chin, her throat, the swell of her breasts. The scent of gardenia wrapped around him like a soft, sinful mist. He didn't think, wouldn't allow himself to think, because then this would have to end, and he was starved for the taste and touch of her.

It wasn't her passion that shocked him or even his own. He was no stranger to passion. But needs he had never imagined existed and could not articulate acted like a powerful narcotic on his unfailing control.

She had melted against him so that he could feel her soft breasts pressing against his chest. As for his wound, it might never have existed for all the attention he paid to it. And her hands were everywhere, threading through his hair, stroking his neck, testing each bunched muscle as she slid them from his shoulders to his flanks.

Was she trembling or was he? It didn't matter. He kissed her hair, her eyes, her ears. He murmured something, he didn't know what. Then he sucked at her lips, swallowing her little cries of arousal like a drunkard with his first drink after a long drought.

She was so soft, so giving, so right for him. His hands slipped to her bottom, kneading, pulling her flush against his hard groin.

It wasn't enough for him, not nearly enough. He wanted her naked beneath him; he wanted to be inside her. He wanted her long, shapely legs to lock his body to hers as he took her on a wild ride to rapture.

She should stop him. He should stop her. Why couldn't they stop?

This shouldn't be happening. She had provoked him and he had responded in typical male fashion. This had to stop. This had to—

He jerked back, frantically groping for what was left of his sanity. Rosamund reached for him, but he had just enough control to take another step back. Her eyes were still heavy-lidded; her lips were parted.

"Richard, what's wrong?" she cried.

He didn't want to hurt her. God, he didn't want to hurt her, but he didn't have a choice. If there was anything between them, it had to end right here. And it would have ended if he hadn't lost his head. He marveled at her power over him. What was it about this woman that made her so different? He'd never lost his head over any woman.

When his breathing had evened a little, he scratched his chin, trying to look casual. "What's wrong," he said, "is that our harmless good-bye kiss got out of hand. It happens that way sometimes between a man and a woman. I should have known better." He managed to sound both amused and apologetic. "Don't build it up to something it wasn't. It didn't mean anything."

He wanted her to slap him, rant at him, spit on him— all of which he knew he deserved. She did none of those things. After a frozen silence, she tipped up her chin and said quietly, "Good luck, Richard. I hope everything works out well for you." Then she went through the door that gave onto her dressing room.

He felt like a worm.

In the hallway, he came face-to-face with Hugh Templar. Hugh took one look at Richard's scowl and chuckled.

"Good grief, Richard," he said, "what has the Amazon been saying to you?"

"She gave me my just deserts. And don't call her the Amazon."

Hugh's brows rose speculatively. "So what did you do to earn her displeasure?"

"What do you think?" he said, snarling the words. "I behaved like my usual, charming self."

"And she annihilated you with her sharp tongue?"

"No. She did just the opposite."

Hugh looked baffled.

They walked down the corridor. At Richard's door, Hugh put his hand on his friend's shoulder and said, "Harper is waiting for us in my room with a bottle of your favorite cognac, and whiskey for me. We have plenty to celebrate, Richard. In fact, I think things have turned out rather well."

"Better than well," replied Richard without enthusiasm.

They walked on. After a moment, Hugh said carefully,

"I hear that Prince Michael is still a prime candidate for Lady Rosamund's hand. Well, it stands to reason, doesn't it? He has the right bloodlines; he knows the right people. They have much in common and—"

Richard halted. He said dryly, "Cut the lecture, Hugh. I've only known the girl a week. Give me credit for some intelligence. And your warning is unnecessary. There's nothing between us."

Hugh's lids drooped to half-mast. "Of course there isn't," he said.

"All the same," said Richard as they continued walking, "you're wrong about Prince Michael. She won't marry him. He's as thick as a door."

"She told you that, did she?"

"He doesn't appeal to her," he replied, avoiding a direct answer.

Hugh was highly amused. "That won't matter, not to women of her rank. They marry for a title and to establish a dynasty. They're not like us lesser mortals. She'll marry where she is told."

Again, Richard halted, and he gave his friend a direct stare. "I hope you're wrong, Hugh." His voice was pleasantly modulated. "Because I wouldn't feel comfortable if Rosamund's family made her unhappy. In fact, I would feel obliged to do something about it."

Hugh was left staring as Richard walked on.

Chapter 16

The caravan of carriages—there were three of them—arrived in Twickenham late on the following evening, after a ride that Richard could only describe as bruising. But that was the least of his aggravations. He had expected that he would have to wear the Devere livery, but he hadn't known that it came with a powdered wig and a tricorne hat.

"I wouldn't be seen dead in that get-up," he'd told Harper that morning when Harper arrived, just after the doctor left, to help him get ready for the journey.

His words fell on unsympathetic ears. "Now, you listen to me," said Harper. "I'm getting tired of your black looks and frowns. By a stroke of good fortune, you've won the favor of the Duke of Romsey. You have Mr. Templar to thank for that. But all I'm hearing is complaints." He made a gesture with one hand, indicating his own livery. "This is a disguise. Think of it as a uniform, just like your dress regimentals. There will be sixteen coachmen and footmen dressed like us, so if we're stopped by the militia, no one will notice you." Then, in his best sergeant's voice, "So move your arse!"

Richard moved.

As Harper helped him dress, he went on, "Remember, we're servants, so don't go drawing attention to yourself by speaking out o' turn or flashing them black looks. Servants don't have no feelings. Just remember your place."

"Yes, sir," Richard answered meekly.

They were in the last coach, along with all the boxes, and, in spite of the garish uniforms, had the deadly earnest job of keeping their eyes peeled for an attack by highwaymen. In Richard's opinion, which he kept to himself in the interest of harmony, there wouldn't have been the least risk of an attack if they had traveled with less show and more decorum. As they drew closer to their destination, however, he saw the logic in Lord Caspar's mode of travel. The militia they met on the road recognized the duke's livery and coat of arms emblazoned on each gilt-trimmed carriage, and let them pass unchallenged. In fact, they saluted and some of them even cheered.

As they swept up the long, curving drive to the house, Harper gave Richard some last-minute instructions. "Remember, your name is Patrick Doyle, on account of your accent."

"That's an Irish name, and I'm Scottish."

"Same thing."

"And I don't have an accent." Richard was serious.

Harper let out a long, patient breath. "Are you listening?" When Richard nodded, he went on, "We're to help carry the boxes into the house. If anyone challenges you, say nothing. Let me do all the talking."

"Who would challenge us?"

"The butler. The steward. The parlor maid. How should I know? But be *respectful*. Remember, this is just like the army, and in this army, we're foot soldiers, at the bottom of the ladder until someone tells us different.

Now, don't pucker up like that. You, of all people, should understand discipline. You're a colonel. In this house, the butler, or whoever, is the commanding officer, and if you assume everyone is an officer, you can't go wrong."

"You mean, I'm to take orders from *everybody*?"

"Aye, that's exactly what I mean, and you can take that scowl off your face, 'cos it won't impress no one."

When the carriages drew to a halt, footmen came out of the house and ran down the steps to assist.

Harper thrust a small box into Richard's arms. "It's empty," he said, "so you won't strain yourself."

Richard grinned. "Rosamund's idea?" He suspected that he had Rosamund to thank, too, for the luxury of traveling inside the coach instead of perching on the box and being buffeted by the elements.

"No. Mr. Templar's." Harper scowled. "And keep your eyes off Lady Rosamund, or we'll both end up in the Thames with millstones tied around our necks."

"A cat may look at a queen."

"Not if the cat's in service, he can't. Right. Follow me."

They had done no more than step down from the carriage when a figure appeared at the top of the marble stairs. There was no question in Richard's mind that he was looking at Rosamund's father, and behind him, the younger brother. The family resemblance was striking.

No one moved. For one brief interval, it seemed that they were all captured like subjects in some painter's canvas, then Rosamund descended from the second carriage and everyone came to life. Flanked by Lord Caspar and Hugh Templar, she ascended the stairs. Richard wasn't sure what he expected, but something more than the bloodless peck on the cheek her father gave her before he put one arm around her shoulders and swept her into the house.

"Some homecoming," he said under his breath, for Harper's ears only.

"That's how it is with the aristocracy," Harper replied, but he sounded disappointed as well.

A footman appeared in front of them. He, too, wore blue livery and a black waistcoat trimmed with gold braid, but his hair, Richard noted with approval, was unpowdered.

"Come with me," he said in exactly the same tone of voice Lord Caspar might have used.

Richard's brows came down. Harper pinned him with a hard stare, then, satisfied that his chief had got the message, obediently followed the footman into the house.

&

They were told to wait in a small anteroom just off the front entrance. Half an hour later, the same puffed-up lackey who had shown them into the anteroom now arrived to escort them to the duke's library on the other side of the house.

"Leave the boxes," he said, "and tuck these hats under your left arm."

When they arrived at the library, he bade them wait outside. He left the door ajar, and Hugh Templar's voice carried to them.

"Robinson and Cook of Mount Street," Hugh said.

"I know them," said the duke. "Good outfit, I'll give you that. But I prefer Sharp and Bland of South Audley. They made things to last. I'm sure my old Lizzie will still be going strong a hundred years from now, and she's thirty if she's a day."

Harper beamed.

"What are they talking about?" asked Richard.

"Coaches," replied Harper. "They're talking about coach builders. Now maybe Mr. Templar will believe me."

The conversation in the library broke off. A moment later, Richard and Harper were ushered in and announced as Doyle and Harper. Seated around a roaring fire were the duke and his sons and Hugh Templar. There was no sign of Rosamund. Richard fixed his eyes on the duke. His hard-eyed stare was returned in full measure.

"So," said the duke softly, "this is the man who abducted my Rosamund."

Lord Caspar stirred but he did not stand. "Your Grace," he said, "permit me to introduce Colonel Maitland, formerly Chief of Staff of Special Branch."

"Step into the light," said the duke, addressing Richard. "It's not often that I'm introduced to a convicted murderer."

"Your Grace," began Hugh, then fell silent when the duke held up one hand.

Richard stepped into the light, and Harper kept pace with him, shoulder to shoulder.

The duke's gaze shifted to take in Harper. "And you are?"

"Sergeant Harper, Your Grace," said Harper, scowling savagely, "bodyguard to Colonel Maitland."

The duke's dark brows winged upward. "And still on duty, I see," he murmured. He passed a hand over his mouth, waited for a moment, then made a thorough and leisurely appraisal of both men. Finally, looking at Harper, he said, "I won't hurt your colonel, Sergeant Harper. A promise is binding. So sit down, both of you."

When this was done, he said, "What is it you want from me, Colonel? Don't be shy. I'm in a generous mood, now that my daughter has been returned to me safe and sound."

Richard had already wrestled with his reluctance to accept help from the Deveres, so he came to the point at once. "I need somewhere safe where I can hide out until things quiet down."

"That was understood at the outset. You'll stay here for as long as you want. What else can I do for you?"

"When I leave here, I'll need money to tide me over. Then there's Dunsmoor. It shouldn't be left empty. When things are settled, I'll repay every penny you've spent on my account."

The duke nodded. "I see. You want to pursue your driving ambition—that is, to clear your name?"

"I do."

"This isn't necessary. Leave it to me and I think I can safely promise that within the week you will be completely exonerated of Miss Rider's murder. Not that I'd do it for your sake, you understand. However, I feel I owe it to Mr. Templar for the help he gave us in tracking you down so that my daughter could be rescued."

"Your Grace," interjected Hugh, refusing to be silenced this time. "I tracked down Colonel Maitland because I was worried about *him,* not Lady Rosamund. I knew she would come to no harm."

The duke ignored Hugh's interruption. "Well, Maitland? What is it to be?"

Richard's eyes narrowed on the duke's face. After a moment, he shook his head. "You're talking about bribing witnesses, tampering with evidence, fabricating new evidence."

"And if I am?"

Richard's distaste could hardly be concealed. "Thank you, but no thank you. I prefer my own methods. And there's more at sake than my reputation. Lucy Rider was murdered. I'm going to find her killer."

From that point on, the duke's questions narrowed on the crime, and how Richard had come to be charged with the girl's murder. In Richard's mind, the duke had taken on the role of prosecuting counsel, and his replies became shorter and shorter, and were not always couched in polite terms.

Suddenly the duke got up and, of course, everyone got up with him. To Richard, he said, "You've been assigned to Lord Justin's care. He has need of a valet, and that will suit for the present. Your duties will not be onerous and you'll be isolated from most of the servants. At any rate, you'll be in livery, and I doubt your own mother would recognize you if she came calling."

To Harper, the duke said, "My daughter tells me that you drove my coach with no one to help you?"

"Aye, Your Grace," Harper answered carefully.

"A remarkable achievement."

Since the duke was smiling, Harper nodded.

The duke went on, "And, Mr. Templar tells me that you like nothing better than to take coaches apart and put them together again?"

"Aye," replied Harper. Then he remembered to add, "Your Grace."

"Splendid! Then I have just the position for you. We're shorthanded in the coach house right now, because . . . well, suffice it to say that I had to turn off some men who let me down badly. How would you like to be head coachman, Harper?"

"Head coachman," Harper breathed out. His face was transformed by his smile, but by degrees the smile faded. "I already has a position, Your Grace. I'm Colonel Maitland's bodyguard. Where he goes, I go."

Richard said, "Don't be daft, Harper. We're no longer working for Special Branch. You're a free agent, the same as I am."

"Then if I'm a free agent, I'm your bodyguard until I decides different."

The duke said, "Perhaps Colonel Maitland wouldn't mind forgoing the position of valet for that of second coachman?"

"It's all the same to me," said Richard, lying through his teeth. In his book, shoveling horseshit was a more manly occupation than acting nursemaid to a dandy who couldn't be bothered to put on his own coat. Harper had inadvertently saved him from purgatory.

"That settles it, then," said the duke. "You'll both be assigned to the coach house. Justin, see to it."

Lord Justin indicated that Richard and Harper were to go with him. Hugh walked with them to the door.

"I wish I could do more," he said, "but it's better for you if I keep my distance for the next little while. Good luck, Richard, and the same to you, Harper."

Richard understood only too well. If Hugh didn't keep his distance, he could lead his enemies right to him.

In the hallway, a superior-looking servant whom Lord Justin introduced as Turner, the groom of the chambers, was waiting for His Grace's instructions. Mr. Turner was in his fifties, with graying hair, shrewd eyes, and a beaked, Roman nose. He wasn't in livery, but in a fashionable gray frock-coat, so Richard knew that he must be pretty high up in the servant hierarchy.

"Doyle and Harper, two new recruits from Devere," said Lord Justin airily. "Mr. Harper is to be head coachman and Mr. Doyle, well, we'll let Mr. Harper decide what to do with him. You might want to show them around and see that they're comfortably settled. Oh, and don't let Doyle do any heavy work. He's not up to it yet."

Turner's appraisal of his two new recruits was as thorough as the duke's, but he waited till Lord Justin had returned to the library before voicing his opinion.

"Don't tell me," he said. "You're out-of-work war veterans looking for an easy life in His Grace's household 'cause you've heard that His Grace has a soft heart. Well, just remember that it's not His Grace you'll be answering to from now on, but to me, Alfred Turner, groom of the chambers. And if you turn out like that other lot, who were wetting their whistles at the Magpie and Stump when they should have been protecting Lady

Rosamund, you'll be out on your arses before you can say you own names. Have you got that?"

"Yes, sir. Thank you, sir," said Harper, flashing Richard a warning look.

But Richard was too relieved to have escaped the indignity of being Lord Justin's valet to put up any resistance. "Thank you, Mr. Turner" was all he said.

In single file, they trudged after the groom of the chambers.

&

Hugh left almost at once. The duke and his sons saw him off in one of the Devere carriages, then returned to the library to talk things over.

The duke was brooding on what might have happened between Maitland and his daughter in the week just past. He'd been so afraid that she would come home a broken woman, cowed, a shade of her former self. But she'd alighted from the carriage and walked into the house as though she'd just returned from a week's holiday with Great-Aunt Sophy in Hampshire. Her sunny demeanor had gone a long way to blunting his rage against the man who had abducted her, as had her insistence that Maitland had behaved like a perfect gentleman.

Maitland, a perfect gentleman? He had his doubts about that.

"Well, what do you think, Father?" asked Lord Caspar.

"About Maitland? Short on charm, but I liked him the better for it."

"He has impeccable references," said Lord Justin. "Hugh Templar and Harper—I'd take their word over anyone's any day."

"Yes," said the duke, "it says a lot for Maitland that he has friends of that caliber. Harper is quite a character, isn't he, though, of course, my view is tempered by the fact that he was on his way home with Rosamund when he ran into you, Caspar. There's something appealing about his loyalty to Maitland, too, wouldn't you say? And he knows about coaches. I was quite impressed."

His last remark had Lords Caspar and Justin exchanging veiled glances.

The duke chuckled. "I would advise you not to make any sudden moves around Maitland when Harper is around."

"And the same goes for Templar," said Lord Justin.

"Yes," replied the duke. "As I said, Maitland is fortunate in his choice of friends."

They fell silent when a footman entered with a coal scuttle and banked up the fire. When they were alone again, Lord Caspar took up the conversation where it had left off.

"Are you satisfied now, Father, that Maitland is innocent?"

"Oh, I don't think there's any doubt of that. When he refused my offer to clear his name, he passed the test. But tell me about Rosamund. What happened between her and Maitland? How did he win her over?"

Lord Caspar's eyes were unclouded. "Has he won her over?"

"All she can talk about is our duty to prove his innocence."

Lord Caspar shrugged carelessly. "You'll have to ask Rosamund. But you must remember that Harper was only acting on Maitland's instructions when he tried to bring Rosamund home. I suppose Rosamund feels grateful to him."

"Mmm," said the duke.

Lord Justin was incredulous. "Father, you can't be thinking what I think you're thinking. You've met the man. 'Short on charm' doesn't do him justice. If you were to put him in the stillroom, one look from him would curdle all the milk and cream. And when you compare him to Prince Michael, well, there's no comparison, and Rosamund turned off the prince."

The duke's gaze rested on his younger son for a long moment. "Justin," he said finally, "you have a lot to learn about women. He's different. Rosamund has never met a man like him."

"You're worrying for nothing," said Lord Caspar. "I have it from the horse's mouth that he wouldn't have our Rosamund at any price. And I believe Maitland is a man of his word."

The duke said nothing, but now he *was* beginning to worry.

৯

Prudence Dryden was a year or so younger than Rosamund and had seemed like an ideal choice for a companion-chaperon when Rosamund first offered her the position. She came of good family—both her father and brother were vicars—and she wasn't awed by a duke's household. Rosamund had thought her a well-bred, sociable girl. She'd hoped they would become friends, but was now coming to believe that she'd misjudged Miss Dryden's character. The girl was either moody, or she, Rosamund, had done something to offend her.

They were in the little parlor, just off Rosamund's bed-chamber, and Miss Dryden's dark head was bent over her embroidery. She was wearing one of Rosamund's gowns, a green gown that Rosamund had never worn because the color made her look sickly. For some odd reason, though she and Miss Dryden had the same coloring, the gown suited the younger girl and intensified the green in her eyes. There were other gowns Rosamund would have liked to offer her companion, gowns that would need very little altering since she and Prudence were about the same size, but she was afraid of giving offense.

Miss Dryden looked up with a question in her eyes. "And that was the last you saw of him, when he locked you in your room at Dunsmoor?"

They were talking about Richard, and her "rescue" by Caspar and Hugh Templar. "Yes," said Rosamund. She had to be careful of what she said, for Richard's sake. "Caspar said they must have missed him by minutes."

Miss Dryden cocked her head to one side. "You're glad he escaped, aren't you?"

Rosamund would have liked to pour her heart out, but she couldn't, of course, not to anyone. She was walking a very fine line. If she said too much, she might put Richard in danger. On the other hand, she couldn't bring herself to make him appear as the dangerous felon everyone thought he was.

She said, "He treated me with respect. I could not believe that he would kill anyone." And because she was afraid of saying too much, she quickly changed the subject. "Now tell me what has been happening here in my absence."

There was little to tell, except that Prince Michael had been out to the house every day to inquire if there was any news of Rosamund.

Rosamund made a face. "I hope this doesn't mean he's still pursuing me." She looked at Miss Dryden. "I hope my father isn't encouraging him!"

Miss Dryden was looking at the door, and her cheeks were turning pink. Rosamund turned her head. Caspar had entered the room.

Caspar said, "Father will see you now, Rosamund."

Oh, no, thought Rosamund. She hoped Prudence hadn't fallen in love with Caspar. Poor Prudence. No wonder she was moody.

੨ઐ

There was no sign of Prudence when Rosamund returned to the parlor, and she couldn't say she was sorry. She felt that her face was cracking from smiling so much. She didn't think she was fooling anyone. Her father, her brothers—they were so solicitous, so uncharacteristically solicitous, that she was sure they knew her heart was breaking.

Her father rarely talked of her mother. It was too painful. He was a man who liked to keep his softer emotions tightly locked inside him. But he'd talked of her mother just now.

His voice had been thick, and there were tears in his eyes. "She would be proud of you if she could see you now," he said. "Damn proud! And I'm proud of you, too."

She had many happy memories of her mother, and the most vivid of all was that her father and mother had had the kind of love most people can only dream about. It was true that Richard could bring tears to her eyes, too, but those were tears of vexation. He really was an impossible man.

At least her father was going to do right by Richard. He could stay here for as long as he liked. But she couldn't speak to him, couldn't do anything that would draw attention to him. Then, in a week or two, when he was on his feet, he would leave here and she would never see him again.

And she would bear it because she was a Devere. That's why her father had told her he was proud of her.

With a little sigh, she began to wander around her room. Her father had reminded her that it was her birthday next week and he thought that they should let her ball go forward. For one thing, the invitations had already been sent out; for another, it would do her good, he said, take her out of herself, and she had smilingly agreed. What else could she do? She couldn't go into a decline just because her heart was broken.

She had to get ahold of herself.

She sighed again. She'd hoped that when she was back with her family and in her own setting, her world would right itself, and she'd see the past week in its proper perspective. But it hadn't turned out that way. Her world seemed much smaller than she remembered.

She picked up her embroidery frame and examined the work in progress. It would eventually become a shawl with a border embroidered in white satin-stitched vines and acorns. She was an accomplished needlewoman, as every room in her father's house could attest—needlepoint cushions, embroidered tablecloths and sheets, monogrammed handkerchiefs for her brothers, wall hangings. And if she wasn't at her needlework, she was reading, or cutting and arranging flowers.

How had she managed to stay sane all these years?

She knew two other accomplished needlewomen, Prudence and Aunt Fran, and no wonder—they had nothing else to occupy their time. But what was there for an unmarried woman to do? Maiden aunts invariably ended up as nursemaids in a brother's household. That's why Prudence had struck out on her own and accepted a position as her companion. She, Rosamund, must be a terrible disappointment to her. At this rate, they would both end up like Aunt Fran, tolerated but with no real life of their own.

Then what could they do?

She already knew the answer. It wasn't only her adventure with Richard that had made her restless. Long before that she'd begun to chafe at the role that had been assigned to her. She was tired of being seen only as a duke's daughter. She'd wanted to be a flesh-and-blood woman; she'd wanted to see things and do things she'd never seen or done before. She wanted to have a real life.

She breathed deeply. The next step, as she knew very well, was to set up her own household, where she could come and go as she pleased.

Chapter 17

Richard looked up from his ledger and glanced out the window of his office. The stable block was on the east side of the house and his upstairs office had an excellent view of the drive and courtyard. As he watched, Lord Caspar, Rosamund, and her companion, Miss Dryden, descended the front stairs of the house, entered the curricle that was waiting for them, and were soon bowling along the drive for their morning outing.

It was a ritual he'd watched for a week now, Rosamund taking the air in her brother's curricle. There was another ritual in the afternoon. That's when a procession of carriages arrived at the house as all of fashionable London came to pay its respects to the duke's daughter, and none more fashionable than Prince Michael of Kolnbourg.

There would be no Prince Michael and no procession of carriages this afternoon. That would wait until tonight, when guests arrived for the ball the duke was hosting to mark the occasion of his daughter's birthday. Meantime, there was a flurry of activity as servants readied the house for the great occasion. From his vantage point, he could see gardeners and their helpers stringing lanterns from trees, and footmen carrying plants from the conservatory to the folly, which overlooked the manmade lake.

He'd been mistaken to think that Twickenham House was like Dunsmoor only bigger. This place was like a miniature palace. As for the people who lived here, however . . . he shook his head. Sometimes he wondered if they'd been born on a different planet.

He was supposed to be the second coachman, but so far his services had not been required, because whenever the duke wanted to take one of his coaches for a spin, he invariably sat on the box beside Harper while he, Richard, traveled inside. And the drive defied description. The duke and Harper were like a couple of maniacs when they got going.

And when the duke and Harper were not taking one of the coaches for a spin, they could be found, more often than not, in the old coach house, commonly referred to as "the infirmary," where broken-down carriages were brought to the duke by their owners—just as though he ran a shop in his back garden—to be lovingly restored to health.

And Harper was in his element.

After dipping his pen in its ink pot, he made a notation in his ledger. This was all he was good for! He'd been assigned to keeping the coach house and stable accounts, but only because he couldn't do anything else. And when he wasn't making notations in his ledger, he'd find himself watching for Prince Michael to arrive in sartorial splendor to take Lady Rosamund for a spin in his equally sartorial curricle with its showy chestnuts.

Two curricle rides in one day was one too many, in

Richard's opinion, but Rosamund didn't seem to mind. In fact, she seemed to enjoy it.

A blob of ink rolled off his pen nib and smeared a column of figures. Richard glared at it long and hard, then let out a furious oath. He blotted it, put down his pen, and got up.

There were no aches and pains when he moved now. A week had made a remarkable difference to him. He felt as good as new. The excellent doctor who tended his wound hadn't raised an eyebrow when he'd first examined him. He'd shaken his head and said something to the effect that it was time that the duke's retainers learned that the war was over and to stay out of drunken brawls.

He debated with himself about going to the tack room to help Harper polish the harness, but last time he'd been bawled out for using the wrong polish, and he'd been told to keep away. He wasn't looking for something to do so much as someone to talk to. He was tired of his own company.

His thoughts drifted to Digby and Whorsley. They'd made the trip from town with hopes of getting a lead on him, or at the very least of arresting Harper and dragging him off in chains. According to Harper, however, they couldn't get Rosamund to say one word against him, and Harper had stuck to his story—that he'd been duped by his chief into believing they were working on a case, and he never would have helped him escape from Newgate if he'd known the truth.

It helped, of course, that the duke had already smoothed things over for Harper by talking to the prime minister. Not only that, but Harper was also to get a share of the reward for his part in rescuing Rosamund! So poor Digby and Whorsley had left Twickenham House gnashing their teeth.

Harper had told the story with great relish, but

Richard was still wary. He didn't think this was the last they'd see of Digby. If the man had only been as intelligent as he was tenacious, he, Richard, wouldn't be hanging around Twickenham House.

And he was still burning to know how Digby found out about Dunsmoor.

There was nothing to keep him at Twickenham now. It was time to move on, time to begin the task of clearing his name. But he didn't want to slip away without saying good-bye to Rosamund. After all she'd done for him, she deserved better than that. She deserved the best.

His thoughts were interrupted when he heard footsteps climbing the outside iron stairs. He automatically reached for his tricorne hat with the pistol concealed inside it.

There was a knock on the door. "Doyle, are you there?"

Turner's voice. Richard put his hat down and went to open the door. "Yes, Mr. Turner," he said respectfully. "What can I do for you?"

His respect for the groom of the chambers came more easily now. Harper hadn't exaggerated when he said that life in service was just like life in the army, and in this army, Turner was the general. Very little missed his eagle eye, and he'd had his eagle eye on Richard for some time.

But there was something different about Turner today. The eagle eyes were softer, as were the thin lips, and there was an air of suppressed excitement about him.

"Come out into the light," Turner said, "so I can get a better look at you."

Mystified and wary at the same time, Richard did as he was told. The groom of the chambers looked him up and down, made him turn around, and examined him from every side.

"You're not as handsome as some, but you'll do," he said.

"Do for what?" Richard was baffled.

"A footman. We're short-staffed for the ball, so present yourself at five o'clock in the footmen's powder room, and we'll get you all rigged out."

"All rigged out? What does that mean?"

"Servants are to be issued with new livery," replied Turner. "His Grace told me not an hour ago. We've been saving that livery for a long, long time, and now it seems it's finally happened." When Richard stared at him blankly, Turner slowly elaborated, "The announcement of Lady Rosamund's engagement."

Richard felt as though someone had punched him in the stomach. It took him a moment or two to remember to breathe. "That can't be true," he said.

Turner's thin lips actually turned up in a smile. "Haven't you heard? Lady Rosamund has leased a house in Bloomsbury. Now, why would she do that if she were not thinking of getting married?" All traces of good humor vanished and it was back to business. "Five o'clock in the servants' powder room, mind, and not a minute before or a minute after."

Richard watched the groom of the chambers as he walked with a jaunty step back to the house, then he stalked into his office and shut the door with a bang.

❧

Lord Caspar delivered his passengers to Callie's house in Manchester Square, then, after promising to return for them in an hour or two, he drove off. Rosamund was glad to see him go, because whenever Caspar was around, her companion, Miss Dryden, would lapse into self-conscious silences. It was obvious to Rosamund that poor Prudence was in love with Caspar. And it just wouldn't do. Caspar had an eye for the ladies, all right, but marriage was the furthest thing from his mind. He wasn't interested in nice girls, only fast ones.

There was another reason she was glad to see Caspar

go. She had something special she wanted to tell Callie, and a man would only be in the way. She had finally done it. She was starting over in a house she had leased just off Bloomsbury.

Though her brothers had supported her in her resolve to establish her own household, in private they teased her unmercifully. They were her brothers, of course, so that was to be expected, but Rosamund had long since decided that men were not comfortable with the idea of women managing their own affairs.

Richard Maitland, of course, was the exception.

As she had done countless times in the last week when her thoughts drifted to Richard—and when did they not?—she banished him to the farthest corner of her mind and thought of something else.

There was a curricle and four in the square just outside Callie's house, with a boy in black-and-silver livery, holding the lead horses' heads. She didn't recognize the livery, but she thought it became the boy very well. In fact, it was the boy who first drew her eyes, not the curricle itself or the four stamping white horses.

Beneath his cap, dark curls framed a face with dark eyes and finely chiseled bones that made her think of the Greek boy warriors she'd seen in Lord Elgin's marbles. She judged him to be about fourteen years old. Tigers, these boys were called—she had no idea why—and they were all handsome or distinguished in some way. As far as she could tell, their real purpose was decorative, the finishing touch to a fashionable gentleman's equipage.

Prudence whispered, "He looks Italian."

"Let's find out."

When they drew abreast of him, Rosamund said, "We've been admiring your horses. I say they're English, but my friend says they're Arabians."

The boy respectfully touched his cap. "I don't know nozing about zat," he said, in the most fraudulent

French accent Rosamund had ever heard. "You will 'ave to ask my master, Monsoor Withers."

"Thank you," said Rosamund.

A few steps farther on, she and Prudence exchanged a quick smile.

Prudence said, "I think that's carrying affectation too far."

Rosamund wasn't really interested in the owner of the curricle. She thought that he might be one of Charles Tracey's friends, or perhaps a visitor who'd dropped in to see Callie. It was Callie she was looking forward to seeing. Since her "rescue," they'd met twice, but both times at Twickenham House, when they were surrounded by people, and could not speak freely. They'd promised each other to have a heart-to-heart talk the first chance they got, and this was the chance she had been waiting for.

When they were announced and shown into the drawing room, they found that Callie wasn't alone. Two gentlemen, with their backs to the window, had risen at her entrance. Aunt Fran was there, too, but she seemed to be dozing in a chair in front of the fire.

Callie came forward to meet them. "Rosamund!" she said. "Isn't this your birthday? Shouldn't you be getting ready for the ball this evening?"

"There's nothing to do," said Rosamund, masking her disappointment behind a smile. She had hoped to find Callie alone. "We're just in the way, so Prudence and I thought we'd make ourselves scarce. So here we are."

Callie laughed. "Many happy returns," she said. "Now let me introduce you to my guests. I don't think you've met Mr. Withers."

"Lady Rosamund," said that gentleman, bowing. "May I, too, wish you many happy returns?"

Rosamund felt her heart skip a beat, and she hazarded a guess that Mr. Withers had this effect on many ladies. He was in his early forties, by her reckoning, but he had the vitality of a much younger man. She thought he had a beautiful smile.

"Thank you. And this is my friend, Miss Dryden," she said.

"Charmed," said Mr. Withers, and Rosamund knew that he meant it. So, by the look of her, did Prudence. She forgot to curtsy.

"And," said Callie, "Major Digby of the Horse Guards. But you've met already, I believe."

Rosamund's heart skipped another beat, but for a different reason. Major Digby had questioned her long and hard about her abduction and what she'd gleaned about Richard Maitland in the week she was with him. She regarded Digby as a very dangerous man.

The first few minutes were spent in small talk, and Mr. Withers did most of the talking. He was English born, he said, but had spent most of his life in and around Charles Town in South Carolina, and that's where he would be returning as soon as his business in England was concluded. He was here to buy thoroughbreds for his stables and look up old friends.

"It will be a wrench to leave," he said. "I'd forgotten how beautiful England can be, and how lovely its ladies."

He smiles too much, thought Rosamund, and there flashed into her mind a picture of Richard with one of his rare, quick grins.

She wanted to smack herself for the errant thought.

Major Digby said, "What will you do with your tiger when you leave England? I ask because I know a number of gentlemen who would give their eyeteeth to have him."

"Oh, I'll be taking Roland with me. You might say we've become attached to each other."

And just when Rosamund thought things were going smoothly, Callie jumped in, as was her way, and gave them a stir. "We were just talking about you, Rosamund," she said, "before you arrived. Major Digby tells me that you're convinced Maitland is innocent, but I wouldn't believe him."

Her father had warned her to use extreme caution when Richard's name came up. They didn't want anyone thinking that the Deveres were too friendly with a fugitive of the law, or they might take a closer look at Twickenham House. So Rosamund chose her words with care.

"I don't remember saying that."

Digby gave a small, mirthless smile. "Not those words exactly," he said, "but it was very evident to me that you were—are—on his side."

Withers chuckled. "Charming brute, was he? I've known men like that. You think they're your best friends, and all the time they're robbing you blind."

Rosamund felt a slur on her intelligence and was stung into a reply. "I would never call Mr. Maitland charming. What I will say is that I think the authorities decided he was guilty right from the beginning and did not push themselves to discover the truth."

Digby bristled. "And why do you think that was, Lady Rosamund?"

"I think he'd made powerful enemies. I think they were glad to see him take a fall."

"Nonsense," retorted Digby, visibly checking his anger. "The evidence against Maitland was incontrovertible. Anyway, the military wasn't involved at that point. If you have any complaints, take them to the civil authorities. The magistrates at the Bow Street Office handled the case. My people came into it only after Maitland escaped from Newgate."

His sneer, his supercilious manner, irritated Rosamund, and she forgot to be cautious. "That won't help. What's needed here is to start over. If we work on the assumption that Colonel Maitland is innocent, as your people should have done from the beginning, all sorts of questions will arise."

"Such as?"

"Such as who hated him enough to engineer his

downfall? Who were Lucy Rider's friends, besides the people she worked with? How can two people, a man and a boy, disappear from the scene of a crime with no one the wiser, when there were so many people about?"

Digby's face was twisted with fury. "The question I'm asking myself is, why did you go to Newgate, Lady Rosamund? Was it a coincidence or were you perhaps there by design? Mmm?"

Callie was on her feet. "Major Digby, you forget yourself! Lady Rosamund went to Newgate at my invitation. Ask my brother-in-law. Charles will tell you, as will Aunt Fran. It was my idea. How could we possibly have known that Maitland would try to escape?"

It was Prudence, painfully shy Prudence, who deliberately drew the fire to herself. "My brother thinks Mr. Maitland is innocent, too."

Digby turned his head slowly and stared at Miss Dryden as though she'd suddenly become visible. "And who might your brother be?" he asked with a faint sneer.

"Peter Dryden," she answered pleasantly.

Mr. Withers said, "Is that Peter Dryden the banker?"

"No. He's a vicar."

"Ah. Then I don't know him."

Rosamund was glad of the interruption. This small aside had brought the temperature down by several degrees. She was afraid she'd said too much. The last thing she wanted was for Digby to suspect she was aiding and abetting Richard.

In a voice that was considerably more subdued, she said, "If he is a murderer, why didn't he kill me? He had nothing to lose. That's what makes me doubt that he murdered Miss Rider."

Digby shook his head. His voice was more subdued as well. "You are Romsey's daughter, Lady Rosamund," he said. "Lucy Rider was a nobody. Maitland is no fool. Your father would never rest until he had avenged your death. Who is there to avenge Miss Rider's death?"

Richard! she wanted to shout. *Richard will avenge her death.* But she dropped her eyes and said on a sigh, "That's what my father says."

Major Digby relaxed a little. "Your father is right."

Not long after, Mr. Withers got up and said that he'd left his horses standing too long and it was time to go. He looked at Digby. "If you're going to the Horse Guards, it's on my way. I'll drive you there."

They left together and Rosamund was in no doubt that Mr. Withers had offered to take Digby with him so that she would be spared further badgering. He really was a gentlemanly sort of man.

Callie went to the window and watched the gentlemen drive off in the curricle.

Rosamund said, "I'm sorry if I was rude to one of your guests, but I cannot like that man."

Callie laughed. "Be as rude as you like. You're not the only one he's practically accused of helping Maitland escape from Newgate. He's obsessed with Maitland. I can't think why."

Rosamund said musingly, "There was something about Newgate, though, wasn't there?"

Callie turned from the window. "What?"

Rosamund shook her head. "I don't know. It may come to me, it may not. Callie, look out the window. Tell me what you see."

Callie dutifully looked out the window. "Nothing. Wait a moment. I'll tell you what I *don't* see. I don't see your father's coach or his coachmen or his postilions."

This was the moment Rosamund had been waiting for. "They're a thing of the past," she said. "From now on, I shall travel in my own modest carriage, just like any other lady. Of course, I haven't got the carriage yet, but that will come. And I refuse to be hemmed in by footmen who just get in the way. I'm going to live like an ordinary girl."

Callie shook her head. "We've had this conversation before. Nothing ever comes of it."

"This time, I'm serious. You see, I've finally taken the plunge. I've leased a house just off Bloomsbury. If I like it, I have the option of buying it before the year is out."

No one knew when Aunt Fran had wakened, but she suddenly exclaimed, "Bravo, Rosamund. That is a real accomplishment. Bloomsbury, you say? That's not far away. Why don't we go right now and see it?"

"Aunt Fran, you took the words right out of my mouth," said Rosamund.

&

George Withers banged into his study and went straight to the table with the decanters and glasses. He bolted his first drink, poured himself another, then walked to the window and looked down upon Bond Street without really seeing anything. His hand was trembling, not in fear, but in rage.

Digby was incompetent! The man was a fool if he imagined he would ever step into Maitland's shoes as chief of staff. He waited for things to happen when he should be *making* things happen.

He sipped at his brandy as he sifted through the conversation at Mrs. Tracey's house. *Peter Dryden,* the vicar. He was the only person in England who posed a threat, because Dryden had known the real Withers. A moment's reflection calmed him. He wasn't likely to run into the vicar, not in the circles in which he moved. All the same, he'd met the sister. These things happened.

If things had gone to plan, Maitland would have hanged and he would have left England by now.

Maybe it was time to cut his losses and run.

That's what enraged him. And Lady Rosamund Devere. It sounded to him as though she could cause a great deal of trouble.

He took a long swallow of brandy as he considered his

choices. Unlike Digby, he didn't wait for things to happen. He'd deal with Lady Rosamund first, then he'd think about Peter Dryden.

ə.

They all piled into a hackney, and though it was a bit of a crush, it didn't take them long to arrive at the house.

"You said Bloomsbury," said Callie. "This is Somers Town. I don't call this convenient for shopping or making calls on friends."

"Nonsense," said Aunt Fran. "Bloomsbury is only a short walk away. And there are shops in Bloomsbury, aren't there, and hackney stands? We passed them on the way here."

"All the same," said Callie, "it *feels* isolated. I like to see what my neighbors are doing and vice versa. It's safer that way."

Rosamund paid off the hackney, knowing that she could get another only a five-minute walk away, and she joined the others at the great wrought-iron gates.

"I don't have the keys yet," she said. "That's why the gates are locked. But there's a caretaker, Fenton. He'll let us into the house."

They entered by the wicket gate, and strolled up the drive. It was a two-storey house, built in the Georgian manner, with long windows facing south over a vast expanse of lawn. Rosamund began to point out the various features; the pasture for horses, the stable block, the woods where deer roamed.

"That's where the house gets its name," she said. "Woodlands."

The caretaker was a grizzled, amiable fellow who obligingly offered to make tea and serve it in the rose salon. And half an hour later, that's where they were, sipping tea and planning a shopping expedition to order material for curtains and upholstery.

After a while, Callie and Aunt Fran went through a door that gave onto a little sunroom overlooking the front lawns, leaving Miss Dryden and Rosamund alone.

Miss Dryden said, in her usual restrained way, "I want you to know how much I admired the way you defended Mr. Maitland. Back there, with Major Digby, you were splendid! I only wish I could have said those things."

Rosamund looked at her companion with interest. "Do you believe he's innocent?"

Miss Dryden nodded.

"You never mentioned it to me when the trial was going on."

"No. But that was because you said he was as guilty as sin, and I didn't like to contradict you."

The price of being a duke's daughter! "You have my permission to contradict me as much as you like."

Miss Dryden's fleeting smile was impish. "Thank you. But as I said, I think he's innocent, too."

Rosamund sighed. "Not many people would agree with us."

"My brother does. Then, he remembers Mr. Maitland from their Cambridge days."

Rosamund sat back in her chair. "Your brother *knows* Mr. Maitland?"

"They were at Cambridge together. Peter says that though Maitland was difficult to know, he was as straight as an arrow. He could never have murdered that girl. You see"—Miss Dryden hesitated before going on—"there was some trouble at Cambridge, and Maitland was blamed for it." She looked directly into Rosamund's eyes. "But he was exonerated. And Peter deeply regrets that he ever mistrusted him. He vowed to himself that he would never make that mistake again."

Rosamund felt her excitement mounting. "Did your brother ever mention a boy called Frank Stapleton?"

Miss Dryden spoke slowly. "The other boy."

"Where is he now? Do you know?"

"He went to Canada right after he left Cambridge. Peter heard he died there."

And that, thought Rosamund, was that. Or perhaps not. It wouldn't hurt to talk to Prudence's brother. Maybe Frank Stapleton had a friend who wanted to avenge his disgrace. Maybe Peter Dryden wasn't as innocent as his sister made out. Not all vicars were saintly.

And maybe she was clutching at straws.

Miss Dryden said, "If only there was something we could do to help Mr. Maitland. It's a terrible thing, isn't it, to be convicted of a crime if you did not do it?"

Rosamund was reminded of her resolve to work tirelessly to clear Richard's name, a resolve that had wavered because her father had warned her that Richard would not thank her for meddling.

"Perhaps there *is* something we can do," she said.

Miss Dryden was startled. "What?"

"We can do what I suggested. Go back to the beginning and interview witnesses again, but this time on the assumption that Mr. Maitland is innocent."

Callie wandered into the room just then. She said archly, "I think this is Richard Maitland's doing, Rosamund. I think something happened when he abducted you, and that's what finally provoked you into setting up your own establishment."

Rosamund made light of it. "You're right, of course. There's nothing like believing that one's life is hanging in the balance to make a lady think about what kind of life she really wants."

Callie laughed. "There speaks Miss Fainthearted! If only Richard Maitland had abducted *me*, I would have *relished* every minute of it."

Rosamund had no desire to listen to Callie eulogizing Richard Maitland, so she exclaimed at the time and said they would have to get back to Manchester Square because that's where they were to meet Caspar.

Chapter 18

*I*t was the oddest birthday party Richard had ever attended. The guests brought presents, not for Rosamund but for the parish poor. It was a tradition, it seemed, to collect money for the poor whenever a Devere celebrated a birthday, and the duke would double whatever was collected.

Such were the ways of the rich.

The weather, as usual, was perverse. What had started out as a glorious day was chased away by a sudden gale blowing in from the North Sea, bringing spotty showers in its wake. Ladies who had dressed to the nines in diaphanous gowns for Rosamund's ball were forced to wrap themselves in shawls to stave off the chill. And that was inside the house.

Outside, footmen with umbrellas hurried down the steps to offer shelter to newly arrived guests while they got in out of the rain. The marquee had blown down and every gardener and groundsman was under orders to batten it down so that it did not blow away, and all this in the rain. Tempers were becoming frayed.

Richard's temper was already frayed. He was made up to look like a fop who had stepped out of the last century, with a powdered wig that was making his scalp itch. He was beginning to wonder if it was infested with lice, but even if it was, there was nothing he could do about it without drawing attention to himself. It was just like the army, just like being on guard duty. He was at one end of the long ballroom, stationed in front of the glass door to the conservatory, where supper would eventually be served, and it was his job to keep guests out until everything was ready.

The duke had been right—even if his own mother came calling, she wouldn't recognize him. No one recognized him, not the duke, or Lords Caspar and Justin, or Miss Dryden, or Rosamund's friend, Mrs. Tracey, whose harebrained idea it had been to visit Newgate. They were all here, in the ballroom, their eyes passing over him without really seeing him. Even Rosamund failed to recognize him.

He, on the other hand, had no trouble finding her in the crush, though the younger ladies were all dressed much the same, in gowns that looked as fragile as tissue. He didn't care how many maids it had taken to dress her or do up her hair in a swathe of dark curls that were pinned to her crown by fresh flowers. It was worth it. She had never looked more lovely.

It wasn't the first time he'd been struck by her beauty, but tonight she was different. She didn't look haughty, or bored with the company. She seemed animated. He'd been watching her all night. She'd opened the ball by dancing the waltz with Prince Michael, and everyone had stood around gawking as though they'd never seen a man and woman dance the waltz before. She'd never missed a dance. But now she was standing at the edge of the floor with Miss Dryden and Mrs. Tracey.

He hoped the change in her wasn't because of that blockhead Prince Michael. He wondered what she was thinking.

What Rosamund was thinking about was finding a partner for Prudence Dryden. She wasn't exactly matchmaking; she just wanted Prudence to see that there were other men in the world besides Caspar. With this in mind, she'd encouraged all the eligible young gentlemen who'd come calling on her this last week to come again, and she'd tried to bring Prudence to their notice, but Prudence was her own worst enemy. She didn't mope and she didn't give herself die-away airs. She smiled, she was polite, but no one could get past that wall of reserve.

Even she couldn't get past Prudence's reserve, and it puzzled her. They'd returned home from their outing that morning closer than they'd ever been, and now they were back to being polite acquaintances.

Maybe Caspar had something to do with it. Maybe the pain of unrequited love made Prudence the way she was. It didn't work that way with her. She was determined that she would not be seen as an object of pity, especially by the man who had rejected her.

Which was why she had agreed to let her ball go forward instead of succumbing to the strong temptation to lock herself in her room and go into a decline. She didn't want her family or friends to worry about her. But above all, she didn't want Richard to feel sorry for her.

Not that they had exchanged more than the obligatory greetings between a servant and his employer. Her father had impressed upon her the dangers of singling him out. Richard's safety depended on complete anonymity. So she had tried to ignore him. But at night, she could see his cottage from her bedroom window, and she could not go to her own bed till the lights in his cottage went out.

Her brother Justin arrived on the scene at that moment, right on time for his dance with Prudence, the dance Rosamund had arranged beforehand that he would ask for. In fact, she'd lectured her brothers on their duty—no slinking off to the card room, the billiard room, or the terrace to smoke their foul-smelling cigars. She wanted no wallflowers at her ball.

"Well, Roz," he said, "here I am. The trouble is, I forget which—"

His words died away when he saw the anguished look on his sister's face. He blinked, noticed Miss Dryden because his sister's compelling stare darted to that lady then back to him, and he finished lamely, "I forget where I put my dancing gloves."

"Try your pockets," said his sister, feigning a laugh.

Justin delved into his pockets and came up with his white gloves. As he put them on, he bowed to Prudence. "Miss Dryden," he said, "may I have the honor of this dance?"

Miss Dryden curtsied, murmured that the pleasure was hers, and allowed Justin to lead her onto the floor.

Callie, who had been watching the expressions chase themselves across Rosamund's face, said abruptly, "Very touching, Rosamund, but it won't work. Your Miss Dryden will never become the belle of the ball."

"I don't expect her to become the belle of the ball," murmured Rosamund absently. Her eyes were trailing Miss Dryden as Justin led to her to a set. "I just wish I understood these sudden changes of mood that come over her."

Callie wasn't interested in Miss Dryden, or her moods. She said, "You do realize that everyone here expects your father to announce your engagement to Prince Michael before the night is out?"

Rosamund was startled. "Then they'll be disappointed."

"Then what is he doing here?"

"I couldn't take back the invitation to my ball, nor did

I want to. Just because I'm not marrying the man doesn't mean I have to be rude to him."

"Careful, Roz, or like it or not, one of these days you'll find yourself married to the prince."

Rosamund turned to look at Callie. "Why do you say that?"

Callie shrugged. "You're the kind of girl to whom things happen. Even when we were girls, you did exactly what was expected of you."

Rosamund was on the point of taking umbrage, but from the corner of her eye, she saw Prince Michael at the edge of the dance floor in his dress regimentals, white tunic and black trousers. He was glancing around as though he were looking for a partner. "Let's take a little walk," she said.

She and Callie slipped through one set of doors and entered the cavernous, marble hall. Though there were chairs set out at intervals, there were few people about, for the orchestra had started playing, and couples had left to join the new sets.

They strolled to one of the long windows that had a fine view of the park. There wasn't much to see in the dark, but they could hear the wind whistling through the pillars in the entrance courtyard.

Groundsmen came into view and began to light lanterns that had been blown out by the wind. Callie was speaking, but Rosamund wasn't really listening. She was watching the groundsmen, trying to determine if Richard might be one of them.

"Did you hear me, Rosamund?"

"What?"

"I said," said Callie, "that it wouldn't surprise me if you know more about Maitland than you're telling."

Rosamund's heart picked up speed. "Like what, for instance?"

Callie smiled. "I don't know. But when you talk of him, I get the distinct impression that you and he became quite cozy in the week you spent together. Did he confide in you?"

"Don't be ridiculous!" said Rosamund, managing to sound as though she meant it.

She heard footsteps, turned, and sucked in a breath. There was someone there, a man who looked faintly sinister in the candlelight, then he took a step toward her and she recognized him. It was Charles Tracey, Callie's brother-in-law.

"Charles," said Callie, "you gave us a fright. Don't you know that eavesdroppers never hear good of themselves?" Her eyes narrowed on his face, then she said wearily, "It was a joke, Charles. You were supposed to laugh and come back at me with a witty rejoinder."

He did laugh, briefly, then he looked at Rosamund. "I believe you promised this dance to me. We're not too late. There are still sets forming."

To make up for Callie's rudeness, she smiled at him warmly. He looked like a sick puppy. Having come down with the same sickness, she was becoming an expert on unrequited love.

If only she knew the cure for it.

It was only when the dance was over that she realized she hadn't promised that dance, or any dance, to Charles Tracey. She had the oddest feeling that things were not as they seemed—Prudence, Callie, Charles— but she couldn't put her finger on what was wrong.

Shaking off her unease, she went in search of Aunt Fran, knowing that she would find her in the card room. Wrong again. Aunt Fran was nowhere to be found.

❧

At midnight, the doors to the conservatory were opened and supper was announced. It was an informal affair, with the food laid out on long tables so that guests could help themselves. The original idea was that they could take their plates outside and eat in the marquee, and afterward stroll down the numerous walks to view the lake with its waterfall, or visit the rotunda or the folly. But the weather wasn't cooperating and only a few brave souls ventured outside.

Rosamund knew she couldn't eat a thing. That was one of the symptoms of unrequited love, this loss of appetite, but at least her vague feelings of unease had vanished. Everything was as it should be. Aunt Fran was with the other dowagers, circling the supper tables like twittering swallows, diving down for tidbits when something caught their fancy; Callie wasn't eating, but talking, holding her audience enthralled, Charles Tracey among them; and Prudence, well, maybe Prudence *was* the belle of the ball. She was flanked by Justin and Prince Michael, and each seemed to be vying for her attention.

As for herself, she was moving from table to table, spending a few minutes with each guest, not so much in small talk, but in an effort to get to know them better. She had taken Richard's words to heart, when he'd accused her of being haughty and unwilling to lower herself to mix with the other ladies at that ball in Lisbon. She saw now that she'd been thinking of herself, when she should have considered the feelings of others. It was hard work. Some people would never see beyond her rank, and their empty blandishments and ingratiating manners were almost enough to make her retreat into her private world.

She was moving to the next table when a footman stepped in front of her, blocking her way.

"A glass of wine, Lady Rosamund?" he intoned respectfully.

She looked at the silver tray he offered with its array of crystal glasses. "Thank you, no."

When she tried to get past him, he blocked her way again. "Take the glass of wine, Rosamund," he said in a fierce undertone.

She would know that voice anywhere.

Her eyes flew to his face. It was Richard, but not a
Richard she had ever seen before. There was lace at his
throat, and lace at his wrists. His broad shoulders were
hugged by an emerald green frock coat with gold frogging and huge turned-back cuffs. His white powdered
wig did something wonderful to the harsh planes of his
face.

He was gorgeous.

She took a glass of wine from his tray, put it to her lips,
and took a healthy swallow.

"The folly in five minutes," Richard said, and he saun-
tered off with his tray.

She watched him go. White satin breeches and silk
stockings completed his livery. Her eyes lingered on his
legs. After a moment, she took another gulp of wine.
Then she looked around for her shawl.

❧

The folly wasn't far from the house, but it took her
some time to detour around a group of gentlemen who
had come outside to smoke their cigars. The groundsmen had given up on lighting the lanterns that had
blown out, and seemed to be concentrating their energies on clearing away the marquee. She heard them cursing the rain and making jests about the inside servants
and what a soft life they had.

By the time she reached the folly, which was nothing
more than a glorified gazebo, she was wishing she had
taken an umbrella as well as her shawl. The rain was no
more than a drizzle, but her silk shawl was no protection
against it.

Richard was already there. He'd doused all the candles but one, and she saw that he'd removed the powdered wig and the lace at his throat and wrists. When he
said her name softly, her pulse jumped.

"I could not leave without saying good-bye to you,"
he said.

Whatever she had expected to hear, it was not this. Eventually, yes, but not yet. He'd only been a week at Twickenham. He was supposed to stay for two weeks at the very least, until the search for him was called off or had died down. Harper should have told her, or her father should, or her brothers. She should have had time to prepare for this.

Her chest tightened as she looked at him. Couldn't he see what this was doing to her? Of course he couldn't. He didn't know what love was. It wasn't his fault. It was just how things were.

Don't turn into another Charles Tracey, she told herself fiercely. She swallowed the thick knot in her throat. "Does my father know?"

"Not yet. I thought I would speak to you first."

She nodded, though she didn't know why, except perhaps that she knew there was no arguing with Richard Maitland when he'd made up his mind about something.

"Where will you go?"

"It's best if you don't know."

She managed to keep her voice light. "We've had this conversation before. Same question, same answer. You'll note that this time, though, I don't take offense."

Smiling a little, he said, "If I gave offense, it was because I didn't know you. Now that I do know you, I respect and admire you. I think you are a credit to the name you bear."

She was disappointed in him. He was beginning to sound like all those people who went in awe of her just because she was a duke's daughter. Could this be Richard Maitland speaking?

He was being polite and gracious, that was all, and she had to meet him halfway. "So this time, it really is goodbye, Richard?"

"Yes."

Someone had to leave first, but she couldn't get her

feet to move. "I should go," she said, hoping . . . hoping
. . . that it wouldn't end like this.

It didn't. He took a step toward her. "Before you go, I
want to talk to you about something."

Her hopes were dashed. There was nothing loverlike
in his expression, voice, or manner. Her father adopted
the same benign look when he was about to lecture her
for her own good.

There was nothing she hated more than to be lectured for her own good.

"Oh?" she said.

He smiled. "It's about Prince Michael."

She didn't return his smile. "What about Prince
Michael?"

There wasn't a gentle way of saying it, so he came straight
to the point. "Don't marry him, Rosamund. He's not the
man for you. I'm telling you this for your own good. And
the same goes for all those other puppies who have been
sniffing around your skirts this last week. They're not for
you, either. Why rush into marriage? Give yourself some
time. One day, I'm sure you'll meet the right man."

"And how," she said sweetly, showing him her teeth,
"will I know he's the right man?"

Richard folded his arms across his chest and studied
her thoughtfully. Her cheeks were flushed, her bosom
was heaving, and there was a tempest in her eyes. She
had positioned herself by the door so that he couldn't
leave without removing her. Well, she'd better watch out,
because he'd had his fill of watching her cavort with a
succession of popinjays this last week. He was trying to be
reasonable. All he wanted was for her to be happy. Why
couldn't she see that?

He wasn't ready to give up yet. "It won't be Prince
Michael," he said. "For a start, you'll be as stifled in the
role of princess as you were as a duke's daughter. You
need a man who will encourage you to take charge of

your own life, who will teach you to live a little more adventurously."

"Thank you," she said, "but I intend to take charge of my own life whether I marry Prince Michael or not."

"You could never be happy with him! Oh, I'll give the man his due. On the dance floor, he has no equal, but there's more to marriage than that. He'll come to your room every night. He'll come to your bed. Are you ready for that?"

When she'd entered the folly she'd been chilled to the bone. Now, she was steaming hot. She draped her wrap over a chair and turned to face him.

"Oh, bed," she said, making a face. "From my limited experience, I would say that what a man and woman do in bed is highly overrated. Now a man who can dance is a decided asset. Do you dance, Richard?"

"No, I do not!"

"Pity."

His eyes darkened. "When you talk about your limited experience, I presume you mean your experience with me?"

She smirked. "You surely don't think you're the only handsome man I've kissed?"

"You told me, in the bothy, that I was."

"That was a week ago," she said airily. "I've been making up for lost time." She relished the sudden sizzle in his eyes, and rashly added another coal to the fire. "Frankly, I don't see what all the fuss is about. One man's kisses are pretty much the same as another's."

Her barb found its mark. He'd never claimed to be the world's greatest lover, but bloody hell, his kisses weren't as unmemorable as all that. He'd had his share of women, he could tell. But what really stung was that the last time he'd kissed her, he'd been shaken to his very foundations. And his kisses didn't rate higher than the next man's? Who else had she been kissing when his back was turned?

There was only so much a man could take.

His whole body seemed to harden when he put his hands on her shoulders and pulled her close. This was one kiss she would never forget.

Rosamund braced for the shaking she could tell was coming, a shaking she knew she had provoked, but if he was angry, so was she. She loved him. Undeserving as he was, she loved him. He must know it. And he had cheapened that love by reducing it to its lowest level. *Bed*. Was that all men could think about?

"Now, just a minute—"

Whatever she was about to say was cut off when his lips took hers with a passion that bordered on fury. Her fury was no less than his. She gave him back angry kiss for angry kiss. When he ground his body against hers, she ground her body against his. His tongue plunged into her mouth and she fought to master it with her own tongue. And when he raised his head to look at her, the storm in her eyes battled with the storm in his.

They were both breathing hard, both fighting for every breath. And as their eyes held, all their tempestuous emotions subtly changed. She whimpered. He groaned.

He kissed her again, but it wasn't temper that heated her blood this time or made her heart pound. Her whole body quivered with need. It came to her that until that moment, she had never truly understood how it could be between a man and woman. This wasn't pleasant. This wasn't sweetly erotic. This was heat and melting and aching and wanting all mixed together. It was almost like pain.

Richard felt her body clench in pleasure and his control slipped another notch. Only a kiss, he told himself, but he knew that he lied. Kisses, yes, but he was raining those kisses on every pleasure point he could find without disrobing her. He kissed her breasts through the fabric of her gown and sucked strongly on first one nipple then the other, coaxing then exulting as they hardened like small pebbles in his mouth. And his hands were as busy as his lips, kneading, molding, claiming forbidden territory as his own. It wasn't enough.

He was yanking her skirts up, brushing his fingers along the insides of her thighs when the sound of her name penetrated the mist in his brain. He raised his head and listened. Her name came again. He knew that voice.

"Prince Michael," he said, almost snarling the words.

"What?" Rosamund hadn't come to herself yet. She steadied herself by placing both hands on his chest.

"Prince Michael," he repeated. "He's looking for you."

The thought of Prince Michael was the perfect cure for his desire. Richard straightened Rosamund's clothes (because she was still in a daze) then his own, then he took a step back.

"Passion, Rosamund," he said. "If you marry Prince Michael, that's what you'll have to give up. You're a warm-blooded woman. Don't settle for a cold-blooded fish."

And with that, he turned and walked out.

Her legs felt like quivering jellies, but she managed to totter on them to the nearest chair. And there she sat, wide-eyed, fingers touching her burning lips, then palming her breasts to ease the ache his mouth had started there, and finally moving over her abdomen to that other ache between her thighs.

All this from a kiss?

She was on the point of leaving when Richard marched back in. "I forgot to wish you a happy birthday," he said, "and give you your birthday present."

Her hand came out automatically to receive the object he pressed into it.

"There was a fire," he said, "and this is the only piece that survived. I've had it since I was a boy, to bring me luck." And with that, he marched out.

Rosamund opened her hand and looked at the object he had placed in it. It was a chess piece, a medieval king carved out of ebony that was scorched around the edges. His expression was very grim.

She didn't know whether to laugh or cry.

⁂

Richard was drawing level with the house when he heard men shouting. It seemed as though a fight had broken out. When he turned the corner of the house, his steps slowed. The deflated marquee had freed itself from its moorings and looked as though it was going to blow away. The head groundsman was directing men this way and that, in an effort to get it tied down again.

Some of the inside servants had been brought out to help, and that's where the trouble lay. There was no love lost between inside and outside servants and a shouting match had started up. If the head groundsman didn't get control of his men, at this rate there would be a full-blown riot. What this lot needed was Harper. But Harper had his hands full looking after visiting coachmen and their rigs.

He wasn't in the mood to resume his duties in the house and he doubted if he'd be missed, so he turned up his collar and made for his cottage. The paths should have been well lit, but half the lanterns had either burned out or been blown out by the wind. There were lights in the stable block, however, so he took his bearings from there.

There were other lights, some of them marking carriages that were lined up on the driveway, waiting to take their owners home, and on the other side of the lake, lights winking on carriages that were already leaving.

If the party was over, Rosamund should have been at the house for her guests to take their leave of her. She should have been there for the announcement of her betrothal. That's why Prince Michael had been looking for her.

Well, he hoped he had taught her a lesson.

His mouth twisted in a humorless smile. He was the one who had learned a lesson, and it made him writhe inside. He'd always regarded himself as a rational man, but for the last half hour, he'd behaved like a sulky schoolboy. He hadn't been thinking of Rosamund's happiness when he'd warned her off Prince Michael. He'd been thinking of himself. If he couldn't have her, he didn't want her to marry at all. But he didn't want her to die an old maid, either.

There was no pleasing him.

Jaw clenched, he walked on, kicking wet leaves out of his way. He was almost at his own door when he heard it. There was no mistaking that sound. It was the report of a pistol shot, and it came from the vicinity of the house.

He did an about-turn and began to race back the way he had come. He tried to assure himself that the head groundsman had fired off a shot to quell his unruly men, but all his training warned him not to accept the first facile answer that came to mind. If there was a killer on the prowl, he was the most likely target.

He was breathing hard and fast when he reached the men who had been working on the marquee. No one noticed his approach. They were standing about, staring silently at the crush of guests who had exited the conservatory and were now milling around on the terrace.

"What happened?" he asked one of the groundsmen.

"Someone in the folly was shot at," he said. "I think it's Lady Rosamund."

Richard stood there rigidly, his throat working. Then he saw them: Prince Michael in his white coat, with a dark-haired girl in his arms. *Rosamund.*

Heart thundering, his mind paralyzed with fear, he started forward.

Chapter 19

Richard had taken only a few steps when a shadow came barreling down on him, a substantial shadow whose impact sent him reeling back on his heels. Before he could do more than find his balance, a voice, fiercely angry, told him not to be a bloody fool. It was Harper's voice.

"I must go to her!" Richard said savagely.

He tried to throw off Harper's hands, but Harper wouldn't be thrown off. He dragged Richard farther into the shadows so that they were a little apart from the other men. "It could be a trap," said Harper. "Have you thought of that? Even now, someone could be waiting for you to show yourself so they can finish the job. And they won't let you near her. What did you think you was going to do? Walk into the house and demand to see the lass? They're more like to lock you up and hand you over to the constables and magistrates. Now put that pistol away before you draws attention to yourself."

Richard hadn't even been aware that he had his pistol

in his hand. He automatically tucked it into the waist-band of his breeches. At Special Branch, they thought he had nerves of steel. He never panicked, never lost his head. He was close to losing his head now.

"How badly hurt is she?" he demanded.

"It's not mortal, if that's what you're thinking. They've sent for the doctor, so that's a good sign."

Richard nodded, though Harper's words did little to relieve his fears. *Not mortal* covered a lot of ground. He was torn. If he wanted to get inside that house, nothing could stop him, but he'd have to do it at gunpoint. He couldn't see himself walking into Rosamund's room and holding everyone off with a gun.

Harper said, "I'm telling you the truth. She's not seri-ously hurt."

"How did it happen?"

"I don't rightly know, except that someone took a shot at her in or near the folly. But this is wasting time if we wants to catch the bastard who did it."

Richard's focus shifted a little. After a moment, he said, "We're never going to find him in this crush. It's like looking for a needle in a haystack."

By Richard's reckoning, there were about forty groundsmen shuffling around on the lawn outside the conservatory. On the terrace, there was an equal num-ber of guests and inside servants, who were now shuf-fling back into the conservatory. Carriages passed them in a steady stream to go to the front of the house to pick up their passengers. The task of finding Rosamund's at-tacker was damn near hopeless unless they were lucky.

"What do you wants me to do?" asked Harper.

Richard let out a breath. "First off, question the groundsmen. See if they know anything. Find out if any-one is missing. Then, if that leads nowhere, organize a search of the grounds. If anyone objects to your giving orders, tell them you're acting on the duke's instructions. If you find anything, let off a shot. I'll do the same."

"Now you're talking," said Harper, sounding happy that his chief was acting more like himself. "And where will you be?"

"I'm going to start with the folly. Give me a few minutes before you come after me."

❧

The folly was deserted, with no one guarding it to preserve any evidence that might have been left behind. Richard had brought a lantern with him and he held it up as he scanned the small interior. It was like an outdoor dining room with a fine view of the river. He could see why it was called a folly. It was like a miniature Greek temple, with Greek columns at the entrance.

Everything was as he remembered: there was a small table, several upright chairs, and potted palms beside the long windows. He remembered that Rosamund had removed her wrap and draped it over a chair, but she must have put it on again, unless Prince Michael had wrapped her in it before carrying her into the house. The floor was made of marble, and there wasn't a drop of blood on it, only the mud that he and Rosamund had tramped in, and perhaps the prince as well.

He found the blood outside on the gravel path—leastways, he thought it was blood, but it was hard to tell. There wasn't much, and what there was had been diluted by the rain. He went down on one knee, removed his glove, and touched the gravel reverently. In the next instant, a wave of rage surged through him. He fought to master it. Rage would not help him find Rosamund's assailant. He had to act as though this was just another case. He had to stop his mind wandering to the house, imagining the worst. He had to focus all his powers of concentration on finding this cold-blooded killer. Then, and only then, would he let the rage take him.

He made a search of the area around the folly and found nothing to help him. The grass was trampled and twigs on the lower branches of trees were snapped in places, but that could be the result of the crush of guests who had come to investigate. He wasn't done yet, though. He stepped off the path and tried to think himself into the mind of the person who had fired the shot. The first question that came to him was, who was the shot meant for, Prince Michael or Rosamund? The second question was that, having pulled the trigger, how did the would-be killer plan to make his escape? Normally, the groundsmen would have been patrolling the area to keep trespassers out. When they heard the shot, they would have quickly converged on the folly. But every able-bodied groundsman had been ordered to help with the marquee. Had the killer known this? Or had he depended on luck to help him evade capture once he made his presence known?

Maybe. But Richard sensed a clever mind at work here, clever and quick to seize any opportunity that presented itself. The villain couldn't have counted on finding Prince Michael and Rosamund in the folly. He must have followed them.

Prince Michael would have been easy to follow. He was in dress regimentals, with a white tunic, and he was calling Rosamund's name. But what was the motive? It didn't make sense. Rosamund didn't have any enemies, and Prince Michael was only third or fourth in line to the title. Now if someone had shot at him, Richard Maitland, it would have made perfect sense.

He was done here. As he debated what to do next, he saw lights flickering among the trees. Harper and his groundsmen were approaching. It was miserable work. It was still raining; everything was sopping wet, and the wind was beginning to whip itself into a fury. A gale was brewing, the kind of gale that uprooted trees and blew down chimney stacks.

The incipient storm found an answering beat in his blood. He would do more than topple chimney stacks when he found the person who had hurt Rosamund.

His thoughts flitted to the house. *Don't become distracted!* he told himself. *They'll never let you see her! Think!*

There were only two ways in and out of the grounds of Twickenham House—by river and through the gatehouse, where porters were always on duty. He thought for a moment, made his decision, and moved swiftly in the direction of the riverbank.

❧

He was bent with cold and fatigue when he finally gave up the hunt. He'd combed the riverbank, he'd questioned the porters at the gatehouse. Nothing was out of place, nothing to indicate that a trespasser had been among them. The exhaustion he was fighting left no room to speculate on what this might mean, not yet.

The ground floor of the house was in darkness, as it usually was late at night when the shutters were drawn, but there were plenty of lights upstairs. He took shelter from the gale in a stand of pines and stood there, staring at the house, thinking, wondering, angry that he didn't have the right to be with Rosamund, and it made him still angrier knowing that his anger was misplaced. He was nothing to the Deveres except a fugitive from the law. If he were Rosamund's father or brothers, he wouldn't want Richard Maitland near her either.

As his breathing evened and his exhaustion ebbed a little, he let his gaze wander. He noted dully that he wasn't the only one to give up the search. There were no groundsmen and no flickering lanterns moving among the trees. There were no coaches wending their way home. There was only the persistent drizzle and the wildness in the wind aggravating the wildness in himself.

He left the shelter of the trees and in a stumbling gait began to make his way toward the stable block. If the searchers had given up, then Harper would be in his cottage. If there was any news of Rosamund, Harper would know it.

He didn't have to force himself to go on now. His feet moved of their own volition, up, up the steep incline to the row of groundsmen's cottages. No light in Harper's cottage, his brain registered, but there was light in his. He dashed the droplets of rain from his face with the back of his sleeve, found the latch, and stumbled inside.

He expected to see Harper, but it wasn't Harper who was kneeling in front of the blaze in the grate. She turned and rose at his entrance. A gust of wind from the open doorway sent sparks from the fire hurtling up the chimney. He slammed the door shut.

"Richard!" she cried out. "Where have you been? Harper and I have been worried sick about you."

His voice was no more than a thick whisper. "Rosamund?"

There wasn't a mark on her, not that he could see. She'd changed her gown for something warmer, something dark that had lace at the throat and cuffs. Tears glistened on her lashes and streaked her cheeks.

"It wasn't me," she said, quickly crossing to him. "Harper told me what you both thought, but you were wrong. It was Prudence who was walking with Prince Michael. We think that someone shot at the prince and hit Prudence by mistake. It's only a flesh wound. She's sleeping now . . ." Her voice trailed away. "Richard, I'm fine, truly I am."

Like a man in a daze, he reached for her. She was warm to his touch, warm and glowing with life. He closed his eyes, wrapped her in his arms, and held her in a crushing embrace. She wrapped her arms around him as well. No words were spoken; no words were needed.

She pulled away first. "You're soaking, you're shivering. Here, let me help you with your coat."

She tugged his rain-soaked coat from his shoulders and draped it over a chair to dry by the fire. When he simply stood there, his eyes following her, she led him to the bed.

"Take off those wet clothes," she said. She was becoming worried. She'd never seen him like this. "Is there brandy?"

"In the dresser. But I don't want brandy."

He sat on the edge of the bed and held out his arms. She came to him at once. She said shakenly, "Oh, my darling, I thought something awful had happened to you. I thought I'd lost you."

"I've been such a fool," he said, and kissed her.

A damn fool, he thought as he stretched out with her on the bed. All his life he'd been surrounded by people, in school, at university, as a soldier, but he'd always been alone. Until Rosamund came hurtling into his life like a meteor. He never wanted to be alone again.

He tightened his hold on her. He didn't expect things to be easy. He didn't know if he could make her happy. But never again, he promised himself, *never again* would he stand outside a locked door, like a suppliant, not knowing whether she lived or died. There would never be a locked door between them again.

Rosamund knew that he was in the grip of some powerful emotion, but so was she. When she learned that Prudence was shot, she'd been deathly afraid that the assassin might still be out there stalking Richard, so the first chance she got, she'd slipped away to make sure that he was all right. Harper had found her in the cottage, and their anxiety had turned to alarm. In the last hours, all kinds of grotesque scenes had played themselves out in her mind, till she was close to panic. He'd come back to her safe and sound, but she was still shaken from all the strain and tension of that awful night.

She'd learned that time didn't stretch out into infinity. All those books in her father's library were wrong. Time could run out at any moment. All they had, all they could count on, was the present, and she wasn't going to waste one precious second of it.

They clung together for a long, long time. His hands were still trembling when he cupped her cheeks and studied her face. There was a question in his eyes.

"Yes," she said simply.

Unsmiling, he began to disrobe her.

She didn't want pretty words or promises. She wasn't thinking of pleasure. She was long past the need for modesty. What she wanted was this ultimate intimacy, bare skin against bare skin, and heat, and to be so close to him that nothing could separate them, not even a shadow.

His mouth and hands were not gentle, but she understood. The pent-up emotion of that night was too desperate for gentleness. Their coupling was swift and fierce, and in spite of the flash of pain exactly what Rosamund needed.

When he slipped from her body, he pulled her hard against him. "Don't leave me," he murmured, and as though to make his point, he anchored her with an arm around her waist. A moment later, he drifted into an exhausted sleep.

※

He awakened with a start, thinking in that first disoriented moment that the gale had blown off the roof of his cottage. When he hauled himself up, he saw that the cold blast of air had entered the cottage through the open door. Rosamund was at the door. He heard her say something to someone outside, but it was too dark to see who it was. She was wrapped in a cloak, but her toes were bare and so were her arms.

"Was that Harper?" he asked softly as she closed the door.

She turned without haste. "Yes," she said. "I thought he might be shocked to find me here with you like this." She pushed her unbound hair back from her face.

His lips curled. "And was he?"

"Not shocked. I think 'resigned' is closer to the look that came over his face."

"Did he give you a message for me?"

"Now, let me see." She looked at the ceiling as though Harper's words were written on it. "If I've translated it right, he said that if you went off on your own again without letting him know where he could find you, he would do you a serious injury." She dimpled. "He was very angry, but of course he was relieved, too."

He smiled. "Is that all he said?"

"No. He offered to escort me to the house, but I told him I wasn't ready to go home just yet."

At these words, the small knot of tension across his shoulder blades gradually relaxed. There was no wariness in her eyes, nothing to suggest that his ardor had embarrassed or shocked her. Any other woman . . . but there was no point in comparing her to any other woman. Rosamund was unique.

"I put the kettle on to boil," she said. "Why don't we get dressed, then we can talk while we have our tea."

"I don't want you to get dressed."

The intensity of his gaze made her heart begin to thud. "Oh."

"And we'll talk afterward. Come to bed, Rosamund."

When he held out his hand, she went to him without hesitation. That simple act of trust brought an odd tightness to his throat.

All at once there was a crack overhead as the wind tore through the trees. They heard a thud, as if a heavy branch had fallen or a tree had been uprooted. Then the wind's howl died to a moan.

When Rosamund shivered, Richard pulled her onto the bed and held her in his arms. Something fierce

moved in him, something fierce that was edged with fear.
She looked up at him with such trusting eyes. He wanted
to protect her from all the ugliness and evil that was to
be found in the world, but he had never been more
aware of his own mortality, or hers.

He kissed her long and slowly. "What would make you
happy?" he asked.

"Being with you. That's what makes me happy." She
gazed up at him, her mouth trembling. "Take me with
you, Richard, when you leave here. I can't face not knowing where you are, or what's happening to you. We could
start fresh, somewhere else. That's what would make me
happy."

"Then that's what we'll do, but not before I speak to
your father."

She stared at him for a long time, saw in his eyes that
he meant every word, and whispered, "What would make
you happy, Richard?"

"You," he said fiercely, "only you."

His embrace was anything but fierce. He kissed her
brows, her cheeks, her ears, and finally, at her urging,
her mouth. When he heard the slight catch in her
breathing, he helped her out of her cloak. She wasn't
wearing a thing beneath it. Her body was smooth beneath his hands, smooth and supple and welcoming. He
wanted to show her that there was more to loving than
his frantic possession. Loving was slow, easy, and tantalizing. Loving was pleasure.

It was like floating in a warm river, she thought, only
this time she wasn't a novice. She knew where the current was taking her. She followed his example, and returned caress for caress. Her heart began to race. Her
breath began to catch in her throat. The warm river became a little more choppy.

Richard buried his mouth in her throat as he struggled to hold on to his control. But her throat tasted sin-
fully of the perfume she had dabbed there, and his

senses began to swim. *Easy*. he told himself, but he couldn't get his hands and lips to obey the commands of his brain. He had to touch, had to taste.

She gave a low, keening cry when his mouth closed on one distended nipple. Heat raced from her breast to her loins. She couldn't get air into her lungs. Then his lips moved to her other breast, and her breath came out on a strangled sob.

He raised her knees and probed gently between her thighs. The soft sounds she made had him shuddering in response. He held himself in check for only one reason. That first time he'd been too desperate to have her to bring her to climax. This time, he was thinking only of her.

She wanted to touch him as he touched her, but he wouldn't allow it. She writhed, she shuddered, she struggled as the rising tide of sensation threatened to sweep her away. "Richard," she cried.

At that cry of helpless need, something primitive and entirely masculine moved inside him. No one else had ever made her feel like this and no one else ever would. She was his. It worked both ways. He had never wanted so much, needed so much.

His chest rose and fell as he braced himself over her, and carefully entered her. "Rosamund . . ." That awful tightness was back in his throat, and he couldn't speak.

Her eyes glazed over. Her nails scored his back. "Why have you stopped?"

He had to smile. She was a sheer delight to him. But his smile disintegrated when she moved beneath him. He rose above her, and slowly pushed into her, making their joining as deep as he could make it.

Never had she been so aware of her body, or so aware of the pleasure she could give and take. In that moment, she felt she understood what had baffled philosophers since the beginning of time. She knew why the universe existed. It was for this.

Then he moved, and rational thought slipped away. She gave him kiss for kiss, thrust for thrust, until the pleasure sharpened, crested, became unbearable, and shattered like an exploding star.

❧

Hands tucked behind his neck, he lay in the aftermath of spent passion, drowsy and content. He knew there was a smug smile on his face. He'd never bothered to judge his performance as a lover. Middling to adequate, he'd always thought, and hadn't felt the need to improve his standing. But that was before Rosamund. With the right woman, he could reach heights he hadn't known existed.

With a sigh of masculine satisfaction, he rolled to his side so that he could watch the light of his life as she made the tea she had promised him. A week, two weeks ago, she wouldn't have known how to light a fire or boil a kettle of water. And now look at her. He was impressed. At the same time, it wouldn't have mattered a straw to him now whether she knew how to light a fire or boil water. Two weeks had made a remarkable difference to both of them.

She was fully dressed. Because she'd laid out a fresh shirt and black trousers for him, he decided to put them on, but he did it to please her. He had looked at his watch and calculated that there was enough time to make love to her again before he saw her safely back to the house.

And, of course, they had to talk.

But when he was dressed and ready to sit down at the table, he found that it wasn't that simple. He had to touch her, had to pull her hard against him and undo the buttons of her bodice so that his questing fingers could find bare flesh. He had to kiss her. It wasn't all one-sided. This woman really knew how to seduce a man.

Those little catches in her breath drove him crazy to have her. She was so warm, so generous, so giving.

When he pulled back, he was breathing hard. "Tea or bed?" he said.

"Bed!" she answered at once.

And with a whoop of laughter, she dragged him to the bed.

Chapter 20

*H*alf an hour later, they had their tea.

"So," he said, "tell me what happened tonight after I left you."

She put down her cup. "Now, this is shocking," she said. "We weren't the only two who had arranged to meet at the folly. Prudence, my sweet, innocent, butter-wouldn't-melt-in-her-mouth Prudence, had arranged to meet Prince Michael! I have never been more misled in my life. I thought she was pining for Caspar, and all the time it was Prince Michael. That's why she was so reserved with me, and with Caspar, too. We didn't exactly sing Prince Michael's praises. I'm sorry to say that sometimes I was quite scathing, and she was hurt on his behalf. And it seems he loves her, too. He's swearing that he'll give up his place in the succession so that he can marry her. He hasn't left her side since the accident—that's what we're calling it up at the house, an accident, but that was just to stop everyone panicking."

"Why are you so cross?"

"I'm not cross, I'm disappointed. I mean, Prince Michael is nice enough, I suppose, but Prudence is an intelligent woman. She could do so much better."

He thought for a moment and said, "But if he loved her, why was he going to become engaged to you?"

A pained expression crossed her face. "That was all in your imagination. How could you believe I would marry that—no, no, I won't call him a bore, because he really is a nice man. It's just that we have nothing in common."

He wasn't going to argue that point. The prince was no longer a problem. That was the main thing. He held out his cup and watched her refill it. "So you're all alone in the folly. What happens next?"

"I was in no state to see anyone right then, so when I heard Prince Michael calling my name, I left the folly and went round to a side door on the far side of the house. My hair was a mess, so I went upstairs to fix it. Meanwhile, I gather, Prudence had entered the folly to wait for the prince. When he couldn't find me, he went to meet Prudence."

"Why was he looking for you?"

"Some of my guests were leaving and I should have been there. My father asked the prince to find me. When he couldn't find me in the ballroom or the conservatory, he tried outside. Of course, he had to go to the folly to keep his tryst with Prudence. They didn't stay there long. They left together. A shot rang out and Prue was hit. The prince fell on top of her to protect her. That's all I know."

"The prince fell on top of her? I think there may be more to the prince than I gave him credit for."

"You wouldn't say that if you'd seen the bruises on Prue. I think Prince Michael did more damage than the bullet did."

He shook his head and chuckled. "I don't suppose he saw anyone or heard anything to indicate who fired the shot?"

"Unfortunately not. Nor did any of the servants or guests who ran to the folly when the shot was fired."

Something else occurred to him. "What about your shawl? Did you leave it at the folly? I remember it over a chair."

"No. Why?"

He shrugged. "Miss Dryden has your coloring, and you're about the same height. It struck me that if she picked up your shawl and was wearing it, she might have been mistaken for you."

She was shocked. "Why would anyone want to shoot *me*?"

"No reason. Just as I can't see any reason for anyone wanting to shoot Miss Dryden." When her expression changed, he said, "What is it, Rosamund?"

She shook her head. "I'm sure this has nothing to do with it, but I learned from Prudence today that her brother, Peter Dryden, was at Cambridge with you. He's recently become the vicar of St. Marks in Chelsea. Do you remember him?"

"Peter Dryden?" Richard took a moment to think about it. The name had a familiar ring, but he could not put a face to it. Suddenly it came to him. "The poet!" he said. "That was his nickname."

"So you do remember him?"

"Yes."

He remembered a young man with spectacles whose head was never out of a book, but that was about all he remembered. Which meant that Peter Dryden had not been a member of the inner circle of young men who had set themselves up as judges of manners and morals. Their names were forever branded on his mind.

He looked at Rosamund. "What about him?"

"Prudence says that he's absolutely convinced you could not have murdered Lucy Rider. He told her about Frank Stapleton and how you were blamed for his crimes. He also said—but Prudence didn't sound sure about this—that Stapleton had gone off to Canada right after he left Cambridge and that's where he died.

"It's worth looking into, isn't it? Especially after what happened here tonight."

"Oh, yes. It's worth looking into."

He wasn't only thinking of Frank Stapleton. Dunsmoor was closely connected to his Cambridge days, and he was beginning to think of Cambridge more and more of late. Peter Dryden was definitely worth a visit.

After that, he went back and forth, drawing her out on one point then another. Prince Michael, he learned, was convinced that the bullet was meant for him. There were always agitators and hotheads in Kolnbourg who liked to stir up trouble. One less prince to worry about would be a cause for rejoicing among that lot.

"And those were his exact words," Rosamund said, and Richard laughed.

"What does your father think?"

She took a long sip of tea before replying. "He hasn't said very much. I know he wants to talk to you. He sent Justin to find you, but when Justin returned and said that all the outside servants were combing the grounds and he couldn't find you, Father decided he'd see you first thing in the morning."

Richard nodded. "Good, because I want to talk to him, too."

"About me?"

"Especially about you."

She fiddled with the lace on one cuff. She checked to make sure there was tea left in the pot. Finally, losing patience, she said, "Well, what are you going to say to him?"

Her question surprised him. "I'm going to tell him that we're going to be married, of course."

She sat back in her chair. "Tell? Not ask?"

"Tell," replied Richard forcefully. "If I ask, he might

say no. He probably would say no. I'm not giving him a choice."

"Isn't it usual for a gentleman to ask a lady first, before he approaches her father?"

She said the words as a joke, but there was no humor in his expression when he answered her. "I'm not giving you a choice either."

She looked into his eyes, and the intensity of his gaze made her catch her breath. Her heart began to thud. She tried to drag her eyes away, but he wouldn't allow it. There was something primitive in that look, something possessive and utterly masculine.

His dark lashes flickered, releasing her from his gaze, and she let out a breath. He said in a bantering tone, "It would shock Harper if we did not marry, and we wouldn't want that, would we?"

She did her best to follow his lead, but her heart was still thudding against her ribs. "I think Harper may be shocked anyway. He told me that you were pining for your lost love."

He looked baffled. "What lost love?"

"She doesn't exist?"

"No."

She nodded. "That's what I thought. Harper was sure, you see, that your heart was already taken, and that's why no woman could hold you, not even the admirable Mrs. Templar or Jason Radley's beautiful wife, but I saw at once that that's not the reason. Harper is a romantic. I know better than that."

He smiled. "Harper is a meddler. He told you that for your own good, so that you would forget me and take up your life again. Well, you had your chance and you didn't listen to him. And it's too late now."

She rested her chin on her linked fingers. "Richard," she said, "don't you want to know why I think no woman has ever held you?"

If there was one thing Richard disliked intensely, it was dissecting the workings of his relationship with a woman. Women seemed to relish it. Not only that, they excelled at it. What good it did was more than he could fathom. No one was ever the happier for it.

"Not particularly," he said.

She sealed her lips.

He heaved a sigh. "All right. Why?"

"Because," she said, "you had not met the right woman, not until I came along."

He grinned. "You're sure of that, are you?"

"Perfectly sure. And it's not that no woman could hold you. Let's be frank. What woman would want to? It's the other way round. What woman would put up with your black moods, your lack of gallantry, and, dare I say it, your blunt way of expressing yourself? Only me." Her eyes sparkled. "And do you know why?"

"I'm all ears," he said woodenly.

"Because all my life, I've been surrounded by people who flattered me. You don't flatter. You don't try to charm. You don't whisper sweet nothings in a lady's ear. When you say something, you mean it."

The smile went out of his eyes. "You're right about that. I do mean what I say. I won't give you up, Rosamund, so if your family makes you choose, you're coming with me."

She cried out when he suddenly reached for her and swung her into his arms. He kissed her long and hard. She tasted passion, and she also tasted desperation. If only it could be this simple, his kiss told her.

It wasn't simple. A dark cloud hung over them, a malevolent cloud that could swallow them up. They might have a future together, or this might be all they would ever have. A bittersweet ache clogged her throat, and her kisses became as desperate as his.

Their lovemaking was slower this time, the urgency

gone, but it was prolonged. Just for a little while, they shut out the world and thought only of themselves.

ॐ

Long after he had seen her back to the house, Richard tossed restlessly in his bed. He told himself that he had no regrets, that he'd tried to give her up, but he'd been fighting a losing battle. Sooner or later, it would have come to this. The shock of thinking he had lost her had only precipitated things.

But now that she had committed herself to him, he was plagued by fears and doubts. What if he could not clear his name? He would be a fugitive for the rest of his life. What would happen to Rosamund then?

It wasn't his way to agonize over what might have been, but to work with what he had. There was no going back for Rosamund and him, so the possibility of not clearing his name was unthinkable.

Having settled that problem in his mind, he concentrated on sifting through the sequence of events that had led to his downfall. He thought about Cambridge, moved on to Lucy Rider's murder, then finally to the attack on Prudence Dryden.

There was something nagging him, something similar about Lucy Rider's murder and the attack on Miss Dryden tonight. What was it? He fell into an uneasy sleep as his mind groped for the answer.

Chapter 21

Richard's interview with Rosamund's father had to be postponed until the magistrates' work was done, and they didn't leave until the dinner hour. They questioned key witnesses and took copious notes, but they didn't look farther than their noses, in Richard's opinion. According to below-stairs gossip, they were satisfied that Prince Michael was the target and that the most likely suspect was some unknown fanatical countryman who had a grievance against Kolnbourg's royal family.

The delay gave Richard plenty of time to think about the question that had teased his mind before he'd fallen into a restless sleep last night. What was similar about Lucy Rider's murder and the attack on Miss Dryden was that in both cases, the assailants vanished without a trace, and this in spite of a crush of people rushing to the scene almost as soon as a shot was fired.

It occurred to him that these killers hadn't tried to slip away. They could have been there in the crush, perhaps even first on the scene of the crime. There would be nothing to attract anyone's notice to them, because they were not outsiders. They were where one would expect to see them.

It wasn't a blinding revelation so much as a theory that should be looked into. Or maybe he was just clutching at straws. He had one solid lead he was going to pursue. Major Digby had known about Dunsmoor. Who had told him about it? Who knew all the private details of his life? Only someone who had gone to a great deal of trouble to find out.

It wasn't much to go on, but it was the only lead he had.

He spent the day helping groundsmen clear away the debris of the storm. Harper was there, too, grim-faced and watchful. Though he had no theories of his own to put forward for the attack on Miss Dryden, he wasn't satisfied with the magistrates' verdict. All his instincts were telling him that Twickenham was no longer healthy and it was time to move on.

Lord Justin came for Richard when he and Harper were clearing away after their evening meal. He'd decided not to wear livery on this occasion and was dressed in black trousers and a dark coat. When he met with the duke, he wanted it to be man to man, not servant to master. Besides, servants got time off, and he'd decided this was his night.

Harper's presence wasn't required, but he insisted on going along. His instincts were still at full pitch and he slipped into his bodyguard mode. Lord Justin thought it was funny. Richard didn't. Like Harper, he had his hand in his coat pocket where he kept his pistol. He trusted Harper's instincts as well as his own.

The duke was waiting for him in his library, and only the duke. Gesturing with one hand, he indicated a chair. His Grace, Richard remembered, was a man of few words, and every word counted. He took the chair.

"You'll have a brandy?"

"Thank you."

Richard had been prepared to find the duke stiff and formal. He knew Rosamund would have told her father that they were going to marry. He couldn't say the duke was friendly, but he'd obviously been warned to be on his best behavior. As indeed, had he.

The duke handed Richard a glass half filled with brandy and took the chair opposite. "You'll note," he said, "I can be as egalitarian as the next person. I don't always stand on my dignity."

Those were Rosamund's words, thought Richard, and would have been amused except that he felt all the awkwardness of his position. He wasn't exactly the catch of the marriage mart, and he was sure the duke would drive home that point. He must remember, too, Rosamund's parting words to him last night: he was to be gracious and keep a civil tongue in his head.

"First off," said the duke, "tell me what you think about this monstrous business of last night. You've heard, I suppose, that the magistrates are convinced that Prince Michael was the intended victim?"

"I've heard," said Richard. He shook his head. "It's too early to come to any conclusions. But the motive seems far-fetched. If he were the crown prince, that would be different. What I'd like to do, with your permission, is interview both Miss Dryden and the prince. We can tell them that I'm an agent from Special Branch. They won't know who I am."

"It's out of the question—"

Richard's back stiffened.

The duke took a breath. He didn't know why Maitland was always so quick to take offense, especially when he, Romsey, was the injured party. "Because," he went on testily, "the prince decided that Miss Dryden would be better off with her brother. They left right after the magistrates did. But I can tell you that they saw and heard

nothing after the shot was fired. Miss Dryden has no enemies, why should she, a young woman of good family?
And the prince has other enemies—husbands, would
you believe, whom he has cuckolded over time? I was
never more deceived . . . well, that's beside the point. He
swears he's all reformed now that he's met Miss Dryden."

Richard relaxed against the back of his chair. He was
thinking that one of the first things he would do when he
left Twickenham was go out to Chelsea and interview
both Miss Dryden and her brother.

A pulse began to beat in the duke's temple. He fixed
his gaze on Richard. "My daughter tells me," he said,
"that you have something particular that you wish to say
to me."

Richard's stare was as unwavering as the duke's.
"Rosamund and I are going to be married," he said.

"I might have something to say about that!"

"Whatever you could say," said Richard, "I've already
said to myself. Believe me, I'm no more happy to have
the Deveres for relations than you are to have me!"

"At least we see eye to eye on something!" snapped the
duke. "But unlike you, we Deveres do not judge others by
their position in society. Oh, yes, I had that from
Rosamund. There is very little that my daughter does not
tell me."

"Then she will have told you that our marriage is in-
evitable."

"Imperative is the word I would use."

Richard said nothing.

"*Imperative!*" repeated the duke. "That's what Rosa-
mund told me. Do you know, I'm disappointed in you,
Maitland? Oh, not so much for compromising my daugh-
ter. The circumstances, she tells me, were exceptional.
She is determined to have you with or without my consent.
I suppose that's why she told me you were lovers. What can
I do? She's not a child. She has made her choice and I
have to accept it."

"Thank you," said Richard, letting out a relieved breath.

"That doesn't mean I have to like it! You may believe I did everything in my power to make her see reason."

And to every argument he put forward, Rosamund had countered that she was of age; she wanted his blessing, but with or without it, she would marry Richard Maitland.

She was just like Caspar after he came home from the war. There was a steel in her that he could not bend. He knew well enough that he could prevent the marriage by sending her to Castle Devere and keeping her under lock and key, but the cost was more than he was willing to pay. She would never call him Father again.

The duke wasn't finished yet. "What disappoints me is that I misjudged you. I thought you were a fighter. I thought your driving ambition was to clear your name."

Richard frowned. "That hasn't changed."

The duke gave a short bark of laughter. "Oh? And how do you propose to clear your name when you're living in Italy or wherever you plan to run off to?"

"What," said Richard slowly, "has Rosamund been saying to you?"

"That you're to be married at once and run off to Scotland or some equally inaccessible place and live, one supposes, happily ever after, though how——" He noted Richard's appalled expression and stopped. "You're not going to run off to foreign parts?"

"I can't think how Rosamund got that idea. Oh, hell!" Richard visibly winced as a memory came back to him. "We talked of starting a new life, but I meant *after* I'd cleared my name. And it was never in my mind to leave England."

There was a prolonged silence as the duke digested this, then he said, "Then isn't this conversation premature? Wouldn't it have been better to wait before approaching me for my daughter's hand? Why the haste?

It's unlikely that she is pregnant. Clear your name, then marry her openly and with my blessing."

"No. This is the right thing to do. For Rosamund's sake, we must marry at once. I don't want to sound melo-dramatic, but we have to face facts. In another week or two, she could well be a widow. If there's a child, it would crush Rosamund if we were not married."

The older man's eyes flared in shock. Finally, he said, "It would crush her if anything happened to you, mar-ried or not. What is it you intend to do that will put you in such jeopardy?"

Richard replied quietly, "It may not come down to it, but if all else fails, I may have to set myself up as bait to entrap a killer. And I'll need your help."

&

It was brazenly done, with no attempt at subterfuge. Lord Caspar procured a special license in Richard's own name and found a little, out-of-the-way chapel in Cheap-side with an ancient cleric who had trouble remember-ing the time of day. They were married in the presence of Rosamund's brothers, her father having begged off because he was too well-known and was afraid his pres-ence would draw attention to their little party. Rosamund knew he was right, but her father's absence cast a small shadow on the happiest day of her life.

There was no celebration. As soon the ceremony was over, Rosamund removed her wedding ring. It was her mother's and she had always intended, if she ever married, that it would be her wedding ring, too. Then they took a hackney to the coaching inn where they'd left their carriage in case someone might recog-nize it at the church, and they made the return journey to Twickenham House.

With her brothers in the carriage, there was little chance of Rosamund having the heart-to-heart talk with

Richard she so much wanted, but at least everyone was civil, and that pleased her. Her family had not exactly been civil that morning when she'd broken the news to them.

She'd talked to her father first, then her brothers were brought in, and she'd faced the three of them as they put forward one good reason after another for, at the very least, postponing the marriage. So she'd given them the one good reason why the marriage had to take place. She had gone to Richard's cottage, she said, and seduced him.

"You love him," her father said finally. "But does he love you?"

"Yes," she said. "Richard loves me."

He had never actually said the words, but she did not tell her father that, because he would have made too much of it. Richard was not sentimental. That's why he found it hard to say the words. He'd tried to keep her at arm's length because, she supposed, he had too much pride to marry so far above him. As though she cared about that! And he would still be keeping her at arm's length if he had not believed that she, and not Prudence, had been shot at last night.

He had been shaken to his very foundations. That's what had broken his control; that's what had unleashed his emotions. What he felt was in his eyes and in the way he trembled when he touched her, in the way he had loved her. Just thinking about it made her ache to be loved again.

Since her brothers and Richard were conversing about Twickenham's stables, she relaxed against the banquette and took a moment to study them, especially Caspar and Richard.

In appearance they were so very different: Caspar, dark-haired and tall, with his gypsy good looks; and Richard, brown hair shot with gold. Richard looked the more English of the two, though she doubted he'd take that as a compliment. They had one thing in common. They had presence, that indefinable air of men who were sure of themselves and knew what they were about.

Her gaze moved to Justin. He was munching on an apple. He was a younger version of Caspar, but he had some ways to go before he attained the kind of presence that distinguished his companions.

She liked Justin just the way he was. There were no shadows in him. He was as transparent as a mountain lake.

She felt a sudden chill, and shrank into the folds of her cloak.

❧

"I don't understand," said Rosamund. "I thought we would leave tonight. I've packed my boxes. What's happened, Richard? What's made you change your mind?"

They were in the conservatory, with Harper guarding the door to the gardens and Lord Justin patrolling the picture gallery, where the ball had taken place. No one could get in or out of the conservatory without their say-so.

This was the first time Rosamund and Richard had been alone all day. It was dark outside, but lanterns inside the conservatory had been lit. The light wasn't good, though, and she found it hard to read his expression.

"I haven't changed my mind," he said. "There's been a misunderstanding. Shall we walk?"

He cupped her elbow, guiding her, and they began to stroll down one of the stone paths. Exotic trees with drooping branches towered above them, and the flower beds were a riot of pinks and lavenders, but Rosamund wasn't interested in the plants. Her heart had started to race.

"Then when are we leaving? Tomorrow? The next day?"

He didn't know how to break it gently, so he said, "I'm leaving, you're staying. But it won't be for long. In a week or two, I'll come back for you, and we'll start that new life we promised ourselves."

She halted and turned to face him, her brows puckered. "And where will you be?"

"In London," he said. "Rosamund, I don't know how you could have misunderstood. I've never made any secret of the fact that clearing my name comes first with me."

He could tell that he had taken her by surprise. Her eyes were huge and her breathing was quick and shallow.

He tried to soften the blow. "I won't be far away, and Harper will bring you regular reports on how things are going."

He looked so calm, so sure, so unaffected, while a wave of mingled hurt and fear was spreading through her. The fear was stronger. "You may never clear your name."

"I have to try."

"How long am I supposed to wait? A month? A year?"

"I told you. A week, maybe two. Not much longer than that."

"How can you be so sure it will be over by then?"

He massaged his temples. "Because I'm going to set a trap for the thug who wants me dead."

A white haze floated before her eyes. She staggered, and was prevented from falling because he steadied her with his hands on her shoulders. The white haze cleared and was followed by a white-hot anger.

She shook off his hands. "I'm your wife," she cried. "We're supposed to decide these things together. And I say we should leave England until things settle down. It need not be forever. We can come back in a year, if you like. Then you can start your investigation."

He said incredulously, "A year? By that time the trail will be cold."

"Then leave it to my father and brothers!" She stopped when she heard the note of hysteria in her voice. "Leave it to my father and brothers," she repeated quietly. "If you stir things up, you'll be putting yourself in mortal danger."

He passed a hand over his eyes, straightened, and shook his head. "I thought you, of all people, would understand. This is something I have to do. It's not just about clearing my name. Have you forgotten that Lucy Rider was murdered? I swore to myself that I would avenge her death, and that's what I'm going to do."

If she had not been savoring dreams all day of setting off with Richard to begin a new life, she would have been in a calmer frame of mind. But disappointed hopes and something close to panic were fueling her anger.

She took a step back. In a low, quivering voice, she said, "You choose a woman who betrayed you over me?"

He was beginning to lose patience. The melting, giving woman of last night, who seemed to understand him with no words spoken, was turning into a virago. "Rosamund, stop this," he said. "I hardly know you when you are like this."

"I can't say the same about you! I should have known better! You're a lone wolf. That's what Harper told me. If I'd listened to him, this conversation wouldn't be taking place."

Stung, he retorted, "Then maybe you *should* have listened to Harper." He regretted the words as soon as they were said. "Rosamund," he said, and reached for her.

She evaded his hands, and with a little cry picked up her skirts and hurried away.

He started after her, stopped, then slammed his hand against the trunk of a decorative palm tree.

                             *

When she pushed into the picture gallery, it was to find that Justin had been joined by her father and Caspar. They were all standing about, smoking their cheroots.

She pointed a shaking finger at each one in turn. "You are responsible for this," she cried. "You put him up to it."

They exchanged uneasy glances. "No," they chorused in unison.

"Well, you had better make him change his mind, or I shall never forgive you," and she stalked off.

The duke blew out a stream of smoke. "I'd like to meet the person," he said slowly, "who can make Richard Maitland change his mind when he has decided on the course he must follow. I couldn't make him change his mind about marrying Rosamund, and I have no desire to embark on another futile exercise."

"Do you regret the match?" asked Caspar.

"I regret the timing, but as we all know, there was a compelling reason to give my consent."

Justin said, "Still, it's a bit of a comedown, isn't it? A few weeks ago, the papers were calling Rosamund 'the perfect princess.' She's gone from the sublime to the ridiculous."

The duke said, "*Ridiculous* isn't a word I would ever use in connection with Maitland. *Single-minded,* perhaps. *Relentless,* certainly. He never gives up. But he is a man of honor. I respect him." He thought for a moment, then went on. "I could arrange for a title. When he clears his name, I mean. They can be bought if the price is right, and the prince regent is always strapped for money. Baron Maitland. That has a nice ring to it."

"Father, I wouldn't," said Caspar.

"What? Not even a knighthood?"

"Not even a knighthood. He won't thank you for it. He's more likely to take offense. He's the kind of man who likes to earn things on his own merits."

The duke studied his older son for a moment, then said, "You like him, don't you?"

"I wouldn't go that far," Caspar replied with a grin. "Let's just say that he improves on acquaintance. Maitland is the kind of soldier you'd want standing beside you, shoulder to shoulder, in the thick of battle. Naturally, you'd want Harper on your other side."

"What about me?" demanded Justin. "I was a soldier."

Caspar watched the spiral of smoke he exhaled slowly dissipate. "Yes," he said, "but you were spared Spain. It was a brutal, filthy campaign. That's one of the reasons Maitland and I understand each other." He looked at Justin. "Don't look so glum, little brother. You acquitted yourself well at Waterloo. You earned your spurs."

"But that's not the same as fighting in the Spanish Campaign?" There was a challenge in Justin's question.

"Spain is not something to boast about," replied Caspar easily. He crossed to the fireplace and threw the stub of his cheroot into the grate. "It's something most of us try to forget."

When he came back to the others, he was smiling faintly. "It's time," he said.

The duke looked at the clock on the mantel and let out a breath. "Yes," he said. "And I don't think my son-in-law likes to be kept waiting." He clasped Caspar's right hand. "All this talk of war makes me uneasy. You will be careful?"

"I'll be careful."

Justin was next. He said simply, "Good luck, Caspar."

With that, Caspar entered the conservatory and shut the door softly behind him.

There was a moment of silence, then the duke, uncharacteristically, threw one arm around his younger son's shoulders. "Why don't we repair to the library," he said, "and console ourselves with a bottle of my best cognac."

As they began to walk the length of the gallery, Justin said, "Father, what happened to Caspar in Spain?"

"Nothing," replied the duke, "nothing that did not happen to every soldier. It was just the war."

❧

Rosamund lay in her lonely bed and tossed restlessly from side to side. Some hours had passed since her quarrel with Richard and she wasn't feeling nearly as self-righteous as she had then. It was shock that had sharpened her tongue to a razor's edge. She didn't feel that she was in the wrong, though. What she wanted now was for them to sit down and talk about their differences like two rational, civilized people and reach a compromise.

She hauled herself up. Richard Maitland didn't know the meaning of the word *compromise*! She held on to that thought to keep her wrath warm, but as hard as she tried, her wrath gradually slipped away. He had never pretended to be something he was not. The misconception was all on her part. From the outset, she had known that his good name was his most prized possession. There were some lines in Shakespeare that expressed it better than she could; but she couldn't remember them word for word.

Then there was Lucy Rider.

You choose a woman who betrayed you over me?

She winced as her own words came back to her. How could she have been so unfeeling? "I'm sorry, Lucy," she said into the silence.

This was her wedding night. What was she doing here, tossing in her chaste bed when her husband—she savored the word—was probably doing the same thing in his lonely cottage? This wasn't how she'd imagined her wedding night would be, and neither had Richard. Whatever their differences, he didn't deserve this.

On that thought, she pushed back the covers, got up, and began to dress. Ten minutes later, she crept from the house and slowly made her way to Richard's cottage. There was no light shining from any window, and she imagined him tossing in his bed as she had tossed in hers. She felt very contrite when she used the key he had given her to unlock the door, and pushed inside.

"Richard?"

No answer. She knew at once something was wrong. The cottage was ice cold and there were no embers in the grate. She felt her way to the fireplace, found the tinderbox, and soon had a candle lit.

The bed was stripped bare, and there was nothing in that small room to show that someone had recently occupied it. She went quickly to the dresser and opened every drawer. They were all empty.

Heart thundering against her ribs, she went outside and crossed the cobbles to Harper's cottage. It was unlocked. When she entered it, she was met by the same frigid temperature that had met her in Richard's cottage.

Slowly now, in something of a daze, she retraced her steps to Richard's cottage and sat on one of the chairs.

He had left her without a word of farewell.

The villain had left her without a word of farewell! Maybe she had walked out on him before he had the chance to say anything, but he could have come after her, forced her to listen to reason. Something.

I'm going, you're staying.

"Hah!" she told the empty room. "That's all you know, Richard Maitland!"

He was going to London, he'd said, but had not told her where she could find him. It was obvious he did not trust her, obvious he did not think she could help him clear his name. After all they had been through together, he should know how capable she was.

Well, it just so happened that she had a house in London. She didn't have the keys yet, but she could stay at the Clarendon until the lawyers settled things. She'd

make Richard come to her, and then she would tell him
exactly what she thought of him. He was treating her as
though she were a useless ornament, something that had
to be left on the shelf because she was fragile, the kind
of woman, so he always said, he had no use for.

And now neither did she.

She walked back to the house, dry-eyed and with a
straight spine.

Chapter 22

George Withers was taken aback when Major Digby and Captain Whorsley were shown into his study. It had always been understood that they would meet on neutral ground—at one of the gentlemen's clubs or at social events. He didn't want anyone to get the impression that their connection was anything but casual.

On the surface, he was welcoming, but behind the mask, he was livid. Anything that connected him to Richard Maitland was a cause for alarm, and Digby was still in charge of the search for Maitland. Withers had done his part by advising Digby where to look and whom to interview, but he'd done it under the guise of a curious bystander who picked up interesting tidbits of gossip in his social circles and passed them along as any law-abiding citizen would. It worked two ways. Digby kept him informed on how the investigation was progressing, but it was done at a distance, and that's how he wanted to keep it.

For all the good it had done him. There was no progress, and that's what enraged him. Three weeks had gone by, and there was still no sign of Maitland. He wouldn't be lying idle, not the Richard Maitland he knew. Once before, he'd left a trail for Maitland to follow, and he'd bitterly regretted it. He'd be a fool not to learn from that lesson.

"Sit down, sit down," he said, indicating chairs.

As Digby and Whorsley seated themselves, he went to the window and looked out. It was late afternoon, and Bond Street was at its busiest. Carriages of every description slowly wended their way to either Oxford Street or Piccadilly. Well-dressed pedestrians strolled from shop to shop. He could not detect anyone or anything out of place, no one watching his door to see who might be visiting him.

Digby said, "No one saw us enter the building. We used the back door."

Withers fixed a smile on his face as he turned from the window. "I'm glad to hear it. Do you know, Major Digby, I'm beginning to regret that I ever got involved in this Maitland affair? I don't think I understood the kind of man we were dealing with. I've heard since that he deals brutally with anyone who betrays him—well, of course, we know that from the trial. I hope to God you've been discreet. I wouldn't want a man like that to think of me as an enemy."

There was a distinct edge to Digby's voice. "Rest easy, Mr. Withers. I never betray my sources, or those sources would soon dry up."

That's exactly what Withers wanted to hear. He looked at Whorsley, who vigorously shook his head. "We have many sources of information," he said, "and we keep all of them confidential."

"Anyone I know?"

Whorsley laughed at Wither's little joke. Digby remained stony-faced.

"You'll have refreshments?" Withers offered. "Coffee? Brandy?"

"Thank you, no," replied Digby.

Withers seated himself. "Then how may I help you?"

Digby breathed deeply. His face taut with anger, he said, "I have two days to find Maitland, and if I don't, I'll be replaced."

"That's absurd!" exclaimed Withers, and his shock was genuine.

"Nevertheless, that's what will happen. The deputy minister called me into his office not an hour ago and told me straight-out. They think I've bungled the job." Digby's right hand curled into a fist, as though he wanted to strike someone. "What they won't accept is that I've been ambushed by the very people who want to see results."

He began to suck air into his lungs as his anger mounted. "I begged them to bring Lady Rosamund in for questioning, and Harper, too, but Romsey has the minister's ear, and he insists that if they're to be questioned it must be at Twickenham and in the duke's presence."

"You think Lady Rosamund and this Harper may be concealing something?"

Digby gave a mirthless laugh. "Maitland did a masterly job of convincing the girl of his innocence. I think she may know more than she's saying. As for that turncoat Harper, I think he was in it up to his neck. He helped Maitland escape from Newgate, all right, but when he heard about the reward the duke was offering he saw a way to claim it and clear his name at the same time. I'm not surprised he's thrown himself on the duke's protection. I'll bet he's afraid to say too much in case Maitland catches up with him one of these fine days."

Withers nodded sympathetically. He'd already reached these conclusions independently, but, unlike

Digby, he didn't want Lady Rosamund to be questioned by the authorities. A week ago, he'd held the opposite view, but now he was worried. She was convinced of Maitland's innocence. What did she know? What could she possibly know?

He said, "I hear there was an attack on one of Lady Rosamund's guests the other night. Could that have been Maitland's doing?"

"Hardly. Prince Michael was the target. One presumes his assailant was a disenchanted countryman."

Withers had never had a high opinion of officers of the law or intelligence agents, but now their credit sank to a new low. At least he didn't have to worry that they were closing in on the boy.

"What about Hugh Templar?" he asked.

"Whorsley?" said Digby.

Whorsley cleared his throat. "He and his wife have retired to their estate in Oxfordshire. All aboveboard. We have him under surveillance, though, so if he puts a foot wrong, we'll be the first to know."

Withers nodded. He'd forgotten that Whorsley was there. He was the kind of character who faded into the background. No one really saw him. But he knew as much as Digby. If he decided to do something about the major, he'd have to include Whorsley.

He looked at Digby. "I appreciate your frankness, but I don't see what this has to do with me."

Digby seemed not to hear. He uncurled his hand and held it out. "I had Maitland in the palm of my hand," he said. His fingers closed and tightened. "But I was overtaken at the finishing post by Templar and Harper."

"You think they let Maitland get away on purpose?"

"They might, for old times' sake." Digby paused, then looked directly into Withers's eyes. "What I need is another Dunsmoor."

Withers's heart jumped. This is what he'd been afraid of. His connection to Richard Maitland was beginning to surface.

Digby went on, "I have no choice but to insist that you tell me who told you about Maitland's house."

Withers spread his hands. "I told you, I heard about it in one of my clubs. Does it matter?"

"It matters. I must have a name."

"Well . . ." Withers looked down at his hands and fixed a rueful expression on his face. He looked up at Digby. "I don't want to get anyone into trouble."

Digby clenched his teeth. "No one is going to get into trouble. What I need is information. If your friend knew about Dunsmoor, he may know where else I should look for Maitland. Good God, man, I've only got two days."

Withers shrugged helplessly. "I'd like to help, but this would be a betrayal. I won't give you my friend's name without his permission."

"Now, you listen to me!" Digby sat forward in his chair, his whole body tense. "We're talking about my career. If I don't find Maitland, I could end up in some godforsaken outpost at the end of the world. This is too important for niceties, do you understand?" He got up. "You have until eight this evening. You know where to find me. Bring your friend or bring me something to go on, but don't come empty-handed."

The implicit threat had Withers's blood surging to his face. No one had talked to him like this since he was a callow youth. Digby would pay for it, he promised himself. He would pay for his arrogance.

He forced down his temper, found his control, and said mildly, "Who else will be there?"

"Just Whorsley and I, so you can tell your friend no one but we three will ever know his identity."

After seeing his visitors out, Withers returned to his

study. He was breathing hard and his lips were pulled back in a savage grimace.

Everything was falling to pieces. He hadn't intended to hang on in London after Maitland was executed. He should have kept to his original plan and set sail for Charles Town. There would have been no tracks to cover then. He was beginning to feel trapped.

If the boy were here, he would be disappointed in him.

The thought gradually brought a measure of control. The boy looked up to him, thought he was invincible. But the boy was becoming a problem, too. He was getting too big for his boots, and he knew too much.

He breathed slowly and deeply. All he had to do was examine his problems one by one and the solutions would come to him: Lady Rosamund; Peter Dryden; Whorsley; Digby; the boy.

That was better. Eight o'clock in Digby's lodgings. And there would be no witnesses. This was one problem he would enjoy solving.

☙

As they strode along Bond Street toward Piccadilly, Whorsley said, "Do you really think a friend told him about Dunsmoor?"

"How else could he know about it? He hasn't been in England that long."

"Odd," said Whorsley carefully. "Very odd."

"What is?" demanded Digby, his patience thinning.

"Dunsmoor. That Withers should know about it when no one else did. I was wondering if, maybe, there's more to Withers than meets the eye."

Digby frowned. "It's too late to think about that now. We've only got two days to find Maitland. And just remember, if I'm posted to some godforsaken outpost, you'll be coming with me." He let out a long sigh.

"Look," he said, "let's get Maitland behind bars first, then we'll take a closer look at Mr. Withers."

❧

Later that same day, as dusk crept over the city, Richard and Caspar sat down to play a game of chess to while away the time until Harper got back. They were in the parlor of the suite of rooms they'd rented in the Black Friar, just off Covent Garden. Their first night in town they'd stayed at another inn, but Richard hadn't liked the layout of the rooms. There was no back exit, and if it came to the worst, he said, they would be caught like cattle in a pen.

Caspar was concentrating on the game, but Richard's mind was elsewhere and he wanted to talk.

"Tell me again," he said, "exactly what the landlord told you when you asked him about the night Lucy Rider was murdered."

Caspar looked up with a scowl. "Do you mind? I'm trying to think out my next move. Besides, I've already told you all I learned."

"Caspar, it's only a game. I can't believe you even bothered to pack it."

"It's a traveling set. It went with me all through the Spanish Campaign, and I saw no reason to leave it behind this time around."

Richard couldn't argue with that. Soldiers were often supersitious about such things. He wasn't exactly superstitious, but tucked into his boot was the hunting knife his father had given him on his fifteenth birthday. And there was the chess piece he'd kept and given to Rosamund on her birthday. He'd carried them with him all through the Spanish Campaign, too.

Caspar gave a sly smile and moved his queen's rook to support his knight for the attack on Richard's king. "Your move," he said. He was within three moves of winning the game.

"Not until you tell me what I want to know."

Caspar let out a breath, glowered at Richard, and folded his arms across his chest. Since Richard dared not show his face in the inn where Lucy Rider was murdered, Caspar had been given the job of questioning the landlord, which he had done that morning. There was nothing suspicious in this because the inn had been practically mobbed by curiosity-seekers since the trial, and the landlord seemed to relish his role as a celebrity.

"Poor Lucy," he'd said, then his face brightened. "But I can't complain about business. Now, what would you like to know, sir?" And he'd pocketed the sovereign Caspar had set on the table.

The sequence of events was exactly as the landlord had related at the trial, but Caspar had a question for him that had never been asked. "Who was first on the scene after the shot went off?"

"Mr. Frank Smith and his son," Caspar told Richard for the umpteenth time. "Or at least, they were among the first. The landlord ordered the boy out, thinking it scandalous that one of his tender years should witness such a gory crime."

"Was there blood on the boy's garments?"

"According to the landlord, it was hard not to get blood on you in that room, and the boy was right by the bed. Yes, there was blood on him, but the landlord thought nothing of it. He ordered the boy out and his father led him away."

"They were guests?"

"You know they were. I already told you. The father was a regular guest. This was the first time his son had accompanied him. But since the murder, they've never set foot in the inn and they left no forwarding address. We'll never trace them."

"Probably not, but I wish I'd known this before. It makes sense, don't you see? How did the man and the boy who were with me in the room manage to slip away unseen? Why did no one notice them leaving the hotel? Because they didn't slip away; they didn't leave the hotel. They were amongst the first on the scene. Then, when the landlord ordered them out, they simply walked back to their own room."

"Mmm," said Caspar. "It's possible, I suppose. But weren't they taking a chance? What if you hadn't lost consciousness?"

"There is that." Richard grinned. "It's just a theory at this stage of the game. But I think those two like taking chances."

"And you think the same thing happened after the attack on Miss Dryden, that whoever fired that shot simply walked back into the conservatory?"

"I'll reserve judgment on that until after I question Miss Dryden tomorrow."

He glanced at the chessboard, idly picked up his queen's knight and moved it to queen's knight six. "What about—"

Caspar cut him off. "I can't believe I missed that. This is a bloodbath! Where did you learn to play chess?"

Richard smiled. It wasn't often he felt superior to his glamorous brother-in-law. "Checkmate in two moves, I believe." He replaced Caspar's rook with his own knight and set the rook beside the pawns and knights he'd already captured. "In Spain. My teacher was our code breaker, you know, cryptographer. Nobody could beat him. Ordinary chess was too slow for him, so he changed the squares on the board to make it a faster game. Now, that game was worth playing. You see—"

He broke off when he heard a knock at the door.

"That will be Harper," said Caspar.

Richard answered the door with his pistol in his hand. It was Harper who entered, but not a Harper who was easily recognized. He was dressed in crimson livery, complete with immaculate white wig and white gloves. For their part, Richard and Caspar were dressed as professional men, well turned out, but not in the height of fashion.

"Were there any messages?" asked Richard.

"One."

Harper handed over the note he'd collected from Caspar's club in St. James. This was their way of keeping up with what was going on at Twickenham House, and if there were developments they should know about.

Richard broke the seal and quickly scanned it.

Caspar said laconically, "The last time someone opened and read my mail, I was a schoolboy at Eton."

"What?" Richard was absorbed in the note.

"My letter. I believe it has my name on it."

"A mere formality," replied Richard. "It's from Justin. He's in town, putting up at the Clarendon." He looked at Caspar. "And Rosamund is with him."

Caspar took the letter from him and read it. "She's come up to town to get her house ready for occupation."

"What house?" asked Richard, frowning.

"Didn't you know? She leased a house in Bloomsbury. That was before she became a married woman. It's very nice."

Richard nodded slowly. "Yes, I remember. The groom of the chambers said something to me, but it had slipped my mind."

"She won't come to any harm refurbishing the house. It will give her something to do, and Justin will look after her."

Richard made an effort to relax. "I suppose. All the same, I'd feel happier if she were in Twickenham. I don't want her to . . . ."

"To . . . what?"

"Get in the way, put herself in danger, I don't know." Richard smiled grimly. "I think I should pay a visit to my recalcitrant wife and find out what she's really up to."

Caspar laughed, but Richard was far from easy in his mind. This wasn't a child's game they were playing. In another hour, when it was dark, he was going to pay that long overdue call on Major Digby. Things were beginning to move and he wanted Rosamund well out of the way if and when the dam burst.

When Harper moaned, his companions quickly got up. "What is it?" asked Caspar urgently.

Harper held out his left hand. His white glove was spotted with the Madeira he'd been pouring from the decanter into a glass. Harper liked his Madeira almost as much as he liked his beer.

"Is that all?" asked Richard, and he began to laugh.

"I don't have another pair," replied Harper with a pained expression. "Oh, you may well laugh, but Mr. Templar and me, we caught a killer because he didn't know how important white gloves is to a manservant. I'll have to wash them stains out or everyone will know I'm an imposter."

He was still at it when Richard and Caspar left to go to Digby's lodgings. Richard insisted that he and only he would show his face to Digby. He was grateful for Caspar's help, as he had no hesitation in admitting to his brother-in-law, but there was no sense in having the authorities out for Caspar's blood, too. He could be transported to the colonies for aiding and abetting a felon, if not worse.

After this little speech, Caspar clapped his hand on Richard's shoulder and squeezed. "Who says you're not charming?" he said, and laughed when Richard glared at him.

When their hackney drew level with Digby's lodgings, they saw a number of men milling around outside. "Bow Street runners," said Richard. "I recognize one of them. Officer Rankin." Then to the driver, "Drive on and pull up at the corner."

Caspar, who had nothing to lose if he was recognized by the runners, walked back to the house to find out what was going on. He returned in a few minutes and climbed into the hackney before saying anything.

"It's Digby and Whorsley," he said. He sounded shaken. "They've both been murdered. Whorsley was shot in the head, and Digby's throat was cut. There's more. The body of a young boy, an adolescent, was found in the garden. His throat was cut, too. They don't know who he is."

A shaft of pure energy shot through Richard's brain. Questions and impressions followed each other in quick succession.

"What do we do now?" asked Caspar.

"We get Rosamund."

❧

"I don't know how many times I have to say it," declared Rosamund. "I am not going home to Twickenham, and that's final."

There were five of them crowded around the little table, eating a late supper in Richard's rooms in the Black Friar, Rosamund and Justin having now been added to the group. Richard and Rosamund had eyes only for each other. Everyone else was concentrating on the food on the table.

"I hate brussels sprouts," said Justin, just for something to say to break the awkward silence that had fallen.

"Try the salad," suggested his brother. "It's very good."

"Salad with beef stew?" Justin made a face. "They don't go together."

"Then have a slice of bread," Harper interjected rudely.

Justin accepted the proffered bread, dipped it in his stew, then happily chewed on it.

Harper was amazed. That's how he usually ate his bread, but in this exalted company, he'd been trying to mind his manners. He gave a huge grin, reached for a slice of bread, tore off a piece, and followed Justin's example.

Richard said, "Digby and Whorsley were both murdered tonight. I think the person who murdered them is the one who set me up. And the boy, well, I think he may be the murderer's accomplice. Maybe they quarreled, or maybe the boy outlived his usefulness. But you see the kind of person we're dealing with?"

"I understand," said Rosamund quietly. "But I have no connection to any of them. There's no danger to me."

She was surprised at how calm she sounded, considering that her nerves were shot to pieces. She'd had the fright of her life when Richard and Caspar had entered her bedchamber at the Clarendon, like two stealthy panthers on the prowl. She'd thought they were intruders and would have screamed if Richard had not pounced on her and put a hand over her mouth. Her second fright came when Richard told her about Digby, Whorsley, and the boy. She wasn't frightened for herself but for Richard, frightened and sick at heart. She had known there was evil in the world, but it had never come this close to her before. She'd known Digby and Whorsley.

If she went home to Twickenham, she would never have a moment's peace, wondering about Richard and what he was up to. She hadn't asked to be brought to the Black Friar, but here she was and here she was determined to stay.

"You can't stay here," said Richard. "I'm a danger to anyone who associates with me. And I don't want you in London. I can't be distracted, and I *will* be distracted if I have to worry about you."

"You think Twickenham is safe?" She picked up her fork, looked at the food on her plate, and put her fork down again. "Have you forgotten what happened to Prudence?"

Caspar sighed. "This is all very interesting," he said,

"but some of us would like to eat our dinner. May I suggest you take your quarrel somewhere else?"

Richard got up, snagged Rosamund's wrist, and half dragged her out of the room.

Justin shook his head. Barely above a whisper, he said, "If they're like this at the start of their marriage, what will they be like in a year or two?"

Harper said, "They'll be cooing like turtledoves in no time at all."

Justin looked skeptical. "How would you know, Harper, a crusty old bachelor like yourself?"

"I don't know what gave you that idea," said Harper indignantly. "I've had three wives in my time, all without benefit of clergy, mind, and I know the signs. Does anyone want that last slice of bread?"

❧

He dragged her to a small chamber with a narrow bed, a dresser, a chair, and little else. The curtains were not drawn and the only light came from lanterns in the courtyard. The fire was not lit.

He shut the door with a bang, leaned against it, and pinned her with his hands on her shoulders. He was breathing hard, and the flickering light cast harsh shadows on his face.

"Rosamund," he said, making the word part plea, part rebuke.

She took his hands from her shoulders and cupped them around her cheeks. Tears leaked from her eyes. "I'm sorry about that stupid quarrel," she said. "You were right and I was wrong. I should have known better. It's just that if anything happened to you, I don't know how I would survive. But I never, *never* want us to part with foolish, angry words between us. Life is too short for that."

All the arguments he had marshaled to persuade her

to listen to reason went clean out of his head. He muttered something savage under his breath, then his lips
were on hers and his arms wrapped around her, bringing
her flush against him, as though he could fuse their
bodies into one.

There was no end to it, he thought: the killing, the hatred, the ugliness in men's souls. He felt sullied by it, because he was part of it. Rosamund was like the pure
springwater that was to be found in the Highlands of
Scotland. When he immersed himself in her, he felt
cleansed.

The same need that drove him drove her. When she
was in his arms, the world seemed to retreat, and all its
ugliness with it. There was comfort here, and strength to
face whatever might come.

They couldn't get close enough. Still locked together, they took the few paces to the bed and tumbled
onto it.

He rose above her, his eyes straining to see her. She
was beautiful, he thought, her dark hair spread on his
pillow, her finely boned features like pale marble in that
dim light. He lifted her hair with one hand and let it run
through his fingers. She was beautiful, and brave and
generous. He knew he didn't deserve her, but he could
no more give her up than he could willingly give up the
air he breathed.

When she slid her hands up the strong muscles of his
back, desire began to tighten his body. She arched when
his mouth opened on her throat. He tasted her scent,
something flowery and uniquely Rosamund, and breathing became difficult. He filled his hands and his mouth
with her velvety softness, then sucked her little cries of
arousal into his mouth. He wasn't aware that she'd un-
done the buttons on his shirt until her hands slid over
his bare flesh.

He came out of that embrace like a drowning man
coming up for air. He had brought her here for a

purpose. They had to talk. But Rosamund hadn't finished with him yet. Her fingers were undoing the closure on his trousers. She was hitching up her skirts and spreading her legs to take him.

"This won't make me change my mind," he said fiercely.

She looked up at him, her face stricken. When she finally found her voice, it was husky. "You think I would use this to . . . to control you?"

She pushed at his shoulders, trying to free herself from his embrace, but he refused to budge.

"I'm sorry," he said. "I'm a clod and everyone knows it." He kissed her swiftly. "You should have married someone else, someone who understands women. I'm hopeless."

The hands that were pushing him away now tightened on his shoulders. "Don't talk like that!" she cried. "You're not a clod. You're not hopeless. You're decent, and brave, and the most honorable man I know."

"I'm also on the brink of insanity. Rosamund, let me?"

He brushed her skirts aside, adjusted her underclothes, and pushed her knees high. Eyes locked on hers, he guided his sex to her body and slowly entered her. Gasping his name, she moved against him in involuntary response.

"Ah, Rosamund," he breathed out.

He held himself in check, gritting his teeth with the effort. He didn't want their pleasure to end. He loved to feel her go wild for him, loved to feel those tiny tremors shake her body just before he brought her to climax.

His movements were slow, easy, tantalizing, drawing out the pleasure until the ache was almost unbearable. When she gave that little keening cry he was coming to recognize, he let himself go. Unfettered now, he drove into her, thrusting, plunging, riding her hard and fast. He could hear her gasps of pleasure, feel her muscles straining as she met his frenzied rhythm. And at the last, her cry of release as he emptied himself into her.

৯৯

She stirred first. "Of all the underhanded, deceitful tricks I've come across, that takes the prize. 'I'm a clod. I'm hopeless,' " she mimicked. "You said that to distract me!"

The bed was so narrow that he was still half sprawled over her. There was a stupid grin on his face. "It was worth it just to hear your rebuttal." He raised his head. "I'm not going to let you take back one word of what you said." He paused, then hesitantly, "Did you mean what you said?"

Richard Maitland unsure of himself was oddly seductive. "Every blessed word," she assured him, and slowly smiled.

A sudden burst of masculine laughter emanating from the parlor made them both look at the door.

Rosamund sighed. "We should get back to the others."

"No." He tilted her face up and kissed her softly. "I don't know what tomorrow will bring. I don't want to talk about it. I don't want to think about it. Just for a little while, I want to imagine that we're two ordinary people. I want a little time for ourselves."

"So do I," she said fervently.

He got up and adjusted his clothes. "Can you light the fire?"

"If there's a tinderbox."

"On the mantel."

"Where are you going?"

"To get wine and glasses. After all, this is our belated wedding night."

When he walked into the parlor, all conversation came to an abrupt halt. "Rosamund and I still have to iron out our differences," he said.

No response.

Three pairs of eyes followed him as he walked to the sideboard, picked up the decanter of Madeira and two clean glasses, and walked out.

Harper was the first to speak. "Turtledoves," he said. "I told you so."

Chapter 23

*I*t was Justin who went back to Twickenham, though he was loath to go in case he missed anything, and he vowed to be back by nightfall. He was to inform the duke of the murders at Digby's lodgings and bring him abreast of things, especially Rosamund's inclusion in their group. Richard had given up trying to persuade her to go home with Justin, but he was adamant about keeping her out of the investigation. She could stay, but only on sufferance, and at the first sign of trouble, he would send her packing.

She couldn't come and go as she pleased, either. If she went out, Harper was to go with her, and Harper was in charge. What he said went.

"I mean it, Rosamund," Richard said. "He's an old soldier. He can smell trouble a mile off."

"I'm not going to give him any trouble," she protested. "I told you. I've arranged to call on Callie today. We're spending the morning shopping for drapes and upholstery for the house. I thought we had settled this. I thought we agreed that there's no danger to me."

He had agreed on no such thing, but he couldn't win that argument because it was based on vague misgivings.

"Look," she said, "if it makes you feel better, I'll send round a note and cancel the outing."

He let out a long breath. He couldn't keep her locked up forever, and an outing with Callie seemed harmless enough. "Be on your guard," he said. "Don't say anything that could lead anyone to think you know where I am. And remember, what Harper says goes."

Shortly after this exchange, Richard and Caspar left for St. Mark's in Chelsea, where they hoped to interview Prudence Dryden and her brother, the vicar. Harper sat down at the table with an array of pistols in front of him, which he proceeded to check and clean. It was too early to go to Callie's, so Rosamund occupied herself by tidying things away. She came across Caspar's chess set on the sideboard and idly began to move the pieces around.

If these pawns could talk, she thought, *who knows what they might say?* They were shuffled around from square to square, with no conception of the larger picture. She and the pawns had much in common.

Who was winning the game, Richard or his nemesis?

Hard on that thought came a wave of determination. She wasn't a pawn. She was a queen, and a queen didn't sit back when her king was in danger. She found a chink in the enemy's armor and went on the attack.

Maybe she didn't understand her enemy's strategy, but she knew bits and pieces of it, and that's where she would begin.

Her mind went back and forth, sifting through what seemed to be unrelated facts. She picked up the black king and tried to visualize Richard's movements the night Lucy was killed. She moved on and came to Newgate. That's when she had come into the picture, and how glad she was that she had. She couldn't imagine a world now without Richard.

She stopped right there, just staring at the board.

Something about Newgate had always bothered her. What was it? Completely focused now, she began to set pieces out to represent all the characters who had been present in the Felons' Quadrangle that day. She moved them around as the sequence of events unfolded.

Prisoner escaped! Lock up the prison! the guard had cried.

She saw turnkeys trying to pry visitors from inmates so that they could take the prisoners back to their cells. Callie was on her feet crying that nobody ever escaped from Newgate. Tell that to Richard! He was coming right for her. She tumbled over the basket; a shot rang out and Richard fell on top of her.

She went through the sequence again, then she had it, the niggling thought at the back of her mind that had eluded her. Before the shot was fired, there was no panic. And the turnkeys had their backs to her as they separated visitors from inmates. So a panicked turnkey had not fired that shot.

"Harper," she said.

He looked up. "What?"

"Who fired that shot? I mean, when we were all in the Felons' Quadrangle and you and Richard were trying to escape from Newgate?"

"I suppose one of the turnkeys panicked and fired the shot."

"But there was no panic, not until *after* the shot was fired. And the turnkeys' backs were to us."

He scratched his chin. "It must have been one of the turnkeys. Who else could it have been?"

"I suppose you're right, but . . ."

"But what?"

It didn't fit in with the way she'd positioned the pieces on the chessboard. Then who fired the shot? Richard had accused her of signaling an accomplice, but, of course, there was no accomplice. She remembered something else. Charles Tracey had become separated from them. He was in a corner of the quadrangle with the other prisoners, with his hands in the air.

"Well," said Harper, losing patience, "are you going to tell me who fired that shot or not?"

"I don't know," she said, "but I'm going to find out."

His voice rife with suspicion, he said slowly, "And how, may I ask, are you going to do that?"

"We're going to Newgate," she said, "and we'll ask Mr. Proudie, the keeper. Maybe he knows."

❧

Harper thought he must want his head examined. He'd hoped never to set foot inside Newgate again, yet here he was, like a brainless stuffed doll, waiting in the hallway of the keeper's house while Mr. Proudie entertained Lady Rosamund in the parlor.

It wasn't really a house, just a suite of rooms near the main entrance, but getting in and out was a major undertaking. The doors were locked and guarded by two turnkeys. He knew he had nothing to fear from Proudie or the turnkeys even if they recognized him. After all, he'd been exonerated of all wrongdoing. It was just Newgate itself. It gave him the shudders.

He'd tried explaining all this to Lady Rosamund, but had she listened? Not her. She'd got this bee in her bonnet. They had to find out who fired that shot, though what good it would do them was more than he could see.

He should have put his foot down, but that was his major failing. Any woman who put her mind to it could wrap him round her little finger. That's why he gave the ladies a wide berth. His friends all thought he was a woman-hater, when he was just the opposite. He was putty in their hands. Women was nothing but trouble!

Hugh Templar's wife came to mind. "Open the door, Harper," she'd begged, and against his better judgment, he'd opened the door and got them both damn near killed. Jason Radley's wife was another. She'd sweet-talked him into taking her to Hampstead, and look what they'd found when they got there! And now Lady Rosamund.

He didn't know what his chief would say when he found out.

The door opened and Lady Rosamund swept out, followed by the keeper. "You may be sure, Mr. Proudie, my father shall hear of this. Your conduct was above reproach, and I shall tell him so."

"And His Grace will put in a good word for me with the governors?"

"You may depend upon it." Then to Harper, "Come along, ehm, James."

When they were outside, Harper drew in a long, refreshing breath. He'd never thought much about the air he breathed until he'd spent time as a turnkey in Newgate. London air wasn't the freshest, but compared to Newgate, it was as sweet as ether.

As they crossed the road to their waiting hackney, he said, "What kept you?"

"Mr. Proudie," she said. "The poor man's position is coming under review and he thinks he may be turned off because you and Richard escaped from Newgate. I promised to speak to my father on his behalf."

"And will you?"

"I said I would, didn't I?"

Harper smiled. That was one thing he liked about Lady Rosamund. She never reneged on a promise.

She waited until they were in the hackney and on their way to Mrs. Tracey's house in Manchester Square before she told him what she'd found out. "Proudie thinks that you or Richard fired that shot. Of course, I couldn't tell him that he was mistaken, so I asked him

why he was so sure." She spoke eagerly, falling over her
words in her haste to tell him everything. "It seems that
when a shot is fired in the prison, there's always a report
written up about it. None of the turnkeys' weapons was
fired; the prisoners don't have pistols and the turnkeys
had surrounded them and their visitors anyway, so they
know the shot didn't come from them. You see what this
means?"

"Well, I sees the way your mind is working. You're
thinking that leaves five people who could have fired the
shot, and we knows it wasn't Colonel Maitland or me or
you, so we're down to two, your friend Mrs. Tracey and
her brother-in-law."

"Charles Tracey," said Rosamund, her eyes glowing.

"Now, don't go jumping to no conclusions. Things
ain't always what they seems."

"I'm sure it was him."

"Why not Mrs. Tracey?" he argued doggedly. He felt
uneasy with her quick leaps of logic, and he wondered
where all this was leading.

Her lips flattened. "Callie wouldn't shoot at Richard.
She truly believes in his innocence. Besides, I was between Callie and Richard, so she couldn't have hit him
even if she wanted to. She would have hit me. But
Charles Tracey could have done it."

"Then what happened to Tracey's pistol?"

"I don't know. But after the shot went off, everyone
panicked. In the confusion, he could have slipped it into
his pocket, couldn't he?"

Harper shook his head. "Why bother? Why not take
credit for the shot? He would have been hailed as a hero
if he'd shot the chief and stopped him getting away.
There was no need to hide his pistol."

"I've thought of that." In her eagerness to convince
him, she put her hand on his arm. "Maybe he didn't
want anyone asking awkward questions. Maybe he's tied
to Richard in some way. No, listen to me, Harper.

There's something about Charles Tracey that doesn't sit right with me. Last year, his brother, James, died in a bizarre accident—that's what the doctor called it, bizarre. James Tracey was a moderate drinker, but he died alone, choking on his own vomit, after drinking a bottle of brandy. Aunt Fran thought the death was more than bizarre, she said it was suspicious, but she was distraught, so we really didn't take her seriously. But guess who got most of the money?"

Harper groaned. "Charles Tracey," he answered as though the name was dragged out of him.

Rosamund nodded. "Yes. Callie got her widow's portion and that was all. There's something else. Charles is in love with Callie. Oh, I know no good can come of it. He can never marry his brother's widow. But what if he got rid of his brother just so he could have her all to himself? Not that it worked. I think Callie despises him."

"What in the name of all that's holy," said Harper slowly and patiently, "has this to do with the chief?"

"Well, I don't know yet. I'm hoping Callie will be able to help me, or Aunt Fran."

Harper was horrified. "You can't just go in there and start insinuating that Tracey is a murderer."

"I know better than that! I'll be very discreet. I'm not really interested in James Tracey's death unless Richard is involved in some way. Maybe, before he died, James spoke to Richard about something. Maybe Charles was afraid Richard would start investigating. I don't really know. But there's something not right here, Harper. I can feel it. If Charles Tracey tried to kill Richard in Newgate, there must be a reason for it."

This was the time to put his foot down, thought Harper. On the other hand, she had a point. There was no getting round the fact that someone had let off a shot in Newgate. If it wasn't a panicked turnkey, who else could it have been but Charles Tracey? And why conceal it?

"You'll be careful?" he said.

"Word of honor."

"At the first sign of trouble—"

"I'll scream for you. But nothing's going to happen, Harper. If Charles is there, I'll keep my lips sealed." Her hand tightened on his arm and she went on appealingly, "If I don't do this, no one will. Richard can't show his face in Callie's house. It was the same at Newgate. Richard may not like it, but he has to depend on his friends now."

After this little speech, Harper was completely won over. It wasn't that women wrapped him round their little fingers, he decided. Sometimes they spoke a good deal of sense.

❧

Peter Dryden's study was as comfortable and as shabby as its owner. Books were piled on the floor and every available surface was strewn with papers. He seemed not to notice. It was the same with his clothes. His neckcloth was askew and the buttons on his waistcoat were at odds with the buttonholes. And none of that mattered a damn, thought Richard, because of the man himself. He was an innocent, in the best sense of the word, a worldly innocent who had seen the worst in men but never gave up on them.

"That's when my correspondence with Frank Stapleton's cousin stopped," Dryden said. "When I went to Liverpool and became chaplain in one of the prisons there. It was just one of those things. He moved, I moved, and we lost touch with each other."

They were waiting for Prudence Dryden to return from a walk with Dryden's wife and their three small children. Richard couldn't help thinking how lucky this bald-pated, bespectacled cleric was. He didn't have much money, but he was rich in everything that mattered.

He hadn't known what kind of reception he would receive when he arrived at Dryden's door unannounced. Dryden might have threatened to go to the magistrates or yelled for help. He need not have worried. Prudence Dryden had not exaggerated. Her brother was staunchly in his camp. The ice had been broken when they'd both admitted that the years had made such a difference that they wouldn't have known each other. They'd both filled out, and Richard's blond hair had faded to a streaky brown, while the vicar had lost his hair entirely.

Richard saw no point in prevarication, so he'd told Dryden straight out that he thought there might be a connection between that long-ago incident at Cambridge and Lucy Rider's murder, and Dryden had reciprocated by answering all his questions frankly and without fuss.

"You'll have another sherry?" said Dryden, breaking into Richard's thoughts.

Richard demurred, but Caspar, who had stationed himself at the window that overlooked the garden, allowed his glass to be topped up.

When Dryden seated himself, Richard said, "You never wrote to Frank Stapleton directly?"

"No. He wasn't my friend. George was. But I was always interested to hear how Frank was doing, and he did very well until that tragic accident took his life."

As they sipped their drinks, Richard went over in his mind what he'd learned from Dryden. Frank Stapleton had left England right after the Cambridge incident and had been taken under the wing of an older cousin, George Withers, who was doing very well for himself in the fur trade in Canada. Frank also had done well, but mainly because he'd married the daughter of one of the richest independent fur traders in Upper Canada. Then tragedy struck. Mrs. Stapleton and her father died in a boating accident, and Frank had inherited a tidy sum.

It wasn't the only tragic accident to have touched Frank's life. His father had died in a house fire just before Frank embarked for Canada. Maybe someone had begun to think that so many "accidents" were highly suspect. Maybe that's why Frank Stapleton had conveniently died in a house fire as well.

Richard said, "Who inherited Frank's estate?"

"George, I suppose," answered Dryden. "He never said. But I know that there were no other close relatives. That was why George felt it was his duty to offer Frank a home. There was more to it than that, though. Frank had always been difficult, was always getting into scrapes. George blamed Frank's father for being too hard on him. He thought Canada would be the making of his cousin."

"And was it?"

The vicar thought for a moment. "Well, Frank prospered. There's no doubt about that. George didn't say too much, but I always got the impression that Frank was a disappointment to him. I can't say I was surprised. George was the kind of person who was very easily taken advantage of. He wanted to go into the church at one time, you know. That's how we met. My father tutored him in Greek. But there wasn't the money to send him to university, so he went to Canada instead."

Richard nodded. Everything was falling into place. George Withers was too trusting for his own good, and his cousin was as trustworthy as a scorpion. Maybe George had become suspicious, maybe he'd started asking awkward questions. For whatever reason, Frank had decided to get rid of him and take his place. Then he could have George's fortune and inherit his own as well.

He said, "When did you last hear from your friend?"

"Mmm? Oh, he wrote to tell me about Frank's death. He seemed very despondent. He said he would stay for the funeral then start over somewhere else, somewhere like Georgia. The winters in Canada were too harsh for him, you see. That must have been about ten years ago."

Dryden went on, "That was the last letter I received, but he's here in England. In town, in fact. It was the strangest coincidence. Prudence met him in Mrs. Tracey's house, not three, four days ago. He said he was in England for business reasons, then he'd be returning to Charles Town. The odd thing is, he didn't seem to know me. I don't think he wants to renew the acquaintance. I must have written something in that last letter to offend him. I'm afraid I wasn't always charitable about Frank. But I can't leave things like this. I must make the effort to make amends, even if he snubs me."

"Was Lady Rosamund there?"

"Of course. There would be no reason for Prudence to be there without her." Dryden gave a wry smile. "And that fellow was there, too, the one who let you get away. Major Digby, is it not?"

At the mention of Digby's name, Caspar turned from the window and Richard's head came up. They exchanged a long look, then Richard looked at Peter Dryden.

"Listen to me carefully," he said. "Last night, Major Digby was murdered along with a colleague and an unidentified boy. Lucy Rider was murdered and someone shot at your sister. I believe that all these attacks are connected to George Withers."

He realized he'd been too abrupt when all the color washed out of Dryden's face. Moderating his voice, he went on, "I'm sorry to be so blunt, but I believe you may be in some danger. If you're wise, you'll forget about approaching George Withers. You should take your family and go into hiding for a few days. Don't tell anyone where you're going, and don't come back here until you read in the papers that George Withers has been arrested for murder."

If Dryden was shocked before, now he was dumbfounded. He blinked rapidly as he struggled to find words. "You can't think George murdered all these people? He wouldn't! He couldn't! If you knew him, you'd know how absurd that sounds."

Richard got up. "I don't think George Withers murdered anyone. I think your friend died ten years ago in that house fire and Frank Stapleton stole his identity and all his worldly goods. I believe the business he came to England for is me."

Caspar said quietly, "That's quite a stretch, Richard, isn't it? I mean, I'm willing to accept that George Withers is who you say he is, but there's nothing to tie him to you, except Cambridge, of course, and that happened a long time ago."

Richard was too impatient to argue what was patently clear to him. "I'll reserve judgment on that until after I speak to George Withers."

Peter Dryden wasn't convinced. "What about his last letter?" he said. "George was staying for the funeral. Frank couldn't show his face at his own funeral. Everyone would recognize him."

"He lied and the letter was forged," Richard said.

"Then why write to me at all?"

"So that you wouldn't become suspicious. If George had disappeared without a trace, you would have made inquiries, wouldn't you? Then the authorities would have become involved, and Frank didn't want that."

Dryden wasn't finished yet. "But . . . but to come back to England as George Withers. Wouldn't someone recognize him?"

"Did you recognize me or I you when we met today for the first time in seventeen years? And I think Frank Stapleton would take some pains to make sure that he wasn't recognized. But there are other ways of recognizing a man. A shared history. Memories. A long correspondence. The last thing Frank Stapleton wants is to meet you in person. That's why you may be a danger to him."

Caspar suddenly exclaimed, "What the devil is Rosamund doing here?"

Richard quickly crossed to the window and looked out. Two young women had entered the garden by the back gate. There were three children with them, and their gales of laughter carried to the open window.

"It's not Rosamund," he said. "It's someone who could pass for her at a distance."

Or in the ill-lit gardens of Twickenham House.

"It's Miss Dryden," said Caspar.

A moment before, Richard had felt the thrill of the chase. It was all becoming clear to him, and very soon he would catch up with the devil who had caused him so much heartache. But as he watched Prudence Dryden approach the house, he felt tremors of alarm ripple through him. Like Rosamund, Miss Dryden was tall and dark-haired, and on the night of the attack she was wearing a shawl, just as she was wearing a shawl now. Most of the ladies had worn some kind of wrap that night, including Rosamund.

His mind was buzzing with questions when Dryden called his sister into the study. He was aware that the usual greetings were exchanged, that Peter Dryden was explaining why they were there, but he was impatient for answers and he cut Peter off in mid-sentence.

"Miss Dryden," he said, "I want you to think about the night you were attacked. Who was first on the scene after the shot was fired? Take your time. Think about it. You were on the ground. Prince Michael helped you up. Whom did you see?"

She glanced nervously at her brother, then looked at Richard again. "There was quite a crowd," she said, hesitating over her words. "I remember Prince Michael ordering them back."

He tried to relax, tried to make his expression un-
threatening. "Is there anyone who stands out in your
memory?"

She nodded and flashed a smile. "Mrs. Tracey, Lady
Rosamund's friend. She thought I was Rosamund and
shrieked Rosamund's name, so of course everybody
thought Rosamund had been hit. Poor woman. She got
quite a fright. Her brother-in-law came up then and led
her away."

"Thank you," said Richard.

When they were outside, Caspar said, "Where to
now?"

"Mrs. Tracey's house in Manchester Square."

૨⚭

When Rosamund arrived at Callie's house, she suffered a disappointment. Callie was not there, but Charles
Tracey was, so of course she could not ask Aunt Fran all
the personal questions she was burning to ask.

"Oh, dear," said Aunt Fran in response to Rosamund's
query. "Callie couldn't remember whether you were to
meet here or at your house. So she went to your house.
She said if you were to come here, I was to tell you."

"That I'm to meet her at my house?"

A look of confusion came over Aunt Fran's face. "I
think so."

"I'll take you, if you like," said Charles.

When he took a step toward her, she backed away.
"That won't be necessary," she said quickly. "I have a
hackney waiting."

Much to her alarm, he followed her out. "Lady
Rosamund," he said, "please wait."

But she didn't wait. She went tearing down the stairs.
He caught up to her on the landing. He captured her
arm, checked her movement, and turned her to face him.

"Charles," she said, trying to sound natural, "what is
the meaning of this?"

He let go of her arm at once. "It's all over Whitehall," he said. "Major Digby was murdered last night, along with Whorsley and some young boy. I thought you should know—that is, if you don't know already."

She was silent, staring at him, trying to read his expression in the landing's half-light. She wondered how old he was. Richard's age or maybe a year or two younger? She wondered which university he'd attended.

His eyes narrowed on her. "Aren't you afraid?" His voice was barely above a whisper. "I know I would be if I were you."

And suddenly she was afraid, mortally afraid. With a little sob, she turned and tore down the stairs, to Harper and safety.

Chapter 24

When she told Harper about her encounter with Charles Tracey on the stairs, he was skeptical.

"He ain't following us," he said. He was looking out the little window at the back of their hackney.

"No, but he knows where we're going."

Harper patted the pistol that was tucked into the waistband of his trousers. "If he turns up, I'll take care of him. I have another in my pocket." He felt in his pocket and produced another pistol. "I could let you have it, if you like."

Rosamund's nose wrinkled. "Harper, it's so big, I don't think my wrist could take its weight. And what would Mrs. Tracey say if I appeared with that monstrosity?"

"She'd be frightened?"

"She'd laugh herself silly! Why do you need two guns anyway?"

"In case my shot misses and I don't have time to

reload." He frowned down at the pistol he'd offered Rosamund. "The first chance I gets," he said, "I'm going to get you one of them dainty French pieces that a lady can hide in her reticule."

As he pocketed his spare pistol, Rosamund took a moment to study him. Harper didn't look like much, but he was sterling. A little tarnished around the edges, perhaps, but sterling all the same. He was still skeptical about Charles Tracey, but he wouldn't take any chances. She couldn't ask for more than that.

When they came to the gates of the house, they paid off the hackney.

"You go on," Harper said. "I'll wait here, out of sight, and if Tracey shows up, I'll send him packing."

"I won't be long."

She entered the grounds by the wicket gate, and struck out along the drive. Just being here lifted her spirits. It seemed as though all the ugliness in the world had been locked out of this small acreage of paradise. She could imagine children playing on the long stretch of turf, and horses gamboling in the pasture, or feeding in their stalls in the stable. She and Richard would take long walks through the woods that edged their property, and count their blessings.

If only . . .

When she reached the house, she found the front door unlocked, and that surprised her. She supposed that the caretaker had forgotten to lock it after he let Callie in, that's if Aunt Fran had given her the right message and Callie was here.

"Callie?" she called out. "Callie?"

A moment later, Callie appeared at the turn in the stairs. "What kept you?" she asked. "I'd almost given up on you."

"I was delayed. Where's the caretaker? He left the front door open."

"I think he went to the stables to fix window frames or

something. I'm in the rose salon. I've purloined a decanter of sherry. I hope you don't mind."

The question was rhetorical. Callie drifted away and
Rosamund went up the stairs after her. Richard would
like this house, she thought. It was solid, unpretentious,
and somewhat old-fashioned, just like him, and she wondered if that's what had attracted her to the house in the
first place.

In the rose salon, Callie was at one of the long windows, a glass of sherry in her hand. She made an arresting picture in her plum-colored pelisse against the rose
velvet drapes. Light filtered through the window, gilding
her delicate features and the line of her throat.

She turned with a smile. "I see you came alone. I
wasn't sure if you would. No ducal carriage, no footmen,
no Miss Dryden. I'm impressed."

"Miss Dryden has gone to her brother's place to convalesce."

"So I heard. This is better anyway, just we two on our
own. Help yourself to a sherry." She nodded to the decanter and crystal glass on a table at one end of the bro-
cade sofa.

Rosamund did not have time for sherry. She came
straight to the heart of the matter. "I went to Newgate today, to talk to the keeper, and I learned something interesting." She breathed deeply. "Do you remember that
a shot was fired the morning we were all there?"

Callie took a sip of sherry. "Oh, yes, I remember it
well."

"The keeper told me it wasn't fired by one of the
turnkeys, or any of the inmates or their visitors. I know
that Richard . . . Maitland," she belatedly added, "didn't
fire it, or Harper or me. You see what this means?"

Callie sighed. "It means that either I fired the shot or
Charles did."

Rosamund was surprised at how quickly Callie
grasped the logistics of the situation. She'd thought she

might have to draw her a map. "Yes," she said, "and I think Charles tried to kill Richard Maitland."

This was greeted with a trill of laughter. "Charles?" said Callie, and laughed again. "Charles couldn't shoot a rabid dog if his life depended on it. He doesn't have the gumption."

"Then who fired the shot?"

"Who do you think?"

After a long silence, Rosamund shook her head. "Not you, Callie. That doesn't make sense. Besides, I was between you and Richard. The shot would have hit me."

"No. You fell over the basket, giving me a clear shot at Maitland, and I took it. I must have missed him by a hair."

Rosamund was speechless. When she began to stutter, Callie cut her off.

"That was my mission of mercy. I went to Newgate with the express purpose of killing Richard Maitland or giving him the chance to end his own life."

Rosamund sank down on the nearest chair. The words were torn from her. "But why?"

Callie was distinctly amused. "If you had listened to me when I told you about Maitland's trial, you would know. I watched him day after day. Didn't I tell you that he was magnificent? Death held no fears for him. His disdain for his accusers, the prosecuting counsel, the trial itself—well, you can tell that he made quite an impression on me. I did not think that a man so far above the common run deserved to die a felon's death. So I made up my mind to help him out of his predicament. I would have left my pistol with him. You see, I was convinced he would have chosen a hero's death to hanging. But fate intervened."

"What pistol?" demanded Rosamund.

"The pistol that was hidden in my muff."

Callie moved one of the drapes aside and pointed to her bonnet and white rabbit-skin muff on the window seat, the same muff she'd had with her the day they visited Newgate.

Rosamund stared blindly at the muff, unwilling to accept what Callie had told her. Callie would dare the devil just for the thrill of it—how many times had she thought that?—but risqué masqued balls and balloon rides were a far cry from shooting a man in cold blood. She couldn't accept it.

"You're not saying this to protect Charles?" she asked.

Callie tossed off the last of her sherry and went to the decanter to pour herself another. "Charles!" she said disparagingly. "He's a weak-kneed woman. He knew I was going to leave my pistol with Maitland. I told him what I intended to do. Here was his chance to impress me with his dash and daring. And what did he do? He tried to put obstacles in my way. You remember how reluctant he was to go to Newgate, how he whined about the rioters? As I said, a pathetic, weak-kneed woman!"

She walked back to the window and sank onto the window seat. After taking another sip of sherry, she said, "When Charles saw that I meant to finish Maitland in the quadrangle, he put as much distance between us as he possibly could." She laughed. "I think he was afraid I would shoot him if he interfered."

"Yes," said Rosamund tonelessly, "I wondered why Charles had separated himself from us."

There was no need to ask why Charles had kept quiet about the whole affair. He was in love with Callie, abjectly in love, and would do anything for her.

She should be more shocked than she was, but she was remembering the little bothy on the downs, when she and Richard thought the militia had surrounded it. *I want to die a soldier's death,* Richard said. *Let me die with some dignity.*

Just thinking of those few moments when she thought she had lost Richard forever, made her eyes burn.

She looked up to find Callie watching her. Rosamund believed her friend now—yet something about Callie disturbed her, something that lurked beneath the surface. *A mission of mercy,* Callie called it. But was it?

Rosamund shook her head. "But Richard wasn't going to die a felon's death, was he, Callie? He was making a bid for freedom. You said you believed in his innocence, so why would you shoot him? Unless . . ."

"Unless what?"

She said the words automatically, as the thoughts occurred to her. "You didn't want him to escape. He had to die."

Callie cocked her head to one side. "I've underestimated you. I didn't think you would work that part out. Oh, I was going to tell you anyway. When I overheard your conversation with Miss Dryden, right here in this very room, I knew it would come to this. You were going to go back to the beginning and start investigating again. And something about Newgate didn't sit right with you. You're right, of course. I didn't mind Maitland cheating the hangman, but I couldn't allow him to escape. I'd always be looking over my shoulder, wondering if he was closing in on me."

Without conscious thought, Rosamund got up. Her mind was racing; her blood was pumping hard and fast. "You can't be Richard's nemesis!" she cried.

"Nemesis?" Callie's eyes glittered. "Yes, you've hit on the right word. This is about revenge. But no, I'm not Maitland's nemesis. I didn't appear onstage until the last act. I had nothing against—Richard? Is that what you're calling him now? But my role was so interesting, I couldn't turn it down."

Rosamund tried to say something, but her tongue was stuck to the roof of her mouth. She was staring at Callie, and everything was becoming clear to her. If Callie was not Richard's nemesis, there was only one part she could have played. And, of course, she was made for it: the delicate bone structure, the small stature; and she had always loved theatrics.

Her mind suddenly conjured up a scene from the past. They couldn't have been more than twelve or thirteen years old. Everyone had to do a party piece on Christmas Eve. She had played the piano, no more than adequately, and received a polite round of applause. Callie had made a quick exit, then returned to the drawing room, making a grand entrance, dressed in boy's clothing. Then she delivered Portia's famous speech from *The Merchant of Venice*, dressed as the lawyer, word-perfect and riveting. The applause had been tumultuous and, of course, Callie lapped it up.

It came to Rosamund that even this was playacting. The stage was set; Callie was giving a word-perfect performance and she, Rosamund, was an audience of one. Callie wanted to astound her with her brilliance, and she was succeeding. She fed on applause.

They were in the last act, Callie had said. How would it end?

A primeval dread sent shivers along Rosamund's spine. Callie wouldn't be telling her all this just to pass the time of day. She was savoring her moment of triumph, then she would end it. And she was prepared. Her muff lay right at her hand. She was brimming with self-confidence, almost giddy with it.

She saw now that she'd been lured here. Callie had known that Prudence had gone to her brother's place to convalesce, and she, Rosamund, had boasted that she was done with ducal carriages and footmen, and all the trappings of her father's exalted position. She just wanted to live like an ordinary girl!

Oh, what a fool she'd been! She'd taken Harper with her, but he wasn't watching the house. He was outside the grounds, watching and waiting for Charles Tracey to appear.

Where was Nemesis?

The thought made Rosamund's knees begin to buckle. She straightened them and tried to get hold of her breathing. Nemesis had to be here somewhere.

"You look pale," said Callie. "Have I shocked you?"

Shocked wasn't the word for it. Her chest rose and fell with pent-up terror. *Don't panic,* she inwardly yelled. She had to take her bearings, think what to do. She had to keep Callie performing until she saw a way out of this.

Harper! She had to alert Harper.

When she spoke, she was surprised that she was still coherent. "You were the boy Richard saw in Lucy Rider's room?"

"I was."

"What made you do it? Does this man have some kind of hold over you? Did he force you to do it?"

Anger blazed from Callie's eyes. "No one forces me to do what I don't want to do. You're so conventional, you could never understand. I killed Lucy Rider for the thrill of it."

Rosamund swallowed hard. "But this man," she said, "he doesn't kill for the thrill of it. He wanted to punish Richard, didn't he?"

Callie's eyes narrowed. "Richard again? I see he made quite an impression on you, too. But you're only half right about Frank. Oh, he wanted to punish Maitland, all right, but that was only part of it. To have the power of life and death over someone is as close to immortality as we'll ever come. Frank understood that."

On a sudden insight, Rosamund blurted out, "You killed your husband!"

Once again, Callie was highly amused. "He was the first. Don't look so horrified. I got him drunk then smothered him with a pillow. He didn't suffer."

Rosamund's horror wouldn't have been so consuming if Callie had sounded more like the deranged woman she was. But they might have been talking about the latest fashions, or who was soon to be married or not.

When Callie stood up and put her hand in her muff, Rosamund rushed into speech. "Callie, this isn't you. What has this man done to you?"

Callie chuckled. "You could never understand. All your life, you've followed rules. Frank and I make our own rules. We live on the razor's edge. We dare everything on the throw of the dice. Life and death have no meaning for us. The first time we met, like recognized like. I told him how I'd killed my husband, and he applauded. He told me how he'd killed his wife, and I clapped. I knew then that I had met my soul mate."

"You killed Digby and Whorsley!"

"No, Frank did. I killed the boy."

"But why? What did the boy ever do to you?"

"Nothing. He just happened to be there. I believe he was collecting on a debt for his master. That's what he told me before I cut his throat. Well, I had to, you see. He'd seen us."

The muff was discarded and a wicked-looking pistol was pointed straight at Rosamund's heart, a dainty pistol suitable for a lady, and easily concealed in her reticule or muff.

Why, oh, why, thought Rosamund wildly, *didn't I listen to Harper?*

Callie said, "Frank must be wondering what's keeping me. This was only supposed to take a moment. But I couldn't resist putting you right about a few things, and now that everything has been said, it's time."

"How can you do this?" Rosamund cried out. "We were raised together. We were like sisters."

"Sisters!" Callie was incredulous. "I was the poor relation! You were the apple of your father's eye! Do you know what my father told *me?* That I must always show a proper respect and gratitude, or he might be turned off and we'd end up in the poorhouse. So I had to smile and simper and pretend to like you. Well, I didn't like you. I despised you, and at last I can say it."

Callie didn't make an arresting picture now. Arrogance gave her features an ugly, spiteful look. Rosamund knew that her own face must be registering her hurt and shock. *Later,* she told herself fiercely, *feel sorry for yourself later. Think of how you can alert Harper.* And where, oh where, was the caretaker?

Her eyes darted around the room, looking for a means of escape or something she could use to defend herself. The decanter of sherry was within arm's reach, and she was only a step or two away from the door, but she'd be dead before she could reach it.

When Callie raised the pistol, Rosamund flinched. "If I'm going to die," she cried out, "I want to know why."

The pistol lowered a fraction. "Because you said you were going to prove Maitland's innocence. I knew you wouldn't give up, and how right I was! You made a beginning with Newgate, but you wouldn't stop there. Even as a child you were immovable once you set your mind on something. I knew I had to stop you. You cheated me once, but you won't cheat me this time."

"I cheated you?"

"Rosamund," Callie said in a chiding tone, "haven't you worked it out yet? The night of your ball, I mistook Prudence Dryden for you. I fired that shot outside the folly."

Rosamund was past being shocked by anything this madwoman could say. She was concentrating on inching closer to the table with the decanter on it.

"You'll never get away with this," she said. "Aunt Fran knows I came here to meet you. Charles knows, Harper knows, and . . . and the caretaker must know."

Callie smiled. "Fenton? Oh, yes, but he will verify my story. I told him I'd given up on you and he watched me leave. Not long after, Frank hit him on the head and

locked him in the coal cellar. I returned, and here we
are. The authorities will think that housebreakers broke
in, and when you discovered them, they killed you.

"No one saw Frank or me. This house is off the beaten
track. You have no neighbors to watch your comings and
goings. I warned you about that, didn't I?"

She'd run out of questions except one. "Who is
Frank? Why does he hate Richard so?"

"It's ancient history. You wouldn't know him even if I
told you his name. I suppose there's no harm in telling
you. It's Frank Stapleton."

There was no blinding enlightenment. She'd already
begun to suspect as much. Now it was time to get out of
there. "Frank Stapleton!" She looked at the door to the
little sunroom and said in a loud voice, "Did you hear all
that, Officer Walters? You'd better get out here before
she blows my brains out."

The pistol swung to the sunroom door, and that was
enough for Rosamund. She snatched up the decanter
and flung it at Callie with all her might. As the decanter
and its contents went flying, Callie dodged away, but she
held on to her pistol. In one bound, Rosamund went
through the door to the hallway, and she stopped dead.
Ascending the stairs was a gentleman she recognized,
George Withers, and he had a pistol in his hand.

Frank must be wondering what's keeping me.

Frank Stapleton. George Withers?

On that panicked thought, she spun around and went
haring along the corridor to the back stairs.

When she flung out of the back door, she flattened
herself against the wall. She'd heard Callie cry out that
Frank should take the front stairs while she went after
Rosamund. She hoped they thought she would hide herself in the kitchens. That would slow them down and give
her a chance to get to Harper, and it wasn't going to be
easy, for they were now on opposite sides of the house.

Her closest cover was the stable block, but to get to it,

she had to go down the side of the house then cut across the sward. If Stapleton came out the front door, he would see her. It couldn't be helped. She had no choice.

When she came to the turf, she kicked off her shoes and took off like an arrow. Everything seemed different now. Distances had suddenly increased tenfold. The grounds were not a small acreage. They stretched out to infinity.

A shout on her right alerted her to the fact that she'd been spotted by Stapleton, and an answering cry at her back told her that Callie was after her, too. She could outrun Callie, but she hadn't a hope against Stapleton. If only Harper would come through the gates, he would see her! She couldn't scream; she couldn't spare the breath.

This couldn't be happening, she thought wildly. The sun was shining; the trees were a riot of color; the pastoral setting was as pretty as a picture. And two maniacs were trying to kill her.

When she reached the cover of the stable block, she stopped to get her breath. She knew she couldn't run any farther. This is where it would end. Harper would hear the shot and come running, all right, but much good it would do her! She had to do something, even if the gesture was futile.

Callie hadn't lied. The caretaker had been working on the window frames. He'd left the job half done. She picked up the plank he'd been working on, then turned back to meet Callie or whoever should turn the corner of the stable first.

Every sound seemed to be magnified a thousand times; the soft footfalls of someone crossing the grass; someone's labored breathing; the lazy drone of a bee; her own panicked heartbeat.

Her timing was faultless. The full force of the plank struck Callie across the chest. Air whooshed out of her lungs. As she toppled backward, the pistol fell out of her nerveless grasp. Rosamund threw away the plank and went after the pistol, then shrank back when Stapleton came round the corner.

He smiled at her, actually smiled as though he were flirting with her, then he transferred his own pistol to his left hand and picked up Callie's pistol.

"Now, that wasn't nice," he said to Rosamund, and clicked his tongue.

Callie was getting her wind back. She hauled herself to a sitting position. Her face was mottled with fury. "You bitch." Then to Stapleton, "Frank, give me my pistol."

"Certainly, my dear."

Screaming was her last resort, thought Rosamund. She opened her mouth, but it wasn't a scream that split the air. It was a pistol shot. Frank Stapleton had put Callie's own pistol to her temple and pulled the trigger.

Rosamund flinched away in horror. Death was instantaneous. Callie's face was frozen in surprise. Her mouth formed a round *O* and her brows were arched above her dark eyes. A small bullet hole disfigured her left temple. When Stapleton straightened, Callie sank back, her lifeless eyes staring at the sky.

Rosamund put a hand to her mouth. She couldn't move, couldn't speak, couldn't take her eyes off Callie. *Get up!* she wanted to scream. *No more playacting! This game has gone on long enough!*

But it wasn't a game. It was all in deadly earnest.

Her eyes jerked up when Stapleton moved. Without haste, he dropped Callie's pistol on the ground beside her and transferred his own pistol to his right hand.

Rosamund's throat worked. "She said you were soul mates," she whispered hoarsely.

He gave a careless shrug. "Mrs. Tracey meant nothing to me. It was the boy I admired, Sebastion. That's how he introduced himself when we met at a masqued ball. It was weeks before he told me his secret. I could never really think of Sebastion as Mrs. Tracey."

She gestured helplessly toward Callie. "But why this?"

"I had to end it. He was becoming reckless. Nothing frightened him. If I hadn't killed him, he would have killed me eventually. He was beginning to lose respect for me. Close your eyes, Lady Rosamund. I promise this won't hurt."

He hadn't lost any of his charm. It made her want to be sick. But she hadn't lost the will to live. She had to do something. Harper must have heard the shot. He must be close by. But close by wasn't close enough.

She made a gesture with one hand. "For the love of God, close her eyes. She loved you. Show some respect."

When he turned and looked indifferently toward Callie, Rosamund seized her chance. She launched herself at him. As they toppled to the ground, the gun was knocked out of his hand, slithered over cobblestones, and came to rest against a stone urn. She bit, she scratched, she pulled his hair out by handfuls, but the contest was unequal. He backhanded her across the face, and before the mist cleared from her brain, he had dived for the gun.

That's when Harper came tearing into the yard with his pistol drawn. He looked toward Rosamund first, and that was his undoing. Stapleton fired his pistol, and Harper went down.

Rosamund and Stapleton had the same idea, but she was closer, and got to Harper's gun first. She would have shot Stapleton dead without a qualm, but he bolted before she could level the pistol.

Harper struggled up, one hand clutched to his shoulder. "Bloody hell!" he said. "How could I have been so stupid?"

Rosamund sniffed back tears. "I thought he had killed you."

"Not bloody likely. What's that?" He grimaced as he got to his feet. "Sounds like horses."

A shot ran out and they heard men shouting. Rosamund started to run and Harper hobbled after her. "Get back here!" he yelled. "Get back here! That villain could have reloaded his pistol! Have you thought of that? And you haven't told me what in Hades is going on!"

She didn't go far, just to the end of the stable block. Three men on horseback had entered the grounds and were galloping across the turf in pursuit of Stapleton, who had almost gained the shelter of the woods.

"That's the chief and your brother," said Harper.

"And Charles Tracey."

It was over in minutes. Richard reached Stapleton first. He leapt from his horse and both men went rolling on the ground. Caspar and Tracey had caught up to them, but they didn't dismount. Richard had his knee on the small of Stapleton's back and his arm around his throat, dragging his head back.

"The chief won't hurt him," said Harper, glancing uneasily at Rosamund, "not really."

"I hope he breaks his neck!" said Rosamund savagely.

But he didn't. He hauled Stapleton to his feet, said something to Caspar, who then dismounted and trained his pistol on Stapleton. Richard mounted up and he and Tracey cantered over to the stable block.

When they reined in, Richard said quietly, "Are you two all right?"

"This is just a scratch," said Harper, holding his shoulder.

"I'm fine," said Rosamund. But she wasn't fine. She was looking at Charles Tracey, steeling herself for what she knew must come next. The curtain was coming down on the last act, but the final scene was nothing like Callie had anticipated.

Tracey dismounted. Grim and white-faced, he said, "Where is she? Where's Callie?"

Rosamund said, "Charles, prepare yourself for a shock—"

"I know she's dead!"

"Take him to her," said Richard quietly.

Rosamund led the way. When Charles saw Callie, he didn't say anything. He simply gathered her in his arms and wept like a baby.

Chapter 25

Rosamund was in her bedchamber in Twickenham House, seated in the window embrasure
that overlooked the drive. A week had passed
since Frank Stapleton had been taken into custody, one
of the worst weeks of her life, not because of Frank
Stapleton, but because Richard had surrendered himself
to the authorities, and he, too, had been incarcerated.

It could have been worse. He could have been sent to
Newgate or the Fleet, but Special Branch had been
called in, and through their influence, Richard was allowed to wait out the investigation in a comfortable cell
in the round house at Richmond, only five minutes from
Twickenham. Today he had been summoned to meet
with the prime minister, and her father and Caspar had
gone with him.

What alarmed her was that the truth might never
come out. Frank Stapleton couldn't deny who he was,
not after she had made her statement to the magistrates

and Peter Dryden had identified him, but the only murder he would admit to was Callie's. He knew he would hang, but he seemed as determined as ever to see Richard hang, too.

Mr. Massie, Richard's replacement at Special Branch, had told her that Stapleton showed no remorse for what he'd done. He killed Mrs. Tracey in a jealous rage, he said, and everybody else was lying for reasons he could not fathom.

"He thinks he's clever," said Massie, "and we're stupid. His arrogance knows no bounds."

She remembered those words when she attended Callie's funeral. It was a graveside service with less than a dozen people in attendance. She couldn't say the right things to Charles or Aunt Fran because she'd felt frozen inside. And bewildered. She still couldn't grasp that the Callie she thought she knew had never existed.

At least Charles Tracey's grief was genuine. He, too, had to make a statement to the magistrates, but all he could tell them was about Newgate, and the attack on Prudence Dryden. He could smell the powder on Callie, he'd said, but he couldn't bring himself to think it was more than one of her outrageous pranks.

When he'd taxed her with it, she'd admitted it. She knew the party would be a bore, she'd said, so she'd brought her little pistol along just to spice things up. And she laughed, because she liked nothing better than to shock him.

But the more Charles thought about it, the more uneasy he became. The bullet had nicked Miss Dryden. It might have killed her. Something else disturbed him. There was no doubt in his mind that Callie had mistaken Miss Dryden for Rosamund.

That's what he'd been trying to tell her when she'd bolted from him and run off to meet Callie. He was going to come after her, and had just had his horse brought round, when Richard and Caspar arrived. So they'd come out to the house together, just in time to apprehend Stapleton.

And from that day to this, she had not seen Richard or spoken to him, not because the authorities wouldn't allow it, but because Richard said that when he came to her it would be as a free man, claiming her openly as his wife.

She was wearing her wedding band now, if only to bolster her confidence. *Richard will be cleared and come back to me.* She repeated the litany now, as though saying it would make it happen.

She almost missed seeing the ducal carriage enter the drive because of the tears in her eyes. She blinked them away, saw that she was not mistaken, and bolted for the door.

"Justin," she screeched, "they're home."

As she descended the stairs, Justin came out of the library and went to meet her. "Calm down, Roz," he said, his words at odds with the excitement in his voice. "Everything will be fine, you'll see."

Hand in hand, they walked to the marble entrance hall, where the groom of the chamber was already stationed. Turner was no calmer than Rosamund or Justin. He was pacing back and forth in front of the door, glancing at the timepiece pinned to his coat each time he made a turn.

"Now!" he said suddenly to the porters on duty.

They opened the front doors and ran down the steps just as His Grace's carriage rolled to a halt.

His Grace was the first to enter. His expression was inscrutable.

Rosamund looked past him. She saw Caspar, but no one else. "Father," she cried out. "What happened? Was Richard pardoned?"

"No," said the duke.

When she sucked in a breath, Justin squeezed her hand.

"He was completely exonerated," said the duke, beaming. "Of course, it must go through the usual channels, but that's only a formality. Meantime, he's a free man. Turner, champagne in the library, if you please, and see that there's ale or beer for every man in my employ and sherry for the ladies."

Richard and Caspar entered the hall, with Harper trailing after them. Servants who, a moment before, had been nowhere in evidence seemed to appear out of cracks in the walls. Richard's greeting to Rosamund was drowned out by their riotous cheers. Everyone was smiling and laughing except Rosamund. Tears were streaming down her cheeks as she walked into Richard's arms.

But this wasn't the moment for tears, and soon she was laughing, too, as they ran the gauntlet of servants who wanted to congratulate Richard on his good fortune.

Caspar was the last to enter the library. He shut the door and leaned against it. "I've never seen anything like it," he said. "Our servants are usually so sedate."

"These are exceptional circumstances," replied the duke. "It's not every day that a member of our family cheats the hangman's noose by the skin of his teeth."

This last remark brought tears to Rosamund's eyes again. She was impatient with herself. She'd been brave all week, and now she was turning into a watering pot.

When they were all seated, Justin said, "Well? What happened? Don't keep us in suspense. Rosamund and I have been biting our nails down to the quick, waiting for your return."

Everyone laughed, then the duke said, "Go ahead, Richard. This is your show."

Richard looked down as Rosamund linked her fingers with his. "What happened," he said, "is that Special Branch accumulated enough evidence to satisfy the prime minister that a grave miscarriage of justice had been done, and that my conviction should be quashed. Massie, he's acting chief of staff, by the way, also came up with the bright idea that Stapleton should be there when the prime minister passed on the good news. You see, there wasn't enough evidence to convict Stapleton of any murder but Mrs. Tracey's, and Massie wanted to get a reaction from him, and by God, he succeeded."

Caspar said, "He exploded. There's no other way to describe it. Then all the bitterness and hatred came pouring out of him like a dam bursting. It wasn't a pretty sight."

"No," agreed Richard.

Stapleton's hatred went far beyond that unfortunate episode in Cambridge. It seemed that he, Richard, had become the focus of every slight and humiliation Stapleton had ever been made to suffer. His mother, his father, his friends at Cambridge had all made him their victim, and none more so than Richard Maitland, who had wreaked a terrible vengeance on him for nothing more than a boyish prank.

"Never again," Stapleton had said, wiping the spittle from his lips. "If anyone was going to be a victim, it wouldn't be me!"

After that, anyone who had found fault with him or made him feel small was seen as an enemy—his wife, his father-in-law, Digby, and last but not least, the boy, Sebastion.

Once he started talking, he couldn't stop. By this time, he'd pulled himself together and lectured them as though they were slow-witted children. They never would have caught him, he said, if it hadn't been for the boy. Sebastion had become too reckless and could no longer be checked. Going to Newgate on a mission of mercy had been his own idea, as had shooting Prudence Dryden in mistake for Lady Rosamund when she came out of the folly. But there was something else. Mrs.

Tracey was angling for marriage, and Mrs. Tracey meant nothing to Withers. That's why she had to die. That's why the boy had to die with her.

If they hadn't all known that Mrs. Tracey and Sebastion were one and the same person, they wouldn't have known what to think.

"He sang like a bird," said Richard, and summarized his thoughts, ending with, "But it was too pat for my liking. I don't think he needed a motive for killing. I think killing had become his sport. I'm not convinced that the wound I inflicted—his words—festered like an open sore for seventeen years. I think he returned to England to buy horses, and when he heard how I had prospered decided that the pleasure of killing me was a challenge he could not resist."

Rosamund shivered, remembering Callie's words. "What about Lucy Rider?" she asked quietly.

Richard's hand tightened on hers, crushing her bones, but she did not flinch. She saw his pain and wanted only to share it.

Caspar took up the story as though no one was aware of Richard's distress, which they all were. "She fell in love with him, and he used her. It's as simple as that. Oh, she was innocent enough to begin with. It was only after Stapleton came on the scene that Miss Rider changed. The poor girl didn't know what she was getting into."

"But how did he find her?" asked Rosamund.

Richard said, "He struck up a friendship with Digby, and got him talking about me. Seems like the major didn't trust me, and kept himself informed of my movements. At any rate, he mentioned that I dined regularly at the George & Dragon and Stapleton took it from there."

Richard breathed deeply, remembering how Stapleton had boasted about how easy it had been to bring the chief of staff of Special Branch to his knees. There was no remorse, not a shred of regret for what he'd done to Lucy Rider.

He cleared his throat. "As Caspar said, Lucy fell in love with him and he used her. She knew that Stapleton—or Withers, as she knew him—wanted to discredit me, but the story he told her was that it was for raping his sister, years before, when we were both at Cambridge. She believed everything he told her, you see, so she followed his instructions to the letter.

"The idea was to convince everyone that I was a jealous lover who attacked her in a fit of rage. She was supposed to start screaming the moment I entered her room. Stapleton told her that he would be there and would hit me over the head with a brass candlestick. Then they'd call in the Bow Street runners, accuse me of attempted murder, and I would be completely discredited. And that would be the end of my career in Special Branch. That's all Lucy thought my punishment would be."

Justin burst out, "But that's incredible! Nobody is that stupid!"

"There goes a man who has never been in love," drawled the duke.

Rosamund said, "Poor Lucy," and shivered.

Richard squeezed her hand. He couldn't tell her the rest, how Lucy had trustingly torn her own garments before she stretched out on the bed. She hadn't even questioned the boy's presence, so great was her faith in Stapleton. Two witnesses would be more convincing than one, he'd told her. Then he'd watched as the boy cut her throat. After the deed was done, the boy had calmly removed his coat, now covered in Lucy's blood, returned to his own room and put on another. Not long after, he was at the top of the stairs, waiting for Richard to appear.

But he wasn't a boy. He was Callie Tracey, Rosamund's best friend. That's what sickened Richard. Rosamund and Callie had grown up together. Corruption on this scale didn't suddenly come into existence.

It must have festered for years.

He looked at Rosamund, and thanked God that Callie's infection had left her untouched, his lovely, innocent Rosamund.

Rosamund said, "I suppose Stapleton told her that he would marry her and that she would enjoy a life of luxury she could only dream about?"

"Something like that."

After a long silence, Justin said, "Did you ever find out how Digby knew to look for you in Dunsmoor?"

"Yes," said Richard. "Because I was careless. Because I was a damned fool. Because, out of sheer sentiment, I kept a painting of Dunsmoor on my study wall."

"That's not it," said Caspar. "Stapleton saw at once that the painting in Richard's study was second-rate, while all the other paintings throughout the house were good enough to hang in the Royal Academy. That, of course, piqued his interest. The name of the house was written, bold as brass, above the front porch. Dunsmoor. And that jogged Stapleton's memory. He's really quite intelligent. He plotted Richard's movements and decided that Dunsmoor was either his destination or close to it."

"It was a lucky guess," said Richard irritably.

"Who is this second-rate artist who painted Dunsmoor?" asked Justin innocently.

"Richard, of course," replied Caspar, and everyone laughed.

The groom of the chambers arrived at that moment with two footmen, who dispensed long-stemmed glasses of champagne. "And there are two more bottles, Your Grace, in the pantry," said Turner. "Just ring if you need them."

When he and the footmen had bowed themselves out, the duke got up. Everybody else, of course, got up as well.

"Will you sit down!" roared the duke. "You're giving my new son-in-law the wrong impression. This isn't a state occasion. There's no need for formality here."

Everyone sat. Caspar and Justin managed not to exchange glances.

His Grace lifted his glass to give the toast, then his eye fell on Harper, who was sitting in a corner, off by himself. "Sergeant Harper," said the duke, "will you do us the honor of proposing the toast?"

Harper reluctantly got to his feet. "I don't know about that," said Harper. "I'm a simple man, Your Grace. I don't have the gift of words like you gents."

"Which is precisely why you should give the toast," responded the duke.

"Well," said Harper, "wife number three was fond of—"

"Harper!" interrupted Richard on a warning note.

Harper cast his mind further back, to his mother and what he had learned at her knee. He raised his glass. "Fight the good fight!" he said simply.

The duke beamed. Everyone got up. "Fight the good fight," they chorused.

❧

Some hours later, Richard and Rosamund retired to bed. They would have gone earlier except that the servants were unpacking all the boxes that had been brought from Richard's rooms in Jermyn Street and others that he'd left at the Black Friar. Now everything was tidied away and they were alone at last.

Richard said, "Shall I call your maid to help you undress?"

Rosamund laughed and dragged her hands through her hair. She'd had more than her fair share of champagne and it had gone to her head in the nicest possible way.

"It's true what they say, isn't it? Men never notice anything. I choose my clothes so I can dress and undress myself now. Callie says—" She stopped.

Richard's smile faded. He wasn't sure what to do or say for the best, so he sat on the edge of the bed and said carefully, "I'm sorry about your friend."

She turned her head and looked at him. "I'm not. Oh, I'm sorry she turned out bad, but what she did was unspeakable. And she did it without remorse, not a ripple of conscience."

"It was the same with Stapleton."

"Her soul mate, she called him," said Rosamund, and shuddered. "For me, she felt nothing but contempt. She's destroyed the happy memories I had of us growing up together. She always hated me. But what's worse is that she seemed to blame me and my family for making her what she was."

When he patted the bed, she crossed to it and hoisted herself up beside him. "When people go bad," he said, "they justify themselves. It's always somebody else's fault. They distort events. Believe me, Callie and Stapleton chose their own paths. No one else made them what they became."

"Oh, I know that! If I'm grieving, it's for something that never was. I'll get over it." She touched a hand to his face. "Thank God there are people like you who have made it your life's work to unmask all the Callies and Stapletons in our world."

It was the opening he had been waiting for. He took her hands in his and pressed a kiss to first one then the other. "I want to talk to you about that," he said. "I think it's time for a change."

"A change?" she said carefully.

He nodded. Trying to sound eager, he said, "Now that I'm a married man, it's time I had a more regular life. Dunsmoor gives me an adequate income, but I think we can improve on it if we take up residence there. There's money to be made in sheep, and we could breed horses.

I've given this a great deal of thought, and though I don't know much about farming, I could learn. I think we would be very happy there, don't you?"

She was astonished. "You, a farmer? A country squire?" She began to laugh. "Oh, yes, I can just see it."

He let go of her hands. "I refuse to live off my wife's money like a parasite!" he said.

"Then we won't live off my money. As you said, Dunsmoor provides you with an adequate income. I can live as simply as you. Richard, I won't let you sacrifice yourself just to keep me in luxury."

"Oh, your father would love that—his son-in-law chasing after murderers and anarchists. When I married you, I knew I would have to give up that life. Your family expects it."

"So that's it!" She slipped from the bed and began to pace. "I thought you were over these silly prejudices. This isn't about living off my money! This is about keeping up appearances." She turned on him, hands on hips, eyes spitting fire. "I'm disappointed in you, Richard, first because you have insulted my family. As though they care how you earn your living. In fact, my father is proud of you. But even if my whole family were as pompous as you make them out to be, that's no reason to kowtow to them. I thought you were a fighter."

He was becoming amused. When she paused for breath, he said, "And secondly?"

She had lost her train of thought. "What?"

"You were enumerating my failings, if I remember."

She let out a huff of breath. "Secondly, a wife likes to be consulted about these things. If you think you're going to bury me in the country while you have adventures, you can think again. No, don't interrupt. That's what's going to happen. I can just see it. Special Branch will call you in to help on a particularly difficult case, then another, and another, and before you know it, you'll be spending all your time in town while I'll be left at Dunsmoor to play Little Bo-Peep."

Now he was laughing. "Come here," he said, holding out his arms. When she was sitting beside him on the bed again, he said, "All right, I'm consulting you. What do *you* want?"

She answered him seriously. "I want you to take up your job as chief of staff at Special Branch. I know the prime minister offered it to you. Caspar told me. Richard, this isn't a job to you. This is your vocation. Without men like you, people like Callie and Stapleton would run amok, and that can't be allowed to happen."

"I'm not the only one who can do that job."

"Maybe not. But it's what you want to do, and if there's one thing I've learned from this horrible experience, it's that we should do what is right for us, not what others think we should do. All my life I've been the duke's daughter. I don't want to be the duke's daughter any longer. I'd feel stifled in that role. So if that's what this is about, if you're giving up Special Branch for me, think again."

He gave her one of his quick, warm smiles. "Supposing I do go back to Special Branch, where will you be? What will you do?"

"I'll be at Woodlands. It's ideal for raising children, and maybe a few horses, and you'll come home to me every night. As for what I'll do," her eyes sparkled, "why, we'll go over your cases together, and I'll help you with them. You can't deny that I have an aptitude for solving crimes."

Smiling, he threaded his fingers through her hair. "If you were a man," he said, "I'd make you my second-in-command."

"If I were a man," she scoffed, "I'd apply for the position of chief of staff."

He gave a hoot of laughter and rolled with her on the bed. After a long, lingering kiss, a thought occurred to him, and he said, "Do you think you could ever be comfortable at Woodlands after what happened there with Callie and Stapleton?"

"What happened? My life was miraculously saved; Harper and the caretaker recovered from their wounds; you avenged Lucy Rider's death, and finally had the means to clear your name; and two remorseless, cold-blooded killers came by their just deserts. If I were superstitious, I'd say that Woodlands is a lucky house, lucky for us and those we love."

She got up, looked around for her reticule, and came back to the bed with the scorched chess piece Richard had given her for her birthday. "Or maybe we owe our luck to this. He goes everywhere with me now."

"*You* are my luck," he said fiercely. "If you hadn't come to Newgate, God only knows how things would have turned out for me."

"It's the same for me." She smiled up at him. "What a story we'll have to tell our grandchildren one day."

He lowered his head so that their lips brushed. "You're ahead of me. I was thinking of our children. That's where we should make a start."

She shivered when his hand cupped her breast. "I've always admired your intelligence," she said, and she drew his head down so their lips met.

ã

She came awake on a cry of panic. Tears streamed down her cheeks. Richard wakened in an instant, and gathered her in his arms.

"Shh," he crooned. "It's just a dream."

"It was Callie," she cried, and clung to him.

"She can't hurt you now."

"No. You don't understand. We were swimming in the

sea. We were too far out. I wanted to go back, but Callie kept on swimming. I screamed for her to come back with me, but she wouldn't listen. She laughed and kept on swimming. Then, I don't know, there was a huge wave, then there was nothing."

Her shoulders began to heave as she sobbed out, "I called and called and called, but there was no Callie. She's never coming back! She's never coming back!"

He pulled her under the covers and cradled her in his arms, rocking her, soothing her with words he might have used to a frightened child. Eventually, she slept.

ॐ

A few days later found them packed and ready to make the journey to Woodlands. Their bedchamber was strewn with boxes. As Rosamund finished dressing, Richard read out extracts of letters he had received from friends and well-wishers.

"This one's from Hugh," he said. "He and Abbie are coming up to town next week and they want to hold a party in our honor. This one's from Jason Radley. I've mentioned him and his wife, Gwyneth, haven't I? They're back from their honeymoon." He chuckled. "I'm surprised the notepaper isn't scorched. Jason has a few choice words to say about friends who don't call on friends when they're in trouble. They want to hold a party in our honor as well."

Rosamund was looking around for her gloves. Finding none, she went to one of the boxes, knelt down beside it, and undid the lock. "Your friends sound like sensible people to me," she said. "Friends *should* call on friends when they're in trouble."

"And this one's from my father." There was a silence, then he went on, "He wants to know why I haven't written to him in over a month. Obviously he hasn't got my letter where I tell him about my trial and that not only has everything worked out for the best, but I'm also a married—" He broke off when he saw what Rosamund had taken out of the box.

"How on earth did this get in here?" she asked.

She was holding a lady's shoe, in pink kid, studded with decorative glass beads, except for the several ugly gaps where a sprinkling of beads had fallen out. The heel was broken and the leather was blotched with water stains.

"The last time I saw this shoe," she said, turning it over in her hand, "was in the cottage in Chelsea, when you gave me Harper's clothes to wear."

She glanced at Richard. He was staring at the shoe as though he loathed it. Suddenly bounding up, he pounced on her and wrestled it from her hand.

"There is no pleasing women," he said, "until they have wormed all a man's secrets out of him." He dropped the shoe in the box and shut the lid. "This is my box," he said, "not yours."

She was bewildered. "Richard," she said, "the shoe is a wreck. It can't be repaired, and even if it could, I've lost its mate. Don't you remember, I lost it in the riots? Give it to me, and I'll dispose of it."

"Oh, no, you won't!"

Her hand dropped away. "But why? It's worthless. You don't imagine those are real gems? They're made of glass. Now, give it to me."

"I will not!"

Enlightenment slowly began to dawn. "Richard, you're not keeping that broken-down shoe out of sentiment, are you?"

He folded his arms across his chest. "What if I am?"

She thought for a moment, then shook her head. "But that means you've kept it since the day you abducted me.

You despised me then. You made fun of me. You terrorized me."

He made a small sound of derision. "There's more than one kind of terror."

She stood up. "We're not going to leave it there," she said. "I want to know why you kept that shoe."

He glowered at her. "If you laugh, I'll beat you."

"I promise I won't laugh." She pressed her lips together, but her eyes were dancing.

He let out a breath. "How do you think I felt when just a few hours after I abducted you, I was lusting after your beautiful body like any callow youth? I was disgusted with myself! And before the day was out, I admired you more than I've ever admired any woman. It went from bad to worse. I was falling in love with you, though of course I didn't recognize the symptoms. How could I? I'd never been in love before. All I knew was that you were the source of all my irritation. 'The Perfect Princess'—that's what the papers were calling you. I knew that you would go to someone like Prince Michael, and that I could never have you. And my feelings for you petrified me."

She took a step toward him, then another, and suddenly she was in his arms. Her face was radiant with happiness. "Richard, are you saying you love me?"

"Don't you know? Isn't it obvious? The whole world knows it—your father, your brothers, Harper, the servants."

"Of course I know it! But I thought *you* didn't know it."

He made a sound, half laugh, half groan, and gave her a shake. "I love you," he said. "Why else would I have kept your shoe? If you only knew how many times I tried to throw it away. I couldn't do it. It was the symbol of something beautiful and brave that came into my life with you."

"But Richard, the shoe isn't beautiful. It's a wreck.

Couldn't you have saved one of my handkerchiefs or something else?"

"I didn't want something perfect. I wanted that shoe or what it symbolized. Are you perfect? Am I?"

"No," she said softly. "We're not perfect. We're just perfect for each other."

About the Author

Best-selling, award winning author, Elizabeth Thornton, was born and educated in Scotland, and has lived in Canada with her husband for the last thirty years. In her time, she has been a teacher, a lay minister in the Presbyterian Church, and is now a full-time writer, a part-time baby-sitter to her five grandchildren, and dog walker to her two spaniels.

Elizabeth enjoys hearing from her readers.
If you wish to receive her newsletter, e-mail her at:
elizabeth.thornton@mts.net

or visit her web page at:
http://www.elizabeththornton.com

or write to her at:
Elizabeth Thornton
PO Box 69001 RPO Tuxedo Park
Winnipeg, MB R3P 2G9
Canada

**Read on for a preview
of Elizabeth Thornton's next
thrilling historical romance. . . .**

ALMOST A PRINCESS

Chapter 1

December 1816

It was moving day for the members of the Ladies' Library in Soho Square. Their lease had run out, and one of their staunchest supporters, Lady Mary Gerrard, had offered her mansion in the Strand. The house was buzzing as an army of ladies and their helpers set to work to transform their new quarters, room by room, from a palatial residence to a library with lecture rooms, reading rooms, and a bright and airy tearoom.

Lord Caspar Devere stood just inside the marble entrance hall, taking it all in. He was a harshly handsome man, thirtyish, well above average height, with dark hair and gray, gray eyes that, for the moment, were distinctly amused.

He left his hat and gloves on a hall table and wandered into the main salon. Some of the men who were helping the ladies were known to him, and that brought a smile to his lips. Not many gentlemen wanted it known that their wives or sisters were members here.

As the Viscount Latham passed close by, carrying a chair, Caspar called out, "Freddie, where can I find Lady Octavia?"

On seeing Caspar, the viscount registered surprise, quickly followed by amusement. In a stage whisper, he replied, "I won't tell anyone I saw you here if you don't tell anyone about me." Then in a normal voice, "Try next door. That's where she has set up her headquarters."

Caspar wandered into another salon, and there she was, the library's founder and driving force, Lady Octavia Burrel. Dressed all in white in something that closely resembled a toga with a matching turban, she directed her small army as they came to her for their orders. Though there was much coming and going, there was very little confusion.

Caspar was not there to help but to gather information, and when the crush around Lady Octavia thinned, he quickly crossed to her. He was sure of his welcome because he'd known her for as long as he could remember. She and his aunt were close friends.

When she saw him, her chubby face lit up with pleasure. "Lord Caspar," she said. "This is a surprise! I had no idea you were interested in our cause."

As Caspar well knew, there was a lot more to the Ladies' Library than its innocent name implied. The cause to which Lady Octavia referred was improving the lot of women by changing the antiquated marriage and property laws of England. The Library was also involved, so rumor went, in helping runaway wives evade their husbands. In some circles, Lady Octavia and her volunteers were seen as subversives. In the clubs he attended, they were frequently the butt of masculine laughter. But there were others who supported the aims of Lady Octavia and her League of Ladies. His aunt was one of them. He had never given the matter much thought.

"I suppose," said Lady Octavia, "I have your aunt to thank for sending you to help us?"

He avoided a direct answer. "I left her in Soho Square, directing things there. I'm looking for Miss Mayberry. My aunt told me she might be here."

"She's in the pantry. Turn left and go past the green baize door at the end of the hall."

As Caspar walked away, Lady Octavia's gaze trailed him. He was easy to look upon, she reflected, this young man who appeared to have everything. His aunt, Lady Sophy Devere, had kept her informed from the day he was born. As heir to his father, the Duke of Romsey, wealth, privilege, and position were already his, and it showed, not in arrogance exactly, but in something close to it. But it wasn't unattractive—just the opposite, especially to women.

There wasn't a woman born, his aunt said, who could resist Caspar, more's the pity. It would do him a world of good to taste rejection. Lady Octavia wondered how Lord Caspar had come to meet Jane Mayberry. Jane didn't go into society.

She frowned when another thought occurred to her: Lord Caspar and his volatile mistress, La Contessa, had recently parted company.

She dithered, debating with herself whether she should go after him, just to make sure that he did not have designs on Jane, when Mrs. Bradley came up and said that she was wanted in the old earl's library.

This request cleared Lady Octavia's brain. She was letting her imagination run away with her. The poor man was just trying to help.

૨૭

He found her in the first room past the green baize door. She hadn't heard him enter, so he took a moment to study her. She was perched on a chair, on tiptoe, fiddling with crockery on the top shelf of the cupboard. The first thing he noticed was a pair of nicely turned ankles. Unfortunately, they were encased in blue woolen stockings. He should have guessed. He'd made a few enquiries about Jane Mayberry and had learned, among other things, that she was a very clever young woman. Clever women, Lady Octavia and his Aunt Sophy among them, wore blue stockings as a badge of honor, a kind of declaration that their minds were set on higher things. "Bluestocking" was a derogatory term that had been coined to describe such women, and they wore that like a badge of honor, too.

With Caspar, it was silk stockings or he wasn't interested.

Her fine woolen gown was a muddy green, "olive" his mistress would have called it, but it was not a color he particularly liked. All the same, it suited the honey-gold hair streaked blond by the sun. The gown was well cut and revealed a slender waist and the long, graceful line of her throat.

He coughed to warn her of his presence, then shifted his gaze when a tawny, bristling mass rose from the floor and positioned itself in front of him with bared fangs.

As she turned from the cupboard, Caspar said softly, "Call off your dog or I shall be forced to shoot it."

"If you do," she said coolly, "it will be the last thing you do." Then to the dog, "Lance, down."

The dog, of indeterminate pedigree with perhaps a touch of wolf thrown in—and that didn't seem right to Caspar because there hadn't been wolves in England for three hundred years—sank to the floor and rested its jowls on its immense paws. Its gaze never wavered from Caspar.

"He doesn't like men," said Miss Mayberry, stepping down from her chair. "Lady Octavia should have warned you. I'm Jane Mayberry, by the way."

It sounded as if Jane Mayberry didn't like men either—a pity, because he found her direct manner and unfaltering stare oddly appealing. She wasn't beautiful, yet she was anything but plain. She had a strong face with straight dark brows and large, intelligent brown eyes.

"I'm Caspar Devere," he said. He would have bowed, except that Miss Mayberry turned away without bothering to curtsy.

"You're tall, that's what matters," she said. "At least you won't have to teeter on the chair."

She had the kind of voice a man could listen to day in, day out, and long into the night. But he'd ruffled her feathers by threatening her dog. If he wanted information, he'd have to tread carefully now.

He took the stack of plates she offered him and set them on the top shelf. When he turned back to her, she had another stack waiting for him. He gave her the smile that never failed to make a lady's heart beat just a little faster. He spoke to put her at her ease, but he was interested in how she would answer all the same.

"How did you come to be involved with Lady Octavia's library? I mean, you're not married. You can't have any interest in changing the marriage and property laws of England."

Not a flicker of a smile, not a blush. His charm, he saw, was wasted on this woman.

"Your aunt isn't married either," she said. "Why don't you ask her?"

"So you know my aunt?"

"Everyone at the library knows Lady Sophy. She's a dear. Would you mind?" She shoved the stack of plates into his arms. "You can talk and work at the same time."

Caspar took the plates and turned away to hide a smile. This was a new experience for him—being ordered about by a young, unmarried woman. He knew, without conceit, that he was a matrimonial prize. Young women usually tried to flirt with him or fawned over him.

He could be charming, but he could be cruel when he wanted to be, as any overambitious young woman who had marriage on her mind could testify.

Obviously, this wasn't going to be a problem with Miss Mayberry.

He said, "Lady Octavia is my aunt's closest friend. That's how she became converted to the cause. And you?"

She could avoid questions as well as he. "Last stack," she said, "then we can start polishing the silver."

He was taken aback. "I can't believe the silver in Lady Mary's house is tarnished. She wouldn't allow it."

"Then it won't take us long, will it?"

Now *she* was smiling, and it was *his* heart that was beating just a little faster. When she opened a drawer and began to assemble her materials, he decided it was time to come to the point.

"Miss Mayberry," he said, "I didn't come here to help you move into your new quarters. There's something I want to ask you."

The change in her was almost imperceptible. He might have dismissed it as a quirk of his imagination if her dog had not lifted its head and whined low in its throat, as though uneasy with some implied threat to its mistress.

She said, "Lady Octavia didn't send you to help me?"

He smiled. "That was a misunderstanding. I don't mind stacking dishes, but I'm hopeless with silver."

When the dog made a movement to rise, she pointed to the floor, and it sank back again. *She's afraid,* thought Caspar, amazed. *What on earth have I said to frighten her?* Not that he could tell by looking at her that anything was wrong. It was the dog that was on edge.

She pushed back a stray tendril of hair. "This is the wrong time to ask me questions, Lord Caspar. As you see, some of us are busy. Why don't you come back later?

Thank you for stacking the dishes. Now, if you'll excuse me, I have a silver paste to make."

He didn't know whether to be amused or annoyed. He wasn't in the habit of being dismissed like this. "One question, Miss Mayberry, then I'll leave you to your . . . ah . . . labors. Where can I find Letitia Gray?"

Her back was to him and he could see the tension across her shoulder blades gradually relax. "Letty?" she said, turning to face him. "You came here to ask me about Letty?"

He nodded. "I was told that you and she were friends."

"Who told you?"

"Does it matter? All I want from you is Mrs. Gray's location."

"I'm sorry. I can't help you."

"You can't help me or you won't?"

"I won't help you."

Now his patience was beginning to wear thin. "Do you mind telling me why?"

"Because it's against the library's rules. What I *can* do is ask Mrs. Gray if she wants to see you, or you can write a letter and I'll see that she gets it."

"That could take days! If it's character references you want, ask Lady Octavia or my aunt. They'll vouch for me."

"They'd give you the same answer as I. It's against the library's policy to tell strangers where members live."

"I'm not a stranger!"

"You are to my friend."

"How do you know?"

Her brows rose fractionally. "Because she would have told me, of course. Your name has been in all the newspapers. Your brother-in-law is the head of Special Branch, isn't he? You and he brought a murderer to justice. The papers called you a hero."

"An exaggeration!" he declared.

Her lashes lowered, veiling her expression. "I don't doubt it, but I'm sure my friend would have told me if she'd met the hero of the Maitland affair."

He didn't know how to take her. Was she poking fun at him or was she serious? Both, he decided, and grinned.

"You're right. I don't know Mrs. Gray, but I know her brother, Gideon Piers."

"You *know* him? That's odd. Gideon has been dead these three years."

"I mean I *knew* him. We served together in Spain." He realized that his voice had developed an edge, and he made considerable effort to soften it. "This really is urgent, Miss Mayberry, or I wouldn't be badgering you like this."

She seemed to soften a little as well. At any rate, in spite of the rising temperature of their conversation, her dog seemed satisfied that nothing was wrong. Its head was resting on its paws again, and its alert eyes were shifting from Miss Mayberry to him, as if it were a spectator at some play in Drury Lane.

"And I don't mean to be difficult, Lord Caspar," she said, "but you must understand that the information you want is confidential. Our members expect us to abide by the policy. I'll tell you what I *will* do, though. If you write a letter right now, I'll see that it's hand-delivered and that I have a reply, oh, shall we say by four o'clock? That's only a few hours away. Surely you can wait that long?"

Stubborn was too mild a word to describe Miss Jane Mayberry, but at least she was gracious with it. She'd learn soon enough that he could be just as stubborn.

"Thank you," he said. "I can't ask for more that that. Now, where can I find pen and paper?"

"Ask Lady Octavia. She knows where everything is." He was almost through the door when she stopped him by saying his name.

"You didn't answer my question," she said. "Who told you that I was Mrs. Gray's friend?"

"I remembered that Piers had a sister who was a teacher at St. Bede's Charity School. I went there yesterday and met the woman in charge." This was the shortened version of events and he saw no reason to enlarge on it. "Miss Hepburn—that was her name. She said that when Miss Piers married and moved away, that was the last they saw of her. But you continued to visit the school from time to time." He grinned. "I got the impression that you were the apple of Miss Hepburn's eye. She told me that any letter addressed to the Ladies' Library in Soho Square would reach you."

"But you decided to come in person."

"As I said, the matter is urgent."

❧

Jane waited until the door closed behind him, then she let out a huff of breath. Her hands curled into fists. There was something about Lord Caspar that rubbed her the wrong way. He hadn't exactly coerced her, but he'd come pretty close to it. If she hadn't given in when she did, he wouldn't have given up. He would have found another way to get what he wanted.

He'd been to St. Bede's. She wondered how much Miss Hepburn had told him. Not that the headmistress would have gossiped about her, but she might have let something slip inadvertently.

She'd told him where to find her.

No harm done, Jane assured herself. Lord Caspar hadn't come for her. It was Letty he wanted to see, and Letty had nothing to hide.

There was no point speculating on what Lord Caspar wanted. Letty would have to see him, of course. He wasn't the kind of man one could ignore. She'd known that even before she'd met him in person. Lady Sophy was very proud of her nephew and the man she described didn't know the meaning of defeat, whether he was pursuing his light-skirts or fighting battles.

A plainspoken woman was Lady Sophy Devere.

Jane wondered how Lady Sophy would describe *her*, Jane Mayberry. A young woman who never went out in society, but devoted all her energies to the cause? A bluestocking? At twenty-six, a confirmed spinster who went out of her way to avoid men? Someone who kept herself to herself? A lone wolf?

Mirrors reflecting mirrors, that's what these glimpses of someone's character were—not illusions exactly, but not revealing the whole truth either. She supposed much the same could be said about Lord Caspar.

A whining sound brought her out of her reverie. Lance's watchful eyes were on her. "I'm not sad," she told him. "I'm just in a reflective mood."

She knelt down and scratched behind his ears. "Some help you turned out to be. I thought you had a sixth sense about people. Didn't you hear what Lord Caspar said? He said he would shoot you. *Shoot* is a bad word."

Lance thumped his tail on the floor.

"Well, at least you didn't fawn all over him. Not that he would let you. Mustn't spoil that immaculate tailoring with a few stray dog hairs."

Lance gave her his doggie smile.

She looked down at her gown and made a face. Her skirt was covered in dog hair. "Did I forget to groom you today?"

Lance's response was to cock his head to one side.

She sighed. "I know. I've been preoccupied lately, but not for much longer. We're going home, boy. Just think of it—open spaces, meadows, trees, badgers, foxes. You'll have a grand old time."

But before that happened, she wanted to make quite

sure that she'd shaken off Lord Caspar. His lordship was a complication she could well do without.

❧

Caspar went in search of Lady Octavia, but it wasn't to ask where he could find pen and paper. He had not known that Mrs. Gray was a member here until Miss Mayberry mentioned it. Now he saw a way of circumventing her. Not that he would have left anything to chance anyway. Mrs. Letitia Gray would see him whether she wanted to or not.

He found Lady Octavia in the library, overseeing the disposal of a portrait that hung above the marble mantel.

"Lady Mary's father," she said to Caspar by way of explanation. "The old earl, and a most objectional man. His treatment of his wife and daughter was reprehensible. We can't have him presiding over our assemblies. He would act as a blight."

To the two footmen who had removed the painting from the wall, she said, "Take him to the attic," then to Caspar, but this time with a twinkle in her eyes, "There's a lesson for you here, Lord Caspar. Consider how your wife or daughter will dispose of your portrait when you're gone."

He answered her with a smile, but he was thinking that Lady Octavia and her ladies were all touched in the brain. They had this thing about men.

"Lady Octavia," he said, "I'm trying to find a lady who is a member here—Mrs. Letitia Gray, or perhaps you know her as Letitia Piers. Can you tell me where she lives?"

"We never give out that kind of information," she said. "It's the library's policy."

"But you know me! All I want is to speak with Mrs. Gray. What harm is there in that?"

She regarded him steadily. "We have these policies for a reason, you know. Experience has taught us that it's safer this way. Anyway, before you try to persuade me to change my mind, let me say at once that no Letitia Gray or Letitia Piers has ever been a member of the Ladies' Library."

"You're sure of that?"

"Perfectly. Our membership list is small, and each lady on it is personally known to me. You've been misinformed."

He'd been misinformed, all right, deliberately misinformed by Jane Mayberry. It had come down to a tussle of wills. There was no doubt in his mind who would win the contest. Then he'd find out why Miss Mayberry was so determined to protect her friend.

"Miss Mayberry," he began, and let the name hang there, inviting a response.

"What about Jane?"

He smiled and shook his head. "She puzzles me. I don't know what to think of her."

"Oh?"

This was not the response he was hoping for, so he took a more direct approach. "How would you describe her?"

Until that moment, he had not known Lady Octavia's placid, fading blue eyes could pierce like the point of a blade.

"Look away from Jane Mayberry," she said. "She is not for you, Lord Caspar. You can have any woman you want. Leave Jane alone."

And until that moment, he had not known just how far his jaw could sag. He took a moment to gather himself, a moment to rein in his formidable temper, to assume all the dignity and arrogance of his rank. "You are mistaken, ma'am," he said. "You must be confusing me with someone else."

"Jane," replied Lady Octavia, regarding him thoughtfully, "has not had an easy life since her father died. I think she has found a measure of peace with us. I don't want to see that peace disturbed."

He didn't know where elderly ladies got their gall. It was the same with his Aunt Sophy. Once they passed a certain age, they thought they could say anything they liked to anyone.

"I doubt," he said, "that Miss Mayberry and I shall have occasion to meet again, and if by chance we do, I shall endeavor to look the other way."

"I'm very glad to hear it."

Gritting his teeth, he stalked off.

Five minutes later, he returned to the pantry with the letter in his hand. Jane Mayberry was assiduously polishing a silver tray. The dog rose at Caspar's entrance, but this time there were no bared fangs, only a bark of welcome.

"Your dog is very intelligent," said Caspar as he handed her the letter.

"That's a matter of opinion." She pointed to her dog, who then sank to the floor and gazed at her with soulful eyes.

"Till four o'clock then," said Caspar.

"Four o'clock," she replied.

He bowed. She curtsied. The moment he left the room, however, his smile faded. Whatever had put that maggot into Lady Octavia's mind? And what role did she think he had planned for Jane Mayberry, his mistress or his wife?

He tried to picture her in one role then the other, and when he realized what he was doing, cursed furiously under his breath.